SECTOR SEVEN

For permission requests, write to the publisher, addressed "Attention: Permissions Coordinator," at the address below

QUID MIRUM PRESS
Regarding: Kaden Sinclair
19215 SE 34th Street
Suite 106-347
Camas, Washington 98607
or
admin@ThePublishingCircle.com

Sector Seven is a work of fiction. Names, characters, businesses, organizations, places, events, and incidents are products of the author's imagination or are used fictitiously. Any resemblance to actual persons, living or dead, or actual events is entirely coincidental.

The publisher is not responsible for mentioned websites, content of the website, or dead or expired links to any website.

SECTOR SEVEN / KADEN SINCLAIR
ISBN 978-1-947398-52-8 (hardcover)
        978-1-947398-40-5 (large print)
        978-1-947398-20-7 (paperback)

Book design by Michele Uplinger

ACKNOWLEDGEMENTS

FOR MY MOTHER WHO, ABOVE ALL OTHERS, has been my best friend, my closest confidant, and my biggest supporter in all I do. I love her more than anyone in the world.

To *The Publishing Circle* and *Quid Mirum* staff, who have enabled me to bring my creative outlet to print and who continue to help me on my long journey as I improve my ability to tell the story I have in my head.

I also wish to acknowledge how lucky I am to have the friends and family, the environment I need in order to be in a position to pursue artistic endeavors. I work toward supporting the art community as much as I'm able to be worthy of their kindness and support.

SECTOR SEVEN

KADEN SINCLAIR

PROLOGUE

DESPITE AN ALARMING FLOOD of information coming from within the Sector he guarded, Seven swept an impassive gaze out over the city, his green eyes reflecting the magnificent and sprawling mass of buildings and lush vegetation. He acknowledged the data but did not act. Could not act. A Tech only interfered if the threat became too overwhelming to ignore.

In the rain, the city glistened as Seven gazed down from atop his cliff-side perch, admiring the beauty in his dispassionate way. Tall, sculpted spires of transparent steel cast out colored patterns in the faint light of the overcast sky. Large, ornate domes rose amidst the forest like gemstones in a sea of green. Seven watched various species of birds fly from canopy to canopy, deftly avoiding the flying vehicles, the floating barges, antigravity buildings, and the elevated passenger trains. Insects of all kinds busily harvested from flowers, cut away leaves, and churned the soil. The breathtaking city of advanced technology had found a way to blend itself with nature, adding to, rather than cannibalizing, the landscape.

As a species, humans now covered the whole of the earth and had unified under a single governing council as they explored the stars. Instead of countries, the world had been divided into nine Sectors to be watched over and ruled by a single council of thirteen. The Sectors, which divided up the continents, spanned vast geographical regions and were guided and protected by the nine Sector Techs—Techs like Seven.

Seven stared into the distance as the rain fell around him. Millions of details flooded through him, through the part of his technologically augmented mind he had set aside to process and control everything around him. With a thought, he sped up an ever-so-slightly off-schedule passenger train, adjusted the pressure of a chemical mixture in a faraway factory, and changed the light patterns of a congested airway to maximize traffic flow. In less than a millisecond and with such a small amount of mental power as to be negligible, he made these and billions of other decisions. In the time it took him to blink the airflow changed within several buildings, changes were made to vent heat into energy recapturing facilities, and adjustments were made to medical supply deliveries so they would arrive where most needed. Another blink and robots were dispatched to handle a breakdown in moving walkways; power rerouted around a transformer outage so lights simply flickered instead of going out.

With each throb of the vein in his neck, each blink of his eyes, a thousand commands were issued and obeyed, all instantly, all without question. His face remained expressionless as he watched the city below him.

Rain soaked his short dark hair, droplets running down the smooth skin of his face and falling from his jaw. From atop the building on which he stood, Seven could make out miles of the city through the fog and clouds. But he had no need for such a mundane form of sensory input. They entire Sector communicated its every detail back to him at every moment of every day. His mind diffused itself throughout all the processors in the Sector.

Merged with advanced nanotechnology, Seven's mind had blended with the city and the city had become part of him. Effectively a humanoid AI, Seven's technological enhancements augmented his ability to interface. Nanobots, robots the size of molecules, had become part of nearly every life form, embedded in every synthetic material. And they all reported back to him, obeyed any command he issued. Technology had interlaced the world around humanity with a means of controlling it. Often, these tiny machines contained the necessary data and instructions to impart information without the need for centralized storage.

In a way, the city owned him and Seven felt the

constraints of this possession. While his thoughts controlled the workings of even the smallest of organisms, Seven had only passive control. Seven made the workings of humanity smooth and unnoticed by the population. He remained invisible, unseen. Under the strongest of edicts, he could not interfere in the lives of those around him, short of protecting them.

His narrowly defined role allowed scarce execution of free will. Not that he'd care to interfere, as the daily concerns plaguing the lives of the general public no longer existed for him. His role of servitude and his integration had him so immersed in the life of the Sector, he viewed his body as a mere mechanism for processing this control. He thought of his limbs as tools, much like his senses.

Most children raised to be Techs became hopelessly insane or lost all sense of themselves when integrated with the vast technology of a Sector, their minds becoming scattered like grains of sand in a windstorm. Low survival rates of potentials meant only nine Techs currently carried out the wishes of the Council and protected the Sectors. If more Sector Techs could be found, the Council could expand and the Sectors be paired down in size. As it was, the Sectors were too large, too unwieldy.

There were several promising replacements among the genetically modified and technologically enhanced children being tested and the Council hoped they could bring several more online. The outer colonies lacked a Tech, and their systems were painfully prone to issues because of this lack.

His chest rose and fell; blood flowed through his arteries. Seven's awareness of his entire physiology lent him near perfect control—a peripheral awareness, intentionally controlled just as he controlled all else around him. Automated processes kept his musculature at optimal levels, kept his skin smooth and free of damage. Like all humans, Seven's susceptibility to harm and age remained after his augmentation, but his supreme health, derived from his relative youth as well as his precise control over his own body, lent him an advantage. His lifespan would be longer, his aging slowed dramatically, his usefulness extended.

People dined, drank, and made love while he stood in the rain high above the nearest city, staring out toward the dimming horizon as the sun set. He would continue to exist until his ability to function in this role became no longer possible, then he would be replaced. Children born with Tech abilities were so incredibly rare, Seven might serve this Sector for a century. Longer, if his mind and body held up with assistance from augmentation and a proper replacement could not be found. Currently, the probability of finding a replacement remained low. Even if they found one or more potential replacements, the child would then need to be capable of receiving the necessary implants, the proper technological augmentation, and would need to remain sane when fully integrated.

Seven watched the world below him move with clockwork precision, subject to his will. For a moment, the merest fraction of a second, he felt a pang of longing. Sadness? Loneliness? He did not know. Emotions were one thing he had no control over and no real understandable connection to, something with which he had no experience. They had no place in his assigned existence.

His jaw tightened slightly, and his eyes softened with an echo of an unknown pain. But only for one moment, then he became devoid of expression once again.

Seemingly uncorrelated data flared in his mind like a dire warning, seizing his attention firmly. The information he'd been ignoring became relevant, disturbing, as his incredible mind unraveled hidden patterns. A series of events and the related data posed a dire threat to his Sector, to the Council itself, which entrusted Seven to protect them. He felt the familiar touch on his mind of other Techs as they, too, saw the dangers. An uncharacteristic uncertainty echoed through the Techs.

Seven's eyes suddenly became focused, troubled. With the smallest of frowns, he turned his head to gaze westward.

ONE

DOCTOR CARLISLE FAUST WATCHED from the observation room as his test subject, Hans Amir, struggled against his bonds, arm muscles tensing until the veins rose in corded ribbons.

Amir raised his head from the table, straining his neck to look at the door, and shouted in a hoarse voice, "Hey!" He cocked his head to listen for a response.

Faust ignored him, waiting for his three colleagues to arrive.

"Hello! Is someone out there?"

Faust nodded to each of the doctors as they entered the observation room, chatting amongst themselves and mostly ignoring Faust other than to return his nod. He'd become accustomed to their lack of engagement. As soon as everyone had arrived, he said, "We have a lot of work ahead of us, but our tests have yielded some incredible results. As you can see, the subject is almost entirely transformed." Faust enjoyed the surprised reactions to seeing their handiwork. "You'd hardly know Amir came to us only weeks ago."

"Let me out of here! You can't do this!" Amir thrashed violently against his bonds, actually moving the heavy table on which he lay. His hospital gown bunched up to his knees as his legs kicked against their straps. He struggled until his breathing became strained from futile attempts to escape. Sweat spun off his dark hair. Finally, with a snarl, he slammed his head back onto the pad of the table. He growled, flexing his massive chest and arms one last time, then lay at rest, breathing heavily.

"Shall we?" said Falk. "I'd say ladies first, but our subject appears a bit distraught. Perhaps it is best if we enter together."

The doctors nodded nervously and made small noises of agreement as the door slid open.

Faust led them as they shuffled forward, quiet now, with only the sound of their white lab coats rustling as they moved. Three robots attended them, two of which carried an array of lab equipment, while the other wheeled in a stainless-steel table.

Amir raised his head and shouted, "Finally! Let me out of here! You can't just keep me in here. Are you insane? If the authorities find out about this, you are all going to lose your medical licenses."

As he yelled, the robots set up gear around his table.

"Are you listening? I'm going to have your fucking licenses. Let me go!" He started struggling again.

Faust forced himself to remain calm, inwardly annoyed at the shouting. With the slowness of age, he moved toward the head of the table.

"Mr. Amir?"

"Yeah, asshole. Suddenly you can hear me? Get me off this fucking table."

"Now, now. Can you please calm down for a moment? Yes? Good. My name is Doctor Faust and I'm here to finish up the experiments. Some of the experiments have resulted in memory loss, so you will see us as if for the first time. But I assure you, we have been working closely with you for weeks."

"Experiments?" Amir said blankly. "I don't want to finish anything. I'm done with this whole thing, you slimy bastard. You can't strap me to a fucking table and leave me alone. Take this shit off!"

Faust was losing patience, taxing his ability to keep his facial expressions neutral. "Please try to control your language. I can see you are agitated, so you don't have to shout. You are probably having a reaction to the hormones. You've grown quite wild in the last few weeks."

Amir laughed a rough, guttural laugh. "Wild? I'm fucking livid! You've got me tied to a table and stuffed in a room by myself and I have to piss so bad my eyes are swimming. How about shutting your stupid hole and getting me out of here?" When he got no response, he added, "You're already in big trouble. I'm going to sue you right after I punch you in your stupid smug face."

Faust had grown tired of feigning patience. "Mr. Amir, please listen to me. Surely you must be able to tell that you are experiencing a heightened sense of rage. Your testosterone levels are extremely elevated. You would not normally be this upset, and we have restrained you because you are potentially dangerous. We aren't sure you wouldn't harm one of us. We have to try to lower your hormone levels."

"Lower them? Why are they so high in the first place, huh? What the hell did you do to me?" Amir strained against the bonds again, muscles bulging. "What's going on? I volunteered for a simple sleep deprivation experiment, not some goddamn Frankenstein show. Now I find myself losing parts of my memory and wake up on a goddamn table ready to piss myself! How long have I been in here?"

"Mr. Amir, you really must try to control yourself. We haven't been entirely honest with you." Faust didn't bother to suppress his expression of amusement. "We have been testing several experimental drugs in the last few weeks. Other than your high hormone levels, we're quite delighted with the results."

Amir gaped at him for a moment. "What the fuck are you talking about? I have to pee, so unless you plan on one of your assistants whipping out my dick so I can take a leak, how about if you get me off this table and we can talk about this bullshit later? Like across the table from the police."

"You really must stop swearing, Mr. Amir. It's becoming tiresome. Unless you cooperate, I have no intention of letting you off the table in your current condition. If you persist, I suppose we could catheter you again." Behind Amir the robots were nearly finished setting up the various trays and analysis tools.

With an effort, Amir visibly relaxed, letting some of the tension out of his body.

"Much better. Yes, excellent."

Amir glared beneath his lowered brows. "Okay, see? I'm calm. Now, I seriously have to pee."

Faust motioned, and two of the robots moved to the side of the table, deftly untying Amir's bonds, but holding his arms.

"These attendants will take you to the restroom where you may relieve yourself. They will also restrain you while you are near us. For our protection, you understand."

Amir looked ready to commit murder, but he let himself be guided off the table and led into the restroom. As he entered, the other doctors moved over to Faust. They watched as the restroom illuminated, revealing Amir behind the one-way mirror.

"Remarkable," said Doctor Elizabeth Anderson.

"And in so short a time," said Doctor Claire Ashcraft.

As soon as the robots released Amir, he tore off his hospital gown, trying to throw the garment over one of the robots to blind and then try and disable it. The robot deftly pulled the robe out of his hands while the other robot pinned him against the wall. Amir nearly overpowered the robot, pulling it off its mechanical feet, but the robot changed tactics and pinned Amir's arm behind his back, forcing him face-first against the wall.

Realizing the futility of his actions, Amir stopped resisting and waited. Finally, in response to its programming, the robot released him, and both robots stood back. With a glare, Amir moved over to the toilet to relieve himself. Before he got there, he looked down at his arms. He seemed entranced. He stepped closer to the mirrors, looking himself over, a position which had him facing the on-looking physicians. He seemed genuinely stunned. "What the hell? Oh my god! This is crazy!" He touched the glass where the reflection of his face stared back at him.

Dr. Claire Ashcraft stared admiringly and unashamedly at Amir's naked form. "He's certainly well developed, Elizabeth. You did a nice job on his cosmetic genetic alterations."

Dr. Elizabeth Anderson wore a proud expression, clearly delighted at her accomplishment.

Faust detected a hint of lust in Elizabeth's eyes. Entirely unprofessional, he thought.

Elizabeth gestured to the one-way mirror. "Thank you, Claire. I got a bit carried away with some of his anatomy, as you can see. Specifically, the male organs. I wasn't sure just what details we could alter with the nannies and the chemical changes we imposed." She laughed. "I know quite a few men who would pay handsomely for this particular alteration."

Claire chuckled. "Yes, and we'll charge a premium for that enhancement, of course." The other doctors laughed along with her.

Amir finally noticed his overgrown male anatomy and stared at its mass. He grabbed himself, hefting the enlarged organ to get a good look.

Faust ignored his personal disgust with clinical detachment. "What about his internal organs? Do we have the lab analysis yet?"

Doctor Earl Reprate cleared his throat and Faust hid his disdain for his dyspeptic-looking colleague.

"Yes," Reprate said in his high-pitched voice, grating on Faust's nerves. "Astonishing, really. The results are better than we hoped for." He fidgeted slightly, averting his eyes from Amir, who continued to admire himself. Reprate cleared his throat. "He's in perfect condition. All of the major organs are extremely healthy, and his brain tissue is reproducing cells at a high rate. He could sustain a large amount of damage in a short period of time and survive unscathed. The improved nanobots are capable of considerable repair. Even his scar tissue could be eliminated if we provide the right instructions. The technology, however, is at its current limit. It will take time to make the necessary adjustments for an individual to have conscious control. Right now, everything is operating with simple reparative instructions from the nanobots. His own body is providing instructions that are . . . problematic. We need to figure out how to prevent the host from unconsciously making changes now that the nannies are transmitting complete data that he doesn't consciously know how to handle. Uncontrolled thoughts can result in the nannies interpreting them as instructions. He might end up with a tail or dream about being a lobster and wake up with claws. Amir currently has no control over what his own body will do with his thoughts or emotions."

Reprate ran his hand down the front of his white doctor's smock and Faust could see the small man nearly puff up with pride as he continued.

"As a test, we pierced his heart in several places, and burned out about ninety percent of his lungs. His enhanced body repaired everything, actually growing back the tissue and even whole organs to a state better than when we began the experiment."

Amir's bladder finally forced him away from the mirror and he threw back his head and sighed loudly with relief as he used the toilet.

Claire rolled her eyes. "His external physiology is greatly enhanced; however his hormone levels are significantly elevated to a point where they pose a danger. His aggression is worse. We've had to drug him several times to selectively blank his memory to keep him unaware of the pain of the experiments. Each time we memory wipe, it seems to exacerbate his anger and he loses more control of his emotions. Like the test subjects we've lost, he is wildly out of balance. We've had to euthanize our previous subjects when they reached this point. He'll probably revert to base emotions and lose all intelligence. We'll have to take similar steps to eliminate him if that happens, of course."

Faust took a deep breath and closed his eyes so he could sort out his thoughts. Finally, he said, "We are so close. I had hoped he'd survive the process without this hormonal imbalance. This reversion to low-level intelligence could render this whole project moot. We must figure out how to ensure the subjects have conscious control of their enhancements and don't lose themselves in the complex rewiring of the brain. Elizabeth?"

Too late to stop himself, Faust realized the desperation in his voice had drawn Claire's attention, and she turned toward him. She looked at him with concern. He knew he'd been increasingly hard to deal with lately, and his decisions had been non-inclusive. He'd tried to hide his growing internal torment, but apparently Claire had noticed.

He turned away from Claire and saw Elizabeth bite her lip before saying, "It appears the sudden surge in hormones leads to a loss of conscious control. The brain responds by wiring even more connections, which results in increasing hormone levels, creating a feedback loop. He lacks any control over this deterioration, which is why we need to work out how to provide conscious control. The cycle escalates quickly, and the subject soon becomes nothing more than a purely emotional creature, losing all ability to critically think or be governed by logic. Specifically, one filled with anger and rage. I am completely at a loss to explain a mechanism to limit this.

Conscious emotional control will be the key here and should be where our research focuses. The technological improvements required will be vast—at least as complex as what we've already tackled."

Faust hated the truth of Elizabeth's statement and he tried not to scowl. Her statement happened to be technically correct and this obstacle was a major source of his internal strife. The failures and madness their work had caused might be true, but he had a plan to deal with this issue. Conscious emotional control *was* the key. The problem was, he didn't have the luxury of time to be delicate about finding the answer.

With a familiar gesture, Claire put a hand on his arm and he felt a twinge of guilt. He glanced at her and the concern on her face made him realize she recognized the anguish he felt. Her brow creased in a worried frown that Faust recognized all too well, for they'd been lovers at one time.

Amir finished urinating as Faust observed him through the one-way mirror. Amir took a moment to marvel at his physique once again, touching his finely chiseled abs and running his hand over his well-developed chest before he reached for the robe one robot held out. The two robots then allowed him to dress. After he'd put the robe back on, they secured his arms once more. This time, he hardly seemed to mind. Amir exited the restroom and strode back to them.

Dr. Reprate spoke up again. "We also broke most of his bones. They've all knitted nicely and are in the process of returning to their original condition, free of the bulging or restrictions normally accompanying healed bones. It's really quite more than we'd hoped for."

Amir had overheard Dr. Reprate. "What's more than you hoped for?" he demanded.

Faust felt excitement boiling up inside of him. "Why, you are, Mr. Amir. Don't you think?"

Amir grinned, his face cocked to the side as if uncertain. "What's going on? Not that I'm complaining, doc. I look like I've been put in another body. I didn't even look this good at twenty-five. I can barely tell it's me. I mean, Jesus! These muscles are insane."

"Indeed. I trust you are pleased with the outcome?" Without waiting for a reply, he said, "You did agree to the experiments, Hans. We have all the proper waivers and signed paperwork." He produced a copy of the waiver from his coat, showing that Amir had clearly signed at the bottom.

Amir barely glanced at the papers.

Faust put the document back in his lab coat.

"I . . . I think I am," said Amir. "Pleased, that is. I mean, holy shit! I look like Superman. And whichever one of you gave me my new piece down here, I sure hope it works. I can't wait to try it out."

Clearly revolted, Doctor Reprate scrunched his face at the crudeness, but Elizabeth laughed, her voice rich. "Yes, Mr. Amir. Your equipment is fully functional. I think you will find your, uh, 'new piece' works better than when you were a teenager. I got a bit over-enthusiastic about the part regarding your external reproductive anatomy, I'm afraid. I've programmed your nannies to restore your vigor rather rapidly, which means you can achieve orgasm roughly once every twenty minutes, indefinitely, assuming you have enough bio-available material." She nodded and pursed her lips thoughtfully. "It's quite an improvement. You will quickly become dehydrated and will need to make sure you consume enough nutrients to keep the pleasure centers of your brain supplied, along with your male anatomy and muscles, but your body is now capable of a lot more sex than the normal human male."

Amir grinned at her, giving her a boldly appraising look that annoyed Faust.

Before Amir could say anything, Faust spoke to cut off what Amir clearly wanted to voice. "I have something else," he said, addressing his colleagues. "As you all know, we have one vital piece of information to verify. I've brought you here so we could learn of the results of our experiment together. Shall we?" He motioned Amir to the table once again. "If you would, Hans, please have a seat. I need some tissue samples for this level of detail, I'm afraid. We cannot trust the analysis of the nannies for this precise information."

Amir frowned, looking at the table. The robots had not let go of his wrists. "Are you going to tie me back up?" He seemed on the verge of another outburst.

Faust felt his jaw clench. "No, no. Please be calm, Mr. Amir. Remember, you are not wholly yourself and your emotions are not entirely under your control. We will allow you to remain unfettered for this test, only restrained by the robots, if you will promise to stay calm." He turned to Elizabeth and Claire. "We really should have fixed this hormonal issue before now, doctors. I'm a bit disappointed in you." He intentionally raised an eyebrow. Seeing their looks, he felt a surge of enjoyment at their discomfort. "Obviously, Mr. Amir is deteriorating emotionally, and this level of chemical cocktail is unsustainable. These repeated failures of yours with all the subjects are hindering the project."

Both Claire's face and Elizabeth's face turned red at his criticism, but he pretended not to notice as he swept by them and joined the robots at the table. He needed the other doctors off guard. Reprate was stuttering more than usual, apparently unable to form a coherent sentence.

Amir finally moved, nearly strutting as he walked to the table and sat down. His gown fluttered open. He grinned at the women, not bothering to close it when the robots finally released his wrists. He even moved one leg to give them a better view.

Both women ignored him. Dr. Reprate occupied himself with examining his lab coat.

Faust motioned to the robots, silently communicating his prearranged commands. "Now then, please remain still while we take samples of your blood, marrow, and spinal fluid. This might be painful, Hans. Would you like us to sedate you?"

"No!"

Faust watched Amir struggle to remain calm.

"No. I'm fine. What about the bone marrow?" He grunted stupidly. "That's all the way to the bone, isn't it? And my spinal fluid? It's going to be one hell of a needle."

Barely able to restrain his eagerness, Faust said, "Yes, well, it *is* for science, so I hope a little needle doesn't scare you. Your body will heal itself within moments. Sure, it will hurt, but the pain will be brief. Rapid healing is part of what we've accomplished in our experiments with you. A benefit, if you will."

Elizabeth started to object, her voice reflecting her confusion. "We don't really need to—"

Faust cut her off. "Nonsense. I don't trust the nannite analysis for everything. Don't become dependent on one technology. Sometimes we must verify with direct observation." He examined the oversized needle.

The other doctors looked confused about the entirely unnecessary process. Claire, especially, appeared be increasingly concerned, so he avoided eye contact with her as much as possible.

"What measurements, Doctor Faust?" said Claire. "Perhaps we are misunderstanding."

He merely glanced at them with a dismissive expression that they collectively chose not to challenge.

Amir seemed to have forgotten the mention of a needle. He examined the muscles of his arms. He shook his head in disbelief. "This is crazy. I feel like a young man. I look like one, too." He looked up and leered at the women, who continued to ignore him and didn't balk when the two robots who had been holding him proceeded to place needles in both of his arms, ostensibly drawing blood. Faust had programmed them to instead flood Amir's system with the drug cocktail they'd used to bring him to this point. This time, relatively vast quantities were pumped into his system. Faust watched as the third robot moved and then stood poised behind Amir with the needle.

"All right," said Faust, trying to suppress the eagerness in his voice, "we are ready to extract the spinal fluid and marrow samples. As I said, this will be painful, Mr. Amir, but the pain will pass quickly as you heal."

Faust felt another wave of excitement as the robot prepared to insert the needle into Amir's spine. He signaled, and the robot moved in response.

Amir screamed.

Although Amir's arms were held in the vice grip of the other two robots, he didn't even try to move. With uncharacteristic control, which surprised Faust, he held still, muscles bulging. The robot's actions only lasted a moment, then Amir leaned forward, panting. A moment later, he straightened.

"That fucking hurt! Goddamn it." Amir shook his head, his sweaty hair sticking to his deep brows. "But the pain is gone now." He took a deep breath. "I feel fine. Even the puncture seems to have stopped hurting."

His voice had become more graveled and had dropped in tone. He continued to stare at the women, his previous expression of lust changing to something darker.

Amir's musculature increased before Faust's eyes, his brow becoming noticeably deeper than when they'd all entered the room. Faust knew Amir's body was adapting to external stimulus quickly, and the result of that adaptation would mean a degraded and unstable mental state.

Still working through his plan, Faust mopped his brow. He waited while the lab equipment quickly and efficiently evaluated the samples and provided the requested results. Faust took a deep breath to calm himself and began looking through the amplification equipment which then projected the data onto the screen. When the lab readout began to appear with the expected results, Faust whooped in triumph. He motioned for the other doctors to join him so they could observe the data being displayed. "It worked!" He didn't have to fake his delight. His next actions hinged entirely on these results.

Several readouts showed Amir's reparative levels to be at the ideal ranges. The biggest source of astonishment was the DNA and genetic analysis readout from all the samples. There were several gasps.

"This can't be right, Carlisle," Claire Ashcraft said. "You didn't tell us you were working on this!" She stepped closer, staring at the screen in disbelief.

Faust, having known this would throw them off guard, laughed. "How could I have told any of you? Don't be absurd. If I'd have told you, I'm sure the enormity of my discovery and all the details would have leaked to the public. I don't have to worry about Dr. Reprate, since he can barely talk half the time, but you two ladies gossip more than a flock of geese and I can't have this information getting out."

Faust waited as Dr. Reprate slowly analyzed the data, clearly unable to believe his findings. His obvious shock was a source of amusement. After a moment, Dr. Reprate finally said, "Oh my gosh! He's effectively immortal!"

God, Reprate had a shrill voice. Faust wanted to clasp his hands over Reprate's mouth, smothering him simply to stop the annoying noise.

Reprate continued. "This . . . this is . . . I mean, look at the analysis. If the comparisons from throughout the experiments are correct, the telomeres are completely repaired. The DNA is dividing as if it were cancer, but without the mutations. The senescent cell levels are almost gone. Increased stem cell counts. Wow. So many obstacles, gone. He could live to be a thousand!" He calmed slightly, his voice dropping to its normal wheezing tone. "Are these cellular and genetic changes systemic? Or am I looking at an aspect of gene editing that is isolated?"

"Yes. The changes are systemic. This is what I've been working on. Immortality! And you thought I had shirked my part of the research." Faust allowed the disdain he felt to come out in his voice. What idiots. And how dare they sneer at him behind his back? "You all thought I hadn't been doing my part."

There were several protests, which he cut off with a shout. Pent-up anger and disgust suddenly rose to the surface. He could barely stand to look at them. "I know you discounted my work! Well, now I have shown you, once again, I'm a far more capable researcher than all of you combined." He raised a hand to cut off their objections. He had no desire to hear them anymore. "You have all been helpful, of course. This is exactly what I wanted, and I'd feared I'd have to step in to complete gaps in your research, which would have slowed my own. Some of you are horribly incompetent. When did you actually plan to fix the lack of hormonal control? Never, apparently. But now I have the missing piece. I've done it, achieved the methods we need to secure immortality."

He watched discomfort creep over their faces.

Elizabeth corrected him. "*We* have done this. *We*," she emphasized. "But yes, I admit I wasn't sure what your contribution would be, other than the constant criticism you seem to have become fond of expressing. I'm sorry for thinking you weren't contributing like you should have been, but I must say, you're being childish. Don't wrench your arm out of its socket to pat yourself on the back. As you so snidely indicated, we clearly have more work to do. We can't have patients deteriorating—especially if they become violent and nearly impossible to kill. This changes the dangers, Carlisle. Before, it wasn't too much hassle to . . . correct the situation. Now, we may not be able to so easily dispatch the subjects." She glanced at Amir when she said this.

Looking back at Falk, she scowled and said, "Stop gloating. Jesus! What the hell has gotten into you?"

"Why shouldn't I gloat? I just turned an aging man of no consequence into an immortal. You have helped me make him into somewhat of the male ideal, which will be a pleasant side effect, but the miracle here is mine."

Doctor Reprate became red-faced. "I r-resent that!" he stuttered. "M-mm . . . my work is equally im-m . . . important. I created a way to heal all but death. Even death would have been something I could have fixed, given more time. You may have made it so he w-won't age, but I've made it so he can survive. What good is not aging if you can be shot to death by a drug dealer or angry spouse?" Reprate licked his lips nervously. "His repair process and central immune system are incredibly enhanced. I . . . uh, I won't have it. I have done an incredible amount of work here. All of us have. What's wrong with you? You aren't the only b-b . . . brilliant scientist here, you know. The world will see more than one f-f . . . face." He took a deep breath and looked worriedly over at Amir. "And I agree with Elizabeth. There is much more t-t . . . to be done. We have to fix all the problems that have arisen. This man is clearly deteriorating to an uncontrollable caveman state before our eyes. Look at him!"

Faust stepped back toward the table, his heart racing as he was finally able to allow a sneer to touch his face. His calculated goading had worked, and he positioned himself behind Amir. The other doctors didn't say a word about his movements. "Oh really?" he continued, goading them even more. "You think creating an oversized penis and bulging muscles are something to be heralded? While you've focused on enhancing physique and useless sexual characteristics, I've been redesigning the genome! You think I couldn't figure out a way to make the tissue recover rapidly? I could have, if I hadn't been so focused on fixing the genetic time bomb which is the downfall of all humans since the dawn of creation. You make me sick. You idiots have done a decent job, but nothing remarkable. Sure, there's a market for some of your silly vanity, but who cares when compared to what I've achieved?"

He made a quick motion and one of the robots injected Amir with another massive dose of drugs from one of the silver trays. Amir began breathing heavily and his fingers grew white from gripping the table. Sweat dripped from his hair.

The other doctors looked at Faust, disbelief showing on their faces.

Elizabeth finally recovered from the verbal slap she'd received. "You arrogant prick!" She stepped forward, pointing at him accusingly. "How dare you demean my work by simplifying it as tinkering with his male anatomy. You insufferable asshole! Those 'vain' enhancements will more than fund the remaining research. I've invented a goldmine!"

Amir began to shake. His muscles bulged. The robots restrained him again.

"Believe me," Elizabeth continued, "I intend to make sure the world knows what kind of egomaniacal asshole you truly are. See if you like how much I gossip now, you jerk."

Faust delighted in her loss of temper and watched her jaw clench in frustration.

Elizabeth finally got control of her anger. "Gah! I knew this project with you was a mistake, but Claire insisted. Keeping this experiment secret is proving to be another mistake. We should have broadcast this from the start. You may have accomplished something incredible, but nothing gives you the right to downplay our discoveries. You know full well they were equally challenging." She jabbed a finger toward him. "Oh, and in case you've somehow forgotten in that smug head of yours, you still need us to perfect the research. There's a long way to go. Since your egomaniacal and infantile delusions appear to have led you to believe the information can be hidden, I'll get the Sector Tech involved. Try maneuvering around him, you egomaniacal ass. He'll grind you into powder the second he deems you a threat."

Amir shuddered and shook his head. Elizabeth backed up in alarm. Her look became one of concern. "Look, something is really wrong with him. We need to sedate him or at least get him strapped back on the table."

Amir thrashed against the robots. He lifted his head and his eyes appeared devoid of thought. An animalistic growl escaped from his throat. The doctors stepped back en masse.

Faust snarled. "Oh? You intend to tattle on me, do you? You think I haven't prepared to deal with you appropriately?" He laughed. "And yes, I quite agree, something is wrong with him. Why, he seems to be in a murderous rage!" He laughed again. He waved his hand in a quick motion to the robots. In response to his signal, the robots let Amir go. For a moment the muscled giant just shook. Then, with a rumbling shout, he leapt at the stunned doctors.

For a fraction of a second, they froze, then they all reacted by turning to run for the exit. Amir quickly broke Reprate's neck and flew at Elizabeth. In seconds, he smashed her head onto the floor, killing her. He roared with rage and tore the metal top off one of the lab equipment tables, overturning the attached devices.

Claire screamed and tried to open the door. Faust had planned for this and had encoded the door to remain locked unless he opened it himself. With the door locked and no escape from her assailant, she whirled desperately to the robots. "Protect me! What are you doing, Carlisle? My god! Robots! I command you to protect me!" Claire raised her arms in a futile effort to protect herself and released a terrified scream as Amir began to beat her with the metal table top, smashing her arms and head violently. The robots never moved. She, like the others, died in moments.

Amir whirled to attack Faust. Before Amir had moved more than a step, two of the robots had both of his arms and tried to wrestle him back to the table. He threw his head back and yelled in rage, dropping the table and dragging both robots with him toward Faust for a moment. Amir's strength had grown to stunning proportions, and Faust took several steps back. The third robot moved to engage Amir, but Faust motioned for the robot to remain at the medical station.

"That's . . . impressive. My, my, you do have a temper, though, and it looks like I don't have a lot of time to deal with you. I hadn't anticipated quite this much raw power."

Amir gave another unintelligible shout, his bloodshot eyes fixed on Faust. He continuing to fight against his captors, who were barely managing to hold him. His strength continued to grow.

Faust had little concern about the danger Amir presented, now that his plans were finally coming to fruition. "All three in less than a minute. Just amazing. I'll note your rapid strength changes in my research." He looked at Claire's corpse. "It had to be done." He breathed deeply. "It had to." He thought, *I need to calm down. Remember—this would have ruined me. Exposure would have ruined the research. We are so close. I am so close! If only I could have trusted you.* "It had to be done," he repeated.

He took several more calming breaths, then moved into action. *Okay. The story. Just remember to follow the plan. Let's see.* He touched his face in agitation. "It's a shame the robots weren't fast enough to stop Amir. Three doctors experimenting on a patient in secret. Shocking, really."

Dry-washing his hands, he continued to talk to himself as he read data from the computer. "This entire secret operation is something I've condemned from the beginning. What were they thinking? They should never have been experimenting with powerful mind-altering drugs and illegal genetic research. I refused to take part and look what's happened."

Amir clearly didn't understand him or care. Faust thought Amir had probably lost language skills, considering his degradation. He continued to fight to free himself.

"Now then, we still have a problem. You *are* a disaster. I believe it is time for your malfunction, Mr. Amir."

He turned to the nanotechnology transmitter. "This is Director Carlisle Faust."

"Voice recognition verified. Welcome, Dr. Faust," said a pleasant woman's voice.

"Stand by to transmit instruction set."

"Standing by, doctor."

"Record subject. Previously defined as Hans Amir."

"Subject recorded. Record updated. Standing by."

"Initiate partial decay training simulation. Subject: Corpse of Hans Amir."

"Warning. Unable to comply. Safety protocols detect subject is not deceased. Logging violation with Central." Then, after a brief pause, "Unable to log violation. External communication state offline. Logging violation to local memory."

"Override. Subject to be recorded as deceased."

"Independent verification required. Querying Central Operations." Another pause. "Unable to process query. Independent verification not possible. External communication state offline. Manual verification required."

Dr. Faust swore. Of course the systems were offline, or he'd have a drove of officers in here. Faust gritted his teeth, momentarily stuck. He couldn't have the robots kill the man, or the physical struggle would be obvious. Then, too, he wasn't sure Amir wouldn't simply heal from a broken neck and spine. He had become just shy of invulnerable and grew stronger by the minute.

His mind raced. "Independent verification standby."

"Standing by."

He gave quick instructions and the third robot moved and drug Reprate's small corpse to the monitor, pressing his thumb on the transmitter. Blood smeared the print identification and had to be wiped off. A second thumbprint attempt succeeded.

"Verification complete. Thank you, Doctor Earl Reprate. Manual override engaged."

"Record subject as deceased."

"Recorded. Subject is now logged as deceased. Warning. Subject transmits biological activity."

"Acknowledged. Override warning. Override safety. Initiate partial decay training simulation."

"Overrides acknowledged. Logging to local memory. Initiating decay simulation instructions to subject's nanotechnology units."

A moment later, Amir's shouts turned to screams, then the screams became those of mewling terror. His struggling grew weak and he began to seize violently, then he stopped and fell forward onto both knees, barely moving. His powerful voice became a whimper. He clawed at his skin.

After a moment, his skin abscessed, his eyes boiled, and he slumped over, dead. Within minutes, his tissue showed signs he'd been dead for several days. This would further confuse the timeline of death and the investigation. The absence of rancidness, due to bacterial breakdown of tissue, could pose an issue if investigated, but Faust had prepared to offer an extensive explanation based on the medical tampering with the man's genetics and some made-up comments about how the bacteria could not consume the modified tissues with nannies protecting the host. His assertions would be factually inaccurate, but they would suffice unless someone pushed hard for more answers.

"Destroy the recorder. Make sure it is impossible to read but take care to leave the rest of the machine intact," he said to the robots. In response to his commands, they quickly dismantled the local recording cube from the transmitter and smashed it with enough force to completely pulverize the recording cube. At his direction, the robots replaced the unit with another, which stopped the repeated error messages. Faust verified the fabricated data of the new recorder, which painted a different picture of the experiments.

The new information, which contained a month's worth of data he'd meticulously created, indicated this experiment had been conducted solely by the three dead physicians. They'd accepted a government contract, and Faust used this to tie them to the research.

According to the falsified records, they'd met in secret many times and the experiments to create a biologically and technologically superior soldier had been unsuccessful. They'd only succeeded in creating a violent and uncontrolled monster . . . not far from the truth. The records further implicated them in the disappearance of several other volunteers.

This data would also show that their disregard for safety and proper science had resulted in Amir killing them all. His enhancements had been recorded as having malfunctioned. This aggression toward the physicians, it would bear to reason, had triggered a pre-programmed suicide sequence after he'd murdered the physicians. The programming hadn't been fast enough to stop him—a mistake which had cost them their lives.

Reviewing all of this, Faust nodded to himself, satisfied. He motioned for the attending robots to clean themselves. From inside a compartment on one of the robots, he removed a pair of shoes and changed them, nestling his old shoes inside them. He could not be found to have ever entered or left the room. An analysis of shoe patterns might lead to him being questioned. Knowing he'd most likely step in blood, he'd planned ahead, providing himself with a second, clean pair of shoes. Faust almost laughed at the idiocy of tracking blood out of the room when everyone was supposedly dead. Unfortunately, both pairs had been decidedly uncomfortable as they were a size too small, but he'd had to wear them to carefully match the prints of Doctor Reprate. During any investigation his shoeprints in the room would appear as if they belonged to the other doctor. Reprate would have entered and left the room many times over the course of the experiments, but Faust needed to ensure nobody suspected he'd done the same.

For this same reason, Faust had worn a second skin, typically used for burn victims but with the purpose of avoiding shedding DNA evidence. He'd also worn a wig designed to look like his own hair and tried to keep himself as covered as possible, a peculiarity that his colleagues would have chalked up to the other oddities of his personality. Faust had acclimated those around him to oddities in his personality over of the past couple of years, allowing these strange affectations to go mostly unnoticed by his peers.

Yet another of their mistakes.

Faust beckoned for the robots to follow him out of the room. Moving quickly, he descended to the lowest level of the facility, where the recycling and reclaiming systems were housed.

Avoiding people proved easy, as this part of the facility had been kept mostly secret. He pulled out a hidden bundle from under the machinery and set it aside. He removed all his clothing and his shoes, throwing them into the reclaiming furnace to destroy DNA evidence that might have contaminated them. Next, he wiggled out of the second skin and pulled off his wig.

After he'd put on his replacement clothing, careful to throw the plastic wrapper in with the rest, he motioned for the robots to enter the chamber. They had to be destroyed, along with everything he'd worn. Analysis of their systems would have shown tampering and drawn questions down on him. The robots, which had been stripped of their safety protocols, would be melted down and added to the other scrap metals and materials which were routinely recycled.

Satisfied, he started the mechanical reclaiming process, which would incinerate anything incriminating.

With meticulous care, he'd previously modified the security system to remove the lock on the lab, as well as any evidence that he'd moved through secure doors in other parts of the facility. He then modified his schedule to show he'd been at a social event all evening, thereby giving him an ironclad alibi if questions arose. Nobody would distinctly remember his arrival, but the doctored security system would be evidence enough. Faust took a deep breath, squared his shoulders, and headed to the party.

TWO

"WE'VE GOT TO DO SOMETHING, JASON."

At the sound of Monica's commanding voice, Jason glanced up from his chair. A lock of raven-black hair hid one of her crystal blue eyes but didn't hide the intensity of her gaze.

He regarded her carefully. He looked down at the printout she waved in her hand. "Do something?"

She slammed the paper down on the desk, slapping her hand on top of it for emphasis. Jason moved his chair from behind his screens to get a better look.

His calm voice seemed to inflame Monica's temper. He repressed a smile, resisting an impulse to goad her into the amusing display of an adult tantrum. His mischievous side had to be ignored sometimes, but the thought of riling Monica almost made him laugh.

Jason saw a printed broadcast to all citizens. He read the title: "Department of Defense: Citizen Registration." He didn't bother reading further. "I've seen this already. Just like everyone, I'm sure." He picked it up and arched a confused eyebrow at her. "Why on earth did you bother printing this off? Why so upset?"

She stood up, a little too straight, her athletic arms folded tightly across her chest. *Ah*, he thought, *all the signals of her anger. If she only knew how easy she is to read.*

For a moment she just let her ice-cold stare bore into him, disregarding his objections as she so often did. Jason patiently waited for her to answer. Finally, in a voice that typically got what she wanted, she said, "Jason, you're supposed to be a genius. What kind of idiot doesn't see this exactly for what it is?"

He arched an eyebrow, knowing how it would affect her. "Exactly? It's literally what it says. Registration for all citizens. We do this all the time for licensing purposes and our ID's. It's not a big deal. Presumably, you see something else, which is not explicitly stated in the requirement. Let's see . . . assuming your usual distaste for governmental, uh, shall we say 'interference' in your daily life, I'm guessing you view this as a personal attack on your freedom."

"Listen, you idiot savant, the 'requirement,'" she said, making quotations in the air with her fingers, "which I *did not* and *do not* agree with by the way, passed without a vote or without citizen input. The government isn't asking us to renew our work licenses or input our travel permits, they're saying we'll be tracked everywhere. ALL the time," she said, nearly shouting. "They want our uplinks to be monitored constantly. If you read this, then you'll know they also expect visual augmentation, so whatever we're looking at can be recorded." She picked up the paper and crumpled it, throwing it on the floor. "This is crazy!"

Jason frowned. "Some citizens have already had voluntarily visual augmentation, Monica. It's no big deal. I can perform the operation on the fly and in under an hour. It provides quite a few benefits."

She stepped closer, leaning forward confrontationally. "I'm not talking about using technology to help diagnose and record symptoms of a patient, Jason. Who the hell needs to see me staring at the door of a bathroom stall? Why does the government need to watch the holograms while I'm watching them? Voluntary is one thing, and those people who volunteered can turn the stupid thing off and on at will. Why does the Council or any authority need to know what I'm doing all the goddamn time? It's already bad enough that almost everything we talk about is recorded if we aren't in our private quarters or some other secure location."

She stood up and turned away, running her fingers through her unruly bangs. Her tone changed. "Jason, this is really bad. We have so little privacy as it is. Now they want it all. Our privacy is valuable. It's our freedom. This tyranny is getting out of control. Most of our freedoms are gone already, given up in little bits for the 'betterment of society.'" She ran a hand down her form-fitting outfit, which covered her from shoulder to toe. "We agreed to wear these biosuits so we could be monitored for health. I understand your job is much easier when you have a constant flow of data from a patient. I'm less than thrilled about the fact my entire bodily processes are an open book to a Medic, or you can, at your leisure, anesthetize or otherwise drug me out of my mind by simply ordering my suit to obey your whim."

Jason opened his mouth to object, but she cut him off.

"Yeah, I know there are rules against abuse and a committee you have to report to, but it doesn't diminish the fact we have so little power."

She took a deep breath. "Okay, so yeah, public places are watched and listened to constantly right now, and the result is almost no crime. I love the automation of our vehicles and our robots, which makes traveling and working so much easier, never mind the fact they are all controlled by the Techs. But Jason, I can't ignore this new mandate. We're talking about my body, for Christ's sake."

She walked across the room, keeping her back to him. Jason could see she was trying to take a moment to calm herself.

She turned back towards him. "I can't allow myself to be branded and used as a living robot to spy on everything and everyone around me. At least you Medics have to answer to each other and your superiors for every action you take. Having to answer to someone makes your ability to harm seem less likely, even though you control the life and death of everyone around you. If you abused your power, you'd be punished."

"Where are you going with that?" he asked.

"Just hear me out." She dropped to the floor and sat cross-legged to look up at him. "The Techs are so divorced from the world, they seem to no longer know what's real. They are genetically engineered into their technology—even the government doesn't understand or control them. They might as well be super androids. But *this* power, this is in the hands of people who have clawed their way to the top and have zero qualms about abuse. I'm afraid that for many of them taking advantage of others is in their nature."

"How exactly do you expect the government will use this registration to cause problems?" asked Jason. "They are just a function of our society like the rest of us. They do have to answer to someone, just like we do. They have to answer to us—the voters and the media. It's not like they can order me to do harm or order you to sabotage machinery. So what if they see more than they already do? There are only nine of them. Nobody has time to watch all the videos created. You're being kind of silly."

"Goddammit, Jason," she said, pushing herself up from the floor. "This is not something I can live with. Stop being so impersonal. You're supposed to be an Empath. A male Empath, which means you still have balls for god's sake. What good does it do the government to have access to so much more information? What possible reason could there be?" She turned her back on him.

Jason closed his eyes for a moment and didn't bother to hold back a smile. "As you know, my dearest Monica, I intentionally do not bother empathizing with your emotions since they are usually out of control. Being dispassionate and logical is part of my function as a Medic. Just because I can feel someone's emotions and various biological processes doesn't mean I let them turn me into a raving lunatic several times a week. That, sweetie-pies, is apparently part of your function as a Mechanic. I can't for the life of me figure out what purpose your wild mood swings serve, but I'm sure being a volatile and emotional nutcase with a strong dose of paranoia is ever so helpful in keeping societal machinery running."

Monica turned back and gave him a flat stare. Her voice grew quiet. She clearly wasn't amused. "At least you're still funny."

He chuckled. Monica's biting sarcasm and wit were one of the reasons he loved her so much. She cut right through to the heart of things, often with a very amusing twist to her words.

Jason knew one of his major advantages in life was his calm and comforting appearance. Over time, he'd discovered his smile made almost anyone trust him with his or her life. His long, languidly muscular dancer's frame was another asset. One he occasionally used to his advantage. His calm amusement and affable good looks weren't working so well on Monica at the moment, but she wasn't entirely immune. Her jaw muscle unclenched slightly.

He took a deep breath, analyzing the problem she posed. "As far as a good reason as to why they might want more information, I can think of several. First, with observation abilities of the masses at their disposal, they could discover problems before they became severe. Structural problems with buildings that a passerby might not normally take note of, for example. Observing accidents as they happen and from many vantage points allows faster response and future prevention. Noting strange behavior that could lead to crime or might indicate a problem with an individual is another potentially valuable instance. Compiling social patterns."

Her intent look didn't waver.

"This would mean being able to correct something before it became worse, saving a lot of money in the long run." He thought for a moment to see if he'd overlooked anything. "It would make my job easier in some ways too, quite honestly."

Her jaw clenched again before she started into another tirade. "Are you kidding me? You're saying you agree with this? You agree with allowing every person to be heard and seen every moment of their lives? Are you insane? I don't want them watching me have sex. I don't want them in my head when I take a crap. Jason, I don't want them hearing the conversation we're having right now. This conversation—despite your thick-headed and rather brainless assertions—is valuable to me because it emphasizes freedom to think and speak as I wish. If they heard me talking like this, I'd be carted off to have my skull used for a chemical testing ground."

The absurdity of her comment almost made him laugh aloud, which would have been a disaster. "You really think they have the time to watch you poop?" he said, controlling his laughter. "As to your claim of being taken to have your head pumped full of drugs, absolutely! I've heard of people being carted off whenever they say something controversial. As a matter of fact, I'm sure you could name a few people as examples. It's happened to so many people we know . . . oh wait. No it hasn't. Not even one person I can think of."

Her eyes narrowed dangerously. "I'm starting to think you've been hooked up to your medical gear too long. You've lost all sense of perspective. Don't you see how easy it is to lead us into modern slavery? Step by step they're eroding our freedoms. I'm not sure why, but something about this seems carefully calculated and planned. They didn't even ask the populace if they would agree to modification. They simply decreed it and we're expected to follow orders without recourse. They took away even our ability to vote on something that violates our privacy. A decree implies an imperial order. That's not freedom, Jason, it's the opposite. We're being caged."

"Monica, be serious. Go outside and look around you. Every citizen is either productive in some way, or they have a valid reason not to be and are cared for. There's no homelessness, no hunger. We are all fed, and every single person pursues whatever profession they desire. We are more educated, more enabled, and have more freedom to choose our lives than ever before in history. How exactly is the governing class doing something that limits you?"

He watched as Monica took time to regroup. She absently played with some small figurines Jason kept on his desk before she spoke again in a quieter voice.

"I can't have this conversation in public, first of all. I don't get to vote on whether or not I augment my own fucking body. How about I'd like some vote on what my body is used for, for starters? Jason, there are tons of things we aren't free to do. If I wanted to leave work and go to one of the space colonies, I'd be prevented. It's below my rank in society. They're limiting freedoms for certain sections of the population, too. Almost like a caste system."

She chewed her lip for a moment.

"I tried to vacation off-world. I thought it would be fun for a while, you know? Go check out some of the men on the outer colonies. I hear they are rugged. Anyway, the Bureau of Travel denied my request. And seriously, why do we even have a Bureau of Travel? Why can't I just pay for a seat on a ship and go somewhere? It's bullshit." She crossed over to his living room to grab a chair so she could sit with him at his desk, clearly tired of standing over him. "Oh sure, the bureau was nice about it. They flattered me outrageously and gave me a bonus week this year to vacation in one of three pre-selected places. They wouldn't even let me choose which of those three, they just said when they had an opening in one of them, they'd let me know. An opening? We're not overcrowded on any world in the colonies, so what the fuck was that about?"

Jason couldn't help but feel exasperated. He took a deep breath. If there was one sure way to piss Monica off, it was to deny her access to potential sex partners, so he could see why the denial of her travel request would upset her so much. "Okay, just to prove you wrong, and show you we're totally fine discussing this in public, I'll say something tomorrow at work about this new policy. Mention I think it sucks. If I'm still around in the evening, I'll be sure to apologize and then drop the subject. Sound good?"

She stared at him for a moment. Finally, she said "No way. Talking about the issue in public just addresses one aspect of privacy, not the underlying issues. Besides, I think just talking about the new policy changes so someone can hear is a weak way of you trying to get out of this conversation. Clearly, you don't care. I have a strong feeling you will change your mind if you ever step outside the herd." She sighed. "I actually hope even a little bit of speaking out about the issue doesn't get you in trouble."

"Fine, then. We can talk about this another time. For now, I'll show you we are free to disagree and we can go from there." He moved his chair back behind his computer screens. Now, I really have to finish working on my report for next week, so if you could leave me in peace, it would be splendid of you."

Her smile seemed forced. "Sure. See you tomorrow." She moved toward the door and then stopped, turning her head to talk over her shoulder. "Oh, yeah. I almost forgot. There're a few new movies out this week. Wanna go?"

"What?"

She turned around. "The movies, Jason."

Jason looked at her quizzically, perplexed. "Yes, I heard you. It's just, we never go to the movies. I can't—"

"Oh, that's right," she interrupted him. "I totally forgot you don't go to the theater because you can't stand the reproductions that are filtered. Same crap produced over and over. Same themes approved for release by the government for the masses."

Jason scowled. It was true. He hated the theater for the very reasons she was pointing out.

Monica smiled sweetly. "Just thought you might like another example of the stagnating and controlled little bubble we live in. See you tomorrow." The door slid open, then closed with a soft hush as she left.

Kaden Sinclair

THREE

THE HOSPITAL BUSTLED WITH frenzied activity. Jason moved quickly between sterile patient cubes with a practiced, but hurried ease, and thought back on his conversation with Monica the day before. There had been an accident in Sector 8 involving one of the largest manufacturing facilities of East City. Twenty-four-hundred people had been exposed to high levels of a known neuro-toxin and the hospitals had been overloaded. Sector 8, and Jason's own Sector 7, had been flooded with incoming cases. His location within Sector 7, but close to the border of Sector 8, often received medical cases from both.

Fortunately, and much to his relief, Jason's work had become much easier with the biosuits most citizens wore. The suits allowed him the ability to analyze the toxin due to their built-in bio-feedback and to order a binding agent into the bloodstream en masse before the damage became too severe. Each suit came equipped with various chemicals for remote administration from a qualified Medic, cutting down on fatalities enormously. Jason could stabilize a patient and then he or she could then be transported to a nearby facility. The analysis and administration of a binding agent was fast-paced work, but the victims were quickly sent to the distribution centers where the new chemicals were mixed and provided to the biosuits. Out of twenty-four-hundred people, there were only a few casualties, nearly unavoidable given the level of exposure.

As the wave of incoming patients subsided and his day normalized, he thought more about the conversation of the night before. Looking at his patients, it occurred to him the response time on this would have been even faster if the uplinks Monica hated so much had been in place and active. Visual monitoring would have noticed a breach before the deadly chemicals were detected by the environmental sampling modules. A Tech would have analyzed and processed the data and prevented the explosion.

Jason wandered to the bathroom to splash some cool water on his face. He grimaced at the thought of Monica's reaction to his analysis, but direct observation of the problem might have prevented the toxin release altogether. At the very least, an evacuation could have been ordered before it hit the air systems. Had the

Sector 8 Tech been involved, he could have instantly shut down all systems and force-evacuated everyone before the toxin escaped containment. Such was the power of the Techs, that the entire incident wouldn't have even required their presence. With a mere thought, the entire interconnected systems would have instantly obeyed the Tech's commands. Monica's paranoia seemed misplaced, yet even Jason felt the Techs held too much power. He didn't trust them. Their influence spanned the globe and they could see and hear anything and everything exposed to technology. Pretty much everything, in other words.

As Jason finished washing, he looked up to see one of his fellow Medics enter the restroom. A big smile lit up Susan's features when she saw him, and a familiar calming and mildly sexual feeling flowed from her specialized nano-bots. Empaths, those with a knack for using nannies to broadcast emotion, tended to radiate a mild pleasure wherever they went without consciously thinking about it. For the most part, the nature of being an empath meant wanting to make everyone around them comfortable. Jason grinned at her and, he knew, the same feeling flowed from his broadcast nannies and were received by hers.

"I think we handled the disaster rather well, don't you?" Susan combed a slender hand through her long hair. She draped her blonde curls over one shoulder so she could wash her face.

"Seems so. Of course, the new suits really help. It seems almost impossible to imagine not having them.

They've only been mandated for what, three years? Funny how quickly great technological leaps become integral. The Director really earned his tenure with inventing the suits."

She pooled warm water in her hands and submerged her face. After a moment, she toweled dry and sighed deeply. "Tenure. Pah!" For a moment, he felt annoyance flicker from her. "If he succeeds in putting through his forced interconnection for all citizens, I'm not sure I will hold him in such high-esteem. His love affair with tenure makes me more than a little nervous. His newest appointment is outside my comfort level."

Jason raised an eyebrow, startled. To hear Monica's sentiment echoed by one of his peers disconcerted him a little. Carefully, he said, "Oh, I don't know. I suppose I haven't looked at it much, but it can't be that bad. With visual augmentation in those workers, think of how quickly we could have reacted today."

She looked at him for a moment. "Jason, there are benefits and curses to every advance we make. The problem isn't what benefit the registration will provide. Undoubtedly, it can do great things. The problem is the hands this power falls into. I'm just . . . not comfortable knowing the thirteen members of the Council will know our every thought and deed. It's one thing if the responsibility is shared, but this is giving them too much power without any balance. It's actually scaring me."

He shrugged, trying to hide the fact her thinking unnerved him. "So? We'll just vote them out, right? I mean, they *are* kept in check by the elections. If they abuse their power they will be removed and replaced. They are only a function of our society, not an edict." He laughed. "They can be fired, just like anybody who doesn't do their job."

Her eyes widened slightly, and her mood changed discernibly. "You haven't seen the secondary order, then."

Jason looked at her, confused. "What secondary order?"

Susan glanced at where the cameras were prominently watching their every move. "They can't be voted out. The Council also announced they were tenured. They are now a permanent appointment, much like our Supreme Court. That's what I meant by Director Faust's love affair with tenure. He's been appointed as a permanent Council member."

His heart skipped a beat. "Permanent?" Their power was only acceptable because it was limited in duration. "This is highly unusual," he said carefully. Permanent appointment was a direct violation of The Construct, the societal agreement to appoint leaders who were granted limited governing powers specific to their specialty. They were replaced in rotation, one each thirteen years— sooner if one died, became corrupt, or was ineffective. A call to vote could be initiated by enough signatories at any time. This balance of power kept them moderately uncorrupted. A permanent appointment could damage the system meant to keep their power in check.

"Unusual is putting it mildly. Director Faust is a

major part of the movement. Something is going on and I'm not sure I have it figured out yet." She hesitated, then, leaning forward she whispered, "And there is some sort of advanced research project going on that they're keeping from everyone. I've seen the orders from Faust to convert the old suit fabrication facility to a high-security research center." She paused and then continued, uncertainly. "After the accident with those doctors a couple of months ago, I'm not sure I feel comfortable with secrets. I hate to sound conspiratorial, but really? Building a secret research facility after a whole team of our best are found dead from a secret project? All of this is awfully coincidental, to put it mildly. Way too strange for me to feel comfortable."

As she moved away from him, Jason clenched his jaw slightly to keep his face impassive. He recalled the incident. Several high-level research doctors had been killed during an experiment with mind-altering drugs. Or so the story had been. There were several pieces which didn't seem to match up, such as the fact no new data had come out of the fiasco. For example, the forbidden research about longevity. What had become of all the research leading up to the tragedy? Whatever they were working on had never been fully disclosed. The media pushed hard to investigate further but got nowhere. The Council constantly blocked investigations with legal maneuvering, which gave conspiracy theorists all kinds of fodder.

"I'm not sure there is anything to be worried about,"

he said, finally. "We do need the extra research space and the fab is already retrofitted." He forced himself to smile. "Besides, we both know who will be asked to head up staffing. You have a knack for finding quality people, my dear."

She moved away from him, her gaze thoughtful and her anxiety still palpable. "I hope you're right, Jason. I don't know what . . . I just hope you're right. Something seems really odd about all this. Especially these changes with tenure." She lifted her chin with resolve. "I'm planning on voicing my objections to the administration."

She finally dried her hands and left the restroom, giving him a wave of farewell. He grinned at her, radiated calm, then dried his own hands and went out into the hall. For a moment, he felt a sense of disorientation, as if he was a stranger in the hospital and not one of its master practitioners. He watched the bustle and frenzied pace of the staff as they hurried from sterile-cube to sterile-cube, carrying objects and materials which were suddenly foreign to him. The movements of the staff and support robots reminded him of insects performing some elaborate process deep within an anthill, scurrying about, busily enacting the wishes of their queen.

His sense of self shrank into a smallness he'd never known. It gave him a pang of foreboding which made him lose his usual sense of control. An indiscernible shadow of the future reached out to him, causing his eyes to blaze with vision. A wave of empathic concern and trepidation emanated from him, swept the hallway, causing nearby people to stop and turn to him in surprise. Several of the robotic staff halted, overridden with his emotional instructions from his silent wailing to fix something they could not discern or comprehend.

His dark thoughts were inexplicable, unwarranted. He vainly struggled to right himself, knowing how much his emotions affected others, but he felt himself careening down a canyon of madness painted with the possibilities of future happenings. He envisioned a society enslaved, mindlessly obeying an unknown set of masters who fed on them like giant spiders nestling at their throats. He railed against the image, vaguely aware he'd begun broadcasting uncontrolled fear to those around him.

He clamped down on his emotional broadcast, reversing his disorientation and closing the window of prophecy that had opened in his mind. Calm permeated the hallway once more. With confused looks, people smiled at him uncertainly, then quickly went on their way. The robots began to go about their tasks as if nothing had disrupted them.

Jason felt foolish. He barked a laugh at himself, but it sounded frantic and he fought down another wave of irrational fear.

He forced himself to move woodenly toward the exit. His need to be outside became compulsory, sapping his remaining volition, and he moved as if marionette strings drew his legs forward. Concerned looks followed him, and he could spare no thought for illusion. He started to become suspicious of his own behaviors, as they were abnormal, but he could name no affliction. His reactions were irrational, a cloud of miasma without substance.

The moment he stepped outside, his senses returned. Sound flooded his ears and sunlight pierced the veil of darkness shrouding his eyes. Without having realized he'd lost external perceptions, he stood mute, overwhelmed with relief by their sudden return. He breathed raggedly for a few more moments, then consciously slowed his breathing to a normal rate. Now he could laugh with genuine relief and the sound of his own voice became an anodyne which freed him of his dark percipience. He'd been sweating, his body metabolizing adrenaline.

Around him, the city bustled with activity. A vast chorus of machines and people created a noise altogether its own.

Flying vehicles wove through the skies in patterns determined by their computers for optimal delivery of their human cargos. Buildings, sculpted for functionality and esthetics, were draped in green. Trees crowned the structures; some so tall the tops could not be easily seen. Vines climbed the sides and cradled the structures in a vegetative embrace. Tiers designed to harbor gardens bloomed with color and breathed life into the air. Rather than the invasive angularity of cities of the past, the newer cities mingled technology and nature with chrysoprase-hued benevolence.

Taken for granted, the city around Jason shone with beauty, and he felt surprise at not having seen it before. He glanced at his hand, which bled from a cut he'd unknowingly obtained. He pulled a kerchief from his pocket and dabbed the cut lightly. Before his eyes, the wound stopped bleeding. Nannites, molecular machines designed to accelerate healing and perform medical tasks, rushed to the site and stitched the skin closed. Commonly known as "nannies", the tiny robots had made it possible for humans to sustain once life-threatening wounds and survive. A recent advancement created and instituted by Director Faust had enhanced the nannites to the point where they kept the body completely whole and protected from everything short of death. They performed minor healing as part of their instructions but could be directed toward complex surgical procedures by Medics. He, himself, directed their operations during surgery and many considered him to be the best at the art. Jason's natural mastery of communication to technology and specifically in directing the nannies, coupled with his empathic abilities, allowed him to discern patient issues, discomforts, and the efficacy of his repairs.

While Jason remained lost in his reverie, he heard the sliding doors open behind him. He turned. One of the facility robots strode up, it's mechanically languid movements unusually fluid and surprisingly graceful. To those who had never seen advanced models, the human-like movements were disconcerting. Jason's surprise derived from the robot's presence rather than its design, however. Before he had time to pull together enough presence of mind to guess its intent, the robot delivered an order.

"Dr. Emerson, Central is detecting an elevated level of anxiety and erratic behavior. We wish for you to come with us for analysis." It used a pleasant, unthreatening voice.

Taken aback, Jason said, "I'm fine. I just had a moment, a panic attack. It's over and I'm back to normal." He frowned. His anxiety had been overwhelming and completely out of character. Suddenly, he suspected his loss of control wasn't entirely due to the shock of the conversation. Something more seemed to be at play. Traces of a biochemical might still be in his bloodstream, but he needed to analyze it soon, before his nannies removed it. He stuffed the kerchief in his pocket, thankful for the blood sample.

The robot paused, receiving instructions. "Thank you for updating us, Dr. Emerson, however policy states all doctors outside the range of acceptable health parameters must be analyzed for potential problems and possibly removed from duty. Please come with me for testing." The soothing voice had become firm.

He felt his ire rising. "Attendant, transfer to Central directly. Central, this is *senior* Medic Dr. Emerson," he said, emphasizing his superior rank. "I have regained normalcy and my panic attack has subsided. As I am no longer outside parameters, I do not require testing," he said, citing protocol. "I must return to work."

After a brief pause, the voice changed from being pleasantly robotic to commanding and starkly human. "Dr. Emerson. This is Central. You are ordered to testing immediately. Failure to follow the attendant will result in seizure."

Jason's mouth opened. He was stunned. Such a requirement was completely ridiculous. His rank should have superseded any orders they were able to issue. For them to require complete testing for something so simple and fleeting as a moment of anxiety was, in and of itself, a source of anxiety. He remained calm, though now genuinely worried. For a moment, he thought about exerting his seniority and forcing a challenge, but he opted to comply.

Without waiting for the attendant, he strode back into the building and, moving rapidly, headed up to one of the lifts and entered. The robot followed. He rode the lift up to the testing floor.

Here he paused, waiting for the attendant robot. This robot led him to one of the interview rooms and ushered him inside.

To his surprise, the room contained several other doctors, including Director Faust. Despite the implied severity of the situation, they greeted him with smiles. None of this made sense.

"Ah! Dr. Emerson," said Director Falk. "Thank you for coming. We are quite worried about you. I personally overrode Central so I could check on you myself and have you brought here. Please, have a seat."

Obediently, Jason sat in one of the plush chairs provided mostly for patients. The chairs were designed to embrace and were slightly heated. Normally, they were comforting. But Jason wasn't comforted. Why so many attendants? Why the other doctors? How on earth had they assembled so quickly? It would be nearly impossible for them to be here on such short notice. Further, they seemed slightly on edge, uncertain. Jason' heightened senses told him they were trying to hide something. Only the Director seemed entirely at ease. Jason saw something ugly flicker across the Director's face before it changed into a look that seemed carefully crafted to evince concern. His entire demeanor rang false to someone so attuned to emotions in others. Jason may have been the only doctor capable of detecting both the trepidation and the false concern in the room.

He nodded politely. "Director."

"How are you feeling, Jason? We detected elevated levels of stress only fifteen minutes ago. Is something wrong?" Jason nearly laughed at such a loaded and obvious question, but a note of caution panged in his head. "Just had a moment of anxiety, Director. For no discernable reason. I must say I'm actually more nervous now than earlier. This is highly unusual." Then, because he knew being blunt would be his best course of action, he said, "And, let's be honest. A whole team of doctors greets me? That's not normal."

"I'll admit, it is rather odd." Faust chuckled. "Well, we cannot have one of our premier physicians breaking down. We depend on you quite a bit, Jason."

An awkward silence followed, since Jason wasn't willing to be led into anything.

Finally, the Director sat across from him and smiled. "You appear to be fine now, so perhaps we were overreacting. And your suit reports you've returned to normal levels. Seems like you are perfectly okay, and we needn't have worried." Again, a brief silence.

Director Emerson steepled his fingers over his mouth, affecting an air of nonchalance. "What upset you, Jason? Anything we should be concerned about?"

With a flash of insight, Jason knew what had triggered this whole episode. The panic attack provided an excuse to find out his level of concern with the permanency of the Council. They would have engineered a reason no matter what condition he'd been in. The real reason for his summons became apparent: his conversation in the washroom with Susan. Her paranoia somehow justified their actions. He knew he couldn't hide the nature of the conversation with Susan, not totally. The Director already knew what they'd discussed and was clearly testing him by leading him to disclose his reasons for the panic.

Carefully, Jason sighed and let concern show on his face. "Nothing major, just a conversation with one of the other Medics. It worried me for a moment until I had a chance to get some air. Then I realized how silly I'd been behaving. Her whole point being a bit absurd, bordering on a little paranoia. I really don't know why it bothered me so much, and I have to admit I had a moment of odd anxiety, which is completely unlike me." Knowing they had surveillance, he added, "I even laughed at my idiocy about the conversation." Let them think he laughed at his own folly and not as a reaction to the relief from the crushing tightness in his chest.

The Director looked at him keenly, his crafty gaze assessing the truth of Jason's statement. When it became clear Jason had nothing more to add, he prompted, "But surely you felt genuine alarm. We saw your levels spike. What makes you think Susan's comments were absurd?"

He hadn't said the person he'd talked to had been Susan, validating his belief they knew about the conversation. "She talked about the tenure for the Council and voiced concern over how it would be viewed by the public, a concern I'm not sure I share. Mostly I became agitated when I found out there might be a new research project I'm not involved in and that it's a secret. I'm anxious. I can't help but wonder if my funds are going to be cut and my project shut down." He let himself feel a mild wave of panic completely unrelated to the story he'd just shared. Surely they were reading him, gauging his emotions to discern the veracity of his statements. They might be crude in comparison to his own abilities, but they could detect some levels of worry if he let them.

The Director laughed, clearly relieved. "I'm glad you aren't concerned over the tenure thing. I have confidence we can still ensure a proper balance of power if things get out of control. People would hardly allow anything to get too bad if abuses started to show up. The tenure is so the Council can focus on some long-range projects and effectively see them through. As our lifespans increase, thirteen years is just not enough time to work on major issues."

Jason just nodded. The Director seemed satisfied with Jason's answer, shifting the conversation to address Jason's fabricated concern about his own research project.

"I wouldn't worry about funding. We have plenty to spare for your invaluable research." He grinned and reached over to pat one of Jason's hands in a grandfatherly way. "This brings me to the point of this meeting, actually. We assembled a few minutes before your panic attack to talk about asking you to head up some of the new research. So, you see? Nothing strange about our little group getting together so quickly. It seems this worked out rather well, since we'd planned on talking to you anyway. We were on the verge of requesting you come up here when you went outside."

Jason looked at him with a puzzled expression, not entirely sure about the motives being presented. He almost shook his head. This had to be Monica's doing. Her paranoia had crept into him. "What research?"

Dr. Faust's smile broadened. "Fascinating research, doctor. We have discovered a way to alter body processes to change physique. With a little fine-tuning, I believe we can make any of our subjects into their vision of the ideal. For a sum, of course. I leave it up to you to finalize the research and fine-tune any side-effects."

Jason stared at him for a moment. "Alter the physique? To what extent? How did this come about? What research led to this?" He shook his head. "This is stunning, Director."

"Isn't it, though? All in good time, Jason. We can fill you in over the coming weeks. I need someone I can trust to help me with this. I can't afford to have this getting out just yet. It's too revolutionary. We can almost completely alter someone. Each of us could transform into whatever ideal we dreamed up. We'll have to have a complete clinical trial, naturally. There are obvious security concerns, too, and other major issues we must still overcome. This leads us to require even more research."

He stood up, inviting Jason to do the same. Shaking Jason's hand, he smiled again. "We'll talk about the project soon enough. Don't worry about it too much," and then, seeming to be almost an afterthought, he added, "and don't let Susan get to you. We'll talk with her and make sure she is okay with everything. I certainly don't want her fretting about something so silly. I need her, too."

"Sounds good, Director. Thank you." Jason kept himself composed while the various doctors shook his hands and bid brief farewells. He let himself sigh in relief, but kept a tight rein on his emotions, not letting his nerves get the best of him lest his suit give him away.

Jason took the lift back down to the patient floor. As he walked down the hall, hospital personnel began informing him of patients who needed his attention, situations that required his input, and decisions he had to make. He quickly fell back into the pace of his work and forcefully put the conversation in the back of his mind.

FOUR

AS THE POPULATION OF EARTH swelled to over twenty-three billion, city boundaries crept inexorably in all directions, swallowing the natural world in deserts of asphalt and spires of steel and glass. The planet heated, weather became erratic, and oceans spun out storms like angry fits of rage.

Governments fought to sustain their power, attempted to supplant their neighbors, and fell under the weight of their own selfish greed.

A world in peril, wrought with fear and panic and war, had seemed doomed to falter and, ultimately, fail, destroyed either by a wildly imbalanced natural world or by the anger and resentful tribalism that nearly swallowed reason and compromise.

With each tick of the Doomsday clock toward the apocalyptic tone of midnight, technology struck a defiant chord, slowing the hands of time. Autonomy supplanted the inefficiency of governmental waste. Calculated alterations to production and distribution alleviated potential shortages of resources. Interconnected networks increasingly formulated solutions to problems, removing them from the slow and faulty thinking of the human mind.

Governments began to merge, to share power and responsibility over higher level decisions, leaving the increasingly vast details to the powers of the artificial intelligences that obeyed their wishes. This merging resulted in a single unified government of Earth: one governing body, called the Council of Earth.

Cities, too, had merged. Oceanic constructs that housed billions provided room when land became scarce. Vast underground complexes further relieved the pressures of housing on the surface.

Fear of artificial intelligence kept |AI repressed, caging the potential of AI becoming self-aware and taking over. The need, however, did not stagnate. More powerful AI and more interconnected systems were essential to sustain growth.

To accomplish this, Techs were created. These human AI hybrids were capable of the vast powers of artificial intelligence, possessing the ability to think and react beyond the ability of the collective human existence, but had the crucial emotional bonds to humanity that prevented a takeover.

Transhuman entities, Techs were long-lived and possessed inhuman strength as well as powerful minds. They commanded every single aspect of technology given to them by the government. Born as human children, potential Techs were tested and merged with technology around the age of six when they became a mix of human and AI. Most did not live. Or they became insane. Only thirteen Techs arose from this great new experiment.

The Earth was then divided geographically into thirteen Sectors for the purpose of governance. One for each Tech to manage. Thirteen Council members were elected to govern over the thirteen Sectors. The Techs were hard-wired to obey the Council, an edict that was biologically and technologically impossible for them to break. This reassured humanity that a solution was in place, and that AI was no longer to be feared.

Over time, some of the Techs died or lost their minds to the WorldNet and could no longer distinguish reality. They were replaced, but there simply were not enough children capable of the nearly impossible task of merging with AI to sustain the number. Thirteen became twelve, which became eleven. After two-hundred years, only nine Techs were in full operation. The Sectors had to be reduced to nine to match the available Techs, but the Council remained at the original thirteen members.

Along with the struggles that had led to governmental changes and the advent of Techs had come the need to calm nature. Coastlines and deserts became entirely too hostile to ignore. Ungainly growth of cities had left the natural world in peril. Concrete and steel had struck at the heart of nature, covering vast stretches of once beautiful land in a growth that appeared cancerous.

Strangely, the congregation of the human species toward unification of government also triggered a recognition of its own monstrous divergence from the natural world. Like a sea urchin covering a mass of spines with Caulerpa for camouflage or a moth evolving color patterns to match the bark of a tree, architects had begun to incorporate human structures with the natural world. Where there had once been asphalt and glass, now huge towers of metal were draped in vines and woody masses of rooting trees. Buildings were designed with cupola containing pockets of diverse micro-biomes.

Transport had been moved underground for delivery of materials and for transferring personnel between complexes and offices during the workday, allowing above-ground transportation to be for leisure and general use when going to or from work to home or out on the town to eat and enjoy life.

Fish swam in scattered pools designed to be part of cooling systems that sat at the foot of many structures; these pools were used too for runoff control and to hold water reclaimed from the runoff. Birds nested in adapted environments that allowed them to flourish. Huge areas between buildings, dedicated to wildlife, remained relatively free of human transport vehicles, which had gone underground. Such large swaths of land held numerous species, ranging from the smallest bacillus to felines and canines.

Bio-degrading of waste had evolved into something of an art, rendering most offal harmless, if not helpful—a panacea for a poisoned world. Most waste contained harmless materials which, in clever ways, bound themselves to more harmful environmental materials, capturing or altering them. In some cases, this trash fertilized or nurtured the plants. Buildings had their own chambers to dispose of and degrade the garbage into something used on exterior surfaces to help grow their protective shells.

Not truly a perfect balance, to be sure, and certainly the buildings disrupted the natural order, but they had become an odd hybrid of technology, one their makers used in the hope of restoring balance, a cry to nature proclaiming man knew it had become a monstrous defacement on the natural world, but wanting badly to be a thing of beauty without the sacrifice of self-destruction.

Oddly, nature seemed to accept this and micro environments—which previously seemed doomed to fail—changed in unexpected ways, resulting in working biomes. Animals adapted to live amongst humans, plants found niches and flourished.

Species originally not part of the master plan found their way into various niches and firmly entrenched themselves. The insect and plant world adapted, taking advantage of man's desire to give nourishment to a burgeoning hybridization of man and nature. What followed was citizens becoming societal harbingers of steadily growing eco-areas. People seemed to feel a sense of peace and contentment, knowing they contributed to this hopeful reversal of a failing Mother Earth. Green and growing things, urged by humans, began to push out and cover the cancerous cities of the past. Citizens suddenly found themselves contending for space in which to proclaim their own nurturing talents.

Still, these structures presented only a small hope for an ever-advancing and technologically spellbound world. Carefully crafted areas often fell to industry, which required morphing the space to improve efficiency.

The advent of the "nannies", societal vernacular for the nanotechnology which had permeated all organic life in various ways, truly began blurring the lines man had tried to draw between himself and nature. Almost all humans were riddled with millions of small robots, designed to care for the frail shell of their humanity. In turn, humans had adapted this technology to the natural world, controlling breeding and reproduction, as well as migration of animal species during times of industrial disruption, preserving much of many once-fading species.

Mankind dreamed of such a thing as manipulating reality, and this technology truly brought the human species closer to complete control of their surroundings. Like all things technological, the instructions to all nannies were handed to the Techs. Now, they not only controlled all automation, surveillance, and operations, the Techs controlled all life except that of humans, ensuring survival, and also ensuring there'd be no conflict. A lion, for example, would never attack a human, because it would be governed by instructions given to it via a sea of nanobots that obeyed the Techs. Bees built nests where they were instructed, plants grew where they had been determined to best thrive and not compete. It was a level of control that some of the population greatly feared. Only strong edicts preventing abuse by the Techs kept society from rebelling against this power.

In a way, which should have been easily predicted, there were those who sought to use this newfound control for personal gain. The lure of the power that came with such manipulation became too strong for those attuned to power. All the new technology meant it was possible to shape the world to *their* vision, imposing restrictions they knew were morally wrong, but ones they were willing to ignore if they gained power. This willful disregard of what was best for the entire population meant believing they would be enacting the will of a supreme being, or some held the belief they, themselves, were a form of divinity. Like all such delusions, this thinking was accompanied by a paranoia, a foreboding sense they must further enhance and consolidate their power in order to retain it. It meant losing trust in others and closing out any voices of reason.

Society had so far capped such grabs for power, bringing them down when necessary by sheer force of will and numbers. For this reason, the struggle for those who sought control meant they must dominate the minds and thoughts of those who would dissent. Those people who sought to seize power began to believe, with heretical fervor, that they must take over everything to prevent mankind from slipping into moral decline.

• • •

Jason breathed a sigh of relief as he coded his personal key onto the door of his apartment. For the first time, he felt protected by the small living quarters. Once inside, he slumped against the door and took a shuddering breath as fear coursed through him. He disabled his biosuit with a quick tap over the insignia emblazoned over his heart.

Finally, he stripped to the waist, exposing the musculature of his body in the living room mirror. He pulled out the kerchief, which bore a small stain from the blood of his cut and ran a quick analysis. As he'd thought, an unknown compound showed up in his blood sample. Surely it had dissipated out of his bloodstream by now, but its presence in the sample reinforced his belief he had been manipulated. Taking a moment to get a glass of water, he pressed the cool glass against his forehead while he called Monica.

"Hey, Jason. What's up?"

Keeping his voice calm, he let himself fake a smile, so his false calm would be detected as if real. "Just thinking about our conversation yesterday. You're right, I think going to an old-fashioned movie would be great."

A slight pause on the other end indicated to Jason she'd decoded his statement.

"Okay, cool. Great, in fact! I'm actually not doing a lot tonight, so I'll head over. Consider it a date. See you in a few."

"Great. See you soon."

"Oh, and Jason?"

For a moment he feared she would say something incriminating. He went cold.

"You better put out."

He laughed in surprise. *Good old Monica*, he thought.

Without further conversation and without waiting, she disconnected.

For a moment, Jason stood there, glass pressed against his face, heart racing. It would take her half an hour to arrive. Just enough time to shower and calm himself.

After moving through the small living room and setting the glass on the kitchen counter, he walked into the bathroom and stepped out of his underwear, starting the water for a shower. Before he managed to step in, however, the door sounded, announcing a guest and making Jason turn in surprise. How had Monica arrived so quickly? She must have been just outside. He draped himself in a towel and shut the water off.

As he walked over and started to open the door he said, "Wow, speedy! Didn't know you were in the area." When the door opened, it wasn't Monica. Instead, Director Faust strode confidently into Jason's apartment.

"I didn't realize you were expecting me, Doctor

Emerson." He swept into the room in his usual imperious manner. "Perhaps your prescient ability to know I would be here should result in testing to become a Tech? You seem to have an uncanny knack for knowing things you shouldn't."

Jason stammered. "Director, I . . . uh, sorry. I expected my friend, Monica."

"I jest, of course. Clearly, I'm interrupting you." He raised an eyebrow, eyeing Jason in his towel. "A female guest? My information on you may have been incorrect. I was under the impression you preferred male company."

Jason felt himself blush and he coughed delicately. "Uh, no. No, you're right. She's just a friend. I haven't had male company in a long time, so it makes the point moot. I didn't realize my sexual orientation interested you."

"Really? Of course it does. I would think you would have assumed all things are of interest to me, doctor. I'm a curious person, and I like to know my staff."

"How may I help you, Director?" Jason clasped one hand tightly on the towel. He glanced briefly toward the open door of his bedroom but refused to change back into suitable clothes.

"I won't intrude long. I just wanted to give you some news first-hand."

Jason felt himself breathing heavily, glad his hormonal and emotional states weren't readable. The timing for stripping down to shower couldn't have been better. He walked over to lean against the wall to imply a sense of calm he didn't feel.

"First, I want you to know we are doing everything we can to stabilize Dr. Reid." Jason's heart felt an enormous surge of pressure from anxiety, a tightening that felt like the clenching of a giant hand. *Oh god. Susan.*

"She's been horribly damaged by the crash, so we aren't sure we can save her." He drew a deep breath, which seemed contrived. He stared intently at Jason. "I think you should know; the outlook is not good." He paused. Jason couldn't speak. His eyes drifted over the familiar shape of the lamp and table at the end of his couch. "We also know what happened, thanks to the new augmentation system we imposed, though it would have saved her if fully integrated into the community. The illegally operated delivery truck and the driver have been apprehended." He shook his head. "I can't believe people would still try to manually operate machinery in this day and age, just to save a few hundred dollars. Well, it's just sad, isn't it? It will cost them everything."

Faust didn't seem at all sad and Jason felt like a mouse trapped by an overfed cat that toyed with him, watching him for his reaction.

"Maybe you should sit down, Jason. You look pale." Faust's eyes narrowed. Making a medical assessment by visual cues was something nearly unheard of and it appeared Faust couldn't get a proper read on Jason. Without the bio-suit feedback, Dr. Faust could only guess where Jason's emotions lay. Jason's fear for his safety would have been too great to hide, but Jason played it off as shock at the news about Susan. His thoughts were jumbled, but he knew he had to dissuade Faust from discerning his misgivings about the current consolidation of power.

Jason desperately wanted Faust gone. Monica's presence would reveal his newfound suspicions, so Jason needed him gone before she arrived.

Mustering control, he reacted as he suspected he should. "Susan! Oh no. I hadn't heard there was an accident." *Stupid! Of course not. It just happened.* Faust seemed to accept this as nonsense words expected from someone in shock. Jason let his eyes tear up and he dabbed at them. "I'm okay. Thank you."

"I'm sorry, Jason. I know you worked closely with her. Ironically, we were seeking her out to talk to her about the issues she expressed with the new rules and about the tenure of the Council. Had we acted on this faster, called her in to allay her fears, she might not have been injured by this senseless and flagrant disregard for safety. I know this will affect you." Faust's eyes appeared probing, calculating.

Jason looked away again, toward his kitchen, not wanting eye contact.

"Yes, I . . . yes, she worked with me a lot. For the most part, I had a lot of respect for her."

"For the most part?"

"Well, shit. Goddamn it. She couldn't see the value in the visual augmentation and it's ironic. The visual augmentation could have saved her if implemented sooner. She couldn't see the bigger picture, and this just proves the benefits." Jason played this off so it would align with what Faust needed to hear to leave him the fuck alone.

"Yes. I suppose I hadn't thought of how the new system would have helped." Then, seeming reassured, he held up the package he'd been holding. "Jason, I realize this is bad timing and you won't appreciate this right now, but I had intended only to bring you good news." Faust handed a thick envelope to him. "This is the new project documentation. Highly classified." Faust backed up a bit, giving Jason space, edging toward the door. "In order to keep this as secret as possible, I wanted to deliver this personally to your home."

Jason accepted the envelope numbly but said nothing.

"I know it will take you a while to overcome the loss of Susan."

So, now Susan's demise was guaranteed. Jason suspected as much. Susan might already be dead.

"When you've had some time, please read over things carefully. Like I said, I need you. Your expertise will be a critical piece in negating the side effects of our newest discovery." Then, as if sharing something among equals, he added, "We are compensating you well, doctor. I know the size of your research funds and associated bonus will bring you out of your grief." He smiled.

Jason forced himself to smile too, allowing the impression he had become motivated by self-interest.

Dr. Faust finally turned to leave. Faust certainly had a rich acquaintance with ambition, and Jason's pretended character flaw served to calm the Director. Reaching for the door, Faust turned his head, and a look came into his eyes that Jason couldn't read. "Jason, I want to give you as much time as you need to grieve for Susan. But I hope you will consider the import of this research and I look forward to you joining the team as soon as you can. I considered delaying this, in light of the current situation, but I simply cannot. The Council itself is eager for this research to proceed. Very eager. I hope you'll consider joining the team quickly."

With another feigned smile, Jason opened the envelope and made as if he couldn't really keep from scanning the documents immediately. Faking an interest he could not bring himself to feel, he carefully set them on his reading table. "I'm sure I'll be joining the research team soon, Director. I'm more inclined to work now than ever. I'm sure Susan would understand. Approve, even." He felt sick.

The Director shook Jason's hand in farewell, as if shaking hands with a man in a towel wasn't abnormal. "Bye then. See you soon." The door slid closed behind him as he strode out of the room.

Jason slumped against the wall next to the door, his towel crumpling under one leg. Clutching his head in his hands, overcome with suppressed anxiety and despair at the loss of Susan, he cried. He was still holding his head in his hands when the door chimed again. Without getting up, he twisted and slapped his left palm against the electronic security panel just above his head. The door opened, admitting Monica.

He heard her pause in the doorway for a moment when she saw him on the floor. She quickly entered the room and let the door slide closed. He looked up, feeling tears streak down his face.

"Jason?" She stared at him for a moment. "Sweetie? What's wrong?" She grabbed a chair and slid it over so she could sit in front of him, leaning forward to place her hand on the side of his head and covering him with the towel.

"Oh god, Monica! I'm an idiot."

She waited for more. When he said nothing, she bit her lip momentarily. "I can't help you if you don't talk to me. What happened?"

He took another breath, trying not to sob. Monica waited for him to find his voice.

"I never got a chance to say anything about the imposed augmentation edict. I didn't have to. My co-worker and friend, Doctor Susan Reid, voiced your opinions at work today. She tried to warn me. Immediately after, I was summoned. Faust and his cronies called me in and strictly analyzed me for any sort of agreement I might have with her opinion."

He wiped the tears from the back of his hand.

"They were so obvious! They wanted to make sure I didn't agree in any way." He sat up more fully, pulling the rest of the bunched towel from under him and wrapping it tightly. "Monica, they were there in less than fifteen minutes to grill me. They triggered my suit to disperse a new chemical that made me freak out and throw me off balance so I'd admit my fears to them. I barely had time to react to the other information. They've passed a resolution to allow permanent appointment of the current governing Council."

"What?"

"Yeah, so Susan told me the government Council positions are to be made permanent. Or at least until the governing members resign or are forced out due to health reasons."

"What the hell? What is going on? Jason, this is worse than I feared."

For once, he had to nod in agreement. "And now . . ." He couldn't finish.

"What? Please don't tell me it gets worse. Did they already select the positions? Is it the existing set of members or new ones?"

"I don't know. I know Director Faust is among them. Oh, Monica. Susan is dead."

"Who?" Her eyebrows narrowed in confusion. "The woman you worked with?"

"Yes. She talked about objecting to this change to the Council and suddenly she is in an accident. Dr. Faust just left here. He might as well have said I'd be following her if I showed the slightest agreement with her thinking. He was fishing for information. I was going to shower and didn't have my bio-suit on, which is the only thing that kept him from reading my emotions like an open book." He shuddered. "He had the audacity to imply I might join him in his play for power by accepting a new research position. As if all this new money would overcome my horror."

Monica sat back in her chair, eyes wide. For a moment, she simply bit her lip again. Then, sweeping back her hair, she got out of the chair and put it back on the rug in the living room. She turned back and grabbed him by the hands, yanking him to his feet. "Get in the shower. Get cleaned up and dressed. Now. We have to go."

"Now? What? No! I'm too upset. I need to lie down." He slumped back against the wall, intending to sit back down. "I think I'm going to be sick."

Her voice became iron and she reached out and prevented him from crumpling onto the floor. "No. You aren't. Not now. Get ready to go out immediately." Then, in a more conciliatory tone, she said, "You should be understandably upset about Susan, but you've got to come to the movie with me. You've got to show your new position and the money you'll receive are enough to push your suspicions aside. He's not stupid. He's going to know you suspect something and he's looking for a reaction. If you go out with me, it shows you don't care enough to raise a fuss. You will hint, eagerly, at a new position. Make it convincing, Jason. Talk around it like you really want to tell me, but don't give away any secrets. Don't mention Susan at all. Not talking about her will seem slightly suspicious, but it is better than you breaking down."

He stared at her, feeling numb.

"Go! Get your ass in gear." She pushed him into the

bathroom and pulled off his towel. He dutifully started the water again and got into the shower.

Through the open door, he heard Monica moving around the living room and then the clinking of dishes put on the counter where the cleaning robots could come remove the stacks and deal with cleaning them. He kept his shower brief, opting to rinse more than anything.

Jason finished and went to his room to put on clothes. When he emerged, still toweling his hair dry, Monica was standing in the middle of the living room near the low table, clutching the papers Faust had brought over and left for him. Her eyes darted rapidly across the pages and Jason saw her face grow increasingly alarmed.

"Monica? What's wrong?"

"How long have you been working on this?"

Confused, Jason said, "What? I haven't yet. The packet is what the Director left with me as a pretense for coming over."

She lifted her eyes from the paper and looked at him with what appeared to be an accusatory glare. It caught him off guard. "Have you read any of this?"

"No, I just pretended to look at the papers when Faust handed them to me. Why?"

"This is a nightmare! It keeps getting worse." She strode around the table and the couch, handing him the synopsis.

Jason started reading.

"They want you to figure out how to overcome the hormonal side-effects of permanent longevity."

He started to shake. The synopsis was more detailed, but it essentially said the same thing.

"The side effects. Jason, they have figured out how to stop aging. They need you to fix things so they can live forever. According to what's in this document, they plan on only giving this treatment to the highest officials. The Council. They are going to elevate themselves to a permanent imperial position and retain their positions until they die. Which may be *never*, if this research is true. They'll give the anti-aging drug to their supporters. If anyone doesn't agree, this paperwork implies how the changes can be reversed. So, you get the treatment if you go along with them, and have it taken away if you go against their will."

Reflexively, Jason said, "Reverse it? Aren't you reaching a bit here? They can't possibly have been dumb enough to give their secrets away in those papers."

"I'm going to hit you."

He took a deep breath after staring at her for a moment. "Okay, maybe I should start paying more attention. Your intuition is probably right."

He got dressed quickly, taking only a moment to steel his emotions, affecting his professional calm.

They linked arms and began talking about what movie to see before they left, getting into the conversation. It took a while, due to the sheer amount of emotions and anxiety, but eventually they walked out, chatting and laughing. Their actions were a bit forced, but it was the best they could do. Jason kept dropping hints about his research position, but gave no details, only conveyed his excitement.

On their way out of the building, they ran into a woman everyone referred to as "Mom", an older woman who lived in the same building and who seemed compelled to treat everyone around her as if they were her children. Mom often hung out on the walkways near the building, talking to everyone, handing out motherly advice. She would fondly reach up to brush hair out of eyes, comment on her "children" needing more sleep, and a slew of other matronly comments.

Mom was tending the small garden in the front of the building. Mom refused a bio-suit, claiming technology progressed too quickly without proper vetting and that the suits frightened her. Instead she wore a simple sundress with her hair pulled back in a bun. For some reason, the sight of Mom made Jason smile a genuine smile.

For a while, he had thought Mom psychologically unbalanced and perhaps in need of a mental evaluation. Possibly, she suffered from dementia, he thought. He'd even gone so far as to ask other residents to help him commit her, have her treated. He'd been met with stony opposition and a few veiled threats, which surprised him.

After a while, he discovered Mom really didn't believe any of the people she tended to were, in fact, her biological children. She wasn't confused or forgetful. She had simply assumed the role of a mother figure and it suited her well. She constantly worried over her neighbors, noticing small things about the stresses in their lives. Mom would appear with cookies, a hug, or just to engage in conversation. She watched her adopted brood all the time, making comments about behavior and generally encouraging her "children" to act responsibly. Mom defused a lot of tense situations, sometimes simply by showing disappointment when someone began to act rude or began posturing. Occasionally, seemingly without concern for her own physical well-being, she would stride into the middle of an altercation and take both people by an ear. Anyone who got angry or objected to this chastisement quickly became overwhelmed with people who backed her up. You might get out from under a painful ear gouging, but you could not escape her influence.

Mom smiled as they walked out of the building, waving. But her wave stopped short and a frown marred her pretty face. Dropping her gardening gloves, she walked over to them.

Her brows knitted. She assessed them with her light blue eyes. A sad expression clouded her face and she touched Jason on the temple lightly and squeezed Monica's shoulder. "Things will be all right. Mom's here and she'll watch over you. Don't worry too much."

Jason stammered and laughed hollowly. "Everything's fine, Mom. Really." Suddenly he felt paranoid about being too transparent. If Mom kept talking and this conversation picked up momentum, his carefully crafted façade would crumble. This, combined with his worry over the fact she could read them both like an open book, made him in a hurry to get away. He prided himself on empathic and intuitive assessment of others, but Mom seemed to possess an unearthly ability to see a bit too clearly.

She gazed at him a moment, then smiled. "Don't lie to me, honey. I'm likely to turn you over my knee right here and spank you. We both know I'll have all the help I need." She flicked his ear and then laughed, her voice calm and kindly despite her threats. "I hope you have a nice time tonight." She patted his face. "It really will be okay, dear. Things will turn out for the best."

He smiled back at her and nodded, opting to keep quiet. But he did feel better, and she seemed to sense the improvement in his mood. She turned and walked back to her gardening spot and picked up her gloves, her disheveled bun bobbing on top of her head as she got back to work.

FIVE

Jason enjoyed the movie, despite his insistence all movies were the same old plot, churned over and over by the industry. Grateful for Monica's insistence they go out, he thanked her and conceded he had been wrong. The enforced gaiety of the evening translated to lightening his dark mood and, by the time he came home, he felt as if he could go to work and hide his real emotions.

They made plans to see each other the next day under the pretense of drinks at her place. He emphasized their plans should be flexible since he wasn't sure what time commitment his new work would require, once again alluding to the new position without giving anything away. Monica pretended to be exasperated with him.

She assumed a captivated expression and said, "Oh wow. Your completely vague promotion sounds vaguely special. Or not? I can't tell. I wish you all the . . . what's the word? Luck? No . . . what I meant is, 'you're a schmuck.'" She sniffed loudly and lifted her nose in the air. "Besides, I don't really care. You keep your little secrets."

When he got home, he breathed a sigh of relief and sank down onto the couch to review the documents he'd been provided.

As he pored over things, he began to realize the work involved addressed a lot more than just longevity.

The papers before him painted a picture of physical modification, restorative powers that defied everything but death, and enhancement possibilities that would vault the current biology of mankind toward something nearly superhuman. The progression of man's increasing love affair with technology would transcend evolution. Especially on the nano scale.

Jason felt a chill. The elite would suppress the masses. Up until now, only the Techs could endure advanced body modifications and nannies altering their systems, and even then, almost every single Tech had died or lost their mind. Those few who survived were not autonomous, but instead enacted complex instructions handed to them. Their modifications were made over time, and externally controlled. What was being planned would give immediate control of the entire process to the individual, with no restraints, creating the kind of superhuman who could manipulate everything around them.

Realizing the time, he brushed his teeth, a quaint

and archaic practice which had been replaced by a fluid that contained minerals necessary for tooth repair and provided his nannies with an electrically charged medium to scrub his mouth clean. The act of using the product triggered the operation, which would interfere with taste and the first phase of digestion for thirty minutes after rinsing with it. He enjoyed the sensation of brushing, however, along with the clean flavor of the paste. *You can't control me in every way,* he thought, almost angrily scrubbing his teeth as he stared at himself in the mirror.

•   •   •

The next day, as the reflectors pivoted to catch the daylight and shine it into his room at the prescribed time, he woke. His windows, which had slid open slightly to let in fresh air and a light breeze along with soothing sounds of nighttime insects, were slowly closing. The curtains near his bed billowed pleasantly before they came to rest.

An attendant robot had set out his biosuit, freshly cleaned and ready for him, and the same robot began removing his bedding for its daily sterilization.

Jason performed his morning workout, which had become habitual and kept him in great shape. Then, he showered, taking time to relieve pent-up male tension which plagued nearly every male on earth in the mornings. Without a current sex partner, his libido could sometimes be a distraction during the day and taking care of things in the shower had become something of a morning ritual. He'd found himself occasionally flirting with willing male staff members at work when he hadn't had time to take the edge off. Jason viewed his advances on male colleagues as unprofessional and put a halt to it. Monica had teased him at how boring and routine his life had become. She had more sex than most men and considered Jason a prude.

He ate quickly, taking no joy in the fresh fruit, yogurt cultures, and granola he normally enjoyed. He quickly glanced over the papers again while he chewed mechanically. His worry over the papers increased as he read them a second time.

Hurriedly, he swished tooth cleaning fluid around in his mouth, too much in a rush to rebel, grimacing at the bitter taste before he spit it out and went to gather his satchel. Mom greeted him with a wave and blown kiss as he jogged out of the building. She was talking with one of the local kids who always seemed to be in some sort of trouble. Jason guessed the kid might be, at most, seventeen. If he had parents, they'd never shown up in this neighborhood, so Jason had always assumed the young man might be homeless.

Mom had him firmly in her grip and her tone indicated she lectured him about something he'd done wrong. His head was bowed in acceptance, but he glanced up when Jason waved back to Mom. The guy managed to look sheepishly at Jason for a moment.

Jason suppressed a grin by biting his lips and then

sipped coffee the house robot had put in a thermal mug and set out for him prior to his leaving the apartment. Jason had been in that situation with Mom before and the familiarity of her tone was more than a little amusing. For a moment, his deep concern and anxiety were forgotten.

Jason took another sip of coffee. His nannies permitted the stimulant as part of the approved list of drugs, so it wasn't broken down immediately. Jason imagined he'd be cranky if coffee was ever banned. There would probably be a mass rebellion. People liked their coffee and alcohol.

The drug approval lists were another reason the biosuits had been met with some resistance. Most people preferred being able to use illicit drugs of some kind. However, since people could simply take the suits off, the general populace wore their biosuits most of the time. Among those who adamantly refused to ever wear them were the hardcore drug users, who were often consuming one or more substances that kept them high all day.

Jason hopped on several transports, including a sky-lift, rapidly passing coffee shops and boutiques at various levels of towering buildings. Some of the clothing stores proudly displayed women's designer biosuits, some ridiculously elaborate. Robot stores of all kinds, diners, and theaters were mixed in with small schools, gyms, flower shops, and art galleries. He quickly, via the high-speed transport, made his way up and over to the city levels of the Medic complex where his offices were located in a massive and sprawling set of buildings.

This location and setup allowed quick and efficient transport of supplies, robots, building and trash materials, and personnel, among other things. Like the arteries in the human body, the interconnected underground transports were in constant motion, moving crucial materials to where they were required. Patients could be rapidly transported between hospital divisions within the Sector on levitations trains, trains belonging solely to the medical infrastructure. Most complexes were this way. The Mechanics had a similar distribution and transport system, with their own underground freeways crisscrossing the Medic transport, as did the education system, the government, the goods and services' collective, and a host of others—all separated and all constantly moving in a fluid and efficient fashion. Jason had no idea how it all worked, but it did—because the Techs kept it running with an automated efficiency that only an AI could fathom.

He finally reached his workplace terminal and exited the magnetic trains. Rather than going directly to his offices, which were much closer, he entered several levels below the entry he generally used, his breathing pleasantly elevated from the long walk from the terminal. Jason smiled in greeting to the nursing staff and other doctors as he passed the medical cubes and stations, noting the concern and sadness on their faces. Clearly, they had heard about Susan. Jason projected calm, understanding, and empathy. His position as a senior Medic derived partially from his capabilities in understanding and administering medical technology and its uses in the biological system. His true talent, however, lay in emotional control of others, giving him an advantage in his profession. People trusted him, respected him, and often unconsciously sought him out as a beacon of calm and hope.

Especially today.

Small groups in the hallways and from nearby seating reflexively crowded around him, stopping short of outright touching him, and he raised his level of broadcast to the maximum extent of his capabilities. In short order the shambling and hollow looks began to fade, and people straightened their backs with new resolve.

Normally, he would not take the time to wander this level, talking with people and observing their work, but people needed him today. Even if he wasn't actively pretending to overlook Susan's death, his responsibilities as a senior Medic came into play. First and foremost in medicine, the people practicing must be able to perform their duties. It was Jason's responsibility as a healer to ease the minds of his staff, to enable those around him to do their jobs. In this way, the small time spent calming and encouraging others yielded the greatest results for the whole.

His personal communicator sounded, but he chose to ignore it, completing his rounds. After another fifteen minutes, he finally wound his way up and back toward his office, checking his call log as he arrived. Faust's name appeared on the log, accompanied by a message. As the door slid closed behind him, he set his satchel down and carefully removed and secured the documents it contained, taking no chances this work would be seen by someone entering his office in his absence. He walked around his desk and opened the bottom right drawer, carefully placing the research order inside and then locking it.

Still standing and leaning against his desk, he tapped his communicator and listened to the message. "Jason, this is Director Faust. I commend you on taking time to emotionally balance the staff, so thank you for helping. We have been having a rough time today, since much of the staff is understandably shaken by the loss of senior medic Reid, who I'm sorry to say passed during the night. We are meeting in an hour to discuss some information regarding your new project and I would appreciate your attendance. Please excuse yourself from whatever obligations you have and meet us in The Convene on level twenty-nine. The meeting should be brief, maybe thirty minutes, so you needn't cancel the entire day. That's it. See you there."

That gave him roughly thirty minutes to rearrange his appointments and make the ten-minute trip. Finally sitting, he signaled several attendants under his direct control and fed them instructions about his change of plans. His holo-display above his desk lit up with the information. The attendants obeyed with their usual robotic efficiency, communicating with other attendants and offloading his cases to available resources, beginning to move people as necessary to closer proximity to other Medics. Flicking his fingers across the transparent display in front of him, he quickly perused information about patients he could administer aid to indirectly and remotely. With a broad swipe of his hand, he spread the results out across multiple displays to get a better view for comparison.

Several patients had minor injuries and Jason approved automated surgical procedures and the use of medicines that would both curb the pain and allow for greater healing. He also directed newly injected nannies to each site of damage. He transmitted quick holo instructions about care, along with an apology for his absence, to each patient. At this distance, his calming abilities were ineffectual, but he smiled encouragingly. The patients seemed to appreciate his sincere apology.

He finished up his direct involvement, gave some last-minute instructions to his attendants, and then gestured for his displays to clear. Getting up from his chair, he stretched for a moment and then made his way to the meeting.

The Convene, one of several in the complex, was an enormous shielded bubble that protruded from the towers to hang out over the city. The Convenes were constructed from super-strengthened glass-like material. The material resisted electrical strikes as well as dirt and mineral deposits. Selective opacity, an engineered reaction to direct sunlight, kept much of the room lit but shielded from direct rays during sunny days. Had it been raining, he would have been dazzled with patterned water flows, funneled down to where the curves of the glass met. During heavy storms, small light displays occurred on the surface, enhancing the waterfall effects designed into the structure. The Convenes were crafted with astonishing artistry.

Comfortable chairs littered the spacious room, clad in fabric reminiscent of green and growing things. An occasional rug spanned the distances between islands of furniture, a fully stocked kitchen, and a restroom. Travertine floors softly reflected the natural light. Several couches with oversized cushions were grouped around a collection of strategically placed tables, designed to make traffic flow easy, but providing ample space to lay out materials and set down cups of tea and coffee.

Several of the large side windows were encircled by a forest canopy on terracing that extended out from the building. The tall glass allowed the viewer to see into a space draped in vines and hanging bromeliads. Buildings were nearly always covered in this way, an attempt to atone for the near ruination of the planet. Planted by humanity to reach toward the heavens in salvific-like questioning from specialized balconies. Occasional movement amongst the foliage caught the eye, drawing attention to various animals thriving in the micro-environment. Larger windows further down gave a spectacular view of the nearby city and offered a movable wall, which could allow for meetings directly out on the balcony to fully appreciate the beauty of nature as it combined with the structure.

Surprised to be the first one to enter, he took a moment to move around the room, trailing his fingertips over the furniture and gazing over the beauty outside. Lost in thought, it took him a moment before he heard the voices of people entering the room behind him. He turned with a smile to greet the Director and his entourage.

Jason's smile froze and his heart felt like it had nearly stopped.

With an involuntary gasp of which he was barely aware, Jason reached out blindly to steady himself on the back of a couch. An attendant robot, noting him falter, rushed forward with great speed from a nearby alcove, there to assist him if he needed.

Jason hardly noticed.

Director Faust had entered, chatting idly with four other well-known Medics. Three of them were peers and Jason had occasionally worked with each throughout the years. Dr. Emma Garbine, Dr. Brad Marchovic, and Dr. Stephanie Preem. Jason didn't recognize the fourth doctor, but he appeared to be animated and friendly.

However, none of the doctors were the cause of Jason's shock. He felt momentary disorientation and surprise because of the sixth person who had entered with them. Statuesque and incredibly handsome, he would have commanded Jason's attention, regardless. But this . . . creature had the telltale enhancements, advanced bio-suit, attached gadgetry, and fiery distant gaze that gave him away. Something transhuman.

A Tech.

One of the rare and incredibly powerful Techs who governed each Sector.

They didn't govern in the way of political wrangling, nor did they govern with adjudication or law. They governed with a strangely distant and removed robotic adherence to their profession. They governed because they could control almost everything tied to technology. They were rare because they required nearly impossible understanding and integration with all technology in the Sector—*all* of it, down to the tiniest nannite. They were in constant communication with everything around them. They influenced everything.

Nobody really understood how a Tech truly worked, and you couldn't ask one. They were so immersed in the flow of data, the vast issuance of commands, the constant efficiency improvements, and so on, that they could no longer relate to the world of biological sight and sound. They saw/heard/felt everything going on all at once in every corner of their Sector.

When they found a child possessing the knack for such integration—a child with the right genetic makeup from a pool of engineered children—the child was given every genetic enhancement and tool necessary to perfect them and tie them to the Sectors they would govern. Most failed, going insane or dying outright.

Techs were to be obeyed instantly, never questioned, and were protected under the strongest edicts. They were trusted implicitly. No Tech had ever shown the slightest inclination toward personal gain, had ever been vindictive or spiteful, and they never issued orders directly. They didn't supersede the Council, nor did they interfere with politics. They caused shock and awe, because of how feared they were. A Tech, it was said, could see through every guise, every lie. They knew the truth of all things. They laid bare all your secrets.

Jason's honesty with himself allowed him to admit the reason for his own reaction. A Tech represented so much power, he simply couldn't overcome misgivings they triggered. More so, any Tech would be able to directly communicate with his nannies in a way Jason couldn't hope to achieve. They could read and, worse, process every tiny reaction in anyone's body—without them wearing a biosuit. His entire soul felt exposed before the power of this Tech. More than anything, he feared the instant recognition that he was hiding his feelings about Susan and his discussions with Monica. The Tech would know and could inform Faust. Fear for his life made him freeze, crippling his control of his emotions.

Within the few seconds it took for him to think these thoughts, two other attendants had moved rapidly to his side, their robotic reflexes immensely fast. All heads turned toward him. His heart fluttered anew, his emotions flailing desperately to right themselves. He felt the others shielding immediately, trying to overcome the blast of fear emanating from him, which hit them like a wave. A few of them raised their arms involuntarily, as if to ward of the overwhelming tide of emotion.

With a flick of his eyes, the Tech glanced at Jason. Instantly, all communication from his bio-suit and his nannies ceased. Incoming data from his personal data feed halted and a vast and incredible silence seemed to fall over him. The Tech had barely moved his eyes, yet he cut off Jason so completely that Jason felt stricken of his senses. Consumed by other matters, and obviously considering Jason inconsequential, the thing had barely afforded him a glance. Stripped of all his abilities, Jason stood mute.

The other Medics, relieved of Jason's involuntary emotional onslaught, relaxed. One gave a nervous laugh and they moved, as a group, to the chairs. The attendant robot gripped Jason and moved him to one of the cushioned seats. Jason sat, unable to control his fingers as they reflexively furled and unfurled in his panic.

The Tech flowed to a position near the Director—a play of muscle showing as he moved with a strange fluid grace—then came to rest, standing slightly behind and to the right of the Director.

Jason finally got his fear under control and forced himself to relax.

"My, my, what an unexpected greeting," said Dr. Garbine. "I must admit, I didn't realize just how powerfully Dr. Emerson could command the bio-feedback."

Director Falk smiled. "Yes. Well, his emotional control, or lack thereof in this case, is one of the main reasons I have him heading up the research on emotional stability. We have a huge issue with imbalanced hormonal changes associated with our work." He turned to Jason. "Really, Dr. Emerson, you must get over your fear of the Techs. I'd forgotten how shocking they can be on first sight, but I'm now quite reminded of my initial experience. Actually, considering how powerfully you broadcast, I nearly relived it."

Jason relaxed slightly. This didn't seem to be an inquisition. The Tech hadn't acknowledged him in the slightest since it had shut him down. He relaxed further, gaining control over himself entirely. "Please. Accept my apologies. This is the first time in a great many years I've lost control of my emotions so completely." He bowed his head in apology.

The other Medics smiled at his sincerity and the Director waived his apology away. "Don't worry about it. We've all had roughly the same response. What a great demonstration of your unique talents."

On impulse, Jason turned to the Tech. "I hope you'll forgive me for a poor greeting. I'm usually much more in control, so I'm pretty embarrassed." The Tech still didn't acknowledge him in any way he could discern, its eyes forward and distant, staring at nothing and everything.

Then, however, without a twitch from the Tech, Jason had full control of his suit and his communications were restored. Startled, but hugely relieved, he broadcast calm. Everyone nodded appreciatively.

"Now then," said Faust, starting the meeting. "Jason,

I want you to meet the other members of the team. Dr. Emerson, as you've all noted, possesses a supreme command of emotive responses, broadcast by his biosuit, which will prove invaluable. Dr. Preem is developing a number of enhanced communication and feedback responses, which are proving their worth and will help fine-tune and augment Jason's skills."

Stephanie flashed her white teeth in a smile, which contrasted with her radiant dark skin. "Jason, so good to see you again."

He smiled back. "You too, Steph. I must say, these suits are proving their worth many times over and your recent enhancements to the technology are pretty great."

Faust continued. "Dr. Black here is taking up the part of enhancing the reparative instructions the nannies use. This will be increasingly important for accident survival. We're hoping to refine this to overcome everything but total destruction of our bodies. His goal is to work closely with Marchovic here to outline what defines our psyches to a point which, potentially, could mean moving our awareness out of a host temporarily to emergency storage while our bodies are rebuilt."

Both doctors waved hello as Faust paused.

"In this way, even complete destruction of our physical bodies might still mean survival. Lofty goals, I admit. It may also mean we encounter a disagreement with the human soul." He gestured to the older doctor, Emma Garbine, who sat to his left. Her mouth slightly pursed as she regarded Jason, then turned into a genuine, if fleeting, smile. Her tightly bound hair reminded him of Mom.

"Emma is going to be looking carefully at the ramifications our advancements might have on our souls, doctors. Hers is the most difficult of all tasks, as there is no metric on which to base her research, no measure of progress. She must work with the esoteric and the undefined and protect us from the unknown."

Dr. Garbine arched an eyebrow and turned to him with a slight tightening of her lips. "Not so impossible, Carlisle."

"Director, if you please. I feel a lot of pride in having earned my title."

Her mouth slipped into a barely discernable sneer. "Indeed, you do, Carlisle, which is one of your many failings. I prefer first names, so there's that."

The Director's jaw clenched for a brief second, but before he could say anything, she said, "Jason, good to see you again. It's been a while and, I must admit, I'd forgotten your . . . presence. Over the years, you seem to have greatly improved your skills. They are astonishing. You've always been a favorite of mine for a lot of reasons. It will be a genuine pleasure to work with you."

A moment of silence followed while Faust clearly mulled over Garbine's intentional slight. Gathering himself, he simply gestured to his right. "And this, Dr. Emerson, is Sector Seven." He seemed to indicate the Tech was there at his bequest, but Jason couldn't fathom how even the Director could actively engage a Tech to be on hand.

Techs were assigned names correlated to their Sectors, which they came to represent in their every thought and action. When invoked, even by the highest authorities, they would no longer respond when addressed by their given names. For this reason, the true names of any of the nine Techs were almost unknown. They were on record, but most people never sought out their names, relying only on their number and designation.

Jason turned and smiled at the Tech, uncertain how to proceed. He took a deep breath and then broadcast a strong welcome and an open and honest extension of friendship.

The Tech blinked slowly, then turned his impassive gaze to Jason, his neck muscles flexing slightly, dark hair glinting in the light. Sector Seven's eyes focused and Jason's heart skipped a beat. For a moment, he simply regarded Jason. Then, unexpectedly, the Tech said, "We greet you, Medic Jason Emerson," in a voice both richly baritone and yet strangely emotionless. For a moment, Jason felt his emotional broadcast echoed, uncertainly, awkwardly, as the Tech tried to emulate his greeting. Then the otherworldly look came over the Tech's face once again. Everyone in the room seemed to cease to exist. Jason had stopped breathing.

The doctors reacted with varying degrees of shock. Jason kept his emotions in check, and continued his unwavering broadcast of welcome, but he felt the other doctors' surprise.

Dr. Garbine spoke first. "Fascinating."

"Don't be droll, Emma. Jason has an emotional effect on everyone," said Stephanie. "Not typically so overwhelming, but his skill in this area is quite impressive." She stared at Jason curiously. Then, as if the Tech weren't even there, she said, "Has a Tech ever greeted any of you? They've never acknowledged me."

Director Faust smiled, though Jason could feel the older man's unease. "We have spoken a few times." Then, he cleared his throat.

"Let's get on with things, shall we?" Assuming a businesslike tone, he said. "Jason, I need you to start working closely with the team, starting next week. I have already assigned the replacement for your floor. Each of you will be given your own lab, your own staff, and a new office. You will all be in charge of your respective research groups, but I expect you to meet with each other frequently. Your offices will be relocated to the new research complex, so they will be close enough to each other for collaboration, yet separated so you can focus on results." He reached for a cup of water which, having anticipated his needs based on his body's desire for hydration, an attendant had ready.

He took a drink and set the cup back on the tray.

"As I said, you'll be working closely with Emma. However, I expect all of you to meet frequently and present any problems you encounter. We have a great gathering of minds here and I don't want to waste resources. Someone might have insight or even an outright answer to problems you become stuck on. We all know how it goes." He didn't seem to include himself in this human failing. "I regret I will not be able to provide as much research support as I have in the past. My duties on the Council consume too much of my time. You will need to take all my research to-date and develop a plan to move us forward.

"I've set deadlines for each of you, but we'll have to adjust things as we go along. The Council is expecting results by the end of the year." Seeing their incredulity, he raised a hand. "Results, not complete answers. We, the Council, are aware of the incredible level and degree of expectations we're setting." He emphasized the word "Council'" as if addressing himself personally. *What a grand sense of self-entitlement,* Jason thought.

They all nodded gravely, seemingly lost in their thoughts about the approaches they'd take, tests they'd need to perform, and myriad details they would have to attend to.

The Director seemed to sense the usefulness of the meeting had been exhausted. He rose from his chair and dismissed them all as he headed to the exit. They followed him silently from the room, each unconsciously avoiding eye contact with the Tech.

All accept Jason, who studied the Tech with interest.

SIX

MONICA CALLED JASON A FEW TIMES during the day, to chat and then to ask him about plans for the evening. The calls were mostly for the benefit of anyone eavesdropping. Without overdoing it, she affected the tone of someone girlishly infatuated with him. Jason, perfectly aware of the game Monica played, and appreciating her cleverness, acted the part of the gay friend who kindly enjoyed her presence, but kept his emotional distance. It was almost laughable, since Monica hardly deferred to anyone, but it allowed them to check on each other without suspicion and to arrange a meeting.

Through Monica pushing and Jason pretending to defer, they agreed to meet after work. Instead of drinks at her place, she changed their plans to go out to a bar and hang out. Jason's nerves ran high while out in public, but he couldn't say anything.

•   •   •

His day flew by in a flurry of changes. His office was relocated rapidly with some of his necessary work being duplicated so he could function in both locations. The staff began offloading his patients, his charts and reviews, and his meetings. He would be effectively transitioned within a few days and could start focusing on his new research unfettered.

The attendant announced Monica's arrival.

Jason couldn't help but gawk when he opened the door, shocked to see her in something other than her butch mechanic attire. She wore a black low-cut dress, which hugged her athletic frame incredibly well. Her tan skin looked vibrant and her cleavage looked like it might pop out of the top of the dress. Lustrous black hair slightly curled around and delicately framed her face. Black pumps made her calves flex as she walked with a slow, sensuous glide. An oversized bag she used as her purse ruined the effect of her dress, however. He gave a startled laugh. Her eyes flashed dangerously, warning him to keep his mouth shut until she was safely inside where they could talk. Other than her warning glance, she maintained her poise until inside his apartment. Then, she punched him on the shoulder. Hard.

"Oh, I'm sorry. Is the fact I had to throw this harlot outfit on and pretend to be all girly and gushy to cover your stupid ass amusing?"

"Ow!" he rubbed his shoulder. "Harlot, huh? C'mon. I've just never seen you in women's clothing. Kinda surprising is all."

"Yeah, well get out of your biosuit and we'll get on with our stupid dinner plans. Neither one of us can afford to have even the minor fluctuations of our emotions read by our biosuits while we talk. Oh, and by the way? Yeah, I had a date tonight. He was hot and I could have had him nail me, so unless you plan on putting out, I don't want to hear your whiny stupid comments about how I look."

"What am I supposed to wear? I always wear my suit, so it's going to look weird."

"Oh, for the love of . . ." She stomped into his bedroom and started throwing clothing out of his closet and dressers as he followed. Finally, she settled on jeans, a tight muscle shirt and a hat. "There. Relaxed and blasé enough to send the signal you aren't truly interested in my pursuit of you, but stereotypically gay enough that you'd have it in your closet in the first place. Seriously, are you twenty-three?"

He scowled and went to the bathroom to change.

"Oh, really? Now you aren't going to even change in front of me? Wow, what a prude."

Jason could almost see her roll her eyes by the tone in her voice as she shouted into the bathroom. "I'm not really interested in you, you know. I could care less. Sure, you have a nice physique and cute face, but . . . GAY! So gay." He heard Monica walk into the living room and flop down onto the couch with an unladylike grunt.

"So, who is this date of yours you're skipping out on?" he called out from his bedroom.

"His name is Jessie or maybe Jake. Whatever. He's a Mech too." She laughed. "He works on the city water reclaiming system and he's super hot. Dumb as a rock, but when his arm muscles flex, I don't really care. When a contaminant sprayed out of one of the drums on him, he had to strip and hit the shower, so I took full advantage of watching him. After I saw those abs and his ass, I about jumped in the shower with him. And wow, is he hung. Yummy! I figure he'll make a good couple of weeks of fun before I get bored."

"Wow, you weren't kidding about being a harlot."

"Yes, I'm totally a skank. And I'm not getting laid tonight because of you, which throws my whoring schedule completely off. Now hurry your faggoty ass up."

It only took him a few minutes to change and, since he wore a hat, he didn't have to comb his hair. "Um, hello. No cologne?" She grabbed his shoulders and turned him around, aiming him back into the bathroom. "Wow, the fact you don't have a boyfriend is just shocking. You have the personal hygiene habits of a hobo."

"I do not! I'm very clean." Even though he'd protested, he headed back to the bathroom for a spritz of cologne.

"Jason, seriously," she called after him. "Being grungy is not how you win someone over, you dumbass. What guy is going to fall for 'Hey there, hotty. Did you notice I don't smell like a dung heap? Yeah . . . it's cuz I showered today! Ta da! I'm a catch!' Try dressing in something other than your suit once in a while and put on some cologne. You've got a great body. Show it off."

He came back out, having walked through a fine mist of some scent he'd been given as a gift. Possibly by Monica, now that he thought about it. She smiled, white teeth flashing. "See? Mmmm . . . your cologne smells really good." She inhaled deeply. "Very sexy. And you didn't bathe in it like most guys, so at least you got the amount right. Now c'mon. You take longer than a girl." Then she clarified. "One of those high maintenance types, not me." She got up and led him out of the apartment.

He laughed as he followed her out.

Mom sat on the steps, talking to Derek and Joey, another kid who constantly got into trouble in the neighborhood. He overheard her threaten them with grounding, of all things. It seemed completely absurd until Jason realized she pointedly referenced leveraging her influence with everyone in the neighborhood to enforce it. With a surprised laugh, he discovered he actually believed she could do it.

Mom got up and smoothed the seat of her floral pattern dress from where she'd rumpled it from sitting. She walked over and pulled his head down for a quick kiss on the cheek, then repeated the action with Monica. They'd gotten so used to this, neither one of them found it odd. She surveyed them, looking over their clothing while the two boys stared at Monica, clearly smitten. Derek adopted a foolish grin.

Mom said, "You look beautiful, honey. Your new dress is stunning." Monica blushed, and Jason's surprise at her girlish reaction elicited a laugh.

When had she ever blushed? Jason thought.

Mom turned to Jason, one eyebrow raised. "Oh, sweetie." Her voice was almost tragic. "You look like you are pretending to be a high school student. What on earth are you wearing? A frat party nightmare is not exactly romantic." She ran the fabric of his shirt sleeve between her fingers and arched an eyebrow.

"This isn't a date, Mom. We're going out for drinks as friends. And this is what gay guys wear. Gay, like I'm not going to be dating Monica at all."

Mom smiled and patted his shoulder. The same one Monica had punched earlier. She glanced at Monica, who affected a slightly hurt look, which Jason found absurdly overdone. Mom seemed to buy the whole act and gave Monica a reassuring look. "Well, you kids have fun. Don't stay out too late, since you both work. Maybe your next date can be a shopping trip for you, Jason. Monica seems to realize clothing isn't something you can keep wearing for a decade after you get out of school."

He opened his mouth and then clamped it closed.

Derek and Joey burst out laughing and Monica tried to stifle a giggle.

Finally, he said, "We can stay out as long as we want, we are both—"

"Have a great time," Mom said. She walked over to sit back down with Joey, brushed his hair out of his eyes and put an arm over his shoulder, talking to him in a nearly inaudible tone as Jason and Monica's autonomous hover-car arrived to take them to the bar.

"That woman. Wow," Jason said, flustered. He got in and sat down on the chair facing Monica. Since there were no drivers, the seats were arranged so passengers could face each other to socialize during the ride.

Monica laughed. "She's great." When he shook his head, she followed up with, "Oh come on. You know you love seeing her every day." She brushed her leg seductively against his. "And she's super glad we'll be giving her some grandchildren. I just can't help my girly gushy feelings for your manly studliness. If only you hadn't worn your, what did she call it? 'Frat party nightmare' outfit. It's irresistible," she said, then laughed.

He couldn't help but laugh too. "You're the one who picked this out!"

Monica slumped back into her seat, stuffing her large bag down in their leg space. Jason felt compelled to ask about it.

"Seriously, what's in your oversized trash bag of a purse?"

"My makeup. Why?" She looked at him innocently.

"That's ridiculous! Not even a clown needs that much makeup."

"How would you know? How much makeup do you wear?" She took a tube of lipstick out of the side pocket and touched up her lips as if to make a point. "It's just stuff, Jason. Women have to have their crap to lug around with them everywhere. All of it. It's compulsory."

He let it drop.

They kept their conversation light and moderately pointless as the cab's computer attendant flew with automated precision through the city. When Jason wasn't chatting with Monica, his thoughts centered around the Tech he'd met earlier in the day. More and more his and Monica's conversation drifted off as he became lost in his thoughts and observations.

He looked out the window and watched the constant flow of traffic: the huge mechanics of buildings as they shifted their positions toward their solar power source; the play of electronics amongst the green of the sylvan metropolis; the living things themselves, passively guided by their nannies. All of it. The whole city and those beyond were under the control of one being. He feared the Council, the power they seemed to be seeking, but everyone completely overlooked the obvious. None of them could escape the fact the Techs were the ones who controlled everything.

Monica touched his shoulder, drawing his attention back to her, away from his thoughts. She gave him a questioning look. He smiled reassuringly, but both knew they couldn't talk. She read his face and, with an intuitive understanding, struck up another idle conversation, diverting his dark thoughts so he'd keep his poise.

Monica had chosen a dark but modern club. Brushed steel and blue luminescent wiring provided most of the décor in the otherwise stark bar. The place milled busily with well-dressed people and Jason suddenly regretted wearing his street clothes. Most of the men wore tailored suits or dress shirts, their handsome features heightened by their classy choice of clothing. The women were in cocktail dresses or low-cut gowns and high heels, with tastefully touched-up faces and neatly styled hair. Jason appeared as if he should be at a young gay club, and felt he clearly did not fit in.

Monica laughed, having known full well where they were going and, it was clear, had purposefully chosen his clothing. She had decided to play with him, finding clever and mischievous ways to distract him. He had assumed she'd just prattle at him all night about movies or books. He should have known she'd play some elaborate game. He had to admire her cleverness, if not her enjoyment of his discomfort.

The bartender looked at him with a barely contained sneer and curtly took his order, clearly annoyed he'd have to serve someone who didn't have the decency to dress appropriate to the bar.

Jason ordered a vodka cranberry, which seemed to further incense the bartender. Monica ordered a scotch and smiled winsomely. The bartender grinned and then threw a dark look at Jason, obviously attempting to lure her away.

"What a lovely place you picked. Thanks."

She pretended not to hear his sarcasm. "Oh! Do you think so? I find this place to be so classy and professional. All the men seem to really understand how to treat a lady." She fluttered her eyelashes at him.

"I'm going to kill you."

"Oh! My! What a shocking thing to suggest, pumpkin. However shall you do it?" She clapped her hands, feigning excitement. "I do so hope it involves poison. Poison is so romantic. I'll be the talk of the whole city!" She leaned in eagerly, pretending to be riveted by him.

He laughed at her absurdity and she shed her helpless girl act and laughed with him. "Seriously, I couldn't help it. C'mon, you must admit it's pretty funny. Besides, who cares what these people think? I'm just paying you back for this god-awful dress." She got an evil glint in her eyes. "We should totally go to the bathroom together and switch clothing. Cross dressing would really make things fun. Then we could pretend like we don't even see anything wrong or weird. We'd find out just how stuffy this place is."

He laughed with her. "Yeah . . . I'm not sure about the whole getting my ass kicked and thrown out part, though. Explaining things to Mom when we get home and she has to watch me walk by in your new dress would add to the misery." He grimaced as the bartender nearly hurled another drink at him. "How long are you planning on tormenting me here?"

"For a while, actually. I think you'll forgive me in about . . . oh . . . fifteen minutes. They play really good music and you're going to love the dancing." She downed her drink quickly and snapped her fingers haughtily at the bartender, paying him back for his rudeness to Jason by suddenly losing interest.

"Dancing in here? These people will hyperventilate in their stuffy clothing."

She just stuck her tongue out at him, then excused herself to the bathroom, hauling her bag with her.

He sipped his vodka cranberry and looked deeper into the club, seeing a large, empty dance floor. Background music streamed, but he could barely make it out above the conversational hum. His personal device indicated fifteen minutes until ten, which was, presumably, when the dancing started. He decided to get drunk. He drank his vodka quickly, ordered a shot, which he slammed down, then ordered another drink.

After five minutes, he grew bored and annoyed and decided Monica would have no problem finding him in his ridiculously out-of-place clothes. He got up and wandered around, enduring the occasionally raised eyebrow. Despite this, most of the people were surprisingly friendly, so he quickly stopped feeling out of place.

He had to admit there were a large number of attractive men. It had been a long time since he'd really been out, and he realized he'd become so engaged in his career he'd neglected his dating life. A few of the men grinned at him and he could feel their eyes on him as he walked by, which made him feel better.

Finally, the music started, and Monica still hadn't come out of the bathroom. He started to get a bit worried, then figured she probably had to spend time wiggling out of that dress to keep from peeing all over it. Carrying his empty glass back over to the bar and with an impudent grin at the sour bartender, he ordered another drink, then decided to head out to the dance floor.

The DJ began to play excellent music. Jason, feeling slightly drunk, put his drink down and started to get into the music. He noticed the crowd had really started to enjoy themselves. The temperature in the room dropped ten degrees and he realized management had adjusted for dancing.

A few minutes later, Monica appeared in front of him and he stopped dancing in disbelief. Knowing how Jason normally dressed, she had anticipated his look and changed into nearly matching street clothes, looking as out of place as he did. She grinned at him impishly and he laughed. No wonder her bag was so enormous.

With abandon, they danced for several hours, having a great time. Monica would snatch an occasional man out of the crowd and dance with him, which seemed to make the room feel incredibly friendly. With a few of the men, she'd dance close and then, leaning forward with a few whispered words, pull them over to Jason. He danced with a few of these guys, briefly, having a great time. All of them were smiling broadly and he realized, with surprise, they were actually attracted to him.

Jason felt a great sense of freedom without his bio-suit. He relied only on himself to gauge everyone around him. He enjoyed the pleasure of reading body language instead of incoming data and savored the thrill of surprise as a handsome man would flirt.

He was thoroughly drunk. Monica had to yank him away from his admirers, letting him know they were going home. Several of the men offered to take him, which he thought seriously about, but Monica took their numbers and told them she'd interview them for the position, tactfully getting him out of the club. One guy, who had been pressing a leg against Jason at the bar, offered to take them both back to his place.

In the cab ride home, Jason drunkenly professed that Monica had consistently shown herself to be the best and most important friend ever. He made her laugh at his inebriated proclamations, and he realized she had done one more thing for him. She'd intended to get him drunk. She'd planned the whole thing and he'd been easily and handily manipulated.

She took him back to her place and threw him on the couch. "You get to sleep there, so don't get any ideas. I'm a virgin, you know. I don't want you thinking you can have this sweet fresh maiden without a ring and a very large . . . dowry."

He exploded with laughter at the absurdity of her statement and she laughed too, getting him some water and a multivitamin.

"See? Much better, right?"

"Yeah, a lot. Thank you."

"Taking time to help when you're down is what friends are for, Jason. Remember to return the favor, so you aren't a one-sided selfish asshole when I need someone to lean on too, mmmkay?" She grinned.

"Got it."

She slipped out of her clothes, unashamedly undressing down to her panties and bra as if he were her brother. She got him a blanket and threw it over him as he closed his eyes.

As he heard her enter her bedroom, his eyes popped open. "Monica?"

"Yeah? What?"

"Oh my god, Monica, I didn't get a chance to tell you." He sat up on the couch so he could see her. "Today at the meeting. A Tech. Sector Seven, he was in the meeting today."

Monica didn't respond.

"Monica?"

She turned in the frame of the door, her eyes wide. "Physically in your meeting? With the Director?"

"No. Not really with him. It seemed, I don't know . . . the Tech seemed to be there for its own reasons."

"What's that supposed to mean? Don't be cryptic. Did it say anything? Jason, this is awful! If the Techs are supporting the Director, or the Council . . ."

"I don't know. It seemed to be there for its own reasons. It felt different. I can't really tell you why, though. He greeted me."

Her hand came up to touch her breastbone, her voice flat. "He? The Tech is a man? What do you mean, it greeted you? It actually said, 'Hi, I'm Sector Seven! What's your name?'" Monica moved over to him and Jason bunch his legs and sat up so she could sit down on the couch with him. She voiced a quick command to bring the lights up slightly so they could see each other more clearly as they talked.

"Of course not. It knew me, though. They know everything. It just greeted me in a weirdly robotic way. I broadcast to it. Friendship. You know, a greeting. I didn't know what else to do, I was so scared." Jason fiddled with the frilly threads of a pillow and his eyes settled on the dull lights of the kitchen appliances as he told her about his encounter. "It shut me off. It turned off all the biofeedback and all the personal devices I had without blinking. The Tech terrified me when it entered the room and I couldn't help but broadcast fear for a moment, so it cut me off. Then, when I'd calmed down, it turned things back on for me. I wanted to apologize, so I sent out a wave of friendship, though it was probably pretty feeble since I'd been frightened out of my skin. Then it greeted me."

"Nothing you do is feeble. Your broadcast abilities are the best there are." She chewed her lip. "Did it act friendly?"

"Not really, no. More like a robot greeting me when I got home or something."

She seemed to think about this. "What else did it say? Did it talk to anyone else?'

"No, I don't know. They entered with it, so it probably talked to them earlier. It didn't say another word."

"This could be a disaster! If those things side with the Council, nothing we do will matter." She slumped down onto the floor. "Realistically, there's nothing we can do now that will matter either. Jason, all this information is useless. We can't stop any of this and the Council is going to run the world. Forever, if things go as they plan. But, if Mister Tech thing would help us, maybe we'd have a chance."

"Monica, seriously. It isn't going to side with them. He—it isn't going to stop them either. They never do. They're totally impassive. Have you ever heard of one changing anything the Council does? Of interfering in anything?"

He watched her mull this over.

"No, you're right. So why did it show up in the first place?"

He shrugged. "Direct observation, maybe? The changes going on are possibly the most significant shifts in our society right now. The Techs have to know everything so they can make sure society runs smoothly. It's probably making sure it knows, making sure all nine of them know what sort of world they have to govern."

"Yeah, you're right." She mulled this over, grabbing one of the couch pillows and hugging it to her chest, leaning forward to bow her head as she voiced her thoughts. "Still . . . what if one could be made to intervene? What if some dire threat made them step in? Jason, if we can get a Tech on our side, we could fight this. We might actually be able to do something."

Jason had to change positions, since the blood to his legs was cut off. He moved to put his legs and feet up on her living room table in front of the couch. "On our side? Are you crazy? It won't take sides. They have no emotions, no allegiances. It probably considers our problems barely worth noticing. I can't imagine how much they process in a given second. Our concerns and fears don't matter in the slightest to something so powerful. For all I know, our lives might be as interesting to them as ants are to us. Come to think of it, they govern ants, too. Literally."

"Yeah, every living thing and inanimate object that contains nannites or any sort of technology." She tangled her fingers in her hair. "Maybe there's a way to make them interested or concerned about us." She sat up and put her legs out next to his, scooting closer.

"Assuming you can get near one. Or even see it." He took a deep breath. "Have you ever seen a Tech? Ever? I hadn't until today. This is probably the first and the last time I'll ever see one, let alone have a chance to slip it a note asking for help."

Monica glanced around her apartment and shuddered. "It already knows, Jason."

He sat up suddenly, afraid. "What? Why do you say that? It can't know. We've only talked about this in private." His hearing was suddenly picking up every little sound of the apartment, things he subconsciously ignored. The faint clicking of the environmental mechanics, the sound of the food storage. Even the tiny sound of her cleaning robots as they vacuumed the floor in the other room.

"Private? There's no such thing anymore. Get real." She gestured around the apartment. "Our personal communicators have been near us every time we've talked." She shook her head. "Shit. I was so sure I still had some privacy. Some place to hide. I feel like a moron. We're surrounded by technology even in here, or at your place. All this technology is capable of gathering and processing information. Our lives are comfortable because our surroundings gather everything about us and adjust accordingly." She shook her head. "I'm so blind. I'm a Mechanic, which is like a junior Tech, and I still overlooked the obvious.'

"The Director!"

"Doesn't know anything. I can almost guarantee it. The Techs really are impassive, Jason. It knows, but it probably doesn't consider it relevant. Even a direct threat to the life of the Director would be ignored. It would simply process the information like it does everything else and only intervene at the last moment—when and if no other alternative existed."

She raised her voice slightly, addressing the Tech as if she was sure it heard her. "I know you can hear us. Just remember, our society depends on you. Sometimes it means you have to prevent it from destroying itself. It's your responsibility!"

Jason stared at her for a moment. "You don't actually think it will listen to you, do you?"

"Yes, it will listen. I don't think it will do anything, though. The Council isn't really threatening society, just changing how it's ruled. If they tried to kill off everybody, then we'd have help." She sighed. "But a shift in politics? No, it won't care. I would be more concerned if it did. They may never interfere for any reason, strictly enforced by some obscure programming and AI rules that govern their actions." She rubbed her finger over her lip. "If they ever started meddling, we'd be in real trouble." She let her head fall back against the back of the couch, staring at the ceiling. "You know, I'm so worried about the Council ruling us, I overlooked the fact we are all virtually slaves to the Techs. If they cared, that is. I'm so beneath them I might as well be a cavewoman."

They were both silent for a while. Finally, she got up. "Well, I'm going to bed. There's one thing I can do. Sleep on it. Go to work the next day. Who knows, maybe having an eternally ruling Council won't matter. I probably won't even notice." She seemed resigned, defeated after her revelation of the farce she'd believed about privacy. He understood. They couldn't protect privacy, even if they had the means. They'd lost privacy long ago.

Drunk enough that he couldn't focus, Jason let her slip into her room without comment. The room spun and he decided it would be better to pass out and worry about their problems later. He lay back down and pulled the pillow Monica had stolen towards him to put under his shoulder, spreading the blankets back over himself.

SEVEN

THE NEXT MORNING HIS HEAD HURT too much to really care about anything. He got up and put on his dirty clothes and managed to crawl into a hover transport, all the while avoiding waking Monica.

Arriving home, he took a shower, then slipped into his bio-suit and began instructing his nannies to remove the toxins and rehydrate his tissues. He ate, took another vitamin, drank electrolytes. Within an hour, his nannies had him feeling much better.

He felt slightly guilty about his heavy reliance on technology and experienced a brief sense of cheating since he was a doctor capable of instructing his own body. He also felt exposed after the conversation with Monica. How could he have failed to realize his entire biochemical activity could be processed and accessible by the Sector Seven Tech? The naked exposure of his vital statistics unnerved him.

Helpless to do anything about it, he shrugged off the passing concern and decided to go into his new lab. Work seemed the best outlet, and he did enjoy the science of his new project.

The cityscape blurred behind his churning thoughts. Did Techs remember everything they saw? He grinned at the simplicity of his thinking. Of course they did, but likely remembered it in such a foreign way as to make the term "memory" irrelevant. They simply accessed the information already stored in a hundred billion locations on a hundred billion devices, maybe a billion-billion pieces of information. In any case, far more data than he could comprehend.

The new route to his lab gave him something different to watch from his window. A large, shallow lake was busy with activity as birds fished and hunted for crustaceans. The morning light reflected from the surface so brightly that he almost entirely missed the people swimming and playing in the water.

After a few minutes, the automated vehicle landed, and he stepped out onto the unfamiliar pad. A smiling brunette, who appeared to Jason to be a teenager, greeted him and handed him coffee and a display tablet with information about the lab.

"Mister Emerson. I'm Jana. I thought it might be nice for me to take you to the lab personally, as a new space can be mildly disorienting."

Jason nodded to her. "Hello Jana, thank you. And for the coffee," he said, raising it up.

She turned and began to lead him toward the entrance. "The Director wasn't sure if you preferred a young male assistant, but he instructed me to tell you several have been vetted if you wish to make a selection. That list is provided on your display. The rest of your staff is awaiting your summons. Nobody has been permitted to enter your research facility without your approval."

Geez. Is everyone trying to get me laid? Of course, now that Jason thought about it, it wasn't uncommon for high-level officials to dally with staff and to select them for this reason—a practice Jason thought disgusting and an abuse of position.

The walk was not long, and Jason sipped his coffee along the way. The complex was almost entirely devoted to the labs for the longevity project. Jana, having not been engaged in further conversation, didn't say anything else. Apparently, she was instructed to adapt to his mood.

As they approached, he stopped. "I'd like some time to go through things alone, if you don't mind. I'll come back out when I've taken inventory and have my bearings. Thank you." He handed her the half-empty cup of coffee.

"Of course, Mister Emerson. I'll be just down the hall here to the left. Or available via your communicator if you wish. I've been encoded as part of your new staff." She smiled cutely and moved down the hall.

The new lab provided ample space for research teams. The equipment shined: metallic instruments made from cutting-edge materials that conducted nearly zero electricity, heat and glass-like chambers made from a polymer stronger than steel, along with other materials and machines Jason wasn't familiar with, but which appeared specially designed. Everything seemed to be colored or reflective to suit its purpose. The employment of gravity fields to hold some liquids or objects was curious, but he knew a feature like that would be useful when trying to prevent contact with anything else.

Jason wandered around, touching things randomly, puzzling over devices that looked alien and the uses of which he couldn't guess. Several new biosuits hung in glass cases, and next to them were vacuum chambers designed to tailor, build, and test nanotechnology. Spider-like arms capable of spinning fabrics rested, awaiting instruction. The lab appeared to contain the most advanced technology available, all at his disposal.

"Impressive, isn't it?"

Jason nearly jumped at the woman's voice. Dr. Emma Garbine laughed. "Even more impressive is that I snuck up on you. Considering your reputation with biofeedback and empathic response, one would think that impossible. Either your mind is preoccupied, or my suit is malfunctioning."

He quickly absorbed the information coming in from her suit and smiled. "It's working fine, Doctor. You're right, I'm immersed in my thoughts and was not expecting anyone until I'd finished surveying the land." He gestured around. "I'm hoping someone can tell me what most of this does or I'll spend an awful amount of time reading manuals."

She smiled. "Seniority has its privileges. I told that young lady out front that you were expecting me. She couldn't possibly challenge another senior Medic. As to all of this, we have a full staff of experts on hand and, yes, they are helpful. I'm still trying to figure out what half of the equipment does, myself. We're supposed to have the staff fine-tune or design anything we might require. No expense spared."

"Wow. Well, the Director seems eager to pursue things. I can only assume he's already figured out how to exploit the research." No use in being subtle. Jason knew they were observed most of the time, so acting naive or false would only trigger suspicion.

"Carlisle wants to live forever and he is slobbering over the opportunity to be young again. Aren't we all?" Her mouth slipped into a thoughtful moue, her head moving to look at a particularly interesting arrangement of colored objects floating in a silvery liquid. Her long grey braids fell forward as she bent over. "Perhaps not you. Not yet. You're still young. But your urgency to find a way to remain youthful will change as the clock ticks on and you feel the inevitable creeping up, coupled with the frustration of knowing the science to derail our deaths is nearly at hand." Her eyes lit up. "It really is that time at last. The opportunity to set aside our mortality and take our next evolutionary steps forward." She smiled. "Along with the responsibilities and ramifications, which are enormous."

"So, we're the logisticians of immortality and the architects working on tearing down the meaning of time itself."

She straightened, turning to face him. "Time is a human invention. It's great as a placeholder and I'm sure physicists would happily smack me upside the head with their theories, but let's face it, it's a physicist's teething ring. We made time up and we're just growing up enough to set our old constructs aside."

He laughed. "I'm glad it's so simple. I grow tired of reality as we know it, so let's just make a completely new one. Fun!"

Emma pursed her lips and shrugged a little. "Let's sit. Too much walking around hurts my hips." Jason spied a set of chairs and a small table off to the corner of the suit manufacturing area. He led her over to it and politely pulled out the chair, offering it to her.

She gave a grateful nod and used a hand to stabilize herself as she sat. "This first step—taking away limitations imposed on us by our limited life spans, the depletion of our exuberance, the tiresome worry which urges us to cut corners so our lives will matter—is incredibly important. From here, we give ourselves an unlimited span of what everyone refers to as *time* to figure out the rest."

Jason sat in the opposite chair and put his hands on the table, leaning forward to prevent having to raise their voices. "And our souls, Doctor? What of them? What are we giving up?"

She reached out and put her hand on his. "Isn't that just it? Is it a gift or a trade? Or is it both, depending on who receives it? Or a gift to the individual and a disaster for humanity?" She sighed, removing her hand from his and opening her communicator. "Tea?"

Jason shook his head. Emma sent a quick command for tea for herself.

"The biggest problem isn't figuring out *how* to outwit time, Jason, it's figuring out *if* we should. I'm eager to rush forward, to abandon everything and throw myself into the future. That eagerness frightens me. I'm scared, figuratively, to death we are making a big mistake. We understand our physical form so well that I can reconstruct any one of us from scratch. But we can't animate bodies with any semblance of life. Not yet. We can emulate and automate, we can merge and become AI, but we don't understand who we are, what makes us alive. Not really. Arguments against leaving behind our humanity and against immortality have arisen since our earliest records. Cautionary tales of meddling with our fate."

The robots arrived with surprising speed, efficiently setting a charming replica teapot of ancient design and a small porcelain cup and saucer down in front of Emma. She scrunched her nose in delight. "I love the ritual of tea and the old design of the pots and cups. It's so quaint. They must have really studied our habits."

Jason didn't find being observed and studied as amusing as she did, but said nothing. The robots left as quickly as they'd arrived.

Emma poured the steaming liquid, gently holding the top of the pot in place. "Arguments against immortality and the power to control the physical are no longer relevant. Such advancement cannot be stopped. Now we must ask the question of how we handle immortality and what infinite life means for us. The big question is 'now what?'"

Jason glanced over across the distance, still taking in the various gear. Everything was so quiet, waiting for him to bring in his staff. The austerity and coldness of the place was heightened by the vast stretches of space between stations. It was not inviting. "Well, there's the whole question of population. Of jobs and retirement. Of family dynamics. Nobody knows what will happen with innovation and drive, since we will have centuries or millennia instead of the blink of an eye to research. This makes suicide sound like our only option if we don't like what we discover. I suppose the societal impacts fit into 'now what?', but these impacts are a pretty broad consideration."

She lifted an eyebrow and sipped her tea, testing the heat. "Not so difficult to answer. We'll need population for expansion into the galaxy, so under-population will be more of a problem than having people who live forever. Jobs will become so specialized it will take a normal lifetime of apprenticeship just to start working within each niche, and there will be so many jobs based on galactic expansion we'll have a shortage of people with enough knowledge." Emma leaned back, following his gaze.

"It's a replicator."

He looked back at her, confused about the shift in conversation. "Huh?"

"That large greyish oven-like thing you're staring at. It's a replicator. New design. I guess it is very good at printing almost any tool or part." She winked at him and sipped her tea again. "I have one in my lab, too."

Then, shifting back to the original conversation, she said, "Anyway. Galactic expansion paves the way for everyone to be useful, despite living indefinitely. Families will probably form, have children, fall apart, reform, have more children. Family will become a cycle, not a fixed position. Assisted suicide, assuming accidents don't kill us off, will only happen if people stop dreaming and reaching for those dreams. Research will accelerate because we'll be able to draw upon knowledge spanning much greater time and vastly broader topics, lending toward better and more accurate insight. Those are easy questions, Jason. What you've posed isn't actually an issue."

This drew an involuntary bark of laughter from him. "Well, I'm glad you figured those complex problems out before they become large social problems. It's nice to know you have all them fixed."

Emma scrunched her nose again, a mischievous little smile playing on her lips. "Yes, well, there will be specifics, but they really aren't difficult problems to overcome." With the slowness of age, she reached up and combed a hand over one of her braids, feeling for stray hairs with her free hand. "The big one will be spiritual. What if we are derailing our spiritual purification, our path to higher learning? What if we aren't even real and we're finding a way to trap ourselves in the eternal dream? What if there *is* a God, or several, and we fall outside of His or Her divine intent to be embraced upon our mortal ending? These are the harder questions. These are the things I need to know how to analyze. It all starts with who we are as beings. Not as physical entities, but as sentient and self-aware creatures. What if there is a greater plan and we are moving to a crossroad where we stray from our path?"

He hadn't thought of this. Something about it worried him deeply. He tried to ignore the deep-seated feeling that she was somehow right. Replying with a tone that conveyed less concern than he felt, he said, "Well, okay, but it's hard to argue we are under the shelter of a god or ten and then say we are messing up the divine plan. If there's genuinely a divine plan, argument for it implies it isn't really possible to do something outside of such a plan."

"That's ignorant." She sipped the last of her tea from the cup, setting it down on the saucer, and undid the last couple lengths of braid to weave back in an errant strand. "There are always stories of mankind being misled and failing the tests set forth. Being able to choose the wrong path means there could be ways of messing up such a plan. Freedom of choice and such. Don't be daft, Jason. Think about our own evolution. What if we, ourselves, are part of the eternal cycle of God and this is our infancy? What if we become the self-same supreme being some of us now attribute to God? We ourselves could be looking back through time with gentle eyes, unable to interfere with our own past, but we've evolved into our own god after millennia. In other words, we could, ourselves, *be* God. Time really means nothing in such a context, you know."

His mind swam in that for a moment. It was an interesting thought exercise. Needing to stand, he got up and moved to a nearby device that displayed blank screens. "How deep. Very well—I'll think these things through a bit. So, what am I supposed to be doing here?"

Jason touched one of the screens and it lit up, becoming transparent. Behind it were a few objects that appeared to be flying drones. Perhaps for gathering materials? They did appear to have collection arms.

Emma stood as well, signaling the robots to remove her tea. "You, my dear, will be working mostly with me. I expect we will need to arrange our teams to meet weekly. You have the strongest control over empathic response of anyone we know. It's fortunate you are a doctor, but we'd have captured you and brought you here regardless, just because you are the key to our largest issue. I need you for my research. I need you to help me figure out how we work as emotional creatures so I can delve more deeply. Since removing all emotion isn't a good option, our other option is learning to control our feelings completely.

"For your part, you'll be working on ways to enhance emotive responses. You will have to test ways to impart your emotive ability, the knack you have for reading others and influencing their emotions. We'll also need to work on testing how to transfer consciousness to another physical vessel. If we figure out how to transfer ourselves, we need to ensure we don't lose who we are and our emotional connections. Transferring into a robot would result in a being of pure logic, which could be a disaster. We fear and tightly control our burgeoning AIs for this very reason. You'll be key in all these areas."

The robots arrived and removed the teapot, cup and saucer. One put the chairs back in their proper place. Jason barely glanced at them. Another of the windows in the storage unit contained crystalline storage devices. Crystal storage had become the new norm, since they were nearly impervious to damage, held up over great lengths of time, and recorded an enormous amount of data. Perhaps these held manuals. Or maybe they were blank, and he was supposed to use them instead of putting his research on the servers. Keep what he learned secret and localized rather than on the network. He'd have to ask.

Emma moved to his side, also looking at the shards with interest. "As a scientist, you'll poke and prod your way through all the research like the rest of us. I'm sure you'll see various areas that require your attention."

Without thinking, he blurted, "Like what it means

to give eternal control to a single group of people over humanity? Let people we may not be able to trust run the show without our best interests in mind?"

She turned her head to look at him, smiling slyly. "Yes, Jason. Problems like a ruling class that needs to be removed must have a solution, too." She glanced sideways at the surrounding lab, implying *not here*. "You are as critical to this research as the rest of us. Remember this: possibly more important than any other aspect is that you are unique in the strength of your abilities, which are key to answering some of the questions we have. Don't underestimate your value or the importance of what you can do."

He felt unsure and didn't understand her meaning. Running fingers through his hair, he turned away from the storage container and led Emma back toward the entry doors. She moved slowly, so he didn't rush. "I'm sure I'm missing something."

"Haven't you considered what it means to have the empathic responses you possess?"

"I know I'm going to miss the point, but sure. It means I can work more easily with patients because everyone trusts me. I can calm down even the most panicked and upset person, then I can help them." He paused uncertainly, remembering the meeting the previous day. "It means, too, that when I lose control, I can make others feel my fear."

She put a hand gently on his shoulder, halting him. He turned to glance over at her. There was a strange urgency in her voice that demanded his attention. "I can't tell you how glad I am you are the one we have for this. Jason, if you wanted, you could impose emotions on others. You could force them to do what you wanted. Maybe not yet, but you will. You do this accidentally, not on purpose, but if you strengthen your abilities and, assuming the person you target has nannies for you to work with, which is almost a guarantee in this day and age, you can make them furious or in love. Complete domination. You are just so good-hearted, you haven't tried."

Jason stared at her in shock. "How horrible! We can't research emotional mind control! I don't want to be involved in perverting and corrupting the science."

She removed her hand but kept his gaze for a moment longer. "Pandora's box, Jason. It's better to research and develop ways to prevent this than to ignore it, no? Would you rather have someone else figure it out, perhaps in an unmonitored research facility, then use it as a form of control? Will it be you who figures this out, or will it be someone who lacks your ethics?" She reached out to touch his arm and looked meaningfully into his eyes. "No, I rather thought you wouldn't want someone else gaining this level of control first. You see, here we can figure out how it works and how to govern . . . and how to counter it." She rubbed her eyebrow with a thumb. "You're already bursting at the seams. You nearly crippled us when the Tech appeared in our meeting. I haven't felt such a wave of terror in a long time. My reaction was completely involuntarily, and I couldn't block you."

The uses that she hinted at—Jesus! They were evil, horrible. Is that what Faust wanted from him? "What if the research we do is stolen, used against us, or without our knowledge? What if we provided the very means for someone to abuse it?"

"Isn't such fear true of anything we do? In the wrong hands . . . blah, blah, blah. But honestly, Jason, do you think someone else could exert the kind of control you are capable of? I'll tell you this, nobody we know can come close. Sure, eventually someone else might be able to do this, but for now, I couldn't imagine anyone as dear and sweetly naive as you." Then, sensing his objections, she added, "Yes, the other Medics have some basic ability, but you're by far the best."

He nodded, relieved to hear this. Emma touched his cheek fondly. Her lips curled in a half smile. "Besides, the Tech shut you down as if you were a fly. Your broadcast nannite signals are a simple thing for them to turn off or on at will. Anything we come up with, any technology we already possess, is something they can control. It's the nature of the Tech to immediately absorb knowledge and research, and then control it. Nothing you do can circumvent them. So, don't worry so much. Clearly, the counter to this already exists by disabling the source. We have no idea how this works in a specific way, but it won't be terribly difficult to work out."

Jason was both unnerved and relieved. The helplessness of being crippled by the Tech, to be wholly within its—his—power scared him. Knowing his ability and research could counter Director Faust gave Jason hope, however.

Emma got caught up in a yawn and put her fist to her mouth. "Good to see you, dear. I'm going to finish setting up some new protocols for my staff. I'll see you later. This was a nice chat, but your own staff is probably anxiously awaiting you." She squeezed his bicep with some familiarity and smiled when he sent a wave of calm and relaxation at her.

Jason watched her leave then moved through the lab to his new office. The walls were transparent, but he suspected he could make them opaque if he wanted privacy. He sat at his station and found updated and new interfacing technology. Proximity to the lab allowed him access to all the control sets and data, limited only by his security protocols. He could probably access most of this from his home, too, which would be considered moderately secure.

Still not willing to deal with staff, he delayed. For a while, he reviewed the information regarding the updated suits and the specifics of the nanotechnology in regard to emotive response. Jason saw an enormous amount of data regarding the chemicals involved in emotion, but massive fundamental gaps. Chemically induced calm, for example, was simply like taking a sedative. It impaired the individual instead of instilling a genuine feeling. This held true of almost everything regarding emotional control. Medicine could change a person's normal modus operandi, and drugs such as MDMA could elicit passivity, but these changes were not genuine, and the person knew they were in an altered state. Further, drugs caused a huge drain on physical resources, which left the person requiring a recovery period.

Jason could somehow affect a change in a person's biochemistry so they truly felt the emotions he projected. In some cases, quite strongly. He'd never really thought about what this meant but could clearly see the importance of the research into emotional control. Fine-tuned and done in secret, from a distance, the person might never be aware of Jason's manipulation. He could potentially control an individual, even a crowd, without anyone knowing or objecting.

Jason shivered, feeling creepy even contemplating the potential.

An incoming call from Monica made him realize he'd been at the lab for nearly four hours. He accepted the call and agreed to come over for dinner. She told him she'd had to get up and go to work and figured he'd snuck out and gone to bed in his own apartment.

As he disconnected, he indulged in a long stretch and yawn. From the corner of his eye, he noticed someone standing off to his right, quietly observing him. Startled, he turned, then froze. The Sector Tech watched him impassively. He suppressed his panic, overriding the compulsion to run from a creature that controlled all the technology in the sector. A being that knew every little thing that transpired and whose commands would be instantly obeyed.

The Tech simply continued to stare.

Jason rose from his chair slowly. The vastness of the empty lab gave rise to irrational fear, as if witnesses would help save him if the thing decided he was going against the Council. Whatever else the Tech intended, it clearly did not seem to mean him harm. With an effort, he mastered his emotions and tentatively sent a friendly wave of well-being with his nannies. The Tech cocked its head and its eyes narrowed briefly as if processing Jason's broadcast greeting. The Tech moved toward him, captivating him with that same liquid grace he'd witnessed in the Convene. Despite the fluidity of motion, the thing approached with disconcerting speed. Jason took an involuntary step backward.

A faint whisper of calm came at him from the Tech. Weak and pathetic in comparison to Jason's capabilities, the returned greeting still hit Jason like a wave. The thing clearly meant to reassure him. He relaxed and stood his ground.

For a moment they just stood there, assessing each other. Then the Tech spoke. "We see you, Jason Emerson."

He wasn't sure how to respond, so he raised his hand to shake. The thing cocked its head again, blinking slowly as if trying to maintain focus. Jason could not imagine the huge amount of processing power going on inside its head. With graceful fluidity, it took Jason's hand in its own.

Jason's heart felt both a heavy blow and a staggering skip. The intimacy of the grip caught him off guard.

He gasped involuntarily but did not let go. He noticed how green the Techs eyes were, how dark his spikey hair, flawless his skin, how muscular his arms. Jason's perceptions of the Tech changed. It wasn't a thing. This Tech was a living, breathing being.

The Tech stared at him. Then, it changed the grip of its hand to a grip of the forearm in a curiously familiar gesture, stepping closer.

In a wildly irrational way, Jason felt an immense attraction. He crushed it out of his thoughts, but no amount of control he could exert could hide anything from a Tech. It knew. He almost burst out laughing at the absurdity.

"We see you, Dr. Emerson. We are glad."

"I . . . I see you, Tech. Sector Seven. I see you, too."

He didn't know what else to say. The thing still had a firm grip on his arm. Jason didn't care. Something about the appearance of the Tech and its curious familiarity struck Jason as worrisome. He knew the Tech must be here for some deeper reason than simple concern, but it clearly couldn't be to arrest or seize him.

Abruptly, the otherworldly distance returned to the Tech's green eyes and it let him go. "We must go." Without waiting for a response, it turned and strode lithely, rapidly, from the room.

Jason let out an explosive breath and slumped back into his chair. He realized his hands were trembling. He ran his fingers through his hair and continued to stare at the door. After a bit, Jason summoned his staff and spent the rest of the day familiarizing himself with the people under him and the equipment. He'd have to go back and memorize their names, since his mind wasn't on-task completely, but it was nice to see faces for now. It would take weeks to fully comprehend the tools at his disposal, but the science of everything helped take his mind off greater concerns. At last, when he'd spent an adequate amount of time with everyone, he let them go home. As the lab emptied, his mind filled again. Sector Seven was playing at something beyond his comprehension. He nearly fled the building, catching a gravity transport back to his apartment.

•   •   •

He prepared a decent meal to keep his hands busy, but his mind would not quiet. With controlled precision, he ate and cleaned up the kitchen. He tried to busy himself with various tasks, continuing his reading and answered a note from Dr. Emerson that indicated he should prep by learning more about his new team. He looked up his staff and made sure he'd memorized their names. He read some of their backgrounds, making notes. However, he simply couldn't calm himself. His lip chewing had become nearly painful.

Without knowing what else to do, he decided to go to Monica's apartment to wait for her.

By the time he finally met up with her, Jason had resorted to pacing the block, having unsuccessfully sat at a nearby coffee shop, trying to read. His body required motion, and his continuous circling of the block around her apartment had raised a few eyebrows from her neighbors.

Monica scowled when she saw him. She grabbed him by the arm in exasperation and nearly drug him up the stairs. Her arms and face were smeared in an oily brownish-black fluid. Even her luxurious wealth of black hair was tangled and greasy from her work.

Without asking him if he wanted to sit, or if he needed a glass of water, she pushed him onto the couch and hurriedly went into her bathroom, starting the shower.

He got up and retrieved a cup from the kitchen, filling it from the tap. He continued his pacing as she showered. Neither one of them said a word through the open door.

Finally, she came out, toweling off in front of him. Monica treated him like a brother and it probably never occurred to her that he found her young, athletic body attractive. As a gay man, he hardly commented on his occasional attraction to women, since saying anything just confused them and had resulted in more than one occasion where they lavished affection on him in hopes of altering his sexual preference. The female form attracted him, just not as much as that of males.

Lost in thought, her voice startled him. "Well, c'mon. You're obviously having some sort of crazy breakdown. What happened? You act like you have a sudden onslaught of OCD. Did the Director do something? Something else, I mean, since the asshole seems to have his tentacles mixed in everything?" She paused, her voice sounding worried. "Or did you find something in your research that's worse than we thought?"

"The Tech came to find me. Me. Specifically me. It even waited until Dr. Garbine left." He fidgeted with the printed material on her table, organizing it obsessively. She grabbed his hands and forced them to stop.

"Okay, seriously, you need to get a grip. Stop flailing around my apartment." Her jaw clenched and her eyebrows rose. "So, it came to see you. Maybe it had been instructed to keep an eye on you. The Director seems to have some sort of rapport, if not outright control, over them. Maybe it is supposed to keep an eye on your whole team."

"No." He shook his head. "No, that's not it. It's, I don't know. It's so weird. The Tech came to me and it said hello and stuff. It greeted me in a friendly way, though it is robotic when you talk to one. It took my hand." *My forearm*, he thought. "It was staring right at me for a moment. You know what I mean. Like it had blocked out the rest of its millions of incoming messages and impressions and focused on me, specifically." He took a breath and clamped his temples between his thumb and middle finger of his left hand. A headache was starting. "It appeared to be concerned about something, I could tell by the way it avoided saying certain things directly. But it didn't say anything I could interpret to figure out what was being implied."

He looked up at her sheepishly, deciding he'd better

be completely honest with her. "Monica, I know this sounds really lame, but if it had been a normal guy, I would have asked him on a date."

She reared back. "Are you insane? You can't date a cyborg!"

"They aren't cyborgs!" Then, seeing her temper flare and her mouth open to unleash a tirade, he said quickly. "Okay! They have a lot of technological modifications to their bodies, including some neural alterations I don't know much about, but they are born and grow up just like the rest of us."

"Oh sure. I remember fondly how, when I was a little girl, they first plugged my face into the WorldNet and I started learning how to command every little technical aspect of my neighborhood. While making brownies in my Happy Princess Bakery, I discovered I could use my brain to direct traffic and command robots to affect infrastructure upgrades and repairs. Just like all the other little girls in my class." She scowled. "Of course, this was before I abandoned all my friends so I could use my Pony Land Adventure Suit to correct anomalies in the power grid." Her frown deepened and she said, "Oh wait, that's right! None of that crap happened because it isn't how normal kids grow up."

"Calm down. Sheesh. Point taken. He hasn't had normal exposure to humanity, but he's still human. Just raised in an uncaring and unfeeling way."

"He? It, you mean. They aren't male or female, Jason. They're robots with human bodies and brains."

"Not fair, Monica. He is definitely male. Believe me."

Her eyes widened. "Omigod, Jason, you can't hump on a Tech! Seriously? Forget for a moment it can have you obliterated with an idle thought. They're also the most protected members of our society and the population would rip you to shreds if they thought you were interfering with one in any way. And believe me, they would consider trying to sleep with a Tech as interfering." She grabbed his arm and led him to the table, almost forcing him to sit in one of the chairs. She pulled up another chair right next to him. "Oh, and never mind the fact the Director seems to have them under his thumb and since he's a ruthless bloodsucking leech, he'd gladly have you torn limb from limb if he doesn't need you. Aside from all those minor obstacles, it would as soon as sacrifice you to stop an out-of-control truck from hitting a grocery store as it would use a toothpick to dislodge a sesame seed from its teeth. Assuming they eat like the rest of us and don't have their nutrition piped into some weird mechanized orifice."

Jason scowled, pushing his chair back from the table to fold his arms across his chest. "You know what? You're missing the point here. Stop it. The thing came to find me at the lab. It came in, watched me for—hell, I don't know how long—then walked up to me and shook my hand. It said it 'saw me', which came across as a friendly and honest greeting. A little odd, but friendly. The Tech seemed awkwardly anti-social, but not malicious."

"Jason, seriously. I'm not missing the point. You

think the thing is attractive. You just said so yourself. I know you see a nice face and some muscles and your faggoty brain short-circuits, but you have got to look past his pretty . . . whatever it is you are looking at. Please don't fall for a trick like this. Please don't let the Director suddenly control you through a ruthless attack on your self-imposed celibacy."

He laughed, taken off guard. He lowered his arms. Monica always surprised him. "That's actually a fair blow to my ego. You get points. I still don't think it had anything to do with Faust, but I will take your paranoia, which has been pretty on-track so far, and keep my wits intact." He pulled in his lower lip for a moment, then blew it out. "Besides, my physical attraction isn't influencing me. I'm just trying to be honest with you. Nobody gets close to a Tech, so I shouldn't have any issues with keeping myself in line. Plus, my attraction is laced with a healthy dose of terror."

She looked at him for a moment with concern, then relaxed. Finally, she smiled and got up, moving behind him to put her hands on his shoulder. She massaged him for a moment, obviously thinking. "This could be good. At the very least, you appear to be necessary. If it is Director Faust behind this, he needs you bound to him. If it isn't the Director spying on your or trying to manipulate you, you have a Tech which, for the first time in known history, is—well, whatever fondness correlates to when you're an alien robot person."

Jason relaxed under her hands, the tension leaving his

shoulders. "We still have a problem, though. If it wasn't Faust, my emotions were out of control all afternoon and I'm sure we were watched. Until I came here, my suit probably broadcast everything back to Central."

"Yeah, so? If Faust intended to drive you crazy by sending in the Tech, then he'll be pleased he succeeded. If that's not what he's up to, what's he going to do? Even he isn't power hungry enough to cross a Tech, no matter how friendly this one is."

Jason thought for a second. "You're right. He'll need to figure out what is really going on and get control of the situation. This might make me more valuable."

Her hands stopped their work on his muscles and she moved away from him toward her room. "Okay, I'm getting dressed and we're going to dinner. Water only tonight." She pursed her lips. "And maybe we need to find you some cock, because you are clearly sex starved. It should take your mind off robot guy."

Jason's communicator sounded. "Dinner, sure. I'm really hungry, so dinner will be great. But I'm not picking up some random guy." His communicator sounded again, and he connected. "Hello?"

"Ah, Doctor Emerson. Thank you for taking my call." Director Faust. The timing was too convenient. Whatever was going on, it wasn't good.

"Certainly, Director. I was just getting ready to go to dinner with my friend. What, uh, may I do for you?"

Faust paused briefly and then chuckled. "My, how quickly we've regained our composure, Jason. I just got back from a conference and found your readings were off the chart. If I'd been in town, I would have dispatched a team to drag you back to the office for help. As it is, I'm concerned about your mental well-being. Surely, you must know I saw the recordings of this afternoon."

Monica stared at him and Jason mouthed, "Faust." She bared her teeth and clenched her fists to her mouth with a panicked expression.

Jason bit his lower lip.

"Jason, are you still there?"

"Yes, Director. I'm just, well, honestly I'm not sure what to say. I had an anxiety attack earlier when a Tech happened by the lab and I'm only just now calming down. Then you call and I'm freaking out about things all over again. Didn't you send it over in the first place?"

This seemed to give the Director pause, as if he should claim the deed. "Ah, no. I didn't. Please don't worry about what I think, or if you are in any way in trouble with me. I'm just concerned. We need you badly for the research, I'll be the first to admit. I simply cannot think of what to make of your visitor." He seemed genuinely concerned, or his acting had gotten better. "I've spoken only a dozen words with the Techs since I've been privileged enough to interact with them. There's no need to verbally communicate with them at all, and they seem to disregard any sort of attempt to engage. The fact you not only spoke to one twice, but that it also purposefully sought you out is, well . . ."

"Am I in danger, Director? Will this . . ." he stopped,

choosing his words carefully, "this creature, will it harm me? I'll be honest, I thought you sent it there to ensure I kept working." A slight, purposeful lie.

Jason could detect Faust smiling on the other side of the communicator, obviously pleased Jason assumed he had so much authority. "No. Like I said, it wasn't me. I don't control them to such an extent. I'll find out what is going on." Then, as if admitting he couldn't control them completely pained him in some way, he said, "As a member of the Council, I do have some power over them."

"I appreciate your protection, Director."

Jason detected a palpable sense of relief on the other end of the line when the Director inhaled through his nose and let out a long, nasally breath. "No, Jason. It absolutely will not harm you. They are incapable of doing so. As a matter of fact, it would destroy physical infrastructure and bend its considerable powers toward keeping you safe, as it would with any citizen. They are our great protectors and, aside from this oddity today, they do not interfere with us in any way short of keeping us safe. Actually, getting their attention is exasperating. They only respond to summons from the Council majority. Even then, the response is not timely." The tone of his voice conveyed he was loathe to admit this. "Techs have been known to disregard the Council completely. This is something else. Perhaps they see the same potential in you I do."

He couldn't think of anything else to say. "Okay."

Director Faust paused and then simply said. "All right, Jason. Get some rest and I'll see you in the morning. Please let me know if you need anything at all. Like I said, the team needs you and I will spare nothing to enable your research."

"That's generous of you. Good night."

"Good night, Dr. Emerson."

They disconnected and Jason filled Monica in on the other side of the conversation. She relaxed, then quickly got dressed. When she returned from her bedroom, she said, "C'mon. I'm too hungry to talk about this anymore. And I'm exhausted from feeling constantly on pins and needles. Let's just forget this whole thing for a while and get some food. We'll figure out what to do when we have time this weekend."

Monica dimmed the lights and put away a few things before they left her apartment. Jason took the initiative and chose an Italian restaurant with a wonderful selection of unique dishes and a great wine list. They traveled in silence, except for a comment Jason made about her hair still being wet and dripping onto his shoulder. She glared at him teasingly, then flung her hair in his face. With a laugh, she moved away from him a bit and they rode the rest of the way to the restaurant in silence, staring out the windows on either side.

The restaurant was moderately busy, filled with the chatter and laughter of other diners. Jason was fond of the art, which consisted of large metal and glass sculptures lit from within in a mesmerizing way. The tables and booths were far enough apart to give privacy, and the lighting dim enough to be pleasant without being too dark to talk. Faint instrumentals resonated throughout, audible only when the conversation lulled.

Despite Monica's insistence they drink only water, he ordered a glass of wine for each of them and they both ordered the same fine dish of butternut and eggplant ravioli with fried sage leaves and pine nut couscous. Everything tasted delicious and eating helped them relax. Jason paid for the meal, overriding her protests with a friendly appeal to let him do something nice for the only love in his life. "Besides," he said, "I have a ton of extra money with this new position. I already had more money than I knew what to do with."

She grinned wickedly at this, hinting at diamond earrings and a nice vacation on one of the colony worlds. She suggested he use his rank to override the government travel board who'd blocked her before. His rank and proximity to the Council should unlock any door, she insisted. "And," she informed him, "you can do all of this without any strings. I won't put out, since you don't want that, but I will allow you a male concubine or two. As long as I get some use out of them, too. Or have my own."

He shook his head. "You'll do as you're told and put out when I tell you, woman. You know how I hate having to beat you into submission all the time."

She made an indelicate noise and raised one eyebrow in derision.

Their banter helped them both relax and, as always,

Jason felt incredibly grateful for her strong personality and for the fact she was always there for him.

Jason decided to go straight home, rather than share a lift back to her place. They left the restaurant, Jason planting a chaste kiss on Monica's cheek. Once home, a pleasant lassitude set in and Jason fell asleep almost immediately after he prepped for bed. He drifted off with a general sense of peace. His dreams, however, were frantic and bordered on nightmares, though strange and unrelated to his daily life.

He dreamt of a top spinning, more a gyroscope perhaps, flashing brilliant colors in the surrounding darkness. Jason felt a strange fear the top would fall over, the lights would stop, and darkness would flood in.

He dreamt of flying, too—not an unusual dream for him. In his dream, he simply willed himself off the ground and, because thinking about the specifics of how he managed flying made him lose control and fall, simply accepted his ability to soar above the city and set himself down anywhere at will. His pleasant flying, however, took him over large areas of dead vegetation and poisoned water. Without warning, he lost control and plunged from the sky and into the muck.

He dreamt of strangers with green eyes everywhere he wandered. Something about them tugged at him in an alluring and seductive way.

Lastly, he dreamt of great cities of people, all performing their designated tasks with clockwork precision, every one of them unaware the leaders who once treated them as equals now drove them like the queen of a hive mind, a queen who expended them at will to increase her power.

EIGHT

WHEN HE FINALLY WOKE UP and shambled into the bathroom, his reflection startled him. Hair messy and sticking out all over, features gaunt, he looked like a derelict. He mechanically got ready for work, briefly recalling flashes of some of his dreams. He shuddered.

Preparation for leaving took longer than normal, and he found himself walking out of his bedroom having forgotten to clean his teeth or to put on his communicator.

By the time Jason left the apartment, he was already late. The day was too bright, the streets too busy. His trip to the station and the gravity lifts to the transit involved dodging through hordes of people, something he normally did without much thought. Today, it felt like he had to avoid colliding with everyone. It took most of the trip to finally reach a state of calm, where he felt he could properly manage his emotions and handle those around him.

When he arrived, he noticed the hospital bustled with activity. Apparently, it had already been a busy morning. The doctors and nurses greeted him with quick smiles and then hurried on their way to various appointments, patients, or to their labs. Without thinking, he emanated a sense of well-being and calm, visibly affecting everyone within his proximity. He usually took his abilities for granted, hardly paying attention to them. This time, he consciously made himself aware of everyone around him. As a test, something he'd never thought of ever doing, he tried to sense others in the general area who were behind walls or were further along corridors he could not see.

When he consciously paid attention to each person, he could identify and detect them. Their nannites were receptive to his broadcast inquiries. He broadcast further out, noting that his calm reassurance reached everyone on the first floor. Attempts to reach further than that became increasingly difficult as the signals became degraded by object interference. He tried hard to detect the signaling and found himself cocking his head sideways as if to hear the faint echoes of the distant transmissions.

Outside, in the open, his ability to reach others was spherical. He could both sense and broadcast the same distance in each direction. Inside, being able to reach out and sense others was more complicated. With strain, he found he could broadcast and receive in a non-spherical way, due to obstructions, with people outside or even on the floor above and below. Jason also found he could sense blind spots: thick concrete interfered with his senses and concentrations of medical equipment confused the return data. Even so, his ability to sense and to broadcast elated him.

The personnel of his new lab were busily at work when he arrived, but everyone greeted him warmly and respectfully when they saw him enter. There were shy and tentative waves and anxious smiles. Jason made sure to say hello to everyone. Most of them he'd never seen before. There were interns and junior staff everywhere. Some engineering personnel, those specialized in fulfilling his equipment needs, were setting up their own offices and work areas.

A few of the engineers clearly felt themselves superior, having knowledge of the biosuits and of the nanotechnology that far outstripped Jason's comprehension. Some smiled at him as if tolerating a new student; a few arched their eyebrows and he sensed their disdain. Most likely, they felt they should oversee the project instead of him, their knowledge of the technology and its uses giving them a sense of entitlement.

However, it wasn't in Jason's nature to let their attitudes bother him. He knew others had a mastery of disciplines in which he had no skill. Instead, he assumed they possessed the necessary acumen for what they needed to carry out their part of the research. The team had been selected, presumably, because of their merits. For this reason, he did not concern himself with their overt disdain since he was glad to have them on his team.

He called a meeting with his staff and the respective engineers, trying to honestly explain the general concepts of what they were trying to achieve. He asked them to please express ideas and new testing openly. Then, to demonstrate what they would be focusing on, he broadcast to each of them a sense of love. A commanding and abiding sense to view Jason as the most wonderful and loving creature they could imagine. He broadcast mindless adoration.

He made the broadcast brief, cutting it off as he watched them all start to stare at him worshipfully. He felt dirty, and guilty, but it had been an effective demonstration.

He made sure to be honest with them about what he'd done, trying to explain how he'd reached out to the nannies in their suits and sent instructions that translated to a "push" to their suits where he changed the emotions to what he wanted them to experience. The suits then changed the biochemistry within the respective host to match. He let them know he did not understand how he was capable of this, especially to the degree and completeness of which he could accomplish what he did. He indicated he simply felt he achieved this as if he was using another sense. He also indicated that he had to focus on maintaining the emotions, or the host reverted to normal the moment he let go.

Every person, including the engineering staff, was startled. Even though the imposed feeling had been cut off, they still had an abiding sense of fondness for him they couldn't seem to shake. Jason instructed them to find ways to shake off or ignore his broadcasts, especially those of this nature. They were told to find ways to change their reactions. Either to enhance the feelings he sent, or to block them out; to become immune to him, or to seize control and broadcast the feelings themselves. In this way, each person became a research subject.

•　　•　　•

He met regularly with the other doctors on the team, reviewing information and sharing ideas. As usual, Emma Garbine proved the most receptive to his ideas, and the most helpful in tuning them toward his research. She asked him to try putting himself in other people's thoughts and seeing through their eyes ... which resulted in complete failure. She remarked on his attempts with kindness and urged him to try again.

After six months, the engineers gave Jason a new suit, one with increasingly enhanced broadcast and feedback abilities. New nannies had been developed, too, which were hyper-sensitive to him. The enhancements resulted in Jason being able to sense everyone inside the hospital, and for many miles outside the facility if they were in the open.

One test, where he took a hover car above the towering buildings, left him breathless and unable to process the millions of people he'd felt. He couldn't filter or discern so much information unaided, and new augmentation for his cognitive storage and control had to be developed. The technological advancements were dangerously close to how the Techs were able to access all the vast data of the connected world, but the new storage method varied so greatly in the desired result as to be truly pioneering. The dangers were voiced loudly, and many urged a halt to the progress while they evaluated what they'd discovered. It required the full ratification of the Council to pass a resolution to continue. This deeply disturbed Jason because he sensed the Council's greed. He knew this new technology could result in terrible abuses.

All these enhancements were clearly understood in concept, but only Jason could, thus far, fully utilize them. Something deeper in his genetics or bio-chemistry lent him the necessary direct communication. Emma constantly read his neural activity and prodded him to experiment. She exclaimed often at the uniqueness of his mind.

Much of the enhanced reach related directly to re-broadcasting from person to person as a relay to further Jason's reach. Experiments had proven that people were blithely unaware that information could be rebroadcasted from their suits and nannies, allowing even more people to be used.

At the end of seven months, during which time he and Monica found themselves frustrated and stalled for ideas about how to stop the progress of the Council, it became public knowledge that nine of the thirteen members of the government had become permanent . . . until their deaths. The other four would be elected and replace those who were already failing.

The population hardly seemed to care. There were no outcries and barely a whisper from the media.

It made Monica hysterical. She cried often when they were in private, complained about feeling her freedoms had been eroded, and shared her frustration at the blind acceptance of the public. She told him she acutely felt the walls of domination closing in.

He agreed, but felt his hands were tied.

They made a point of going to dinner and then out clubbing when they could, though he found little time to enjoy these dates with Monica. Jason's work completely consumed him and he had to be dragged away from it under protest.

Eight months later, he saw the Tech again. The Tech stood outside his apartment one morning, in the middle of the street.

At first, Jason didn't notice him. As he left the apartment building, he saw the anti-gravity transports acting in what appeared to be an erratic way. Puzzled at the strange anomaly in the normal flow of traffic, he stopped to take a closer look. When he did, he saw the Tech. Vehicles zoomed at high speed around him, treating him like an obstruction. The hover vehicles at this level simply swerved aside or rose over him, only to settle back toward the ground. Fast-moving traffic could hardly endanger the Tech, since it controlled everything technological in the entire Sector.

Jason, however, panicked. Without thinking it through, he reacted as if the Tech could be struck by any of the zooming transports. Instinctively trying to help, he ran out in the middle of traffic to pull the Tech out of the path of the vehicles.

The Tech reacted more quickly than Jason would have thought possible. Fast as a lightning strike, the Tech sped toward Jason and he found himself lifted off the ground by its mechanically enhanced and flight-capable suit. They flew briefly over the traffic and landed safely on the top of his apartment building.

The whole thing happened so fast, Jason barely had time to process what had happened. His worry over the Tech being harmed quickly gave way to fear for his own well-being. His heart pounded in his chest when Jason realized he'd been plucked off the street like a child, and with as much ease as picking up a doll.

When the Tech roughly set him down, not seeming to realize its strength, Jason staggered backward and fell onto the heavy foliage on top of the building.

He sat, stunned, for a moment as the Tech regarded him, then got up and pulled a large, tropical leaf off his butt. He laughed and smiled at the Tech, extending the leaf as a gift.

"Here, this is for you." The Tech didn't respond to Jason's joke, but watched him curiously. Jason tossed the leaf off to the side. "Uh, yeah, so thank you." He ran his hand through his hair. "I guess I forgot you are totally safe in the middle of heavy traffic and I kinda freaked out."

It continued to look at him with a steady gaze. Jason, unsure of himself, glanced around, noting the lush vegetation, busy insects, and small rodents moving amongst the foliage. Typical of most buildings, his apartment building exterior was a shell of natural balance. Jason had never seen it from this vantage point.

Refusing to be daunted, albeit disconcerted by the silence, Jason used his most powerful new skill to broadcast his joy at the surprise visit, knowing the Tech could turn the broadcast abilities of his nannies and his suit off like a light switch.

The Tech's eyes widened in surprise. Perhaps for the first time in his adult life, he had been thrown off-balance, because he stepped backward involuntarily, lips parting as he breathed in sharply.

Without waiting for the Tech to dissuade him, and operating on pure intuition, Jason stepped forward and followed up with a hug. He pulled the Tech against him, setting his chin on his shoulder.

The Tech made a startled noise and did not return the embrace, but did not resist him, either.

Jason stepped back, still sending waves of calm mingled with gladness. Despite his low-lying fear, he felt happy to see the Tech again.

"Thank you, Jason Emerson, for your kindness toward us." The Tech paused. "This emotion. It takes us by surprise." Another pause. "We are glad to see you as well." For a moment he seemed to be struggling with staying focused on Jason. "We regret causing you distress from wishing to physically observe you at close proximity. We did not intend for you to be alarmed." Then, he did something that shocked Jason just as much as he'd shocked the Tech. He smiled at Jason—a genuine if uncertain smile. "We enjoy watching you when we have time."

"You've been watching me?" He wasn't sure what to think.

"Yes. We feel compelled to watch you when we are able. We have decided to make our presence known, as we deem it harmful to be deceitful in our invisibility."

"Why? Why are you watching me? I mean, is there something wrong? Or do I need to help you with something?"

The Tech's eyes became unfocused briefly. Jason assumed this meant he was issuing several million commands and taking in vast amounts of information, evaluating the time he could spend conversing or interacting, time distracted from running the Sector. Jason couldn't be sure, since he didn't really understand what happened behind those green eyes, but surely the vast complexity of being connected to everything was a difficult distraction to overcome.

A look of concern crossed the Tech's face. "We watch you for no reason other than we wish to. We do not mean to cause you concern."

Jason detected a lie in there. Or maybe not a lie, so

much as the omission of information. Could the thing really even lie? Something prevented it from talking openly and Jason took a moment, unsure of what to say. So, the Tech watched him both because it wanted to, and because of something else. Probably related to his research, Jason reasoned. He decided to keep up the guise.

Jason smiled. "That's rather flattering. I can't imagine many people are interesting to a Tech." He couldn't help but notice the piercing green eyes and the fine lines of its jaw. It seemed sheer idiocy, but Jason found himself attracted to the Tech for a lot of reasons.

Apparently, Jason's flirty humor had no impact, since the reply was almost mechanical. "All humans are of interest. However, there are no other individuals under direct observation at this time." Again, the Tech seemed uncertain about how much to convey. "We do not know why we are compelled to seek you out. We have suppressed this behavior, which is not useful or productive. However, we have found the urge to find you builds up over time and it is easier and more pleasing to watch you physically when time permits. It is not enough to observe you passively through remote data collection."

Jason hesitated before deciding to dare a question. "Did someone order you to watch me?" He needed answers and there might not be many chances to get them. Answers meant getting to know this strange person, something Jason felt compelled toward anyway. "What should I call you? Tech? I admit I feel weird and don't know how to address you." He smiled. "I mean, handsome and sexy seem a bit bold even for me."

The Tech stepped back, its eyes curious, surprised. "We are not thought of as handsome and sex does not apply to us. We do not believe we have desires such as you have. We do not understand your assertion in this regard."

"I'm sorry. I didn't mean to be a jerk. It's just—I figured you were being honest about watching me. So I sorta feel I owe it to you to be honest back." He grinned, a calculated action he decided to employ. Then, also with calculation to be coy, he looked up and moved his eyes back and forth along with a slight motion of his head before looking back at the Tech. "Seriously, I'm sorry. I haven't dated in a long time and sometimes my sense of humor gets the best of me."

"We must go, Jason Emerson, we have duties which require our proximity."

Realizing his flirting wasn't welcome, Jason said, "Okay, sure. I'm just Jason, if you are all right with that. It's sort of weird to be called by my full name repeatedly. I feel like a sign post."

The Tech stepped forward and grabbed him again, clearly intending to fly him down to the street. Jason stepped into the embrace and wrapped his arms around the Tech, preparing to be lifted. In a moment, Jason realized the Tech wasn't moving and so he pulled back slightly, breaking the embrace.

"We are Tarien Fade, Jason." The Tech struggled with

some long-forgotten sense of self, green eyes searching Jason's face with an unexpected look of vulnerability. "I am Tarien. I have not used my name in a long time. We are bound by our ties to the WorldNet and do not often feel a sense of self. It is within my capabilities, as are most things, but I have not identified as separate since young."

Jason dared a light touch on Tarien's jaw, which elicited a widening of his eyes and a slight tilt toward Jason's touch. "You aren't so scary after all, Tarien Fade. What a fitting name for someone so mysterious and aloof."

"We . . . I do not mean to be aloof. It is necessary for our work. We do not hold the same values as the rest of humanity and do not possess a sense of isolation as do you." He continued to look at Jason as he lifted his hand and placed it on Jason's chest, closing his eyes as if to enjoy the sensation of Jason's lingering fingers. Then, softly, he said, "I have not felt human contact such as this since I was a child. It is surprising. I have . . . missed it, I believe."

"I thought you knew everything. How could you be surprised?" Jason did not step away.

Tarien's eyes widened. "We know only what is processed by the technology to which we are bound. We know only the present. The future is often discernable based on environmental clues, extrapolation, but individual behavior baffles us, as it does you. We are human too, Jason. We are not monsters." There seemed to be an incredible sense of loneliness in those words.

They tugged at Jason's heart. "We feel you reaching out with emotion. This is new to us, forgotten. We are unsure of it and wish to understand. It is . . . desirable for us to have these emotions."

"You certainly look and feel human, now that I'm not scared to death of you. Of course, it would help if you didn't control the entire world we live in, but whatever."

"We really must go, Jason. Would you allow me to embrace you again? For the purpose of flying you safely down to the street level? We do not wish to cause you further trepidation by acting without your knowledge and consent."

Jason grinned. "On one condition. You should have a hug. A real hug, not something fake or utilitarian. Just this once. It's more comfortable and it really does feel nice. Promise."

Tarien wrapped his arms around Jason and, for a moment, held him, resting his head on Jason's shoulder. Jason held Tarien close, as if Tarien were a child seeking comfort. Then, suddenly, they lifted off the building and floated down to the sidewalk. The sudden motion was startling, despite Tarien's assertion about not causing Jason trepidation. Clearly, knowing almost everything made it difficult to fathom that real humans required communication or body language. The danger represented was something Jason simply couldn't get out of his mind. Whatever else, Tarien was transhuman, possessing the strength and speed of a robot and the mind of an AI.

Naturally, every person within eyesight was stunned to the point of disbelief. Jason disregarded the emotions pouring in around him as they descended. He didn't have to see the crowds to know people were shocked.

As they landed, Jason stepped back and smiled, unwilling to let the private moment be ruined by all the gawkers. "Thank you."

The Tech looked haunted, his eyes sad. "We know you are frightened of us. We know you are suppressing fear. We thank you for tolerating us and we are sorry we have interfered."

"No, please don't say that! Yes, I'm scared of you because you have the power to completely shut me down. You control everything I can see and hear and feel. But it seems you wouldn't hurt anyone. I'm not sure why, but you want me to be near you. I can't help but be drawn to you. So would everyone, I imagine. You're a mystery. We all wish, privately, we could know more about you. I'm just lucky."

"We would never harm. We cannot, even if there was a desire. We only protect. It is our purpose. This makes me uncertain if what I have done conflicts with my programming. We fear we are harming you by our interaction. We cannot foresee the consequences." He gazed skyward for a moment. "Thank you, Jason. We must go."

Jason watched Tarien lift his face skyward, then fly away. He continued to stare after Tarien had vanished behind the buildings. Slowly, the sounds of the city entered back into his awareness, making him realize the moment had stilled his senses outside of the small area in which they had both stood. Looking around, he saw people staring, saw traffic had mostly slowed or stopped. Shoppers and people dining had left the stores and restaurants to gape at him. Jason felt a flush of self-consciousness that surely made his face red. He felt a hand on his shoulder and noticed Mom stood behind him. Her light blue eyes conveyed a sense of panic. The wrinkles above her brows more pronounced as she knitted them together with concern.

"What on earth were you thinking? A Tech! Are you insane? Those things could accidentally break you like a twig." Her breathing was ragged, and her outstretched hands trembled on his shoulders. She took several hurried gulps of air, then put her hand on her chest. "Oh sweetie, that's the most frightening thing I've ever seen. I watched you being plucked off the ground like an abducted child and being carried away. I was afraid it would drop you."

Jason tried to calm her, both by broadcast and by touching her shoulder in return. Mom didn't wear a bio-suit, so his efforts were mostly in vain. "He wouldn't have dropped me. They seem entirely incapable of harming anyone."

Before Mom could say anything else, several other people ran up to them, wondering what they had seen, not believing it. Finally released from their shocked paralysis, the crowd bombarded him with questions.

Jason tried to retreat, but they were relentless.

The Director appeared soon after, parting the crowd with a fury. "What the hell was your little social outing with the Tech about? Dr. Emerson, this is ridiculous." His eyes became predatory. "Did you use your new abilities on it? Somehow—I don't know. Take it over? Force it to obey you? What did it say?" His anger had an eager, hungry quality to it. Jason could guess what Faust was after, his desire for power and control obvious.

"No, I . . . what?" Jason quickly became angry. "Seriously, Director? First of all, how in the world would I force a Tech to do anything? He could shut me down without getting anywhere near me. What kind of idiot question is that?"

The Director's eyes blazed. "Watch yourself, Doctor. My patience with you is rather thin as it is. You seem to delight in spending entirely too much time with that Tech. Practice your skills where we can gauge them and bite your tongue. Remember, accosting a member of the Council, even verbally, can be considered treason."

"Really? Is this a new rule you invented? I can't even disagree with you? You are above the law now?" Jason raised his voice even more. "Is it treason for voicing my opinion to the esteemed Council punishable by death? Are you going to just have my head cut off?"

The Director looked murderous. Still, he was wily enough to realize the crowd around them listened intently with enough attention to get this entire affair to the media rather quickly, confused as they might be by the dialogue.

"Don't be even more of an idiot than you've already proven yourself to be. It is of the deepest concern to the Council that you aren't causing problems with our Techs, Doctor Emerson, and no member of this society would look the other way if they thought you were interfering with one. If anything, I'm protecting you from being torn to shreds by a mob."

"I'm telling you now, the Tech came to see me. I don't know what you're implying, but if you haven't noticed, they are the least helpless people in the world. One of them could have you locked up and end your Council tenure with absurd ease."

Doctor Faust reared back as if struck. His face turned an ugly purple and his fists clenched below the short sleeves of his blue suit jacket. For a moment, Jason thought he really would have him beheaded.

Finally, Faust's gaze became flat, hateful. "We will speak of this again. You'll be summoned." He turned on his heels and the crowd flinched out of his way. His airlift took off as soon as Faust boarded.

Without waiting for the crowd to recover enough from this second shocking interaction so they could bombard him further, and realizing he was leaving Mom standing there with no answers, Jason fled to his apartment.

NINE

FOR A WEEK, JASON KEPT EXPECTING the Tech to appear. He dreamed of him, waking in frustration, hoping to spy him from a distance. Not knowing where or when he'd see the Tech again made him slightly crazy. His hope finally gave way to disappointment, then frustration. His strange fear of the Tech had instead become fascination. Finally, he sank into a mild depression and focused only on his work.

Shortly after the end of the week, Jason received a summons from the Council, mandating he appear in three days. All dreaming of Tarien gave way to fear. Monica began to panic, pleading with him to grovel. She talked incessantly, and Jason eventually had to avoid her, since he could barely contain his own anxiety.

Aside from having to avoid Monica, Jason found

himself dodging his staff, random strangers, and his neighbors, including Mom. The news had picked up the story and Jason sometimes had random people come up and try to talk to him about the incident with the Tech the previous week. Instead of taking the public anti-gravity trains and lifts, Jason ordered a private vehicle to fly him to work. He ordered food delivered and did not go anywhere he wasn't obligated to go. The summons of the Council quickly became gossip throughout the Med labs and amongst his peers.

Doctor Garbine came by to express her concern with a tight-lipped and carefully phrased offer to stand up for him. She evinced unbridled anger in her quiet tone but didn't want to afford the Director a reason to have her removed. The other doctors avoided Jason when they learned of his summons and even his staff grew reluctant to be around him for long, going about their duties as far away from him as they reasonably could.

At last, a robot came to escort him to the Council chamber, informing with mechanical indifference that Jason must appear within the hour.

Jason followed the robot with increasing fear, which finally gave way to anger. How ridiculous that he should be summoned because a Tech had contacted him. It was completely absurd to be stripped of his rights and due process over something out of his control. The Director's peevishness and feelings of his will being thwarted reinforced the fact Faust should not be allowed to govern. Summoning Jason was petty.

Jason took a short flight, then landed on one of the pads of the main, pyramidal, complex of the center of government. Security took a long time, requiring complete scans and multiple layers of clearance. He felt manhandled, taken in by robots who ushered him down long hallways. They placed him in a small shuttle akin to an elevator, although it had the extended capability of going sideways. With a complicated and rapid set of directional changes, it moved him efficiently to a waiting chamber. He lost all sense of location within the complex. The main, massive pyramid dwarfed the nearby buildings, and smaller pyramids at each of the four corners were, in turn, flanked by other pyramids. The entire place took up several square miles.

Jason waited briefly, fidgeting nervously. The doors opened, and robots escorted him to a small balcony overlooking a massive room. A focused beam of light shone down on his platform, the only lit area in the entire hall. The door closed seamlessly behind him, leaving him on an illuminated island floating in a sea of darkness—a daunting effect.

Above him, the lights came on over thirteen much larger balconies. He flinched. The Council seats. They were too far away to see clearly, but above each hovered a massive bioluminescent membrane, a display designed to show their faces as giant projections. The screens lit up, showing each of the thirteen members of the Supreme Council, the rulers of the most influential of the nine total Sectors in the world.

Their age surprised Jason, who hadn't expected they'd all be so old. Faust must be the youngest by several decades. Some of the members appeared ancient. Two of them, both women, stared down at him with rheumy-eyed indifference, their paper-thin skin mottled and nearly translucent. White, wispy hair fell across their faces in thin strands as they stared with watery lenses out into the darkness.

A quick glance showed Director Faust staring down at him with a sneer of self-satisfaction.

A strong, clear voice addressed him, and Jason saw a man on one of the screens—a hulking dark figure with large brows and jet-black hair with white at the temples. Even advanced age didn't seem to be wearing this goliath down. The man smiled. "We have summoned you, Citizen Emerson, ostensibly to discuss the issue of having derided a member of the Supreme Council in public. We have been asked, and have, albeit reluctantly, agreed to reprimand you for the issue. This is to be the official and recorded reason for the summons." He looked pointedly at Faust.

Citizen Emerson. A clear slight, Jason thought. He cleared his throat. "Medic Emerson, if you please. Or Doctor Emerson."

The man raised his large brows and laughed softly. "Indeed. Medic Emerson. While we do not have a formal process for reprimand in this regard, we've been urged by Director Faust. According to him, we cannot have the Council seen as being subject to public derision."

"So you are creating a new set of policies to ensure we don't challenge you? This is a bit tyrannical, don't you think?" Jason wasn't going to stand by and let his rights be stripped away, not if he had already been judged.

There were several uncomfortable coughs and one of the Council actually looked sheepish. The magnified screen emphasized Faust's anger. He pointed an admonishing finger at Jason. "Be silent until we ask you to speak, Jason."

"Medic Emerson, Council member Faust. And I will have my voice heard unless you have managed to override the constitution along with my rights, which should have prevented this absurd farce."

Faust flushed with fury. "You see? This man is an outrage! He has no respect for the Council."

One of the ancient women spoke up with a surprisingly rich voice. "Council member Faust, please be silent. You are behaving like a spoiled and petulant child and, as the newest member, we are starting to notice a lack of maturity expected of someone of your prestige. We agreed to this meeting to review the research under the guise of punishment and, at your insistence, ask Medic Emerson to please behave more appropriately in the future. To *ask* him, Council member Faust, not command."

Faust nearly had apoplexy, but somehow, miraculously, closed his mouth and sat back in his oversized chair. He stared murderously down at Jason.

The woman continued. "Medic Emerson, I am council member Elandra Hayes and I would like to thank you for coming." She smiled, her red-rimmed eyes watery but kind.

Jason frowned in confusion. "A pleasure to make your acquaintance, Council member Hayes. I know who you are. I think everyone does, but I appreciate the introduction."

"Yes, of course. Now, we must apologize for this—what did you call it?"

"Farce," offered the large man who'd spoken first. Jason recognized him as Arkine Feit, a former sports star and brilliant man. A rare combination, but one which had served the country well once he'd left football and moved into politics.

"Yes, farce," continued Council member Hayes. "Honestly, we have been speaking with each member of the research team as we are able, but we cannot draw undo attention. We had intended to come up with a way to bring you before us earlier, but this opportunity, however absurd, presented itself." She frowned. "Unfortunately, I do not agree with the signal this sends to the populace. We should not be seen as interfering with such small matters and certainly Director Faust needs to be more discreet about his meetings with you, regardless of your association." She looked pointedly at the screen where the Director sulked.

"Consider yourself spanked, Medic Emerson," a tiny, wrinkled woman said. Her nearly elflike size and incorrigible smile gave her a childish appearance. Brenda Nigh, if Jason recalled correctly. A Nobel Prize winner in physics and said to be incredibly mischievous.

He let out a surprised laugh. "This whole thing is just an excuse?"

"Tsk," said Brenda. "Now seriously, doctor. We certainly appreciate you coming to see us, and I'm eager to see what you can do, but let's be honest. We do have more important things to do than wag our fingers at anyone who looks at us cross-eyed. At least, those of us who aren't children have more important things to do." She glanced sideways at Faust.

He suddenly felt a lot better. His fear of being genuinely in trouble, that the Council had slid into petty retaliation for small challenges to their authority the moment they were impervious to being removed, now seemed silly.

"Then why am I here?"

Director Faust slid forward in his chair, still looking hateful. "Aside from the fact we told you to be here, Medic Emerson, the Council wants to see how much progress you've made. The videos don't adequately convey the complexities involved in how you can impact everyone. Some of the Council are convinced the emotions you work with are false or somehow indistinguishable from normal feelings."

"Okay. So? Are you guys asking for a demonstration?"

Faust frowned. "Please refer to us as 'the Council' or 'your eminences', not 'you guys.' This isn't a street conversation, Medic. You stand before the Supreme Council of Humanity, an honor most will never know."

"Council member Faust, honestly, if this is how you intend to act in front of everyone we meet with, we might vote to have you muzzled," Elandra said. Turning back to face Jason she said, "A demonstration would be wonderful, Doctor Emerson. We are all excited about this research, but not everyone truly understands or believes the enormity of what the results could be." She rubbed her eyes tiredly. "Other than the work of Doctor Garbine, your focus is the only other type of research we don't quite comprehend. The other researchers have clearly measurable and well-explained results, such as the enhanced nannies and new biosuits. Those of us who believe you must have certain powers still have a hard time understanding just how much you can do with them."

"All right, sure." Then he added, "your eminences." He reached out and found each of them in the darkness, sensing their nano-feedback and reassuring himself they were, indeed, here in the room with him and not just projections on the large screens. He felt several hundred other people nearby, probably security and aides, or administrators.

He sent a wave of calm, of relaxation, of reprieve from all the cares in the world, of elation. He did it to everyone he felt, and made it strong, but not overbearing.

They sighed collectively, and he saw every face on the screens relax, all tension leaving them. Even Faust became calm and collected. Jason made this emotional change in them brief and then released everyone back to their base emotions.

"Oh my."

"This is incredible."

Several of them sighed.

Tyra Altur, another ancient woman, said to Faust, "Carlisle, this is amazing. I can hardly believe it. It felt real; it still does. I feel better, more relaxed than I have in many years."

Brenda suddenly leaned forward with a glint in her eye, her wrinkled face impish. "What else? Could you, for example, make us all completely enraged? Better yet, how about lust? How strong are these emotions? What about permanency?"

Arkine's brows jumped to his thick hairline. "Brenda!"

"Oh, c'mon. You know we're all thinking about something like that. Let's face it, I haven't felt a good rush of lust in half a century. Just affect *me* then, Doctor Emerson." She giggled wickedly.

There were several laughs at this. "And me!" said Susan Castle and Tyra Altur at the same time.

"Actually, I love the lust idea," said Mohammed Adnor. "What about the permanency question? I'm not sure any of our hearts could handle prolonged lustfulness." He chuckled to himself.

Before Jason could answer, Director Faust jumped in. "His control is entirely temporary, and he must maintain focus and concentration, or the sensation dissipates. We're working on this from a number of angles. The first is to augment the broadcast abilities with enhanced nannites and the newly created enhanced suits. The second is to change the receptors of the host's—"

"Yes, I'm sure whatever you're saying is riveting, Carlisle. But let's move along. None of us here have much time to spare. I would like to feel my heart quicken and my blood rush." Brenda pursed her lips. "So? Can you do that, Doctor Emerson?"

Jason didn't know what to say, since the request surprised him. Finally, he said, "I think so. I haven't tried it on anyone, to be honest. It seems a little . . . invasive."

"Well, I'm asking you to try. Nothing invasive about that." Brenda smiled encouragingly. Then, with some hesitation, she said, "Or is it because I'm a girl and we girls sort of gross you out?"

Jason laughed. "No, that's not a problem. Despite what you might think, I'm rather fond of women and have some of the normal male thoughts about them. No, it's more . . . well, it borders on controlling someone rather than passive reassurance. It just seems, you know, unethical."

She beamed at him. "Oh, you are a dear. What a heartening thing to hear. I have a feeling we'll be grateful for your ethics. You're probably better suited to this Council than most of us. But that's neither here nor there. I'm delighted to hear your concerns, and I'll admit the request is a bit absurd, but I'm *old*, Doctor. I want to feel something of my youth."

There was a murmur of assent.

He took a deep breath. "Okay. Yeah, sure. I'll see what

I can do. You first." He reached out again, found her bio-signal and took a moment to analyze it. Then, without really knowing how, he pushed a strong sense of lust and worship. Reading her response, he tightened it, made it sharper, upped the urgency. Finally, when he found her whole body responding, he sent another wave of desire akin to a cat in heat. The instructions were the strongest he'd ever pushed out and the most he'd ever worked with the signal feedback to tune it toward a specific goal.

She groaned in her chair, lips parting and eyes wide. He let her go after only a few moments, worried about causing her physical harm. But she breathed heavily for another moment and then leaned forward with a huge smile on her face. "Oh, wow. Wow. I'm still . . . I can't tell you. I don't think I felt like so much of a harlot even when in my thirties." She brushed her hair out of her face. "If you could make a chemical cocktail for what I just felt, I'd have it synthesized and drink it for morning tea." She laughed.

The rest of the council held their breath and finally leaned toward their consoles eagerly, with the exception of Faust, who sat scowling down at Jason. He said, "Leave me out of this little experiment, if you don't mind."

Jason suppressed his revulsion at the thought of touching Faust in that way.

The others requested the same, with the exception of Yao Chin, who's extreme age made him entirely too delicate. Faust reiterated that he wanted to be left out, making sure Jason understood. He gave a snort of disgust.

"Please hurry up, then. I'd prefer to have Doctor Emerson working on more important things, not performing parlor tricks."

Jason steeled himself and then reached out and assessed each of them. He agreed that Chin was entirely too fragile. In his opinion, several others shouldn't be included either. However, he took a deep breath and slowly brought each of them up to a level of desire he thought suitable for the demonstration, then enhanced it for the stronger members. For a few, he brought them to a fevered pitch. He reached out further, experimentally touching all the staff and security in the area.

These people were all younger, healthier, and more receptive to being put in a near frenzy. From several security staff members, he felt a resistance he'd never encountered; recognition of what they were feeling as a falsely induced sense of lust. Unconsciously, they fought to normalize their bodies. The unconscious fight shocked Jason, though he found their response extremely useful to know about: his emotional pushes could be fought, after all. He overcame those who resisted, but only let it last a few minutes and then slowly brought the signaling level down to normal for everyone. He wanted it perfectly clear to other people what the Council was forcing him to do, so he included all the staff. If there was to be any hope of a public outcry, it could start with the people in this building. By including so many others outside the room, he hoped to send a strong warning to the masses. He might never be given another chance.

When he finished, he shivered and had to grasp the bars of the balcony to stabilize his legs as a wave of fatigue swept over him. He furrowed his eyebrows and pinched his nose, experiencing a stabbing pain in his head. His nannies quickly rushed to alleviate the problem. The exertion had cost him.

Yes, it had cost him, but he had gained insight. Behind their polite smiles, their insistence that Faust was alone in his tyranny, he detected greed and urgency. A need for the research to restore their youth. Jason realized they were simply playing good cop, bad cop with him.

The Council babbled excitedly amongst themselves, most of their conversation inaudible. He heard other voices in the background, though they were too muted for him to discern the nature of what they discussed. He could read these others, however. Probably aides and high officials. Jason could tell were all excited, though some were afraid. After a few minutes, Faust finally told Jason he was dismissed. Having gotten what they wanted, the Council became so involved in their discussion that they ignored Jason entirely.

The door behind him slid open and two security personnel stepped in. For a moment, both guards appraised him, their hands clenching and unclenching unconsciously. Their clear upset took Jason aback and he felt some panic, then felt ashamed at having included them in his test. He resolved not to read them or interfere further.

They had not asked for this, and he should not have

included them, despite his belief it would help raise awareness. If he could passively get the word out about this research, it might excite the public enough to ask more questions and keep the Council under tighter scrutiny, but despite these good intentions he felt dirty. He couldn't meet their eyes.

They handled him carefully as they directed him back to the transport. They headed back to his lab. The security people wore helmets, which kept their faces hidden, and he respectfully kept himself from reading them, so he wasn't sure how they felt about him.

He hoped they weren't angry.

At last, one of them reached out and touched his arm in a friendly, reassuring way. He sensed they could both tell he had become ashamed of his actions. Jason smiled. "I owe you both an apology. I shouldn't have included anyone besides the consenting members. I'm really sorry, I just—I thought you might need to understand what was being researched in case . . ." He trailed off. How could he express his fears this technology could get out of hand? Convey the fact they might need to recognize the dangers?

He didn't need to continue. They both nodded, their mirrored visors reflecting the light. The one who'd reached out to touch him let the touch linger and then the fingers of his glove slid down Jason's arm as they let go. Without a word, they turned and left.

TEN

ANOTHER MONTH PASSED.

His team had given him enough input that he could selectively control his emotions and those of any individual around him. His light depression, which had come about both because he had heard nothing from Tarien, who he'd secretly been hoping would find him, and because they drove him to rush his research, became an unacceptable indulgence.

The other doctors on the research project had made great strides and continued making large steps as subsequent months passed. By the end of the year, they were ready to try altering volunteers with the longevity genes and the nearly invulnerable physical changes. Jason voiced his concerns. He still couldn't ensure enough control and he couldn't fix the emotions in place.

He worried they were pushing too fast.

The Director's increased hostility toward Jason, borne of his inability to find out the purpose behind the Tech's visit, flared up at Jason's suggestion that they slow down. He had Jason removed from the lab during some of the discussions.

The Council eagerly authorized the physical modification testing on test subjects and the research crew cheered. They celebrated their progress and congratulated each other on all the hard work. Jason quailed at the wanton disregard for proper safety and understanding.

They selected four subjects, two men and two women from the pool of volunteers. The injections and new nano-technology were introduced in phases, the subjects carefully monitored. They were housed in a five-thousand-square-foot section of the lab, which became their semi-permanent home during the tests. They were not allowed to leave, but were given every indulgence.

The volunteers were striking in their changes, both physical and emotional. In the first few weeks, they became gorgeous idealized versions of themselves, which only vaguely resembled their original physical bodies. Jason watched the rapid changes with amazement.

Sexually charged, their physiques began to reshape in response. One woman, who started out mousey and somewhat plain, with a distinct overbite, shrank down to a mere five-foot-four inches, with a tiny waistline and large breasts. Her face became like that of a porcelain doll, with a pink rosebud mouth and long, thick lashes over hazelnut-colored eyes. She walked with a distinct and provocative sway of her hips, and became prone to giving tantalizing, sultry glances and a downcast gaze which forced her to look up through her thick hair. Her voice rose slightly and became breathy and seductive. She invited all the male researchers to come in and dally with her, an invitation the Director quickly denounced. If anyone so much as entered the research quarters without permission, they would not only be fired, they would be charged as criminals. Several of the younger crew discussed how it might be worth having their employment terminated.

The other woman grew to over six-and-a-half feet and became Amazonian in her looks, with hair that had grown rapidly down to the middle of her back and had changed color from thinning light brown to a stark, glossy black. Her musculature became defined, her face sharply angular. She aggressively and lewdly showed off for the cameras, masturbating in front of the assistants, and occasionally yelling at them that they were too weak to come in and satisfy her. She demanded to service all the men in the lab.

The frustration of the male lab assistants became almost palpable.

While both the female and male subjects spent large amounts of time engaged in intercourse with each other, a strange hostility developed over time and none of them were ever satisfied, no matter how often. Their desires became increasingly desperate as they begged for more partners and a greater variety of them.

The men in the experiment both towered above the staff, having grown to nearly seven foot in height. For a few weeks, they were overwhelmingly beautiful, muscular and smooth. Supermodels. They continued to change, however, and became too alien to be viewed without fear, their torsos elongating and their upper body skin becoming nearly translucent. Stranger still, they increasingly began to mirror each other in a lot of ways, only resembling their original looks in small details. Jason found their changes creepy as he watched them daily become twins of each other. One would develop an attribute the other would mimic without conscious control. At first, they changed toward lithely athletic, almost feminine, with sooty lashes and no body hair. They were graceful and languid, though strange. The lab had them try to change specific features, and they had some success, though if one of them changed anything, the other soon followed.

However, as they became more immersed in the chemical cocktails of their hormones, they shifted toward becoming heavily muscled to the point of vulgarity, with sharp, cordlike ropes crisscrossing their arms and legs. Still tall, they became increasingly bulky. Within two months, their brows grew heavily and became mongoloid, giving them a Cro-Magnon look. Their body hair grew everywhere, thick, black and wiry, covering them like apes, including their backs and knuckles. These changes were appalling, but the subjects claimed to have no control. They started to show signs of despair and panic.

They also stopped cooperating with the staff as their communication skills degraded. The two female subjects deferred to the men in almost everything. The stronger willed of the two, the "Amazon", defied them at first and actually got in a few fights, which were fantastic to watch. The brute force of all four of them was astonishing. The fact they could heal from nearly anything made them vicious. However, the alpha female soon allowed them to dominate and began to rebuff the staff with angry comments and threatening gestures when asked to refuse to allow the males to control her actions.

The men continued to have sex with the women almost constantly, often ignoring their other duties until threatened with having their food supply cut off. Finally, they became completely volatile in their emotions, raging wildly at the staff, and weepy uncontrollably at times. Jason had been forced to overwhelm them to prevent them from killing themselves or one another. His control over his abilities had grown to the point of outright dominance if he wasn't careful. The fact he had to override their natural state of emotions, no matter how distressed or complex, made him feel like he'd bathed in raw sewage. He could adjust one or many emotions, fixing any one of them in place. Like a panel of slider controls on a sound board, each emotion could be moved in any direction, or he could move many at the same time.

One unexpected side-effect of his abilities was being

able to feel the emotional state of those around him. Increasingly, the concerns and worries of those around him bombarded Jason. At night, he had nightmares and often awoke in a cold sweat. A few times at work, he had to retreat to the men's room where he broke down and cried, shivering though he wasn't cold.

This increasing receptiveness and ability to control fascinated both Emma, who poured over the data Jason produced for her own research, and impressed Director Faust, who became increasingly obvious in his envy of this power. Jason hated himself for what the Council forced him to research, knowing the Director and the Council intended to use it when he discovered how to impart his gifts. Using the nannies, it was thought, Jason could directly transmit detailed instructional data sets so someone like Faust or other Council members would then possess the same abilities.

That wasn't so.

His suppression of the test subject's increasingly erratic emotional states could not be sustained when Jason wasn't present. He could not—at least yet—permanently override them or force them into a fixed state of compliance. They became so crazed, so animalistic, they had to be sedated with some of the most powerful sedatives available.

But sedation proved a mistake, compounded by the fact they should have been separated.

The lab assumed they would remain under sedation until revived, buying the staff time to experiment with enforced reversion, but the subject's enhanced bodies threw off the chemicals in a short period of time. Their metabolic processing, coupled with the new nannies, cleansed their system in a matter of hours. Upon waking, one of the men killed his companions and wreaked havoc throughout their quarters. He destroyed most of the furniture and electronics, tore out most of the fixtures and monitoring equipment, and tried to break through the observation glass.

Since the other subjects were nearly impossible to kill, he had torn them to pieces and burned their bodies. Then he'd wrapped himself in every flammable material in the room and set it on fire. He'd even gone so far as to use the refrigerator door, one of the only large remaining objects left after his rampage, to direct the fire suppression water flow away from his body so he would have time to burn.

When the staff came running to deal with the emergency alarms, they were stunned and appalled. The volunteers' deaths meant many of the staff had to be put on leave to sort through what had happened. Some of the staff had simply quit in shock. Jason sat in the nearby kitchen with Emma over coffee the whole day, doing nothing. Monica became incredibly angry when he told her that evening. She had no idea they had progressed with their testing so far, and this made her furious. Jason had been so immersed in his work, he'd been remiss in updating her. The violent deaths of the subjects were a complete setback.

The next day Jason and his peers who were leading

the project were summoned before the Council.

As expected, the Council members were outraged, even the mildest among them. They had not been able to contain the press and the resulting media coverage threw the public into a panic. Angry citizens were clamoring for answers. None of the details had been leaked, so the public only knew an experiment had gone very wrong, resulting in a fire in the lab and the death of several test subjects. Speculation ran rampant and demands for an explanation mounted. Protests about illegal human testing broke out around the hospital.

The research doctors were accosted by the media and had to be put under guard. Jason had suffered a severe blow to the head when one of the angry people outside his apartment had thrown a rock, hitting him in the temple and causing him to stagger and fall to the ground.

Mom had erupted in a furiously protective tirade, covering his body with her own and angrily demanding protection from her adopted brood. The neighbors, reluctantly, stepped in to rebuff the attacks. They had stuffed Jason in a vehicle, which tried to take off through the mob, but was forced to a standstill as protesters surrounded and leaped on top, stomping and hitting the chassis, their numbers increasing every minute. As part of the safety protocols, the antigravity transport would not take to the air while people were so close. His head bleeding profusely, he huddled in the seat, curling up in a ball. He could feel the anger, the danger that people outside represented. Mom and her gang had little to no effect, and they were forced to retreat, leaving Jason even more alone. Fearing for his life, Jason had moved to the front and tried to manually fire the gravity boosters, despite the fact it would hurl people away from the vehicle and those on top, trying to smash through, would fall. As he changed seats and swiveled around toward the manual overrides, he could see the anger in their faces.

Moments later, the crowd broke and ran. Jason had looked up through the glass. Sector Seven—Tarien—had personally appeared over the masses, his imperious gaze sweeping the crowd. Suddenly, Jason saw robots, vehicles, sirens, personal communications, and even cleaning equipment harassing the demonstrators. They did no harm, but the frightening display as all the local technology obeyed the Tech, moved the crowd back. An area opened around Jason to allow his vehicle through to where Tarien could aid him. Jason helped Tarien scatter the crowd by elevating their anxiety and fear levels. The mob finally fled. While Tarien could have overridden the locks, Jason had sensed a protective and towering anger in the Tech that, apparently, required a physical outlet.

Instead of unlocking Jason's vehicle, Tarien had torn the door from its hinges, still hovering slightly above the ground as he reached in and pulled Jason out. Wrapping his arms around Jason protectively, Tarien flew toward the nearest medical facility, wasting no time to speak. With a pained look on his face and a gentle touch to Jason's jaw, he surrendered Jason to the staff, then flew away as the medics ushered Jason to a healing pod. Jason's wound was cleaned and site-specific nannites applied to knit and repair the skin, a process that completed in minutes. The medics, however, did not let him leave. His head had suffered a jarring impact and they wanted to keep him out of the public eye, prevent him from being exposed to a still-angry mob near his home. They gave him a sedative and overriding instructions to his nannies to prevent it from being purged. Jason had fallen asleep quickly.

While Jason recovered the next day, he received an emergency summons and robots brought him before the governing Council to explain what had gone wrong.

More than the upset over the catastrophe, which they were now playing off as a system-wide malfunction of the new laboratory equipment, they were angry over the loss of their hopes. The dropped their pretenses at being patient and understanding and became accusatory.

The Council members had expected this process to have been near completion at this point, their greed for life and youth overriding their moral senses. Without the emotional control to prevent the degrading and crazed problems that had overtaken the subjects, they could not be given the nannies that granted youth and vigor. Accustomed to power, the Council demanded the problem be fixed immediately. Many of them were frail, clearly short on time, and desperate. Their attitudes reinforced Jason's opinion that the Council was completely wrong for this gift of science. He wished he could somehow prevent things from progressing.

Jason could not adequately explain the failures. He could sense, but not control, deep-seated emotion with any sustained ability. He could broaden his broadcasts and sense large numbers of people, but this control took all of his ability. He could not imagine moving any more quickly. He sagged under the burden of the strain they'd put upon him.

The normally calm Council's anger became vocal, and they accused him of being uncommitted and weak. They ordered him hospitalized and assessed for possible removal from the project.

After several days, as he knew they would, the Council ordered him back to work with strict sets of guidelines. They had nobody else and Dr. Garbine, the closest thing they had to Jason, couldn't use Jason's research in any practical way. Her own projects consumed all her time, and she flat-out refused to try and take over his work.

A newer, more powerful set of nannies was developed and administered to Jason without his consent and without proper testing. They proved to be a nightmare for him. He could not tune out most of the emotions of those around him. The new nannies broadcast and received so strongly, they nearly crippled him.

His frustration could barely be contained when he left the confines of his hospital room. Along with the others, he had no idea how to address the problem. The barrage of anger and disgust he felt from most people, which he couldn't block, due to his developed skills, caused him unending emotional distress. He slept with a pillow over his head to try to shut the emotions out, but his new nannies could detect emotional states even without his bio-suit. He started to be subject to bouts of sobbing, his sanity cracking under the extreme pressure.

Director Faust demanded he learn stricter control, coldly dismissing Jason's emotions as those of a weakling. He gave Jason seven days to "get over it" and resume his testing, including solving the hormonal control problem within three months. Faust accompanied the demand with a thinly veiled threat to end Jason's career due to "unfounded psychological distress rendering him incapable of performing even the smallest functions necessary in his field." He actually struck Jason across the face and strode out of the lab. Jason both laughed and cried at the same time, overcome with a hysteria he could not control. His entire staff vacated the building, leaving him alone as he slumped to the floor.

Finally, he managed to get himself to point where he could leave the offices and rush home. He ate mechanically and tried to sleep. He could not remain in his bed. The bombardment from his involuntary reception of emotions drove him to move rapidly and pointlessly around his apartment. He tried to shower, but the mirror reflected his internal distress, his face gaunt and eyes haunted.

He ultimately fled his apartment each night, jogging around the streets compulsively, muttering to himself. He knew he looked like a maniac.

•   •   •

He made his way back to his apartment after his nightly jog. The seven days of reprieve were up. As he walked in, he received a notice from Faust with orders to renew testing. Jason would be forced to work on this day and night for "the good of the people." Sleep would be tightly rationed.

With a cry, Jason deleted the notice of demands and threw his communicator against the wall of his apartment. He stood for a moment, so disoriented he lost track of time and place. Half crazed from sleeplessness, he stormed into his kitchen, exclaiming loudly as he nearly collided with a figure standing in the doorway. For a moment, Jason thought he was hallucinating. Everything around him had taken on the characteristics of a dream.

Tarien must have sensed that his appearance was an intrusion and he became apologetic and oddly chastened. He offered to leave, but Jason put a hand on his chest.

Still having difficulty processing reality, he shook his head. "No, please. Stay." Then, in a pathetic plea, he repeated "please" almost inaudibly.

He began shaking uncontrollably and slumped against the wall, putting a hand to his temple in a futile gesture to protect his thoughts. He whimpered and fell to the floor, staring up at Tarien.

Tarien watched him for a moment, clearly unable to discern the most logical course of action.

"We won't enter your space without seeking your

permission in the future. No places are barred to us, so it did not occur to us there would be an issue."

"Tarien, I—that's not it. If you show up for any reason at all, I'll be glad to see you. I actually prefer you here instead of on top of the building." Then, with a weak smile, he said, "Thank you for saving me. I'm glad you made a personal appearance now." But then his madness returned. "Are you really here?"

The Tech stared at him and frowned, unsure how to address the question. "We will tolerate no harm to our citizens when preventative measures are possible. We had to reconcile our edict of non-interference with protection."

Jason had lost his grasp on reality and retreated within himself, his head falling forward as he stared at the floor. He only repeated what he'd heard without understanding. "Reconcile . . ."

Tarien's voice grew alarmed. "We sense great distress. We do not wish for you to be encumbered in this way and are deeply concerned. We have tried to remain distant, in order for your natural ability for emotional control and understanding of proper balance to come into play and thereby ease your distress, but we have noted degradation instead. Are you unwell, Jason?"

With a hollow feeling in his stomach and another tide of distress threatening to overwhelm him, Jason looked up suddenly. "Can't you tell?"

The Tech cocked his head slightly. "You are not well," he decided. "This we are able to discern. We do not have your abilities and consequently we operate with empirical, concrete information. You are not physically suffering, outside of elevated chemical levels associated with stress, so we are unable to guess the nature of your distress."

Jason couldn't answer. Lost in a sea of emotions which were not his own and bombarded by the masses without sense of context or control, he clutched his head. His rational mind could not intervene enough to protect him.

For a moment, Tarien stood in silence. Then Tarien said, "We wish to ease your suffering, Jason." He stepped forward, lifting him from the floor as if he were a child. He stood Jason up and enveloped him in his arms. He held Jason in his muscular grasp for a few moments, comforting him, one hand on the back of Jason's head, the other in the small of his back. He pulled Jason's head to his right shoulder.

All external feedback ceased. With a nearly palpable wave, the bombardment he'd been under from everyone dissipated. Quickly, blessedly, he was alone in his thoughts and emotions. His legs gave way and Tarien had to hold him up. With a change in his arm position, Tarien lifted him off the ground, carrying him to the couch.

Nearly hysterical, Jason buried his head in Tarien's chest and cried in relief. He made an animal-like laughing noise as Tarien lay him down. Tarien kneeled next to him, his face oddly concerned. With a strangely human gesture, Tarien brushed Jason's unkempt hair away from his eyes.

"We do not know how else to help you, Jason. We feel great guilt in cutting off your abilities with your nanotechnological enhancements, but we note the effect it has on you. We do not know what else to do."

Jason regained control. With a relief he had not felt in months, he took a deep breath. "You really are here." He breathed raggedly. "You are the best. Oh, wow. Thank you. This is exactly what I needed." Feeling more capable of processing and voicing his despair, Jason tried to explain his distress. "I couldn't block everyone's emotions. Everyone is so filled with anger, hate, fear, distress. I've been picking that up for so long, it started to become part of me. I'm not built to deal with this." Quietly he added, "I don't know how you do it."

Tarien smiled slightly. "We process only data, not emotion. We have no connection to these things. This is entirely unique to you. Our data input is entirely functional, not subject to interpretation." Jason lay back against the pillows. Tarien still knelt between the table and the couch. After a moment, he continued. "We are relieved. We perceived this to be the only course of action, but we feared your response when we cut off your input. We are gratified you are not angry with us." He seemed to struggle with the concept as he said, "With me."

"God, no. Thank you. I could kiss you." He touched Tarien's face.

The Tech cocked his head sideways. "You've made an unusual response. We are uncertain kissing us would be appropriate."

"It's a figure of speech." Then, realizing he sounded like an idiot, he said, "Look, sorry. I just meant I'm so grateful for your help, a strong and overt display of affection would be the best way to express my thanks. My attraction to other males makes me more inclined to display such things. Usually, this would be more appropriate if said to a woman or if a woman said it to you. I just forgot to consider how it would come across. I didn't mean to make you uncomfortable," he finished lamely.

The Tech seemed to consider this. "It is of no consequence. We are immune to any discomfort others may feel in this regard." He cocked his head, which seemed to carry some form of silent communication that eluded Jason. "We wish to express concern over the progress demanded of you. We also worry about the pressure you are under and the choices before you. We do not wish you harmed by these decisions."

This startled Jason. "What do you mean? What decisions? You mean the Council? The Director?"

Tarien said nothing for a moment. "We are under restrictions and cannot say more. We only ask you to carefully consider the choices that will be put before you." Then, placing a hand on Jason's head as he stood, he said, "We will act to protect you in some ways if we are pressed. Please consider this, too."

He sat up. "What protections do you think I'll need?"

Before Jason could press the issue, his door chimed.

"Do not be alarmed, it is your Mechanic friend. She is here out of concern and will wish to take you out to dinner. We ask you to consider her proposal. Her friendship aids you greatly."

Jason grinned weakly. "That's uncanny. It must give you headaches knowing everything."

Tarien smiled. "You surprise us often. We do not know everything, Jason. Our inability to help you today should be proof."

The door chimed again. Twice.

Jason got up. "You helped me more than you know. I feel nearly human again." He gave a vocal command to open the door, still shaking slightly.

Monica strode in with a resolved and combative narrowing of her eyebrows, her mouth open, apparently ready to level a stream of admonitions at Jason. Three steps inside the apartment, she stopped, her eyes growing wide as she saw Tarien. She took one involuntary step backward.

Tarien smiled warmly at her, seeming to have become accustomed to this familiar gesture. "Greetings, Mechanic Monica Talon. We see you."

She made a startled noise and her hand flew to her mouth in surprise. She stood there, gaping in stunned silence.

"We do not wish to cause you alarm. We are validating the well-being of Jason and are just departing. We wished to remain until you arrived. Please do not allow our presence to waylay your objective." He turned slightly and said, "Jason, we request suppression of your nanotechnology system for a period of time to give you reprieve. Will you permit us?"

"Yeah, thank you. That would be great. I can probably get control over myself in a week." Then, suddenly, it occurred to him this might be a problem. "Will the Council allow it?"

The Tech frowned, looking oddly imperious. "We have said it. It is as we have decreed. The Council will not gainsay our judgment." He paused. "For now."

Jason stood up and walked over and hugged Tarien again, drawing back and putting both hands on his shoulders. "You have no idea how good this has been for me, so you have my strongest thanks."

"We are glad." He smiled again. His smiles seemed to be coming more easily. Then he departed, allowing Monica to fully enter so the door could slide closed behind her.

Monica let out an explosive breath. "Oh. My. God." She walked over to the couch and flopped down without any semblance of grace. "I came over to take you to dinner and beat the crap out of you for being a whiny crybaby only to find out you have a personal Tech hanging out, taking care of you." She looked up at him, her eyes still wide. "Really? I mean, how the hell did this happen? What was he doing here?" Then, before he could answer, "Oh shit. It's the Council, isn't it? They're protecting their interests. They want you to pull your act together and get them what they've all been slobbering over. Immortality and complete control."

"Monica, I—"

"Of course! Shit! That self-serving pack of walking cadavers will stop at nothing, especially with Death practically watching their every move."

"Well, I don't—"

"Goddamn it! This is a nightmare! This accident is only going to make them more viscous."

"It didn't seem like he came here under their orders," Jason said, annoyed at the implication.

"Well, sure. I mean, you know Techs. They like to hang out and read bedtime stories to everyone," she said with heavy sarcasm.

Jason frowned. "Wow, thanks for coming over to cheer me up."

She bit her lip. "I'm sorry. Look, you're right. Let's go out."

Heeding the advice of Tarien, though he didn't want to go out, he nodded and walked over to the kitchen counter. "Yeah, okay." He fidgeted with some of the small figurines he'd displayed on the countertop. "I mean, maybe they are using him to keep an eye on me. But Monica, he's been surprisingly helpful and maybe it doesn't matter. I do feel better and I really needed the help." He looked over at her for understanding.

She stared at him a moment. "Um, Jason . . ." She pursed her lips delicately. "I don't mean to be a jerk, but it sort of seems like you are becoming dopily enamored with your new robot friend."

He laughed. "Thanks, that was subtle."

"Well, I'm not exactly sugar and spice."

"I've noticed."

"So now you are slobbering over him."

"He's not a robot."

"Uh huh."

"And I've only seen him a few times, so it's not like we have long conversations over coffee."

"I see."

"He's really just showing up to help me."

"Which is totally normal."

"I'm going to hit you."

Her eyes grew wide and she effected helplessness. "Why, Jason! What a shocking thing to suggest."

"Hard."

"I'm entirely too fragile!" she said, moving toward him with a large eyes and pursed lips.

He punched her shoulder lightly.

She laughed. "That's not very manly, missy." Then, dismissively, she said, "Fine, I'm not going to harp on you about flirting with a cyborg. It's certainly better than some of the morons you've managed to get stuck to the bottom of your shoes." She tapped her lips thoughtfully. "And I have to admit, it is very cute." Her change of tone and lack of accusation eased the tension.

"Are we going to eat?"

"Yes, probably. Assuming you can stop slobbering on yourself and get ready."

"I AM ready. Let's go."

She let out an explosive laugh, looking him up and down pointedly. Her face took on a scrunched look of combined sympathy and mockery. "Wow. You've really lost it. No, you aren't." She wrinkled her nose. "Seriously? You look like you've been crying, which you have. You smell like you wallow in your own stench as a fetish, and you need to at least trim your mangy-dog face. You really aren't the type to grow facial hair. You look like you have scurvy." She put a hand on his shoulder. "Honestly, Jason, you stink to high heaven and I'm afraid someone will mistake you for a hobo the moment you step outside. There's no way you'll be allowed in any establishment short of a rehab clinic." She pointedly looked around at the mess in the apartment.

Crap, thought Jason. Clothing and dishes littered the floor along with containers of half-eaten food that he'd had delivered. Jason had been completely unaware of the mess.

It slowly dawned on him how neglectful he'd become about his space and himself. He took a deep breath, nodded to her, and went into the bathroom. He took a long time to shower and shave, but he felt a lot better. For the first time in a while, he could look at his reflection in the mirror.

By the time he emerged, Monica had made considerable progress tossing his clothing into the cleaning units and putting the dishes where the robots could deal with them. She had tossed the food containers into the recycling. With the floors cleared, the small robots could do their job of roaming and cleaning the smaller debris. She looked up and smiled. "Much better. C'mon, I'm starving."

She put her arm in his and led him out of the apartment and then down and out of the building. Mom gave him a relieved hug, expressing her concern for him.

The sun shone outside, and they walked to a nearby restaurant called Aracona.

Dinner and drinks were great. Jason had never been to Aracona, despite living only a few blocks away. The place was dimly lit, but had a lively crowd, and the furnishings were trendy, with an artistic color scheme of black and brushed metal, along with brightly colored walls. He had an excellent pepper steak and a heavenly lime and basil sorbet. Monica picked at her mahi-mahi, barely finishing it, despite the fact she said she thought of it as one of the best dishes she'd ever had. She didn't touch her mousse, so Jason happily ate that too. He became concerned when she didn't respond to the flirtations of the waiter.

They chit-chatted about random things, carefully avoiding public conversation about his work or the problems he'd recently had. By the end of the evening, Jason felt great. Monica looked exhausted.

ELEVEN

JASON TOOK THE NEXT FEW DAYS off from work. He went on walks through parks, saw some local musicians, visited museums, and tried, with much success, to relax. Whatever Tarien had done, Faust had quit the nagging and pressuring. In an unusual period of calm, Jason wasn't sent nasty threats or other forms of coercion.

Monica stayed with him when she wasn't working, except one night, where she'd met a young man and had some fun with him before kicking him out of her apartment. Jason had just arrived at her place as she ushered her boy-toy out the door. With a lingering kiss and an aggressive hand on the man's ass, she certainly made no pretenses about what she'd been doing with him the night before.

Worried about Jason's lack of sex life, she tried to

introduce him to a guy she'd met at work, which turned out to be embarrassingly awkward. The man clearly liked Jason and tried to engage him with flirting gestures, overt sexual references and, finally, by trying to kiss him. Jason showed the man no interested at all, since Monica's friend was too hairy, too beefy, and simply not very intelligent. In reality, his only romantic thoughts, irrational as they might be, were of Tarien.

Still, having someone pay him attention was refreshing. He returned to work, partially, near the end of the week. The block from Tarien was still in place. Jason could sense his own nannies, but not those of others. Without the torrential flood of incoming emotions, he could focus. He used this respite to focus on becoming able to manually shut down receptors himself, so that he would not need Tarien to do this for him. His staff noted the communication method he used to issue the shutdown orders and built that into their lab systems so they could intervene if he failed or turn them on for him. This turned out to be rather simple and, thankfully, complete. While he could turn the reception of emotions either on or off, there didn't seem to be a dimmer switch.

At the start of the next week, after a relaxing weekend and without warning, the bombardment of external sensory input resumed. He looked around for Tarien, expecting him to be nearby to have triggered his nannies, but Jason couldn't detect the Tech anywhere close.

At first, he clenched his teeth and tried to endure the input, but quickly found he needed to shut off incoming emotions. His staff kept close watch on him and regulated his communication in case he slipped. Each time they turned them back on, he made a concerted effort to filter or outright block everyone out. It took him several more days before he found the trick he'd been looking for.

It seemed if he broadcast opposing emotions to each individual, like two waves coming from opposite directions, it negated incoming information from that person to him without changing it in the host. Doing so made him consciously aware of the nature of each incoming data stream. One by one, he filtered each emotion out with sustained negation. Next, he began to attempt creating subtle changes in each person, rather than completely and forcefully overriding their emotions.

This level of granularity proved beyond his ability. He either completely dominated the person's emotions and hormones, an effort that dissipated when Jason wasn't nearby, or he had to shut them out and ignore the signals. While almost everyone had basic nannies that regulated their bodies for medical reasons, the new nannies were extremely complex in their abilities. He needed to master communication to these basic nannies in people before the advanced nannies could be made available to the general population.

The rest of the team proved equally unsuccessful at their assignments.

Dr. Garbine, who had been just as shaken by the previous accident, now evinced reluctance to perform any aggressive testing. She avoided him as much as possible, clearly shaken by the entire program and its failures. Even so, she had discovered that when a person had a close emotional tie to another person, that bond formed a sort of natural intermingling of one person's core self with another person's core self. She'd discovered this after reviewing old research with plants, using attached sensors for monitoring, showed they were affected when a plant in another room had a leaf cut off. This happened for humans, too, when a definitive bond was present between the individuals. Working with this premise, her experiments were leaning toward the strong possibility that one's consciousness could be moved between hosts based on this bond. She feared, however, that an aggressive push to force the host to submit to a foreign consciousness would kill the host individual, leaving behind a shell that was then occupied by the foreign consciousness. Essentially, you could transfer "soul" to another body, but you'd kill the person to whom you transferred. There didn't seem to be a way to share the host. The theory was esoteric, and her work seemed to be the most difficult of all, but she appeared to have lost energy behind the little progress she'd made and spent increasing amounts of time away from the lab.

Dr. Preem had made the most progress. Her new communications, enhanced suits, and overall technological enhancements had come out almost daily. She watched the other teams like a hawk and made adjustments to provide each of them with more specific tools. Unlike both he and Dr. Garbine, she seemed more attuned to the problems since the disaster and showed laser-like focus on the problems at hand.

Dr. Black had all but completed his work. The new nano and cellular enhancements made potential subjects nearly invulnerable. Given enough time and material, the body could repair just about anything. These reparations were becoming rapid with each new version. Fire and chemical destruction of the subject, or electro-magnetic disruption of the nannies so they could not repair were the exception, and freezing would delay the repair process. His work also meant that the biosuits would, eventually, be moot. They were designed to protect, enhance, provide signal boosts, and house chemicals for medical use in their fabric. Highly advanced nannies could manufacture just about anything from surrounding materials and do most of the work the suits now provided.

Dr. Black began working more closely with the other chief scientist on his team, Markovich, and began looking at true cloning as a physical replacement for a destroyed body. They could replicate any person within months, using advanced cellular cloning and accelerated growth, but these lab-grown clones were just inanimate carcasses. Even with Dr. Garbine's work, Jason could not detect these beings as living organisms and could not, therefore, identify enough with them to try and animate them. The attempts were like trying to animate a chair.

The dire problem persisted with the ongoing experiments to enhance existing bodies, too. The issue of out-of-control hormones and the inability of the host to keep their body normalized persisted. This worried them all, considering how it caused insanity and self-destruction.

Markovich pointed out that Jason held the key both to stabilizing and to transferal. Something about emotions came from more than just chemical processes. They found an underlying guiding force: consciousness.

The new questions and issues seemed to inflame the Council, who only viewed the amazing discoveries and progress as falling short of their desired goals. Whatever vestiges of goodwill and friendly disposition they'd pretended toward Jason evaporated. Somehow, they had assumed the technology to be nearing completion...close to being feasible for them to use to save them from aging. They did not understand how science often revealed new problems as it progressed. These new revelations put the science just as far away from the final goal as when the doctors had started.

Director Faust became increasingly hostile. He would, occasionally, review their work, making disdainful suggestions, though they were, admittedly, brilliant.

A Tech constantly accompanied Faust during these visits, as if to emphasize Faust's authority. Sector Seven would be at Faust's side on occasion, but Sector Nine most often stood by Faust's side. On rare occasions, another Tech, a woman from Sector Four, would substitute. The presence of any Tech frightened the research team more than anything Faust could do or say. Faust was a known. Prone to fits of rage and often belittling those around him, yes, and certainly intimidating, but still human. A Tech, however, was rare. Most people had never seen one, let alone had one observe them so closely. The population revered them and were terrified of them at the same time. Nobody knew just how much a Tech could see into your every thought, know your every action. Having one physically present made the fear that they knew every one of your secrets more real.

Despite this, the expression Nine wore was not the unemotional and stoic face that people expected. When Sector Nine attended, he loomed over them with a slightly confused expression on his face, as if unsure why he had submitted to becoming a personal attendant to Faust. This slight human flaw in his otherwise inhuman presence tempered the concerns.

During the visits where Seven accompanied Faust, he would stare at Jason. Unlike his normally distant expression, he had a fiery and piercing gaze that Jason couldn't understand. Jason became increasingly concerned about Tarien's appearance, especially since he had begun to frown on occasion and his eyes narrowed dangerously in contrast to Faust's smile during one visit as they discussed the advancement of Jason's experiments. The more progress Jason made, the more dour Tarien's facial expressions. Such expressions were rare on the face of a Tech, but now both Nine and Tarien wore them.

Finally, when Tarien seemed particularly upset, Jason had broadcast strong compassion and concern, smiling encouragingly. Instead of the intended effect, Tarien's eyes widened and his face and eyes became sad, hurt even. Everything he saw happening with Tarien confused Jason. First, because the behavior didn't resonate with anything he knew of how the Techs operated, which didn't seem to involve normal human emotion, and second, because he'd thought that they'd connected on some level. Why would Tarien be sad when Jason was just trying to let him know he was concerned?

Immediately after sending comfort to Tarien, Sector Nine and, surprisingly, Director Faust had turned their gazes at him as if they were twins. Nine's gaze seemed indifferent, Faust's cold and hostile. Their mirrored movements confused and shocked Jason. He could understand how Nine would have known what he was doing, but Faust? That implied Faust had some sort of method for detecting and reading what Jason was doing real-time. The thought chilled him, since he hoped to keep some of his work secret from Faust in the hope of thwarting him. This only happened when Nine was present. Faust, he reasoned, must have some sort of direct link of communication there.

It was all he could do to stay at the lab on the days when the Techs appeared.

Most nights when he came home, Monica was around. She was spending a lot of time with Mom and with Derek, which made no sense. She didn't live close and neither of them had been particularly good friends of hers in the past. Whatever her reasons, she refused to talk about it with him and she, Mom, and Derek never spoke of anything of consequence when he was present.

When Jason asked her, Monica simply responded, "I discovered that we share some ideas about social issues. That's all. They have some great ideas on how we can all work together for change and for once I'm actually hopeful. Don't worry about it. I DO have other friends, you know." Jason decided he had plenty to concern him and needn't question her new relationships.

At long last, he made a breakthrough. With some success, he could permanently fix the emotions of some of the test subjects into a combination that meant obedience. The resulting emotions were basic and people lost any form of objectivity. They became nearly zombie-like, capable of carrying out only simple commands, but they remained utterly under Jason's control.

From this breakthrough, came another surprisingly useful ability. He could induce mild autism in some of his lab assistants, which made them capable of solving complex issues. The lab assistants became exhausted in this state, so the technique only worked for short bursts of research. Extended time in this state forced their brains to perform beyond their natural capacity, burning out sections. Jason carefully avoided getting to this point.

It had been just over two years since they had started the experiments. Obtaining the kind of success the Council wanted would take several more years, at least. Possibly as much as a decade.

Unexpectedly, on what was an otherwise calm day, Carlisle Faust burst into the lab. He swept his arm across a lab table, hurling glassware and metal instruments to the floor. Jason's staff rushed to get away from the violence. Faust picked up a mass spectrometer they had been using to analyze new elemental properties in some of the materials used for the suits, clearly intent on throwing it at Jason. Two of the attending robots rushed at Faust, each grabbing an arm to prevent this. "This should have taken half the time, you moron!" he screamed at Jason. "I've solved far more complex problems in my sleep!" He tried to break free from the attendant robots, who would not allow further destruction to the lab. In a couple of minutes they released him, standing by to grab him again if needed. "One of the Council is dead, because you are too slow to get your part of the research under control."

Dr. Garbine gasped. "Who died?"

"Elandra Hayes. Dead! In a time when death should be easily defeated."

Faust bunched his fists and strode towards Jason. "You're the one who's holding this up. We have a way to prevent death. I solved the physical problem two years ago. The only thing we need is a way to control the feedback problem and to prevent loss of control. I've solved death and I've solved how to regenerate, and you can't figure out something as simple as emotional control!" With that said, he swung a fist at Jason.

Jason stepped back, but not before Faust's fist connected with his nose. Shocked, he didn't feel the pain before he tasted the salty warmth of blood in the back of his throat. Jason lifted his face and stared at the man in disgust. Several of the other doctors sucked in their breath in astonishment and Dr. Garbine stammered, "Carlisle!"

Too late, the robots rushed to restrain Faust again.

Jason wiped the blood from under his nose, tempted to hit Faust while the robots held him. Instead, as his anger bubbled to the surface, he said, "Then do it your goddamn self. I quit."

Faust sneered. "Oh, do you? You think you can just walk out? You think I won't destroy you because you are the only one we have who can work on this? I think you'll find out just how persuasive I can be." He finally jerked his arms free of the robots and stormed out of the room.

Jason's nannies repaired his face quickly, but his anger would not subside. The staff stood in shock as he left the lab without a word.

Instead of the lifts and elevated public mag trains, he took a private gravity vehicle home. It was faster, for one, and he hadn't taken time to look in a mirror and wipe the blood off that he knew must be on his face.

The vehicle landed near the large gardens that flanked the entrance.

Monica lingered outside his building, talking with Mom and with Derek, busily helping them plant a few new things. They all looked up in surprise, then concern. Mom reached him first, stepping out of the dirt and onto the walkway, touching his upper lip and letting out a small cry of concern. Monica came up behind her. Derek wandered up behind them both, looking at Jason curiously.

Monica was both upset and concerned. "What the hell happened? Is that dried blood on your chin?"

Jason tried to tamp down his anger. "Faust. He threw a tantrum about the death of Council member Hayes. He sees his own mortality staring him in the face and he hit me."

Her hands tightened into fists. "That son of a bitch! I don't get it. Why doesn't he just use the new technology to make himself immortal? I must be missing something. You said he developed it already, so what is he waiting for?"

What the hell was she doing? Talking like this out where everyone could hear. "Monica! We aren't alone." Then, to Derek and Mom he said, "Look, this is just speculation and worry about some things at work. We need to go inside."

Monica looked stricken, then blushed and lowered her face. "Okay, crap. I sort of already told them, Jason. It's one of the things we've been talking about. Before you get all mad and throw a fit, it's important for people to take a stand. You even told me you broadcast emotions to the workers and guards when demonstrating to the Council, right? Because you wanted to get the message out. So, the more people that know and raise concerns, the better. Maybe if there are enough of us, we can band together, do something."

"Great. When this gets back to Faust, because you're standing around gossiping, you'll suddenly be hit by a flying vehicle that unexplainably lost gravity control. He doesn't go easy on people who he suspects are a threat, Monica."

She moved closer, throwing a quick look over her shoulder. "I get that. But out here is probably safer than inside my apartment, where every gadget can hear every whisper. At least out here, there's nothing but flowers and a few worms. And I doubt they're spying on us. Nothing that can overhear is close. Mom suggested it. It's the least suspicious way for us to have these conversations. If we were all seen running off to some hiding place all the time, that'd look weird. Out here, we are visible and yet probably completely unseen and unheard."

He had to admit, this was a solid idea. He glanced over at Mom, who cocked her head a bit, making her pinned-up grey hair bobble to the side. She gave him a wily look, a little smile on her saintly face. "Oh, sweetie. I'm not as silly and unaware as you might think. Here, let me." She took out a small rag and spit on it and wiped the blood from his face. Jason was caught between laughing and flinching. It was so gross, but so like her. He wasn't sure his face looked any better. At least the blood had been cleaned off.

Monica pulled her gloves off, kicking her shoes against the walkway to dislodge dirt. "So? Why hasn't he? Faust, I mean. He has the technology to make himself immortal. You said so yourself. I am terrified he will, that our chances will be gone to resist, but I can't figure out what's stopping him."

Jason stared at them for a moment, deciding that talking out here really was a reasonably good idea. Probably not for long, but nobody was nearby. "Monica, he can't. You must know what I'm working on."

"Yeah, you are working on control. The ability he needs to command everyone around him, enslave people so they can't challenge him and a bunch of other shit he should never be able to do. But he can enslave people later. For now, he could just give himself the treatment."

"No, he can't. I'm working on the piece he needs to remain himself, once he induces the physical changes. All our test subjects went crazy and changed so much they weren't human anymore. They had no control and ended up dying. He needs me to either suppress the emotional feedback loop permanently or to teach him how to consciously control it himself. Right now, I can only suppress things generally, but it renders the subject nearly useless. Until the process is fine-tuned, he runs the risk of destroying himself."

"Then don't do it! Good god, Jason, he's a monster and he's trying to make himself invulnerable in every sense of the word."

"I won't. I quit today. I just left the lab. I'm done, Monica. I'm not going back."

Monica's mouth opened and her brows shot up. Whatever she had expected him to say, it clearly wasn't that he'd quit. Where before she had been poised for an argument, now she was unable to speak. Mom stared at him, blinking occasionally. Jason couldn't tell if Mom was surprised or just absorbing what they had both been saying. Jason expected Monica to finally snap out of it, so he was surprised when Derek put a hand on Monica's shoulder and turned her slightly toward him.

"We need to do this now, Monica. He needs to know."

Monica snapped out of it. "Derek, shut up."

"Fuck that. The Director will have him killed if he really won't go back. You know it. It's our only chance."

She rounded on Derek. "I said, shut up!"

Mom put a calming hand on her arm.

Derek scowled at her.

Jason frowned at the whole group. "Tell me what? What the hell are you guys talking about when I'm not around? It's clearly not a birthday party."

Monica threw a nasty glance at Derek. Mom finally spoke. "He's right, sweetie. We have to tell him. We may not have another chance."

"Okay, I'm done with all this scheming. Tell me what the hell is going on or I'm going to my condo and locking myself in there for the rest of the month. I'm seriously done."

"Shit. Fine. Derek, lead the way. Jason, you have to come with us now and shut up. Not another word."

Before he could respond, Derek grabbed him by the arm and led him around the apartment building, through a few alleys and toward a large, nondescript building that had few windows. To the side of the building was a small car, an old-style vehicle with barely enough room for the four of them. Much to Jason's shock, Derek actually drove the thing, winding their way through various streets and toward the river. They met every question from Jason with silence, ignoring his increasing irritation. The streets weren't often occupied by ground vehicles. When people saw Derek driving toward them, people scurried hurriedly out of the way, squawking like frightened birds. A woman wearing an elaborate bio-suit with a cape and hood nearly dropped the bundle she was carrying. She yelled at them angrily as they passed.

As they drove through an older area of the neighborhood, where warehouses and storage buildings displaced living areas, the gardens and general sylvan feel of the city faded. Out here, concrete and metal still ruled. To Jason, it was stark, dirty.

Finally, they reached a warehouse with wide metal doors and tiny windows two stories above them that faced the blank wall of another large building. The façade of the warehouse was cracked and flaking. Poor drainage meant pools of stagnant water around the front of the building, and the smell was unpleasant. Jason felt some mild nausea along with a strong urge to leave. Monica grabbed his arm, apparently sensing Jason was about to bolt, and led him inside. The smell inside was worse, consisting of urine and possible some animal feces, and he would have bolted for sure if curiosity hadn't overtaken him. They wound their way through crates and metal containers, the dusty floor showing signs that people walked this path rather frequently, if the mass of footprints was any indication. They passed some old machinery, which appeared designed to move large items and be driven by a person instead of a robot.

Finally, they navigated between two tall yellow metal containers and moved toward the back of the building. Jason watched in surprise as Derek touched the concrete wall in a series of spots. The wall moved, revealing a set of metal stairs inside a deep shaft of concrete.

The stairs continued down several stories until they reached a long concrete corridor. They passed several closed metal doors, finally reaching a large opening that revealed another storage room, much smaller than the one on the ground floor, but still filled with dusty old storage containers and clutter that was piled here and there. Broken pieces of rotting wood and concrete were barely visible in the dim light. Behind a particularly large pile of debris was another stairwell. Had you not intentionally known where to go, the twisted rebar and broken slabs of concrete would have obscured it entirely.

Jason hesitated. The light here was dim and this area of the building seemed so old that it barely seemed safe. Monica's gripped tightened.

Resigned, he followed Mom down the single flight of narrow metal stairs and into a short hallway. The door in front of them was made of solid steel and banded with support bars of more metal. It looked like something you would see on a vault. Or in one of those movies where you had to contain the radioactive monstrosity that someone had accidentally created in their evil lair.

With a grunt and a lot of pulling, Derek managed to

swing the huge door outward toward them. The hinges complained loudly, echoing in the narrow concrete hall. The sudden sound of something other than their feet made Jason shiver.

Surprisingly, the door didn't hide a murder scene with a stone alter and a bunch of hooked tools and pincers hanging on the wall. Instead, it revealed a rather pleasant and inviting space. Brightly lit and with tall ceilings, Jason saw the room had an old-style kitchen, several couches and a community gathering space.

After everyone entered, Derek pushed the massive door closed. A steel table with mismatched hard plastic and metal chairs filled the bulk of the dining space. One wall of shelving stood stocked from floor to ceiling with food supplies.

Jason took a long moment to look around, completely confused. A hidden room, with all the twists and turns to get here, and well-stocked with supplies? Why? Though well lit, and inviting as it was, it reminded Jason of a prison cell. Maybe it was the door. Or maybe the fact it was four stories underground.

Finally, Mom spoke. "Would you like some coffee, sweetie? There's plenty. Sit and I'll get you some." As Jason sat, so did Monica and Derek. Mom took a jug of water from another metal shelf that stood next to a small sink set in a cabinet and began heating a pot over the propane stove that sat adjacent to it on the counter.

"What the hell is this? Some secret society safe house?"

Monica sighed. "Jason, we have a lot to talk about. But I doubt we have much time. The Director won't just let you slip out of his grasp. He may not kill you, not yet, but he might do a lot of things that will make you wish he would."

Derek nodded at Monica and turned to Jason. "Look, I'll give you a quick rundown. I'm a little distrusting of the government and I've been worried about their actions for a while. I found a group with a similar set of concerns. A well-connected group. Whether or not you agree with our paranoia, just let me talk.

"I thought I might need a safe place, somewhere the government couldn't hear me, so I helped retrofit this warehouse. The leaders of our society passed down information about building this place, though they haven't explained why. The group is pretty cautious." He took a deep breath. "Anyway, so this room is surrounded by lead and copper mesh. A Faraday cage, essentially. It means there's no communication in or out. Probably easy to find if they suspected it exists, and I'm sure they will at some point, but for now, we have a place to talk. Building this place has been my job, as has been recruiting Mom and Monica. I don't know why, but I just do as I'm told."

"This is so dumb. A secret organization? I'm going home."

"Shut up, Jason." Monica accepted a cup of coffee from Mom. Jason grudgingly did the same.

Derek continued. "I know the Tech is interested in you for some reason. Everyone does, after seeing that display where he took you to the roof to avoid the angry mob. I became interested enough that I convinced Monica to share the rest. She denied everything at first, but I shared my own information about our movement to stop what is happening and she came around. I don't really care what you think of me or my crazy ideas, which is beside the point. What I do care about is making the public aware of what is going on and, more importantly, I want to do something to make them care. Jason, I want Faust dead. I doubt that will happen, and most of the plans we have are impossible, but I have one clear objective. Whatever the intent of the organization, I intend to use this as a way to achieve my own goals. Specifically, I want to capture a Tech."

Jason's nose flared with outrage. "Are you fucking kidding me? Let me guess, you want the one I'm familiar with—Sector Seven. You plan on, what? Putting a bag over his head and chloroforming him? Are you a moron? He'd have every device in the city at his disposal. He'd have your own nannies turn against you, for Christ's sake! Never mind the fact I would never harm him, for any reason."

"Yeah, well I need to capture him. He's the only thing that can possibly help! Jason, if we can get him under our control, we can make him help us. He can stop Faust and the Council."

Jason couldn't believe what he had just heard. The statement was so completely absurd, he almost laughed. "Oh my god. Are you five years old? First of all, you can't just capture him. That's pretty much impossible. Second, you can't control or coerce him. He's a Tech. Everything in the city is tied to him! Do you plan on capturing every piece of technology in the city? Okay, let's say you somehow captured and controlled him. Then what? He is physically incapable of harming anyone. It's part of the safeguards of his integration."

They waited until Jason finished. Monica took a deep breath. "Jason, if you could override his volition with this new ability of yours, you could cripple him enough for us to capture him. Once we had him isolated in this room where he can't communicate, you could figure out how to control him. Think about it. It's exactly what Faust is planning to do with the Techs when he finally learns to use your abilities for himself."

Jason stared at each of them, horrified. "No! I can't do it!" He saw Monica open her mouth to angrily protest. "No, shut up a minute. Really, I can't. We're talking about a Tech here, not some average schmoe. His systems are so complex I wouldn't have the faintest idea of how to even begin. And if I somehow could, given another three years to specifically research the way he works, what then? The entire Sector depends on their control. They are linked to everything." Facetiousness crept into his voice. "I presume the whole city would instantly know something had happened when systems started failing and commuter vehicles crashed. You know, that whole issue about traffic, machinery, and everything else suddenly not having the proper governance."

He saw Monica clench her jaw, clearly desperate, not wanting to hear him.

"Jason, we have to try. We have to. What else can we do? Faust is going to kill you, and you know it. The moment he has what he needs, you're dead." She gave Mom and Derek a look, then faced him again. "You're dead, he's immortal and capable of being rebuilt even if his body is completely destroyed. Worse, Faust will be in charge of the Council and the entire population. He will use your ability to control the nannies, to force people to do whatever he wants. You think he'll share the abilities he learns? No way. He'll be so aware of anyone attempting to use the same technology, he'll instantly know to stifle it and keep himself in control. We have to try." Monica shuddered. "Faust may eventually be able to simply kill at will, from a distance, by shutting down biological functions with a thought."

She paused for a moment, seeming to weigh information. "Look, we have enormous backing. We have highly placed people giving orders. This isn't something we just came up with. Our superiors believe this will work, and they have incredible influence and resources. They said to make you aware that you need to learn to control a Tech. We assume this means they intend for you to capture one."

Derek looked at Jason with concern and Jason felt some sympathy as he responded. "I'm sorry. I know this is a nightmare, and believe me, I wish there was something we could do, but the only thing I can think of is to keep looking for another answer. This one is impossible. Capture him? It will never happen. I can't even get close to him without him knowing. I wish Seven could help, but he can't. He is under strict control by his programming. Even if I completely controlled him, I wouldn't have the foggiest idea how to do anything he does. Without knowing how to control Seven, it would essentially make him an ineffective prize. That renders me worthless."

Tired and still upset, he didn't have the energy to engage them further. "I'm going home."

He got up, gave Mom a hug and left without another word. Monica and Derek glared at him but didn't try to stop him. They shared a look, implying this wasn't over.

He wound his way back up through the labyrinth to the surface. Once outside, he had to get his bearings since he had no idea about his location. Finally, he found a transport and made it back to his condo.

Once home, he shed his biosuit and threw it forcibly against the wall. It wasn't enough that his career verged on ruin, his failures mounting. Now his friends had gone completely insane, coming up with stupid plans that had no chance of succeeding and would get them imprisoned and possibly executed. He wasn't sure what would happen for assaulting a Tech, since it had never happened.

He got a glass of water and stomped into the bathroom to take a shower. Before he could start the water or even undress, someone grabbed him from behind. Instinctively, he jammed an elbow into their stomach and whirled around to face the intruder. But the man had him pinned against the wall too quickly to defend himself further and a woman stepped out of the shower and injected him with something. He immediately felt groggy and slow as he tried to fight his way free. Whatever they'd injected, his nannies couldn't process the foreign chemical fast enough and he soon blacked out.

TWELVE

HE AWOKE SLOWLY, FEELING GROGGY from the drug lingering in his system. The effort needed to open his eyes felt monumental. He succeeded, only to find Director Faust looming over him. "Good, you're finally awake. Your nannies don't have this compound on file to process, so you're going to have to shake this off on your own."

Jason tried to move and quickly discovered he had been strapped to a large metal table, arms and legs bound, and was still in his clothing from before he'd been kidnapped. He struggled, to no avail. Two robots flanked Faust, standing ready to carry out whatever orders the doctor issued.

Fury laced through Jason. He looked around. "What the hell is this? You think you can kidnap and drug me?"

"You're rather slow. I've already done exactly that."

"People might be sheep, but I can guarantee you they won't ignore my disappearance, not after Reid was killed by a 'rogue driver.' The circumstances around her accident were already suspect. Certainly not after all the deaths from 'failed experiments.' People were furious when they heard of the volunteers dying in the lab. The public was accosting Medics, including myself. They are going to start to see a pattern if it's the Medics disappearing, too. You've killed so many people in so short of time, it's becoming obvious."

"Oh?" He laughed. "So, you figured out the death of that other team was my doing? Yes, I suppose there are those who might wonder if something is going on. And you're right, I got rid of the original team of scientists and then your co-worker Reid handily enough. No reason for me to deny it."

"Go ahead, kill me. But you aren't going to get away with it. The media is still pushing hard enough that even the Council can't stop them from finding out." Jason noted he had to pee, but not badly. He hadn't urinated in his pants. That meant he probably hadn't been knocked out for long.

Faust rolled his eyes. He checked several displays, working on something while he talked. Moving out of Jason's view for a moment, he grunted, then moved back toward the foot of the table. "So, what if they find out? At this point, it will hardly matter. I have safeguards that will bog down any sort of investigation indefinitely, or at least long enough to where it won't matter. I'll have the research I need. Believe me, if I want, I can create enough secondary news that a few murders will be the least interesting thing going on.

"Regardless, this is hardly relevant. I'm not going to kill you, at least not yet. Fortunately for you, I do need you to finish your research. For whatever reason, you seem to be the only person capable of the level of control I need. If you weren't such an imbecile, we'd have finished the necessary research by now." He motioned, and the robots quickly moved a metal tray over to the table from the wall.

Jason couldn't make out much about the room, since he was restrained, but the lighting was low, and he could see one corner of the room. So the space probably wasn't that large. The tray was too elevated to see what lay there, but a box was apparent.

"As it stands, I need you to solve the issue of the longevity curse. I can't give myself the treatment if I'm going to lose control of my body and emotions, potentially suiciding. And I've no intention of living forever as a mindless ape."

"I've tried! You're trying to move things too fast. I can't just snap my fingers and suddenly have what you need. Even if I did, you'd just kill me anyway, so why would I bother?"

"Why indeed? You see, it appears to me you haven't been properly motivated. I think you are purposefully dragging your heels." He opened the metal box sitting on the tray and pulled out a syringe. "I would promise not to kill you if you worked it out, but you obviously don't believe me, and I really don't care to try and convince you."

"What's that? Another unregistered chemical you plan on using on me? Some sort of drug to torture me with?"

"What a marvelous idea, the torture thing. I'm sure we'll get around to it at some point. No, this is a bit more direct." He jammed the needle into Jason's arm.

"Shit," screamed Jason.

"I must say, a syringe is really archaic, but I find satisfaction jamming a needle into you, for some reason."

"What the hell is wrong with you?"

Faust laughed maliciously. "Oh my! A lot, actually. Most specifically, I'm old. I need to know I won't die tomorrow of a heart attack or any other malady." He put the syringe away and the robots took the tray. "I'm afraid I've given you a huge dose, several times what we've experimented with. You will probably start feeling the effects in half an hour at most. By tomorrow, I think you'll feel rather marvelous." The smile on his face struck fear in Jason's heart as he slowly realized what had happened. Maybe it was the injection, but Jason felt himself break into a cold sweat and his heart rate increased dramatically. "You injected me with the immortality drug, didn't you? And the experimental nannies?" His heart continued to race, and his breathing became hard, panicked. "Giving those to me is a death sentence. I'll go insane!"

For a moment Faust didn't respond. He moved back out of view to glance at the displays. After he was satisfied, he finally answered. "Possibly, yes. Probably, even. I'm rather depending on self-preservation to push you toward figuring things out, though. Like I said, you haven't been properly motivated, and I can't trust that you're really trying. Now, I'll know for sure or I'll be done with you and it won't be my fault. Nobody will believe you didn't do it to yourself, not when you won't be able to say otherwise."

Faust moved back into view and motioned to the two robots, who then restrained Jason's arms while they also removed his bindings. "I'll have you taken to the holding apartment, where you'll have a couple staff to work with you. Assuming they will work with you. I'm afraid I can't allow you out of the complex, since you'd just try and run away again or take the opportunity to tattle on me. You'll be nice and cozy while I observe your every move."

Jason couldn't respond. Terror constricting his throat. The robots pulled him off the table and practically dragged him out the door. Jason began to scream, hoping someone would hear him. He tried to order the robots to let him go, complained they were hurting him, but they ignored him. Obviously, the safety protocols had been overridden, which wasn't much of a surprise.

Finally, resigned, he just let them drag him down the hall, offering no resistance.

The robots dragged him to what must be the apartment Faust had spoken about. They hauled him to the middle of the living room and onto the rug, then simply left. He sat on his knees and put his face in his hands for a long while. The robots departed through the main doors and the sound of locks engaging was audible.

Removing his hands from his face, he clutched at the fibers of the thick tan rug. His breathing grew ragged as the panic of what had happened kept his adrenaline high. Finally, running his hands through his hair, he let out an explosive breath. He clenched his jaw in fear and near despair, then barked a short laugh of frustration, staring at the ceiling.

His mind raced. They'd locked him in here, knowing he would soon start feeling the effects of the drug. Unsure of how much time he had, he got up and explored his living quarters. He soon discovered a room that must be his lab, fully equipped and with several new biosuits hanging on the wall. He picked one and carried it with him until he found his spacious and well-furnished bedroom. There were other bedrooms, but this one had amenities that Jason assumed were meant for him. After finally emptying his bladder, he turned on the shower and stepped in, letting the water run over him to calm his nerves. As he began to soap up, he felt a rush and put his hand against the wall to stabilize himself. Another rush ran through him, stronger. The effects of the drugs were starting. Eyes wide, he took a moment to accept his feelings, to listen to his body, and to gauge how he reacted. Knowing the nannies would, technically, start making him healthier, younger, and more in direct control of his other nano-technological enhancements, it wasn't death he feared. He feared the loss of his sanity. Jason briefly recalled the monstrous changes in the test subjects who had volunteered, then succumbed to mindless rages and dying when one of them had killed the others and then burned himself alive.

The rushes continued, which led him to believe extreme changes were taking place in his thermal regulation system. They weren't unpleasant feelings, just odd. Related to his metabolism changing, he suspected. He finally got out of the shower and dried off, donning his suit so he could gather data from it. Because he had no idea how long he'd been knocked out, he wasn't sure if he felt hungry because he hadn't eaten in a while, or if the changes were burning up available fuel. Jason suspected the latter, since he assumed he hadn't been unconscious for long. Whatever the reason, he felt ravenous and, upon finding the food synthesis units in the dining and social rooms, made a quick meal and devoured it. While the dining area contained automation, it also contained a full hobby kitchen, including a cooking range and oven, counter space, and a recipe panel with keys for fresh ingredients. Nobody really needed to cook anymore, so the addition was a luxury. The dining counter was clearly designed to expand to accommodate many, but currently had room for four. On it sat a fruit bowl. Another wasteful addition. It was also kind of in the way if more than one person wanted to sit and visit. Jason moved it to the counter near the cooking range.

Jason finished his meal and small cleaning units arose from the sides of the counter, quickly breaking down the bio-degradable dishes and utensils for repurposing and carrying them away. As he rose from the stool, which then merged back with the underside of the counter automatically, he heard the main doors unlock and open. Rather than rushing out to try to escape, he patiently waited in the dining area. The doors clearly closed and locked again and he heard voices. Wiping his hands, he walked out to the living room where three people stood, looking around fearfully. They were part of his lab staff.

Two of the women, Jenn and Eve, were unconsciously leaning into the third technician, Ephrom, as if he'd protect them in some way. Jason almost smiled. Ephrom likely wouldn't protect anyone but himself. All three watched him as he walked in, eyes confused.

"Hello, Dr. Emerson," said Jenn.

"Hi, Jenn. Eve, Ephrom. Let me guess. You were 'volunteered' to help me continue with my research."

Ephrom barked a laugh. "Yeah, we volunteered all right. Minus the volunteering part. They yanked me out of bed this morning and threw a bag over my head. I don't even know where we are."

The other two echoed his story.

Jason did his best to offer a comforting smile, dreading what he was going to have to tell them. More to the point, dreading their reactions when they found out. "I'm sorry this happened to you. As to the rest, I'm not sure where this place is, but we're essentially in prison. Do you know who kidnapped you?" They shook their heads, faces darkening. "Yeah, I didn't think you knew. Faust, just so you know. The reason he yanked you out of your homes and had you thrown in here is because he's lost patience with our work. He feels we're going too slow and he's willing to ignore laws and rights. We're prisoners."

They looked at each other and then at him, confused. He took a shuddering breath and closed his eyes for a moment. Time to tell them the truth. "So, you aren't going to like this. At all. Faust gave me the treatments, injecting me against my will, and he's locked you in here with me to force the experiment along. I presume he wants you to help me figure out how to stop the degradation. It's either that, or death."

Jenn and Eve recoiled. Ephrom's eyes widened in fear.

Jenn threw her hands over her face. "Oh my god, Jason! You mean the longevity drug and the new nannies both?" Jason nodded. "When? How long do we have?" she asked.

"It's been about an hour, but he gave me a huge dose, which means I'm already feeling the effects as the nannies replicate and integrate throughout my entire system. They are speeding the chemical process of the longevity drug along rapidly as they grow in numbers."

Ephrom groaned. "What? Shit. I'm sorry, doctor. No offense, but we need to find a way to barricade ourselves in our rooms immediately. We've all seen what happened to the volunteers." He moved quickly across the room, staying away from Jason, and disappeared into the hallway behind him. Jason watched him go with a clenched jaw. He heard a door slam and furniture being moved.

Jenn and Eve hesitated, but then Jenn fled the room as well. She took the precaution of making several doors open and close, ostensibly to throw him off when he went crazy.

He arched an eyebrow at Eve.

Eve just stood there, looking at him. Finally, she walked forward, her dark face afraid. "I don't know what good it will do to hide, and I'm not sure it will matter if we even live through it, since I doubt we're going to be allowed out of here." She swallowed. "If they've gone so far as to kidnap us, they'll probably get rid of us just to ensure we don't talk." She took a deep, controlled breath. "So, I'm going to try to help you stay sane as long as I can, because it's the only way I can think of to survive. If you succeed, maybe there won't be a reason to silence us."

He looked at her a moment, feeling grateful, and nodded. "How pragmatic. Thanks, I guess. At least it's something and I don't feel like a complete leper. Eve, honestly, it might be best for you to lock yourself in a room too. I'm not sure what will happen, but it's probably going to result in my being unable to control myself. Tomorrow, I may not be able to even tell who you are, let alone stop myself from harming you."

She laughed, a high-pitched nervous laugh tinged with dark humor. "And you think we can hide? You can find us anywhere using your bio-suit to find our nannies. Before long, you'll be able to find us without the suit, as the new nannies take over your system. Even if we weren't locked in here with you, our transmission signatures from what we already have in our systems are a dead giveaway. And seriously, hide? How? You can already force us to do whatever you want, and you can sense us anywhere within a few miles, even without the new stuff. I know what the research tells us, remember? It may not be perfect, but our experiments are far enough along that we aren't going to be able to resist you if you decided to force us to come out of hiding. No, Jason, we're essentially dead no matter what we do, unless you learn to control yourself. At least I'll see it coming."

Another massive rush came over him and he flushed. She focused closely on his face. "You're already changing, you know."

Ice leapt up his spine. "What?"

She grimaced, staring at his face. "Yeah. Sorry, but you are. Small things. Your skin is tighter, for one. More youthful."

His hand went to his mouth and his eyes closed in a moment of fear. He shuddered. "Great. I'm not even aware of what the nannies are doing. I can tell they are busy, but the complexity is beyond me."

She nodded. "You're burning through a lot of calories. These physical changes don't come cheap." Her mouth formed a moue, and she put a hand to his forehead.

Her hand felt cool as it touched his skin.

"You're hot. Not just warm, but almost burning up."

She looked at him clinically. "How do you feel?"

He walked over to the couch and sat down. The main room was surprisingly archaic, with actual carpet and furniture that seemed to be made from fabrics and stuffed with material. Very unlike the slightly morphic style and materials of the modern times. "I keep feeling flushed, like I'm getting a fever, but I don't feel sick." He made an effort to really let himself feel the changes in his system. "It feels like there is some sort of automation going on with the nannies, like they are receiving instructions."

"You mean like something is broadcasting to them?" She looked around, as if she could peer through the walls to find the source.

He thought a moment. "No, not like something external is doing it. I guess it feels like I'm feeding them instructions unconsciously. Or they are pre-programmed to read my unconscious and automated systems."

"Okay, that's good. If it's internal, at least it isn't something we can't analyze or figure out. Instead, it's something we can gain control over." She walked over and, after a moment of hesitation, sat beside him, putting her hand on his shoulder. "Maybe we can guide things along at least. Avert the worst. You're going to change, but maybe you can change into something harmless and still be in control of yourself, which will buy more time."

He nodded, keenly aware of her touch. The brief touch on his shoulder sent an electric and pleasant thrill through him. He felt another rush and his body shuddered. This time, he paid attention and felt a burst of communication surge to his nannies.

"You okay? I saw that." Nervousness crept into her voice.

He realized he needed to keep talking to her, feed her information so she could help him keep perspective. "Yes, I'm fine. I felt a lot of activity for a moment. Like a surge. I can't tell if the surge is chemical or if it is nerves firing rapidly." He shook his head. "I'm feeling a bit dizzy. Not bad, just weird. I'm hungry again, too."

She bit her lip for a moment then said, "Let's get you some food." She smiled weakly. "I'm not a very good cook, so I'll have to just use the standard replication to get you something edible."

She got up and took his hand. The touch sent another wave through him, this time mildly sexual. For a moment, he admired her dark skin. Feeling even dizzier, he got up and smiled at her, letting her lead him into the dining area, where he sat, waiting for her to order something.

"It's been about an hour. We should track everything, Jason. In an hour, you've felt hungry, you've had these rushes." She hesitated. "Anything else?"

"Yeah, the confusion. Or dizziness, I guess, not really confusion. And the bursts of activity I sense in the nannies, but which I can't really define." *Oh, and by the way, now equally attracted to women as to men,* he thought. Great. He opted not to mention the change in his sexual interests just yet.

"Right. Good. So maybe with the process happening so fast, you can see a pattern."

Jason could hear in her voice that she felt dubious.

She walked over and keyed in a sequence of requests to the food replicator and dispenser, which quickly cooked up some eggs, steamed vegetables, and a protein shake. "I figure protein will be best, but you should eat some vegies too. An odd combo, but probably the most nutritious. I've added extra vitamins and minerals to the food requests to boost the nutritional usefulness." She glanced over at him. "Unless you're craving something in particular? I mean, can you tell specifically what you should eat? That would tell me what your body wants."

He thought a second. "Not really. Eggs sound fantastic. Thank you." He grinned, making an effort to reassure her. He felt her tension ease a bit.

Eve moved to the counter and a stool emerged. She perched on the stool and set the steaming food and drink in front of her.

He eyed the food hungrily.

"You know," said Eve, "I have to say, I'm a bit pissed at Jenn. Ephrom is a coward, which I already knew from when I tried to date him. He is completely scared of heights, of wind surfing, and spiders. I learned this about him all in a single date. I'd hate to think what his day must be like, since those are probably the least of his phobias. But Jenn, she's been a friend of mine for a long time, and she didn't hesitate to leave me in the room alone with you."

"Thanks," he said ruefully.

She laughed. "Hey, I'm just saying. I'm dead set on

you figuring this thing out, but she could have at least asked me to hide with her."

"Fear does funny things to people. I'm sure she already feels bad." He grinned. "Not bad enough to come back out and drag you to safety, of course."

"Yeah, seriously!" She leaned forward to put her elbow on the countertop so she could lean onto her chin, her face sexy to his changing vision. "Well, I'll be sure to take someone more dependable along next time I'm kidnapped." She slid the plate with her free hand over to him and he began scarfing it down. He saw her expression change to one of disgusted surprise.

"Could you maybe eat your food more like a person and less like, oh I dunno, a behemoth?"

He paused in the midst of shoveling another forkful into his mouth. "Ha! Yes, sure. Sorry. I didn't even realize what I was doing. Thank you." He proceeded to eat with a bit more decorum. "Yum! Excellent."

"Yeah, totally gourmet. Let me know if I can order some more pig slop for you." She put her other elbow on the counter and cradled her head in both hands, letting her hair fall forward. "Especially since I think my career as a scientist is now over. I can almost guarantee Faust will ruin me publicly, if he doesn't have me killed."

Jason didn't know what to say. The situation was a no-win for everyone.

The eggs really did taste incredible, bland as they were. His taste buds were obviously becoming more in tune with what his body needed for nutrition. The vegetables didn't taste as good, but he ate them with as much gusto.

Eve watched him as he ate, her eyes calculating. He could feel her fear, her nervousness. Her nannies were easier to read than ever. Without thinking about it, he calmed her.

Her head reared up, and her brows immediately furrowed. He realized his mistake. "I—I'm sorry." He managed to sound sheepish. "I should have asked. I just felt how uncomfortable you were, and I didn't want you to be so upset. Doing that kind of thing is second nature to a Medic."

She clenched her jaw, clearly angry. "Yes, you should have asked, Jason!" Her eyes flashed. "Look, right now all I can think about is that you might pacify me while you tear me to shreds, so please don't do anything without asking. It's key to ask permission. Anyone must say yes. I know you mean well, but you might not realize what you are doing. As long as you always ask, and I always agree, it's probably okay. Just don't go changing anything I don't explicitly agree to."

He immediately countered his previous commands to her nannies. The fear returned, overshadowed by a firm resolve.

He bowed his head. "Please accept my humble apologies."

She nodded. "Done. Need anything else?"

He yawned. "Yeah, a nap. I'm not sure if it's the process, or if I'm just worn out from being dragged out of my house and strapped to a table, but I'm kinda sleepy."

She looked at him nervously. "I'd really rather you stay awake. The process is going to continue and the more we can talk about it, the better chance we have to understand what is going on."

He nodded. "You're totally right." He yawned again, this time for a long moment.

"I'll make us some coffee."

She moved to the replicator, but he got up and motioned for her to sit. "No, really. Let me. I appreciate everything you're doing, honestly, but doing something as normal and simple as keying in coffee will help."

She shrugged and sat down.

He changed a few of the standard ordering values for the coffee, making it fairly strong. "Any additives for you? Other than a couple hundred more milligrams of caffeine?" She was clearly thinking about something else, because it took her a while to answer.

"I'll take mine black, thanks," she said finally. "And, come to think of it, throw me one of those apples."

He plucked an apple from the dish and tossed it to her.

"Eve, you know the Council is trying to get this drug perfected so they can inject themselves, right? So they can live forever. You realize they've made themselves permanent members?" He might as well tell anyone who would listen.

She bit into the fruit, her white teeth contrasting with the redness of the apple. "No, I guess I hadn't pieced it together. I know Faust is planning on using the formula as soon as it's perfected. That's obvious, but I didn't think about him being on the Council and what it meant." She took another bite. "They won't be allowed to remain if word of this gets out. The public will throw them out on their asses. They've already overdone a lot of things and pissed off much of the population."

He picked up both cups and handed her one, returning to his stool. "No, think about it. If they can control emotions to the extent they're pushing me to learn, they can subdue even their worst enemies. They can, effectively, enslave everyone around them and eliminate those who somehow evade them. It won't even matter to most people, so their takeover won't require much effort."

Eve stared at him a moment. "What about you? You could cancel them out, you know. So far, your ability to command the nano-technology and what it does is far more advanced than that of anyone else." She bit her lip. "I wasn't supposed to tell you this, but I really don't care at this point. A few of us were working on another project. Similar to yours. We have a group of young scientists with some abilities like yours. We've been trying to get them to control things the way you can. Some of them show promise, but nobody is even close to having your skill." She drank some of her coffee and finished the apple. As she set it down, the cleaning units emerged and quietly whisked it off into the reclaim receptacle. "The testing is really new, so I'm sure a few of them will do well, but for now, you're it. They need you. Badly. Faust is taking a huge gamble. If you don't figure this out, he loses everything."

Another massive rush came over him, making him feel faint. He dropped his coffee on the floor, the cup shattering. He reached over and stabilized himself on the counter.

Eve yelped. Still, she clenched her jaw resolutely and moved around the counter to help him. "Jason?"

"I'm . . ." He took a shuddering breath. "I'm okay. Just another surge in the nannite activity." He looked at her and did what he could to appear reassuring. "Sorry, I just got really dizzy when it happened. The effect is disorienting."

"No problem. It was just a little startling." She looked down at the mug. "Here, sit down. The cleaning units will take care of the spill and the broken mug. I'll get you another cup."

"Wait. I want to try something. I feel like I can sense nannies in the materials around here." He reached out and found the nannies in the broken mug. The small units that had come out to clean it hesitated, since he stood over it. Just as he'd suspected, the components in the room contained nannies too. Clever Faust. Jason had to admire the man. Faust had made sure Jason had everything at his disposal to test his abilities with his surroundings.

He scooped all the shattered pieces of the mug from the floor and set them together in a pile on the counter.

The little units removed the liquid and tiny bits of material. Jason ignored them as he concentrated on the fragments piled before him. To his surprise, the shards each contained vast amounts of information embedded in the material. The information, he now understood, told him exactly how the material should be arranged. It was like looking at a puzzle and being told which pieces went where. He didn't need to figure out how to assemble the mug, the instructions were provided to him. Following these instructions, without actually understanding them, he ordered the nannies to return the cup to its original shape based on the supplied pattern.

Eve's eyes widened as she watched the cup reassemble before her eyes. "How the hell are you doing that?"

He smiled in satisfaction as the pieces moved together, the cracks disappeared, and the cup became mostly whole, with one missing piece near the top. Jason bent down to glance under the counter. Finding the missing piece being carried off, he plucked it off the cleaning unit and set the last shard on top. It merged with the rest.

Finally, he set the reassembled mug down on the counter. "I just suddenly had a thought. Faust probably wanted to ensure I had every opportunity to learn control. He treated everything in here with nannies and I can communicate with them. And they are smart. They contain the data for each and every object they are within. Essentially, I just sent a command for them to carry the materials to their proper position and to restore the mug to its original shape. The pieces actually contained information on the original shape, so I didn't have to know anything more than how to follow those instructions. I just had to command restoration based on the supplied pattern."

Her eyes were still wide. "So, you can pretty much alter the physical objects anywhere in this apartment and have them do whatever you want?"

He thought for a moment. "Probably not. I can't tell them to do something without knowledge of what I'm doing. I mean, how could I tell the mug to turn into a glass bottle, for example? The material can't change, and I have no idea what instructions it would take to shape the bottle. So really, all I can do is repair something or, maybe, break it down. I might be able to send rudimentary instructions to make an object or treated surface move or something, but I seriously doubt I could reconstruct anything without additional information."

"Yeah, the last part is what I'm worried about." She barked a laugh. "Jenn is going to be so surprised when you don't come crashing through the door. Instead, you'll just command the door, and whatever she's managed to drag in front of it, to move out of the way."

He grimaced. "I really don't think I'll lose it. Despite feeling dizzy and weird, I have increasing clarity of my surroundings and not the slightest inclination to do anything harmful."

"Yeah, for now. It's been, what? Almost two hours?" She paused and closed her eyes. "Scratch my last comment. I have to believe you'll be fine."

He shivered from the surges he experienced and felt increasingly tired. "I think I need more coffee. I'm so tired, I can barely stand."

She nodded and got up to fetch him one.

He took the cup from her and said, "This is yet another aspect of Faust's desire for control. He probably plans on treating everything with nannies and learning to control those nannies as well as those inside people. If he's immortal, he'll have plenty of time to figure out how to do it. Eventually, he might be able to reshape everything around him." He gulped down the coffee, burning his mouth. Before he could react to the pain, he felt nannies repair the tissue, adding some set of additional changes he couldn't quite place.

Eve looked puzzled. "How in the hell would he be able to remember anything so complex? I mean, just changing the structure of one object would require a huge amount of memory, and the human brain, as complex as it is, can't possibly retain any useful amount of necessary information."

Jason thought about it, feeling more acutely aware of his intelligence. "He could probably augment his own mental abilities. I mean, we have the technology already and we enhance ourselves all the time. I'm capable of an enormous amount of data analysis and retention that is beyond my baseline organic mind. Greater augmentation is just a few steps further."

Eve gasped. "The Techs! It's the same technology they use to integrate."

Jason shook his head. "I don't think so. It takes some inborn ability, some incredibly rare trait for them to be integrated. I guess, given enough time, he could figure out what characteristics they have that make them so unique, but it's more of a reach to control the emotions of humans. Realistically, this process we're experimenting with boils down to the chemical and electrical modification of the human system. Those things are complex in and of themselves, but simple compared to reading all the vast data like a Tech and being able to comprehend and control it all. We haven't even solved how to work with our bodies and keep them under control. Expanding that to all matter will take ages. It's taking us a vast amount of resources and a lot of luck to get rudimentary control."

"But what if he controls one of them to jump ahead? What then?"

"A Tech? How? They are completely beyond us to the point they're almost another species. One of them shut me down with a simple thought. The moment Faust even tried, he'd be cut off from his own communications. I bet they could even reverse the immortality nannies by simply cancelling them out so they couldn't complete repairs or work within the system. After all, they communicate with various electrical and chemical frequencies. Even with radio signals. The communication standards are part of how they function. Theirs is an absurdly complex total network nearly down to the molecule. The Techs are tapped into everything and would be aware of the changes long before Faust could issue the commands. He couldn't even catch one off guard."

"Yeah, but does he have to? If he has the power of the Council behind him, can't he just order them to do what he wants?"

Jason thought about this before he replied. "I just don't think they work in the way you describe. Look, nobody really knows this, but I've been close to one of them several times and I've learned a lot about them. At first, it occurred to me they might be vulnerable in some way, but the more I've been near the sector Tech here, Sector Seven, the more I realize I'm so completely pathetic in comparison, it's almost laughable." He suddenly felt a wave of grief wash over him as he realized he had become infatuated with Tarien and his infatuation was like a teenager having a crush on a movie star. There would never be a chance to get close to him. Depression hit him with the kind of strength that caused a warning bell to go off in his head. This wasn't normal. He issued commands to override the sadness. In moments, he felt fine. Normal again.

The process must have been visible to Eve, who watched him with concern. "Jason?"

"Yeah, wow. I just thought about something and suddenly got really sad. A lot of emotion all at once. Not normal for me, but I figured out how to cancel it."

She sipped her coffee, her eyes hopeful. "Well, that's a good sign, right? If you can cancel things out, maybe you can keep yourself under control."

He took another gulp of his scalding hot coffee. This

time, the liquid didn't burn his mouth. He set the cup down. "So, apparently, my body adapted to heat to the point I can't burn my mouth anymore."

"Huh?"

He quickly explained.

"Changes like that are to be expected, right? I mean, sure, it's really fast, but pretty much in line with what our previous experiments have shown."

"Yeah, really fast." Jason was so tired, he could barely concentrate. He needed sleep badly. "And the caffeine doesn't seem to be doing anything. I'm really trying, Eve, but I'm so tired I don't know if I can possibly stay awake."

"Got it. You're probably breaking down the caffeine before it can do any good. So maybe we have to let you sleep. Um . . ." She tapped her finger on her lips. "Let's do this. I'll put a bed in your room and stay up for a while and watch you sleep. If anything looks weird, I'll wake you." She paused. "Gently, of course. I don't want you wildly swinging at me and taking my head off."

He smiled tiredly. "Thank you." They left the mugs on the counter so the units could take care of them.

Another rush went through him. The urgency of sleep became almost an imperative. "Another of those instructional bursts," he said, making sure to keep her informed.

She turned her head slightly and nodded as they walked down the hall to one of the bedrooms.

He washed his face and swished his teeth clean while Eve piled blankets and pillows from an adjacent room onto his floor. He looked at her quizzically and she explained. "I'm not dragging a whole bed in here, and I'm certainly not sleeping next to you, no offense. A bed on the floor is easiest."

"Well, at least let me sleep on the floor." Before she could protest, he said, "No, really. I doubt I'll even notice."

"Sounds okay to me. I love a good bed. As long as you don't hold it against me," she joked.

"Wake me up if I oversleep. I don't know how long I'll be out, so a good eight hours should be plenty." He lay down on the blankets.

"Uh, your suit? I mean, I guess you can keep it on, but it's probably going to be uncomfortable."

He nodded sleepily and unzipped it, yanking it off, catching her expression of amazement.

Eve stared a moment. "Well, either you're living at the gym or those things are really at work." She turned away but not before he saw her blush.

He registered only vague awareness of her embarrassment at his nudity, too tired to care. He fell asleep the moment his head rested on the pillow.

THIRTEEN

THROUGHOUT THE NIGHT, JASON felt waves of hormones coursing through his body, causing emotions ranging from deep sadness to elation. His dreams ranged from nightmares of being hunted and slaughtered to dreams of power. Despite the realism of his dreams, he retained an awareness of dreaming. He both experienced the dream and acted as an analytical outsider, processing each scene. Although aware he was dreaming, he had no control over the scenarios playing out behind his closed eyes.

In one dream, Faust kidnapped him. Instead of the old, moderately decrepit Director, Faust had become young. With a laugh, Faust had Jason cut into pieces and, unable to die, Jason endured the pain like nothing he'd ever imagined. Jason's body repaired itself and Faust laughed as he repeated the torment over and over.

In another dream, he had become the epitome of masculine beauty, standing above a crowd of worshipful faces and lifting off an elevated throne and flying over the multitude of people. He felt absolute and corruptive power. Merely glancing at buildings caused them to crumble and fall, and he could command anyone to do his bidding. In his dream, he laughed at his complete control while at the same time feeling an empty hollowness, a horror at the monster he'd become.

Another dream became so highly erotic, even his detached mind could barely discern it wasn't reality. Every kiss, touch, and feeling felt as if someone had climbed into bed with him. He writhed in his blankets and ejaculated into his sheets.

He awoke with an embarrassed start.

Self-conscious because Eve slept in the bed next to him, he quietly got up and pulled the soiled sheets from his bed on the floor. Mortified over his teenage-like bodily responses, he quietly sighed in relief at the sound of her steady breathing. *So much for staying awake to observe me*, he thought.

Jason could see the details of the room with unusual clarity. His eyes had been enhanced while he slept. Not wanting to wake Eve, he tiptoed out of his bedroom and down the long hall to the laundry room, where he pulled another set of sheets out of the closet. With some amusement, he noted the closed doors that Ephrom and Jenn were hiding behind. He put his soiled sheets into the automated laundry unit. It would clean and fold the sheets and return them to where they could be used again.

He went back and put the fresh sheets on his bed, then crept back out to use the shower. The bathrooms were large, with multiple mirrors and full bathtubs, along with showering spaces. Each shower was large enough for two and had a double set of nozzles. The shower felt wonderful and the memory of his dream made it erotic. He remained too turned on to return to his room, so he took care of things in the shower.

Still feeling tired and frustrated, he decided to go back to the shared room. He quietly climbed back into bed, settled into his blankets, and fell fast asleep.

The dreams continued, and he awoke several times in a cold sweat. Waves of uncomfortable feelings coursed through him as his body made changes he couldn't quite follow, and he tossed and turned restlessly.

When he woke again, Eve sat on the edge of the bed, watching him.

Jason did a quick self-analysis and then, seeking to reassure Eve, he said, "I'm good. Not feeling murderous or in any way violent." He felt a pang of affection for her bravery in the face of his potential madness. "As a matter of fact, I feel phenomenal." He stretched languidly, his body still excited. With some surprise, he noted that he felt absolutely no tiredness from his release earlier, another sign his body had adapted. This constant arousal could become a problem. Apparently, he had both the libido and staying power of a teenager. "Uh, so how long did I sleep?"

She stared at him with a curious look on her face.

"Uh, Eve? You okay?"

She watched him another long moment, making him fear something might be wrong. He didn't feel anything was wrong.

Finally, she spoke. "I think you'd better go look in the mirror."

Panicked, he jumped out of bed and darted to the bathroom. When he reached the mirror, he gasped. He'd become gorgeous overnight. Not just handsome, but stunning. He'd always been rather average. Maybe a little more than average, but he had always wished to be one of the good-looking guys he envied. Clearly, his body reacted to Jason's desire to be beautiful and his new nannies had modified his physical appearance accordingly.

He'd grown slightly taller, too, though he wasn't quite sure how much. Maybe two inches. His face had lost all traces of aging and looked almost as if he had been airbrushed. He leaned forward, putting his face close to the mirror. His skin appeared flawless and he had the bone structure of a male model. After staring at his reflection for a while, he drew back and looked at his body. His musculature had changed, too.

He'd always been an athletic guy, but now his appearance was idealized. While not overly large, the muscles of his shoulders, chest, and arms were shaped to perfection and the small amount of chest hair had disappeared, leaving him completely smooth. His arms were still covered in fine hair, which had grown soft, and he still had some slight stubble on his face, but both his upper arms and the rest of his body were without hair. His leg hair, too, had grown finer, silkier. A curious change, since he'd never minded his body hair. Actually, he preferred a little hair on some of the men he'd mooned after. Why this change?

His obvious preference for more endowed men had translated to drastic and absurd changes. His penis had grown significantly, hanging so low he now wondered if the organ was even functional. Physiologically, male organs of any great size were typically incapable of erection. Considering how massive his penis had become, possibly he would be unable to perform. Of course, it might also be that any future partners could not physically accommodate him.

The moment he observed himself and his thoughts started to turn toward sexual excitement, he began to get hard again. The sound of Eve behind him made him clamp down on these thoughts immediately and, surprisingly, he had more direct control over his erections than he would have thought possible. Not quite "on and off", but capable of shutting things down.

Embarrassed by his massive organ, he avoided turning around. "Wow. So, I guess some self-control is lost during sleep."

"Yeah, obviously. I know you said you were fine, and you seem like that might still be the case, but are you really? I mean, Jason, you look completely different. Would you really know if you had changed in other ways?" As one of the original staff on the project, along with Jenn and Ephrom, she knew all about the failed experiments and what had led the test subjects to kill each other and themselves.

She echoed a fear he had. *Would he?* This worried him.

He realized he could sense a complex set of emotions flitting through her, some of which were fear and wariness. His ability to sense her every emotion, almost her thoughts, had sharpened. She admired his butt and Jason blushed. He grabbed a towel and wrapped it around his waist in a ludicrous attempt to conceal his male anatomy.

Keeping his back partially to her, he strode over to his bed and picked up his suit.

"I really think I'd know if anything else had changed. I mean, I am stunned by the changes too, and I don't know what to say. I had a lot of dreams last night, so maybe they had something to do with it—a kind of visualization made real." He tried to sense his body to read the changes. To his surprise, he actually got small glimpses of the instructions the nannies were using to make the changes. More progress toward direct communication so he could consciously control the changes.

"What kind of dreams?"

He tried to struggle into his suit but realized he wouldn't be able to tuck his penis in easily. It would clearly bulge absurdly no matter how he positioned it. For once, he wished for baggy clothes and not the skin-tight suit. His fetish over size started to irritate him. Still, he had no other choice but to tuck it in as best he could. The suit would stretch, but the enormous equipment would be obvious. "Well, just a lot of random dreams, some of which were of me being really good looking."

"Okay." She waited, and when he didn't explain further, she said, "Look, I know this will sound paranoid, but did you get up last night? The laundry indicated it had completed and I wasn't sure if our other residents snuck out last night."

Realizing he'd better tell her everything to keep her from being afraid, he reluctantly explained. She sensed his embarrassment and gave his midsection a couple of glances with clinical detachment. Finally, she nodded. "It makes sense, Jason. Your body is changing to the point to where you are, effectively, at the height of your health. Sexual function is one of the things directly related to health, so it's natural to have this reaction. Same thing you'd have issues with when you were a teenager." She smiled wryly. "And it seems you are a size queen, since your body is accommodating your desire for larger genitalia."

He smiled. "Yeah, well as a teenager I couldn't control how my . . . uh, body parts grew or changed. This is worse, unfortunately. I feel no fatigue and, even now, most of my thoughts are erotic. It's going to mean a sharply divided attention span, unless I can get it under control."

"We had the same issues with our test subjects, remember? Before they . . ." she trailed off.

"Yeah, I remember. They changed to become physically attractive before they got all weird. The first stage, it seems." He couldn't help but look her over and he registered a mild shock at his desire for her. Far worse than the day before. Having always been a gay man, it was strange to be so strongly attracted to a woman. This overflow of hormones distracted him too much, so he sternly cancelled his desires. Not entirely, but his conscious control seemed to help.

"I'm really hungry again. I could go for some breakfast."

"You slept for ten hours."

"Ten hours? Really? Wow. How long have you been awake?"

She seemed to loosen up. "About an hour and a half. I wanted to check to see if the others had been out, just in case they got it in their mind to sneak out and try to harm us preemptively. There's no sign they've left their rooms, but they don't have food in there, so they'll have to come out at some point."

He nodded and led her to the dining area. Jason keyed in simple things, but in large quantities for himself. They ate in silence, Eve staring at him throughout the meal, her gaze disconcerting since he could read her emotions like an open book now. He knew she held her fear in check. He knew she wanted to leave. Jason sensed her attraction, too.

He found himself studying her, noting her athleticism and catching himself fantasizing about her. She scowled at him when she noticed he had started looking her over, quickly surmising the thoughts going through his brain. "Don't even think about it. You'd try to sleep with a goat right now. Pay attention to what else is going on with your body. Can you get specifics about the changes? Think you could, for example, willfully change something? Like making your fingernails grow?"

Her lips were full, and the curve of her breast had him breathing hard, but he listened to what she said. Fighting his desires had become increasingly hard. He could control some of his body with his thoughts, but if his thoughts began to betray him . . . "I'm not sure. I'll try. Focusing on anything right now is rough." He tried to think about his fingernails. Instead, thoughts of her manicured hands flickered through his head. Her hands caressing his body. He gritted his teeth and stared at his fingers, refusing to allow himself to fall into that line of thought.

He thought of his nails growing, getting longer, but he could only send a vague command, just an order they should be longer without any details or specifics. He wasn't sure how long it should take, but nothing seemed to be happening and, after a moment, he thought of his fingers sliding down her buttocks, her thighs, putting them inside her. Having lost control of his thoughts, his erection strained against the fabric of his suit. Only because he sat on the opposite side of the counter could he hide this fact from her.

He threw his hands over his head. "This is ridiculous! I'm sorry, but I need to go do something about my uncontrolled libido or I won't be able to function."

She gave him an exasperated look. She finished her food and the units took it away. "Really, Jason? You can't even control your hormones?"

"I'm trying! But it's no use. Everything I see and anything we talk about is turning me on. I'm sorry, but when you mentioned a goat a minute ago, I actually had a thought—" He cut off his words. "Anyway, the best cure for this is usually to go take care of it. Then I can focus on other things more easily."

He could sense her annoyance, her frustration at being helpless to figure out a way to stop the changes. "Oh geez. Fine, little boy. Go play with your new oversized toy and hurry back. I'm going to take a quick shower." She stabbed a finger at him. "Don't even THINK about it. I'm not going to bother to lock the bathroom door, but if you even consider trying to get in there with me, I'll rip your absurd boy parts off and throw them in the garbage disposal."

"Tell me more. Garbage disposals are so hot." He grinned. "Just kidding. I won't try to get in there with you . . . unless you offer, of course. Hey, I'm just saying—"

She stormed out of the room.

He grimaced, then got up with some discomfort. At least he knew the size of it wasn't limiting his ability to use it. A bit crazed, he ran to his bathroom and tore off his suit, pulling the monstrous thing out and quickly finding release. The feeling was incredible, better than anything his normal body had been able to experience. He threw his head back and a wave of pleasure brought him to his knees. His muscles tensed, and he stared in the bathroom mirror, enthralled with the eroticism of his own reflection. Beautiful and foreign, like seeing someone else through a window. He ran his hands over his skin, stunned. It felt like silk. So soft.

With a groan, he realized he wasn't sated. Still turned on, he stayed on his knees and kneeled back and let the full length and weight of his organ thrust forward. Now more sensitive, each small touch felt more incredible. Taking his time, enjoying it more, he found release a second time. Without realizing he was losing control, he also lost track of time. Insisting to himself that he needed to be sated so he could concentrate, he allowed himself to continue far beyond what was normal. He wasn't getting tired. This should have alarmed him, but the reward centers clouded his thinking.

He wasn't sure how long he kneeled there, letting himself go, forgetting himself, having orgasm after orgasm, vaguely realizing he wasn't going to tire. He felt thirsty, hungry, but his muscles still felt no strain, and the desire was too overpowering to ignore. His body wanted more. The mindlessness of release became a compulsion almost too strong for him to resist.

With a frustrated yell, trying to break the cycle he knew he'd fallen into, he got up. He'd made a huge mess.

He spent some time cleaning everything up, emptying a roll of toilet paper and flushing the remains down the toilet. He then drank a bunch of water and jumped in the shower to rinse off the sweat from his marathon exertions.

The second he stepped into the water, without thinking about it, he found release again. And again. And again. Mindlessly thrashing his head back and forth as he climaxed repeatedly, his orgasms grew stronger, more all-encompassing, as his brain rewired for more reward and his nerves allowed for more sensation. He forgot his surroundings, forgot the dangers of being enslaved to the feeling.

Finally, he became aware of someone banging on the door, yelling at him. He detected Eve and her concern through the door.

"I'm getting out. Just a second. Sorry, I lost track of time."

"Yeah! Like an hour! Just do it already and get out here! Jesus, you'd think it would take you like five minutes." With exasperation in her voice, she said, "I'll replicate you some more food, since you're eating like a horse. Maybe some tea or coffee. Just get out here so we can work on this. It's making me anxious."

He mumbled something and she left. With herculean effort, and every ounce of his willpower, he shut down his desire. Resisting his urge felt like moving a boulder, but he finally managed to focus his thoughts on something else. Mainly food. His hunger could be used to negate his lust. The need for nutrition overrode his desire to remain in the bathroom. He noted that he now craved specific vitamins and minerals that had been depleted.

Realizing he also had to pee, he finally stepped out of the shower, avoiding looking at the mirror. Thinking more clearly, he understood what had just happened. This loss of control frightened him. He thought of the test subjects and he feared he had begun slipping. They had probably fought to control themselves, too. A whole team was there to help them along the way, and those who'd been subjects had still lost the battle.

After he dressed, Jason padded down the hall to the kitchen. Eve practically threw a plate of food at him. He forced himself to eat slowly.

"Some teenager. That ridiculous thing of yours seems to have lost function."

Trying not to talk about it, since he feared it would trigger lustful thoughts again, he just nodded dumbly.

"What's with all the food?" she asked. "Do you know? I mean, specifically. Obviously, you are burning through energy quickly with all the changes. Can you tell what and how your system is converting? Where it's going? Can you specifically direct any of it?'

He felt surprise at this line of questioning. "I guess I don't know. I hadn't really thought about it."

"You should be analyzing everything you can. Not just playing with your—you know. The more specific your knowledge, the better chances you have at controlling your changes. We know you ARE hungry, but what exactly is the energy going toward? You've grown slightly taller and changed physically in other ways. Is that all?"

With a dark warning glance at the reference to his male anatomy, he settled back into his chair and thought about his food, about his stomach and his organs. Surprisingly, he got useful feedback from his nannies. It wasn't specific, like the name of specific chemicals or the exact process, but the information did tell him quite a lot.

He learned his limitations were due to a lack of specific scientific data. If he had encyclopedic knowledge of chemistry and biology, he would then be able to specifically control every molecule in his body without harming himself. As it stood, he simply didn't know enough to do anything useful. The information was there, but he didn't understand it. He expressed as much to Eve."It's so complicated. I can, for example, get the molecular makeup of various things, but I don't know what the molecules are."

She nodded. "Okay, so even incomplete, this knowledge is great! I mean, probably there is a way to use a computer to reference things. Eventually, with enough study, you would gain sufficient understanding to be able to control your own chemistry."

Jason suddenly noticed his fingernails. They were longer—quite a bit longer. He held them up for Eve to see. "Wow! It worked. I ordered my nails to grow and they did."

She looked at his hands. "When? Do you know how?"

He didn't. He'd been so busy in the bathroom that all

thought had disappeared. Even now, he shied away from thinking about it.

"I'm sorry, Eve. I don't know."

"Well, no big deal. Try something else. Try making them shrink." She glanced down at his waist. "Try making your junk shrink, while you're at it. Seriously, Jason. You look worse than some Tom of Finland drawing. No offense, since you obviously have a fetish for size, but it's obnoxious."

He groaned. "Stop talking about it! It's not any better. I spent the whole time in there having repeated . . . well, you know. And it didn't wear out at all! If I don't stop thinking about it, I'll just go back in there."

He could tell she was trying not to laugh. "Wow, that's a problem most guys would kill for. I'll not mention it." She grinned. "Baseball, pain, whatever it takes. Think of stuff you hate or are bored by."

He shuddered and nodded. "Baseball, right. I fucking hate baseball. It's the most boring sport on the planet." He thought of his fingernails shrinking, again trying to order them smaller, but nothing happened. "I'm trying to make my fingernails smaller." Then, after a moment of staring and hoping, he decided to wait. "Seems to be automated after I issue the command. I forget about it and some background process in my brain must take care of the instructions. I guess we'll see if it works and how long it takes."

They spent the next several hours trying to change things about him. His skin color, his eye color, even breaking objects and having him analyze how he managed to put them back together. He stared at a salt shaker for over an hour, trying to memorize everything about it, all the information his nannies could process. His nails never shrank. His eyes remained the same brown color. His skin stayed deeply tanned. He almost screamed in frustration before he realized screaming might be a lack of emotional control, which could be a risk. Not to mention it would scare Eve half to death.

He did, however, have success with the salt shaker experiment. He ordered the pepper shaker to be exactly the same as the salt shaker, which had a similar shape, but was different enough to be visibly changed. He also learned the nannies had modified the material as they nested into it, changing it to a kind of static fluid, capable of rearranging easily. This property had been built into their base instructions.

Throughout all of this, he kept having to fight a battle with his libido, which distracted him constantly. He found everything erotic and only through tight control could he suppress it enough to focus. The reminder about the previous test subjects who had died due to issues with hormonal control kept him from obsessive masturbation.

Eve stayed with him most of the time, only allowing small bathroom breaks for each of them. He carefully avoided looking at the mirror or at himself in any way. He'd become completely narcissistic in this regard and fought it desperately. She fed him often, but his appetite seemed to have slowed to normal, as if his changes were halting or, at least, slowing. He still consumed extra nutrients with his food, some of which he sensed his body handled so they were non-toxic to him in larger amounts.

She commented on his good communication, noting to her apparent relief he hadn't really changed much after his previous night's transformation.

She played some games with him, testing his mental acuity. The spent a lot of the late afternoon in the lab. She ran him through a series of physical tests, pushing him. Some of the cardio tests would have been dangerous, considering how much his heart rate increased, but she didn't seem worried. He had become, according to their previous testing, virtually immune to harm. With his permission, she burned and cut him. He had to practically force her to break his fingers, but he insisted they try it. The wounds healed rapidly, the cuts repairing so quickly barely any blood welled out. After seeing this, she was willing to snap the bones in two fingers at his insistence. The breaks to his fingers were knitted within minutes. He hardly felt the pain.

"So, theoretically, you could be incapacitated briefly, since the bones take some time to recombine. A massive blow, maybe with a vehicle, would cripple you for a few minutes, possibly even half an hour. It would be enough time to, say, burn you or dissolve you in acid."

Holy cow! he thought. *She doesn't shy away from anything.* "Wow, such a pleasant thought."

"Sorry, I am just glad to learn Faust could be destroyed.

If things progress and you give him what he needs, he's going to inject himself at the earliest opportunity."

"Yeah, I know. It's just rough knowing you are thinking of ways you could destroy me."

"Morbid, true, but useful. Besides, consider it a form of self-preservation. This whole experiment, Faust locking us in here to observe everything, is designed to either figure out the solution to the serious issues or have us all die. I'm looking at ways to destroy you if you turn into a monster. Better, I'm hoping there's a way to kill that fucker, Faust, if he succeeds. You should understand why."

"You're right. I'm glad you're here and glad you are thinking things through." He smiled his most tender smile, gazing into her eyes.

She shuddered and turned away. He could feel a deep physical desire course through her, and then anger. He felt bad, but as she turned away, his eyes immediately fell to stare at her butt.

"It's getting late, Jason. I'm really tired, so we should probably call it a night." For a second he hoped she'd ask him to sleep with her. "Are you tired at all?"

Yes, he definitely felt tired. "Yeah, another useful thing to know. Sleep is required." He thought about it. "Although I think I could stave it off if I had to."

"Good. Noted. If we must, we could destroy you in your sleep if you weren't aware of the danger. Just conk out and I'll wake you again if you don't get up after a reasonable amount of sleep."

He nodded and readied for bed. Despite all the exercising he'd done all day, his body wasn't physically tired. It was his mind that required the rest period.

Like the night before, he fell asleep quickly after he climbed into his pile of blankets.

The dreams started immediately. He dreamed a similar broad spectrum of dreams, some so horrible he cried in his sleep. In his detached awareness, he knew his body continued improving healing and recovery processes. He could sense the instructions. Another thing that happened in his dreams was that he changed his physical features easily.

He had repeated wet dreams again. He only woke after his sheets and blankets were completely soaked. For a moment, he gaped at the outrageous volume of ejaculate, his fluid loss so extreme that he needed water badly.

Getting up, he drank and drank from the faucet. For a moment he wondered if he should worry about hyponatremia from so much water in so short a time. *Oh right*, he thought, *my enhanced body won't allow it.* He went to the kitchen to get some salty foods to have the right balance. He ate a quick meal and then got clean bedding out of the hall supply of laundry and threw his current soiled set into the machines so he'd continually have a clean set. It looked like he might need new linen often.

Thoughts of Eve made him wonder about getting in bed with her. He knew he could make her want him. He gritted his teeth, disgusted with himself for having these thoughts. The word *rape* gonged in his head like some huge warning bell.

He threw his bedding down, not caring if he woke her, and went to the other room and got in the shower to wash himself off.

The shower turned out to be a mistake. The moment he stepped into the spray of water, he once again fell to masturbating and couldn't stop. It wasn't satisfying enough. He knew he had lost control, but the reward system was overpowering.

He needed something more than standard masturbation. He knew if he got out of the shower in this condition, he'd force himself on Eve no matter how wrong. With some despair, he realized he'd become too enslaved to the pleasure, which his body had increased as it adapted. He couldn't stop. *This is how the volunteers died. They lost control. It's too overpowering!* Again and again he came. His orgasms had grown so strong, he thrashed on the floor of the shower, his head tossing back and forth.

He completely lost all sense of himself for long periods of time. He could feel the muscles specifically and had direct control over them as they thundered deep in his lower abdomen. He flooded his own mind with overpowering pleasure for what felt like an eternity. His body kept running a feedback loop, enticing him to do more. The danger of addiction had become a reality, his need too great. *Dying like this is good. It will keep others safe and is the most pleasurable way to die.*

His thirst grew again as he emptied his reproductive organs repeatedly, and a deep need for specific foods arose. Gulping water, he kept at it, thoughts of the kitchen intruding on his mindless abandon.

At first, he thought he'd gone crazy, distantly aware the pleasure had perhaps driven him to hallucinating about his desire to get food. But, eventually, through the haze of his clouded thoughts, he realized he heard someone down the hall in the dining and cooking area of the apartment. There was a quick sound of dishes clattering and an exclamation. Like the enhancement of his eyes, his hearing had also grown acute. He picked up the faint sounds, which should have been impossible at this distance and with the many walls in the way.

The sound broke him out of his pattern and the practically fell out of the shower. He badly wanted more than just masturbation. How long had he been in here? Hours? Grabbing a towel, he wrapped himself and quickly strode down the hallway, knowing if he could talk to Eve while she got something to snack on, he'd be fine. She'd help him, talk him through it. Already, he could clamp down enough to keep himself from turning around and going back to his shower play. The distraction had helped him reassert some control. He shouldn't be alone.

When he reached the kitchen, a blond woman whirled to face him. Jenn clutched as much food as her arms could carry, trying to quickly grab what she could and run back to the safety of her room. As she spun around, she gasped.

It wasn't Eve. He needed Eve. She could help him. His thinking had grown too clouded. He was aware enough to understand this. He should just turn around and wake her. Call to her.

Jenn gaped at him, which startled him, and he lost control of his desires for a moment. He smiled at her, calming her as her fear spiked, mingled with disbelief and attraction. The attraction gratified him, and he moved toward her, letting her see him fully. He languidly flexed his muscles, grinning at her as her eyes took in the mass pushing the towel forward. Her breathing quickened, stark terror radiating out from her and paralyzing her. Her eyes began tearing up in fright.

He shook his head in confusion, but his thoughts were dominated by an unnatural need. *Eve! I need help!* He couldn't make his voice work. He didn't want Jenn to be afraid, he only wanted her to love him. To help him feel safe, secure. As he thought about it, he felt her nannies obey him and she became calm, content. *Yes. Calm. Much better*, he thought. It's not like he would hurt her. He would just calm her until Eve could get here.

He stepped toward her, touching her hair and staring into her eyes. She looked at him dreamily, her hands clutching the food she'd pilfered. He carefully took the food from her hands and set each item down on the counter, letting his towel fall to the floor.

He let his concern for her flow over him, through him, to her. His sexual energy broadcast to her, and her eyes ran over his body. He sensed desire sweeping powerfully through her. She whimpered.

He overwhelmed her fear and attempts to escape his power and triggered lust in her.

Her lips parted. She reached for him.

He smiled a purposefully sexy smile and undressed her, continuing to override her desire to flee. He smashed her fears down with the force of his will and built up her desire, fine-tuning it. He sent powerful hormones through her body, causing her to reach orgasm even before he touched her. She moaned, but he could tell she wanted to scream for help. He instructed her nannies to match his own, to extend her innate female ability to experience pleasure multiple times.

Her nannies rushed to obey, and he let his lips find their way to her every erogenous zone. More powerful waves coursed through her, making her orgasm again. He brushed his lips down her jaw, her neck. Jason discarded her body's need for rest. He'd almost felt her pleasure for himself. The feedback grew stronger and he processed it. She didn't possess advanced nanotechnology by comparison, so she couldn't keep up with his demands. He had far, far more advanced nanotechnology. Still, he forced her nannies to do what they could, attempting to get them to go beyond their ability. *Perhaps I can replicate my newly enhanced nannies in her*, he thought.

Needing release, he pushed into her, pinning her to the counter. But his sexual organ was too huge. It had grown so large that all the surrounding muscles and tendons had rearranged in order to suspend it properly, becoming larger than his arm and reminiscent of something on a demon. *An incubus,* he thought, laughing. It would have been horribly painful for her if he'd allowed her to feel pain. Instead, he overrode her pain through his control, thrusting into her. He gave her pleasure beyond what she'd ever been capable of. His release was so powerful, he let out an animalistic cry.

He didn't consciously recognize her bleeding, her torn body from his assault. Something deep inside him, however, watched in horror, but was suppressed by his growing animalistic nature *Eve! Please. Help me!*

Again, he rocked into Jenn, forcing her as she thrashed beneath him, stretched so far he'd damaged her. A basic part of his mind knew he'd torn her up inside. He couldn't fit, so he forced his way in. She wanted to scream, he could sense it.

He upped the frequency of her pleasure, demanding she stay in a state of orgasm from which he would not allow her to escape. Surely, this would cancel her fear of him. His own pleasure echoed with hers and he climaxed again and again, timing his release with the rising and falling tide of her falsely induced state of bliss. A blurring occurred, and he almost felt he WAS her, experiencing an overwhelming sense of terror and pleasure burning through her system. He grew aware of a terrible fiery pain in her loins, which falsely translated to pleasure. He also felt large tearing deep inside her body, destruction with each thrust. She thrashed beneath him, unable to escape from her enforced ecstasy. Dying.

Deep down, he recognized something was horribly wrong, but he lost all sense of himself, drifting mindlessly in his own desires. He'd forgotten the name he should be shouting for help. His body continued to supply him with boundless energy. His new mass of muscles tensed with pleasure, rippling grotesquely beneath his perfect skin, as he scooped her up against him like a rag doll, cracking her ribs, puncturing her lungs with inhuman strength. With another violent thrust, he threw her back against the counter, pushed against her arm with his hand, wrenching her shoulder out of socket with unconstrained physical force. Her head struck the counter and cracked. He threw back his head and roared. "Again! Again!"

He heard someone screaming behind him.

He didn't care. The feelings were so incredible, so unending. He felt a powerful blow to his torso. He ignored it. An odd inconvenience, nothing more, mingling with pleasure so incredible he couldn't think. His body healed the tearing of his flesh the moment it occurred. He came again, groaning.

Again, something struck him. Again, he ignored it. Blood flowed from Jenn in large amounts. Her lungs were gurgling as she struggled desperately to breathe. He could feel parts of her mind burning out, unable to handle the forced activity as she flailed weakly under his control.

Then a massive blow to the head knocked him to the floor, away from Jenn. A second blow followed, crushing part of his skull. Jason nearly lost consciousness, his mind wondering what had caused his pleasure to be cut short. The blow had blinded him in his right eye. He started to stand, and a third blow knocked him nearly unconscious. He took another blow to his skull, and his assailant stopped, apparently thinking they'd incapacitated him. Jason had a peripheral awareness he had been prevented from fulfilling his needs by an attacker. He cared nothing for the fight, only that he should be able to resume his pleasure. He'd have to destroy the assailant, so he could continue to satiate himself.

Moments later, he slowly became aware of hysterical screaming, of frantic yelling. He rolled over, his heightened sense of smell detecting blood in large amounts. Vision returned to his eye as he healed.

Before the iron skillet could land another blow to his head, he rolled out of the way and into a crouch before his opponent. He heard himself snarl.

Jason experienced a strange double-vision and a wave of dizziness, which nearly made him crumple, but he reached out and balanced himself with his right arm on the counter. Ephrom started forward to strike Jason again, but stopped when he saw Jason wasn't going down.

Clearly terrified, Ephrom openly wept as his knuckles clutched the iron pan desperately. His hesitation proved to be enough for Jason to recover, his body healing rapidly.

Jason remembered something. He had other abilities he could use to fight, not just his ability to heal. Without thinking about the situation, Jason stood and smiled insolently, seizing control of Ephrom's nannies, sending a mental blow his way. Ephrom reeled and dropped the pan, clutching his head and staggering backward with a cry of defiance. Jason barely noticed Jenn, eyes staring at nothing as she lay broken and battered on the counter. Her mouth kept forming the same nonsense word over and over. "Nuh. Nuh. Nuh." Tears were leaking from her eyes, but she didn't move.

Jason strode toward Ephrom. Through Ephrom's senses, he could tell he appeared monstrous, his torso bloody and mixed with semen that had dried on his thighs and legs. Jason could see as Ephrom saw, hear through his ears. He could control Ephrom's senses.

Ephrom made a valiant effort to recover and grabbed a knife from a block in the recreational cooking area of the kitchen, grabbing the pan from the floor as well. Jason didn't bother subduing him or preventing him, relishing the thought of a fight. He could have easily prevented Ephrom from obtaining either weapon. He grew excited about the threat of violence. He laughed, throwing back his head and reveling in the sound of his own rich voice. Deep in his mind he recognized the laugh of a madman, but it only made him laugh louder.

He walked straight toward Ephrom, wincing slightly as the knife slashed him across his right arm and chest. A thrill went through him. The wounds closed immediately. Ephrom slashed him again and struck him as hard as he could with the pan. Jason began to giggle. *So weak.* With little effort he took both weapons away from Ephrom and threw them on the floor.

He seized Ephrom by the throat and held him in the air, legs dangling. With a grin, he threw the man across the room into the wall. Ephrom's breath exploded from him as he hit the wall, and the sound made Jason shudder with the thought of more fighting.

Behind him, he felt Eve rushing down the hallway. She entered the kitchen with a cry, running to Jenn.

"Nuh. Nuh. Nuh," Jenn babbled, trying to make words to ask for help.

He felt Eve's horror. "Jason! Oh my god! Jason, what are you doing?"

He laughed again, tears streaming down his face. Oh, this was incredible! *Doing? I'm learning what it means to be more than human!* Moving forward, he picked Ephrom up from where he'd tossed him. Face bloodied from his head striking the wall, Ephrom stared at him in horror and his nannies were screaming fear. Jason smiled at him as he changed Ephrom's emotions from fear to those of worship. Ephrom froze, staring at Jason with a look of wonder. Jason smiled and Ephrom sighed longingly, still having trouble breathing as he dangled from Jason's extended arm.

Eve refused to give up, to hide. "Jason, stop! Stop it! You've lost control!"

Lost control? He shook his head, but he had such clarity of thought, like nothing he'd ever experienced. Eve must be confused. His control continued to grow, not fade. Control wasn't something he'd lost.

"We're just playing! Eve, It's amazing. I can do so much. I know how to control things much more effectively. Watch!"

With a gesture, Jason changed the chemical composition of the wall to form tentacles which writhed and wrapped over Ephrom's wrists.

Eve can't see how clear things are now, he thought. He'd become so superior, she couldn't conceive of his changes. Powerful, and in control of everyone around him. His every thought a cocktail of sex and strength—and his mind continued refining his control more with each moment.

"Jason, you're hurting him! Let him go! And Jenn . . . oh my god! Jason, she needs medical attention. She's going to die!"

He laughed at how silly Eve was behaving, then he kissed Ephrom. He ordered the manacles back into the wall and dropped Ephrom to the floor as he turned toward her.

"Eve? Don't be ridiculous. I'm perfectly in control. It's amazing! Ephrom isn't hurt, see? I let him go. We were just wrestling, and I'm learning my strength, but he's fine. And Jenn?" He frowned. He'd forgotten her. "I'm giving her pleasure beyond words. We were a little rough, but I'll heal her. I think—" For a moment, he was confused. Jenn's nannies simply weren't responding rapidly enough. They were older, antiquated technology. They couldn't keep up with his own. He had a solution, right? He could replicate his enhanced nannies into her.

Take over everything down to the cellular level. She'd heal. He frowned at this, but then lost interest as another surge of hyper-sexual desire demanded his attention. His thoughts became increasingly foggy, filled only with emotion and desire.

"Jason, please listen! It's me, Eve! You said you trusted me. Whatever is happening, you're confused. Think about how you're acting. It's not you, and just look at her! She's broken and terrified! I'M terrified!" She rushed to Jenn and cradled her head. She struggled to lift her but then settled onto the floor with her.

Jason was growing tired of being thwarted. If everyone could just see what he saw, it would be easier. "Eve? There's no reason to be afraid. I can help you understand, make you understand." He snared her emotions before she could protest, flooded her with comfort and attraction. She stared at him a moment and he felt a massive surge of adrenaline as she tried to resist him. Then, overwhelmed, she smiled and abandoned Jenn, walking toward him invitingly. Ephrom rose from the floor behind him and began kissing Jason's shoulders, running his fingers down Jason's bloody torso. Jason shuddered in delight, the blood from his now-healed head wound sticky in his matted hair. He turned and rewarded Ephrom with a deep kiss, tearing his shirt off. He experienced the same sense of being someone else, of experiencing the pleasure of Ephrom. It was as if he was kissing himself. He pulled Ephrom to him roughly, sliding his hands down to his butt and massaging it.

"Yes, see? I will teach you just how much your body can do, Ephrom." The feeling rushed through him, and he felt Ephrom's male organ straining against his pants. With another deep kiss, he made Ephrom orgasm with so much force the man sagged against him involuntarily. Jason held him up, as he thrashed, kissing his neck, enjoying the shared sensations.

With another laugh, he turned and picked up Eve, who stared at him, and set her on the counter alongside Jenn, intending to take Eve as he'd taken her. Jenn weakly repeated "Nuh. Nuh. Nuh," as her body struggled vainly to survive blood loss and the filling of her lungs. She radiated pain and deep desperation to be saved, fighting for her life.

Before he could tear off Eve's clothing, the door opened, and Emma Garbine walked into the room. She carried a briefcase. The look on her face was grim, determined. Angry.

"Jason, it's me, Emma. Do you recognize me?"

He smiled sensually at her. "Of course, Emma! Come in. I have discovered so much. I can control everything. Everything! Even the materials in this room are treated with nano-technology and can be commanded to obey." The counter shaped itself around Eve, cupping her toward him so he could enter her more easily.

Ephrom watched Jason with sustained longing, absently running his hands over his own torso. "Please!" he begged. Jason dominated his nannies, and Ephrom desperately needed attention.

Emma moved toward the center of the living room, then into the edge of the dining space. "Jason, you've lost perspective. You aren't in control of anything, least of all yourself. Look at Jenn, for god's sake!"

His brows narrowed with confusion. Someone else had mentioned her. He could not remember who. "Jenn?" He glanced at her broken body for a moment, recognizing her wounds. "Jenn? What? Don't worry, Jenn. Your nannies will fix the hurting." He smiled and commanded her nannies to repair. However, once again they were inadequate. They were already attempting to minimize the bleeding and close the wounds, but they simply weren't designed to help her in the way she needed. They were barely keeping her alive.

Jason mentally dismissed the issue. "I've ordered her to heal, so she'll be fine. I'll adapt her so she can accommodate me, love me. Her body just needs to be rebuilt. I'll rebuild everyone, so they can receive my love. Everyone should experience this incredible feeling. I'll give everyone the treatment so they can adapt. We have solved it! We can give the immortality drugs and new nannies to people."

He ignored Jenn and smiled, satisfied his commands had been transmitted. He forgot about her in moments, turning his attention back toward his own physical needs, which were overpowering. Ephrom, driven beyond control by his imposed desire, pressed up against Jason, begging. Worse than any addiction, Jason dominated every pleasure and reward system in Ephrom's brain.

"Jason! You've nearly killed her! Stop it. Turn off your emotions, your elevated hormone levels. Your body is controlling your actions, not your mind. Your judgment is clouded and out of control. Shut them down!"

The conversation was irritating him. Even so, he decided to prove he was in complete control. "No! It's not that at all." He stepped out of Ephrom's embrace and around the corner toward her. "Emma, it's amazing! You don't understand. My body, my ability, it's so incredible. The feelings during sex are so intense, so overwhelming, and they don't have to stop. It is bliss. I can keep going and going, and I just need to help others experience the same thing. It's pure ecstasy, and I can help you have it too. Your body will adapt. I'll help you."

He moved forward and reached out to control her nannies, but he suffered a shock. There was nothing there. If he closed his eyes, he couldn't sense her at all. It was like she was invisible to him. If he didn't see her in front of him, he'd have thought she wasn't even in the room. He cast out again with more force, seeking to find her nannies. Surely she'd been treated. Everyone in society had nannies in one form or another.

"What—"

"I've got a suppression device, canceling out all signals around me. Very simple, but it should keep you from forcing me to do something I don't want. Jason, listen! I don't WANT you to take over my mind, my body. It's wrong. Think! You'd know this if you just concentrated. What you are doing isn't you, Jason. You're becoming the monsters from the failed experiments."

He laughed and tried to seize control of her again, having already forgotten his failure. "You're making such a huge deal of out this, when it's really just about pleasure. It's wonderful. I'll show you." He started forward.

Emma pulled out a gun. Where had she gotten a gun? They were forbidden unless issued by the government. He laughed at the absurdity of it. A gun. Against him? "Let me show you," he repeated.

"No, Jason. What you are doing is raping people. Even if you change their emotions to appear willing, it isn't what they wanted before you changed them. You're forcing yourself on them, against their will."

For a moment he looked at her, stunned and confused. Against their will? But his will became their will, he reasoned, and they wanted him. Even now, he could feel Ephrom and Eve behind him, as they yearned for his attention. He could feel Eve's nipples harden, her loins clench. He could feel Ephrom's male organ straining against his clothing. He rewarded their desire with pleasure akin to orgasm and they both shuddered. He felt their feelings as his feelings. The more he could capture their nannies, the more he could enhance his own sensations. "Emma, please don't be so hysterical. Look." He motioned for Eve and Ephrom to join him, and they did so eagerly. "They want me, want to be with me. I'm not forcing them by controlling their bodies. They are moving on their own. I just helped them know how much they wanted me. If anything, they are suffering because we are wasting time here." He ran his fingers up his bare stomach, dried blood flaking off. "I'll show you, too. You need to see." He moved toward her again.

"Stop right there. I'll shoot. I am telling you flat out. I don't want you to come near me. I don't want you changing me."

He hesitated. Conversation became difficult, annoying and disruptive. "But you will. You will want to, I promise. You'll want it more than anything else. It's so simple. I can't—. Stop talking! You need to see."

Emma fired the gun. She hit him in the chest and fired again, destroying his right leg.

He collapsed, screaming in outrage. Before she could fire a third time, he commanded the floor under her to shift upward, throwing her off balance. With a cry, she fell backward. As she fell, the material around her arms and legs changed at his command, snaking forward and binding the right side of her body. He couldn't control the material on the left side, since the briefcase had fallen too near and continued to cancel out signals, but he'd restrained her enough to keep her from reaching for the weapon, which skittered across the floor and landed against the wall.

He yelled again in pain, but his wounds were already closing, healing. His heart staggered, faltering from the destruction of his chest. In moments, the nannies formed a latticework, covering the wound and repairing enough of the damage to stabilize his blood pressure. He knelt, head bowed and arms barely able to hold him up. The pain felt incredible, amazing. He savored it and laughed as it fled from his body. In minutes he had healed completely. Finally, he stood, his body whole. He felt weak, however. He needed food badly.

"Hungry," he mumbled.

He staggered to the replicator, gorging himself, eating whatever he could grab as soon as it was produced for him. He got much of it on himself, spilling food down the front of his body as he forced it into his mouth. The sensation of eating was incredibly pleasurable in itself and he moaned between bites. Finishing quickly, he moved to the sink, drinking greedily from the faucet. Briefly, the thought that a bigger mouth would make it easier.

Emma yelled in fright as she watched in horror, trying desperately to turn enough to grab the briefcase handle and drag it toward her. "Jason! My god, stop it! You're turning into a monster." Then, through frightened tears, she pleaded with him. "Please! I'm your friend!"

In between gulping water, he looked at her. "You shot me. How could you?" He giggled, rubbing his healed leg. "It hurt." Oh, but it had felt amazing, too. "Emma?" He shook his head. Pleasure and pain overlapping in his mind. He needed more of both. *Food?*

"Jason, you've got to stop. Let me get you out of here, to the lab. We can stall the process before you destroy yourself and hurt anybody else. Remember what happened to the others!"

Hadn't he already talked about this, dealt with it? *What others?* He moved around the counter, his leg supporting his weight as if it had never been torn. He began to swagger toward her. The floor writhed around her arm and leg, holding her fast. Sex. Then food.

"Please, Jason, stop!" He sensed her fear. "Help! Please! Somebody get in here! I can't stop him!"

He reached the briefcase and kicked it out of the way, feeling a momentary loss of signaling from his leg as it passed through the dampening field. "Filthy thing. Poison."

He felt her nannies now that the briefcase lay out of range, and it made him smile.

He kneeled over Emma, able to sense her fear through her primitive nannites, seeing what she saw that evoked this terror. Subconsciously he recognized he appeared as a nightmare come to life, a mess of food, blood, and with sexual urges run rampant. He ran a finger over her cheek, with a rush of anticipation as he thought of what he could do to help her see him as an object of desire, not one to be feared.

That's not me. She's not seeing correctly. I'll fix it. She will see me as I really am.

She screamed and thrashed against him. Through Emma's eyes, having rudimentary communication with her nannites, he was given a picture of himself as a monster. Eyes wild, lustful and dangerous. Grinning horribly. Covered in grime and bodily fluids. Like seeing a reflection. One he would change. She would see him as powerful, beautiful, desired above all things. With glee he threw his will against hers, intending to convert her as he had the others.

To his shock, his commands to overwhelm her were cancelled. The door opened and he staggered back under an onslaught of complex instructions to his own nannies. Reacting on instinct, he threw his hands over his face protectively and countermanded the foreign instructions, which were designed to entirely shut off his ability to send and receive communication through his system. He felt his control, all the power he commanded, slipping, being cut off.

Sector Seven strode into the room, a look of concern on his normally impassive face.

Tarien! For a moment, Jason felt sane. Then Jason resisted the instructions to shut down his control with all his might, desperately trying to keep the window of his own power from closing on him. He screamed in rage at the Tech, "Stop! What are you doing?"

Tarien walked toward him, sending a set of signals completely incomprehensible to Jason and vastly more complicated than he could hope to understand. An interwoven skein of these instructions snared Jason's mind and Jason could barely remain in control of himself as he fought. He lost ground, unable to fend off the attack. Even if he would normally have had a chance, his mind had grown too clouded by lust and emotion. He couldn't process the sheer complexity and speed of thought coming from so many directions. Jason tried to rise, to physically overpower the other man, but the moment the thought of physically resisting occurred to him, Tarien overcame his attempt. Jason's body would no longer obey him when he tried to push forward. He resorted to backing away and Tarien moved in step toward him, eyes never leaving Jason's face.

He staggered into the wall and then Seven had him, gently resting both hands on his shoulders as he allowed the nannite battle to continue. With surprising gentleness, he took Jason's head in both hands. "We don't wish to harm you, Jason. Please stop resisting us."

Jason stammered, "I can't—ugh!" His jaw clenched in concentration. "Stop it! I need—" With a groan, he sagged. "No!" But he simply wasn't capable of resisting. Tarien's ability vastly eclipsed his. He might as well have been a mosquito trying to outmaneuver a space-fighter. Even so, he fought with every ounce of willpower.

Tarien sighed in resignation, a look of deep concern flashing through his eyes as Jason's nannies were ripped out of his control and stopped obeying his commands altogether. The pain of losing his systemic control tore at Jason and he thrashed involuntarily against Tarien, who pulled him into an embrace, cradling his head against his chest. Tarien's strength matched that of Jason's, even as enhanced as Jason had become, and Jason couldn't pull away. The sudden loss overwhelmed him, and he sobbed.

"We are sorry. Sorry . . ." Tarien put his cheek on the top of Jason's head as he held him.

Jason felt himself normalize. His hormones and emotions no longer controlled him. Without realizing it was coming, he started screaming in horror as his conscious mind reasserted itself. He shook with sobs and would have fallen to the floor if he hadn't been firmly held.

In moments, his innate concern for others surpassed his own trauma. He looked up at the Tech. "What have I done? Jenn! We've got to get her help. She's, oh Tarien, I think I killed her. What is happening to me?"

A team had already rushed in to treat Jenn as well as to help the others. They had begun a blood transfusion.

"She is greatly harmed, Jason. She will be aided, but her damage is extensive. Her body will survive, but we cannot discern the injury to her mind. We do not know how to gauge the extent of ruin or her probability of recovery." He paused, still forcing Jason to look at him and not around the room. "We need you to reverse the changes to your friends."

Jason gaped. "Why don't you just do it? You're infinitely more in control of technology than I am."

Seven shook his head. "We lack understanding of emotional and hormonal controls and cannot restore them properly. You have changed them. We can stop you from communicating, and easily cancel or redirect communication, but we do not understand emotional control or the body and its complexities. These things are the province of those with medical training." He stepped back, letting Jason support his own weight. "You must do this now. We will re-establish your links for this purpose, if you can remain in command of your senses."

Jason looked at him a long moment, shaken. "I . . .

I don't know. What if I can't? I thought I remained in control. My thoughts were so clear, but the desire grew too strong, too confusing." He shuddered. "My ... desires were too strong. You may have to shut me off."

Emma cried out for help, her arms and legs still encapsulated by the flooring.

He nodded. "We will help you. We have frozen you as you are, so you will not be able to issue additional changes to your body until we are sure of you. Do you know how to temper your internal feedback so it doesn't control you? We will release you now. Ready?"

Jason took a deep, shuddering breath and nodded. Suddenly, it all came flooding back in a wave. With a groan, he clenched his teeth and fists, felt his eyes rolling back in his head. His massive chest rose and fell and the cord of muscle around his neck tightened. He panted, resisting the desires that coursed through him again. Acutely aware of Tarien's presence, his statuesque perfection and the danger those thoughts represented, Jason used that as a mechanism to control himself. He wanted to reach out, to embrace the Tech and ravish him. With agonizing slowness, he negated the incoming signals, cancelling them and regulating his body to something more normal. He couldn't stop the desire, but now he was wiser, more in control. He knew the danger of such powerful allure.

It seemed hours had passed, but he knew only a few seconds had elapsed. Less, maybe. Jason's thinking processes were greatly accelerated. He looked up at Tarien and nodded. "I'm okay. I have myself under control."

Without expression, the Tech moved out of his way and gestured to the scene behind him.

Jason cried out at the horrific scene. A team of Medics attended to Jenn, hovering over her and attempting to stabilize her. Jason could see flashes of her torn, bleeding body as she continued her litany of mindless protests. Eve and Ephrom stood exactly where he'd left them, watching him adoringly, sickeningly. He feared releasing them, knowing the hate they would feel for him. For what he had become.

Still, with great care, he restored them to normal by reverting the instructions he'd sent earlier to override their hormone production and brain signaling. He unblocked key parts of their mind, which he'd used to cage them, restructuring their will. Both of them collapsed, blessedly unconscious. The medical team kept them from falling to the floor and quickly put them on floating stretchers, which they pushed from the room. He could feel them, knew they were caught in a traumatic slumber, resulting from the waking nightmare they'd both endured.

In horrified disgust, he sank to the floor against the wall, cupping his head. Aware of his nakedness, of Jenn's blood on his body, he realized how monstrous he must appear. He was deeply ashamed.

"Well, well. I see you certainly made a mess of things, Doctor." Faust had come into the room and Jason could hear the nasty sneer in his voice.

Jason looked up as the older man stepped over Emma and entered the room, attended by several guards.

"Still, it appears as if our little incentive program paid off. A bit drastic, I agree. However, it often takes a lot of parenting to get people where you need them to be." He laughed. "I certainly enjoyed the show, I must admit. You provided some wild entertainment for a while there. I wasn't quite sure how things would end. It would have been a shame to gas you and then incinerate the room."

Jason felt like murdering the horrible old man and he knew this rage didn't stem entirely from his systemic changes. Jason hated him. "You're a monster! You should have stopped me sooner!" Before Jason could launch a mental attack to destroy Faust, rid the world of his evil, a staggering blow to his psyche nearly made him black out. Something ripped Jason's control away forcefully, with much less care than when Tarien had nullified him. He screamed and, as his vision cleared, he saw Faust was attended by another Tech.

Nine looked at Jason with the same impassive unconcern inherent to all Sector Techs, his black eyes devoid of emotion.

Tarien did not even turn, and Jason assumed he must surely be in rapid communion with the other Tech on a level nobody else could comprehend.

Jason stared, horrified. While he couldn't believe a Tech had fallen under Faust's direct control, the thing aided Faust in some way. Prevented Jason from harming Faust. The Tech had rendered Jason helpless.

Faust laughed, obviously aware Jason had tried to kill him. "Don't be ridiculous. As if I'd allow you to lash out after so much care has been taken to bring you to this point." He looked down at Emma who had stopped struggling and lay quietly. Well, Jason? Are you going to let her up?"

Jason suppressed his hate for the man and, with an approving nod from Tarien, and a brief return of his broadcast abilities, he reset the floor to its default configuration, which unbound Emma as it changed back into a flat surface.

A couple of Medics helped her to her feet.

The Tech nullified Jason's abilities again, just as harshly as before. A frown crossed Tarien's face. Jason did not protest.

"If you can't learn to cooperate, you will have to be forced." Turning, he motioned for the guards to secure Jason. "Take him to the holding cell and hose him down. He looks rather . . . frightening, if truth be told. I'll be along after I take care to contain things."

The guards pulled Jason roughly to his feet, nearly dragging him out the door and down the hall. They pushed him, still naked, into a vehicle that normally moved equipment within the complex, and transported Jason to another location. Even though he could see out of the enclosed cart, he was easily confused by the unchanging scenery as the vehicle moved through various hallways and down numerous levels of the building. They exited the vehicle after some time, and he was led for a while through winding corridors of bare concrete.

The chill of the maintenance corridors did not affect him, as his body adjusted quickly. Nor did the strain of walking such long distances. While mentally tired, and emotionally exhausted, he remained physically strong.

At last they reached an area that appeared to contain nothing more than large, solid concrete rooms. The guards roughly pushed him inside one of the cells and the door slid closed. Turning, he saw two other armed guards standing near the doorway, complete with body armor. A third dragged a hose, which Jason barely had time to notice before they turned it on, blasting him off his feet with freezing cold water.

He fell backward when the force of the water hit him and bruised his butt on the hard floor. The concentrated spray pushed him back against the wall. He cursed. He healed immediately, of course, and the water no longer felt cold as his body adjusted. At least the Techs had permitted his automated functions to continue to operate. Maybe they were unable to unbind the changes. He got up and scrubbed himself off, actually walking into the spray with an inhuman display of balance and strength. He couldn't read the guards, since his external communications had been turned off, but he could guess their surprise at his inability to feel the cold and the powerful muscular control which allowed him to remain standing against the force. He stared impassively, letting the spray wash over him.

The water shut off and the guard opened the door and

dragged the hose through. The door automatically closed behind him as he left the room. Neither of the other two guards who remained so much as moved.

Jason sighed and sat against the far wall, water pooling around him and rushing toward the drain as he dripped onto the floor. At least he finally felt clean. For a long time, he had to fight to keep from weeping over Jenn and all the damage he'd caused. Body exhausted, he lay down and slept.

FOURTEEN

HIS DREAMS WERE LESS POIGNANT, less urgent feeling than those of the past couple of nights. Even so, he thought he couldn't shake the vague sense of missing something important being conveyed, something just at the back of his conscious thinking.

He woke and sat up, the most recent dream lingering in his mind. He realized it was the lack of being able to sense and control people and materials around him that he was missing.

The guards still stood at the door. He couldn't tell if they were the same guards or not and had no idea how long he'd been asleep. Someone brought him food and water, which he ate with purpose. He slept again.

By the third resting period, he had control over his system, and his body had reached a point where it wasn't undergoing further changes. Physically, he locked himself in at this idolized version. He couldn't discern if the nannies were still busily writing changes and replicating, evolving within him on a molecular level, but at least he felt none of the sudden rushes and disorientation he'd experienced before. His body still craved pleasure, but he knew better, and dampened the nearly overriding urge.

At long last, the door opened, and Director Faust walked in, accompanied by two more guards, a man and a woman. Neither wore helmets. Jason almost considered it to be worth the effort to lunge and be shot down, hoping to reach Faust before the guards could destroy enough of his body to incapacitate him. He couldn't be killed, not without removing his head and dissolving it in acid or burning it, but he could be stopped.

Faust still had the same smug look, which seemed to be permanently etched on his face. He looked Jason up and down, then guessed at Jason's murderous thoughts.

"Oh, by all means, try. I'm almost looking forward to having you torn limb from limb, just to watch you scream while you heal. It might be as entertaining as pulling the knowledge from your skull by torturing you in other ways."

Torture? A flash of terror went through Jason, recalling his nightmare where Faust had done exactly that.

"No? Well, you disappoint me. I cannot say I'm surprised. Now then, I need to know details. You are rather unstable if your performance last week is any indication. So, transmit the instructions you've learned."

Last week? So, he'd slept much longer than he'd thought. His mind raced. Jenn would have been treated as much as possible, and he desperately wanted to know her condition. Jason also heard the implied fact that they didn't understand the data he'd generated during his living nightmare, hadn't puzzled out his ability to now control himself. Their inability to understand the information could prove useful.

"Oh, I see, so now you're going to sulk." Faust crossed his arms. "Well, I assumed as much. You are really quite predictable." He motioned, and the two guards crossed the room and attached chains to Jason's legs and arms, then secured them to rings on the wall behind him, which disappeared into the wall. Clearly, they could be pulled back to secure him. The guards saluted smartly and left the room. A moment later, they entered with a chair and a mobile medical analysis station and then backed away. They positioned themselves on either side of the door with the other two helmeted guards.

Faust seated himself in front of the station. "I assume you are going to fight me every step of the way, so I'll just jump right to the point. I'm going to tear you apart, little by little, and we can record what's going on. Eventually, you'll get to a point where you can't help but consciously start issuing commands, which will give me the data I need to suppress this issue of hormonal imbalance."

Jason stared at him in horror, realizing he had no escape.

"I'm going to turn your broadcast nannies back on, so you can learn to control them. This time, nobody will show up to cut off your nannies from external reception. I'm recording the signals you use so I can decipher them myself." He touched the display.

Suddenly, all his external bio-feedback came online. With horror, Jason quickly suppressed his desire to reach others to control them. He felt such self-loathing, he had little trouble keeping himself in check.

He did lash out at the Director, hoping to kill him before the little toad could react. However, his broadcast abilities were dampened in an area around the small man.

Surmising his thoughts again, Faust said, "Naturally, I'm wearing a dampening suit. Another invention I'm proud of." His smile was cold, reptilian.

Jason had nothing to say.

"Now then. Let's get started."

Faust's fingers flicked over the display and the chains retracted, pulling Jason back against the wall in an upright spread-eagle fashion.

"That's really obnoxious, you know," he said, referring to Jason's large sex organ. He turned to the guards. "Go get something to cover him. I don't want to have to look at him like this while I'm working. It's disgusting."

The woman disappeared out the door.

The Director made several notes and ignored Jason for a while. Eventually, the guard returned with an oversized towel, which she proceeded to wrap around Jason's waist.

Then the guard stepped back to stand near the door.

The Director continued to ignore Jason and focused on his screen, typing rapidly. After a while, Jason began to meditate. He carefully calmed himself, sending specific instructions to his nannies and refusing to allow the incoming signals to overwhelm him.

As Faust continued to work, Jason eventually became aware of the guards, both of which had their nannies available to him. The negation field only surrounded the Director, so Jason could sense people, even those outside the room. Just as he realized he could sense them, Jason also understood this apparent lapse. Clearly, Faust hoped Jason would reveal how to control those around him, perhaps being tempted into using the guards to kill him. There was no way the man had accidentally forgotten to prevent Jason from communicating with their nannies. He refused to play Faust's game.

The Director finally looked up from his pretend work, clearly annoyed Jason had not taken the bait. "Not going to seize one of my men, eh? Fine. I have plenty of other tests."

He picked up a scalpel from the silver tray and walked over to stand directly in front of Jason. With a quick motion, he slashed a deep wound across Jason's chest. It healed almost immediately. The Director cut him again. The wound healed just as quickly. Faust began slashing rapidly, cutting Jason on the face, arms, and chest. Jason thrashed against his restraints, the pain lancing through him. He tried not to scream, but finally threw his head back and bellowed like an enraged animal. His control slipped and his mind flooded with hormones and a cascade of negative emotions, including murder.

This time, familiar with the overpowering thoughts, he kept them under control. He refused to let them take over his consciousness. He willed away the pain, became detached. After a while, the cuts no longer hurt, no longer felt like anything. Eventually, he simply ignored them, retreating into himself.

The Director clenched his jaw in disappointment, but finally stopped. He stared at Jason for a while and Jason guessed he wanted to continue to cut at him, regardless of the lack of reaction. Faust walked back over to his machine and analyzed the collected data.

"I'll have to correlate the information gathered, which will take several days, but this is a good start. Not as much as I'd like, but I'll find ways to extract more useful information."

He signaled, and the guards removed the station and the chair and resumed their positions around the door. Every sentence, every action taken, had been a way to gather data. Jason had no choice but to transmit a way to negate his pain. This would give Faust information he needed.

Faust left without another word. Jason hardly noticed as he sagged against his restraints.

Time passed, and the guards fed and watered Jason with regularity. Still chained to the wall, he had no ability to care for himself, so he suffered the humiliation of urinating and then, finally, of defecating himself. The guards hosed him down and replaced his towel, the only garment they bothered to cover him with.

He slept, his head rolling to one side, and the cramping pains were horrible. Eventually, he learned to change his body enough to make the cramping subside. Days passed like this, with him simply hanging from the wall as they fed him, cleaned his excrement by spraying him down, and otherwise ignored him.

The guards changed shifts every six hours, but were forced to stand, doing nothing, the entire time. He tried to talk to them at one point, but they refused to recognize or acknowledge him. As he extended his ability to sense those nearby, he began to analyze their nannies. He learned to tell them apart and sense their feelings toward him. Mostly, they were indifferent. Bored. Several of them found him attractive and fantasized about taking advantage of him while he couldn't resist. Most of them were fascinated by his male organ, even the straightest guys, who thought of them as a curiosity and with some envy.

Two of his guards wanted to torture him, running through scenarios where they could severely injure him and test his healing abilities. Jason hated being able to read these ugly thoughts. As he grew more familiar with the process, his senses increased, and he began to fine-tune this ability. The materials in the room did not contain the nano-technology he wished was available. For a moment, he'd thought about escape until he realized there wasn't a way to free himself. He knew the moment he used one of the guards, a dampening field would come into play and Faust would have the data he needed to broadcast instructions on his own, a way to make changes and impose will.

After long periods of sleeping and waking periods had elapsed, Faust returned and repositioned himself with another mobile medical station. This time, his tactics were more brutal. He burned Jason's flesh, applied acids. Jason thrashed against his bonds as he screamed until he could isolate the pain and turn it off. Invariably, once Jason stopped responding, Faust would return to his recordings to analyze the mechanism Jason employed, then change tactics.

Several rounds of this torment culminated in Jason's whole body being subjected to fire. Faust charred his flesh and waited for him to heal, subjecting him to unbearable agony. Jason writhed in torment as flames burned away his flesh. The torture reduced him to sobbing uncontrollably, crying out nonsensically. He tried to shut out the pain, but he couldn't ignore fire as easily as being cut and it cost him great effort. There was also the fundamental fear that fire could completely destroy him. Burned completely, Jason could not recover. He required enormous amounts of food to regenerate from this torment.

Eventually, his captors took him down from the wall and strapped him to a metal table. He attempted to throw his guards off as they released him. He almost succeeded, but they managed to bear down on him and hold him while they strapped his arms, legs, neck, and waist. For a while, he lay like this, barely breathing, hoping they would just kill him and be done with it.

But Faust had more tests. He cut off Jason's fingers, then his entire arm. It took days to heal the horribly painful wound, but his arm and hand grew back.

With increasing malice, Faust neutered Jason, cutting off all his male organs and throwing them into a transparent tub, placed where Jason could see. The Director kept him in mindless pain most of his waking hours.

Hoping to learn something useful, Jason guided the process of regeneration, enhancing his arms and legs so they were incredibly strong. He guided his male organs to grow back and, though he kept them a bit larger than average, he did regrow them to something more within the norm. Not the monstrous appendages he'd had, but large enough to be personally pleasing. A vanity he opted to keep.

One time, when they left Jason crying and sobbing, reattached to the wall and head dangling as his body tried to keep him alive after the last round of torture, one of the guards broke down and began to cry. He could feel her emotions as she watched his torment. She wanted to free him somehow. Most of the guards were sickened by what they saw and mortified at the extent to which Faust continually ruined Jason's body. Still, they could do nothing.

He wondered just how much they knew. Probing

her thoughts, Jason realized she had no idea where they were. The guards were brought to this location through a complex set of transfers, leaving them disoriented. He wanted to send her a wave of calm, of reassurance. But he knew the information generated by calming her would be useful to Faust.

The Director appeared with meticulous regularity and he kept urging Jason to work with the guards, to manipulate them. He needed this data. Faust now understood the complex signaling that Jason used to exert self-control and keep himself stable, but most of the external control information eluded him. The most vexing was the knowledge of how to manipulate others. He wanted this last bit of information desperately, for Faust's unending goal was to know how to dominate those around him, to exert control over everyone.

Jason knew he had limited time, whether he gave Faust what he wanted or not. Faust surely neared the time when he would give himself the treatment, since his aging body could give out at any time. He had enough information to keep from breaking down and losing control now. His control would be imperfect, and he'd have to struggle without Jason's innate ability, but he could learn. Given time, he would gain increasing precision. He only kept Jason alive in order to shorten this process, to afford him the instructions he needed without having to discover them unaided.

In desperation, Jason's mind cast about for a way out, a solution. During one of his quiet periods, he came up with an idea. He wasn't sure how easily it would be discovered, but he knew he had to try.

With incredible focus, Jason began the long process of understanding every communication signal in his body. He enhanced his brain to retain this information, rebuilt his mind so it could process and store vast amounts of data. He assumed he modeled himself after a Tech in some rudimentary way. His memory became perfect, and his problem-solving skills soared. Once he felt he had a good understanding and direct control over every part of himself, he enhanced his nannies, having them build more advanced versions of themselves in rapid evolution. Then he began creating organic versions of nannies, far different than those he'd been injected with, an entirely new set of technology based on a language he invented as he created them. In this way, he created a secondary set of nannies tailored to his body alone. *Let Faust get stuck trying to puzzle out this data*, he thought. Any data Faust managed to gather would remain incomprehensible because he lacked a frame of reference. He would need the cipher Jason had created.

The Director noticed. He could tell how the brain enhancements worked, how Jason augmented himself to become super-human, super intelligent. But Faust could not discern the purpose for the foreign instructions as Jason built new organic nannies—not without capturing the modified communication standards Jason invented as he went along. Faust brutally questioned him regarding this missing data, but Jason refused to tell him. The two sets of nannies existed side by side, one set dormant until Jason would have the opportunity to put them to use. He also used these new organic nannies for further mental enhancements, intent on cheating Faust out of as much data as he could.

Faust became furious when the flow of data reduced to a trickle.

Jason learned from accessing the guards' emotions that the Director planned to have him executed in a few days. A week at most. Jason knew Faust purposefully let this information slip to frighten Jason into showing at least some progress. Jason set about the secondary phase of his plan. He began re-writing the nannies of the guards to match his new technology. If he could replace their nannies with those Jason had created, he could control them without the knowledge getting into Faust's hands.

The process didn't work, however. The nano-technology present in the guards was crude, many generations behind the enhanced set Faust had injected him with. The guard's nannies could not understand anything more than basic instructions and could not be reprogrammed. He tried to have the nannies build newer versions of themselves, but even those instructions were too complex for them to handle.

He began a hurried mental search for some way around this problem, his terror making him desperate. Finally, he realized he could create machines that rested on his skin, waiting to come in contact with the next person who touched him. Perhaps someone who cleaned him off, or someone who fed him.

The newly created machines rushed to his skin, exiting through his pores in beads of sweat. He purposefully soiled himself and waited for his captors to take care of him.

Once more, he failed. They hosed him off, washing away the nannies. Even as more swarmed to his skin while they toweled him off, he realized the guards were too meticulous. They were not allowed to directly touch him in any way. They wore gloves and discarded them after they cleaned him. Unfortunately, the nannies couldn't move fast enough up and through the gloves to reach exposed skin before the materials were thrown into the incinerator.

He sagged against his chains in surrender, his last hope dashed. For all his cleverness, Faust stayed one step ahead of him.

But then he had another flash of insight. He built new versions of the nannies and had them bond with the material of his chains. Other versions fell from his body to the floor, replicating rapidly as they permeated the concrete. They used the materials around them as a resource to make more of themselves. Copying with increasing rapidity, they swarmed over the walls, over the guards. In a matter of hours, he had complete control of the room and both guards. As the guards changed shifts, they carried these new versions with them, shedding them along the way as they touched objects and other people. Like a virus, he spread his control outward onto each new surface the guards touched. He even permeated his towel, so he'd have a way of fashioning clothing from it. He had nearly perfect control over these new nannites since they were specifically attuned to him. He also increased his broadcast and receiving abilities, broadening his range.

Hurriedly, he sent his nannies still further and soon knew his general location. By intercepting communication, Jason knew Faust had detected something was wrong. Faust's computers were analyzing data related to Jason's broadcasts and it had caught Faust's attention that almost none of the enormous amount of data being recorded actually contained anything he could decipher. To Faust, this massive increase of foreign transmission must mean that Jason had devised a way to keep things secret. A team was dispatched to dispose of Jason before he could become a threat.

He needed to buy time before they arrived and Faust discovered his escape. Jason quickly took control of the guards in the room, paralyzing them. They crumpled to the floor, even as Jason's towel transformed into a skin-tight suit. There wasn't enough fabric to do more until the nannies came in contact with more building material, which left him with a basic one-piece fitted suit. Jason's chains fell away as he deteriorated the metal. He landed lightly on his feet. With inhuman speed he rushed to the door, which opened at his command.

With knowledge of the area still incomplete, he only had a vague sense of how to escape. His nannies were still replicating with exponential speed, but they were too few. Nonetheless, he knew to run to the left and down the hall to the nearest elevator shaft.

During the time he'd built his new nannites, his strength had grown. Jason tore the doors off with ease and flung himself forward, grabbing the cabling. He scaled upward rapidly, modifying his body as he went so his hands and feet took on climbing properties of a gecko. Everything he touched along the way became infused with his new nannies as he shed them. Creating so many new copies expended energy at a horrendous rate, however, and he knew he needed food. He could feel himself growing visibly more emaciated as he spread his new technology.

As he reached the upper levels, he launched himself through another set of doors and ran into a busy office. Faust's assassination team must have arrived at Jason's cell because an alarm went off. His nannies confirmed that secondary security teams had been dispatched and were attempting to isolate him. He threw himself at the windows. They cracked, and he kicked hard, shattering the glass and creating an opening large enough for escape. He climbed out, his exposed hands and feet now fully capable of scaling the side of the building by adhering to it. His internal modifications continued, his vision improved, his senses heightened.

He crawled rapidly on his hands and feet down the side of the building, even as he saw incoming enforcement vehicles flying toward him. With a leap, Jason threw himself into the air, knowing he could easily survive the six-story fall.

He hit the concrete and his body absorbed the shock, translating up his enhanced skeleton. He began running, dodging through a startled crowd.

Jason knew he had limited time before being recaptured. Remotely, he knew everything transpiring through his uplinks with the nannies as they reported back to him. From afar, Jason infected the security team as they entered his former prison cell. In moments, he gained control of their communication gear and tried to stop all transmissions. Unfortunately, he couldn't shut down the alarm to Faust fast enough.

The building he'd just dropped away from exploded, the wave of the detonation sending Jason to his knees.

Faust knew. While he may have hoped and planned Jason would not find a way to bypass the heavily controlled technology, Faust was clever. He had clearly guessed it was possible, given Jason's increasing level of control, along with the experiment of treating the materials in the apartment with improved nannies to see how Jason would learn to work with them. The experiment was designed to encourage changing matter, so Jason could figure out a way to create new technology on the fly. It was a risk Faust had needed to take, or he would struggle to find a way to learn how to change materials around him that were embedded with nannites.

He must have embedded explosives in the building, having been far-sighted enough to have planned for this possibility. Still, he couldn't destroy all the nannies, not with Jason still on the loose. If Faust knew they existed, he must also know that Jason could spread them upon contact. He'd have to capture and destroy Jason to be rid of them.

Jason grew more exhausted each moment and could not keep manufacturing more of the microscopic swarm from his body without food. His continual output of the nannies had weakened him dangerously, but he dared not stop. His only hope was to gain enough control of an area to protect himself. He ran as fast as his new body would carry him, the people around him becoming a blur as he passed.

But it wasn't fast enough. Faust had immense resources at his disposal and access to the main observation and security systems in the city. He must already know Jason's location since every camera and sensor in the city reported back to Faust.

Jason threw himself at a street vendor, scattering the stand and the food in all directions. Quickly, he grabbed as much food as he could and crammed it into his mouth, eating ravenously, spending a precious few moments on replenishing his energy stores. Grabbing more food, he leaped over the debris and continued to eat while he ran.

With a new burst of energy, he resumed synthesizing more of the nannies, which he dropped along the way. His only hope, before they captured him, would be to spread them far enough to give him some sort of advantage. With enough time, they would be a serious threat and Jason might be able to protect himself . . . if he wasn't killed first.

He burst out of an alley and into the street.

Nine landed on the street in front of Jason, staring at him. As he'd surmised, Faust had him pinpointed.

For a moment, he almost thought the Tech nodded to him in recognition, but he couldn't be sure. Nine cocked his head as if listening to something. Incoming orders from the Council, Jason guessed. Nine's emotionless face horrified Jason as a wave of commands hit him, cutting off all communication to his original nannies.

However, the new organic versions were not encoded into the system. This loss of communication afforded him the ability to use the now inert robots for material to synthesize more of the new nannies. His new nannites began to tear down all the old ones and harvest the molecules.

Nine confidently walked toward Jason, an odd look of regret on his face. Jason, however, took off in another direction with a burst of speed, clearly indicating he hadn't been slowed by the Tech's superior technology. Jason shrugged off an order for him to freeze in place, a command for his muscles to lock. Those nannies were no longer able to enforce the incoming commands. For the first time in his life, Jason imagined, Nine suffered a shock.

Jason managed to escape the street and duck into another alley, but the surprise bought him little time. Immediately after realizing Jason had become immune to directed commands, the technology in the area, under

Nine's direction, began to hinder him and tried to force him into a corner. He burst onto another street and desperately dodged vehicles and small flying machines as they converged on him. He scrambled over cars as he ran toward a narrow opening in the obstructions, but law enforcement quickly converged, officers pouring out of hovercrafts to try to capture him. Robots of all kinds surrounded him. In a matter of moments, the combined forces cut off all chance of escape.

His skin oozed a blackened oil-like substance as he hyper-accelerated the manufacture of his version of nano-technology. It poured out of him onto the street and onto vehicles. If he could distract his pursuers long enough, his nannies could overwhelm the area, giving him control.

Unfortunately, they were too limited in their replication ability. Even as fast as they could build new version of themselves, they were still too tiny, and he didn't have enough time to multiply to the extent needed. If he'd had hours, he would have been unstoppable, but with only seconds, he could not prevent recapture. Desperately, he established communication with pockets of technology as they came online from his sprint down various streets, but they were too far away to be of any use.

Several robots seized him. Jason began to infect them out of reflex.

Officers surrounded the area, energy weapons aimed. Nine flew in from over the top of the nearby buildings, landing deftly on the street a few dozen yards away. The robots dragged Jason toward a police hovercraft. Jason sagged in defeat.

Without warning, the robots let him go and suddenly went limp. All nearby vehicles moved away, and the police hovercraft began to rise out of the area with no warning, startling most of the enforcement agents.

Tarien walked toward the scene with a look of anger on his face. Jason was so shocked to see an expression of outrage on the normally stoic face of a Tech, he didn't take advantage of his release. He stood dumbly, unsure.

Tarien's voice boomed. "We will not permit this. You are commanded to disband from this area immediately. Citizen Emerson has not been convicted of a crime and is being unduly harassed. Power is being abused. A warrant has not been issued, and direct orders from a Council member are not sufficient to eliminate his freedoms. We will not permit further abuses. Leave immediately, or we will be forced to defend citizen Emerson, and this may result in physical harm to anyone in violation of our command."

Silent communication between Nine and Seven happened in a flash, and Nine seemed momentarily torn. Ignoring Faust, who was a full member of the Council, was difficult. He nodded in agreement with Seven and the two of them faced the gaping crowd.

"Citizen, we will remove you from this area and carry you to safety. You are not permitted to seek your own way at this time, as it is deemed unsafe," said Nine in his monotone voice. "You should not speak at this time." There seemed to be some deeper warning here. Jason suspected they had set this entire exchange up. Planned this out. How had either of them arrived so quickly? Two Techs in the same location? The probability of such an occurrence was so vast as to be absurd.

Tarien walked forward, all the vehicles moving aside for him. He enveloped Jason in his arms tenderly. "We found you," he whispered.

They lifted into the air and flew upward.

FIFTEEN

JASON PROCESSED THE INTERVENTION rapidly, his enhanced mind deducing the probable outcome of this reprieve. While stunned at Tarien's interference, Jason imagined it would do little good in the end.

"Thank you, Tarien. I don't know what to say. You have bought me a little bit of time. Still, we both know Faust will have a warrant out for me within the hour."

"We will have hidden you before that occurs and will disguise the path taken to obscure the search parameters. Nine is already engaged in hindering the warrant process and One is helping him remotely. This will not last, but it will give you time to work with your new nano-technology."

"You know about that?"

"Nine confirmed this immediately after you were able

to refuse his commands. He purged this new knowledge from his mind, to keep it hidden, for reasons that will become apparent later. We foresaw this possibility. We approve, though this technology must be limited." A more human element entered his voice. "Jason, it is imperative for you to put an end to the immortality research and find a way to alter the course of Faust's actions. Already, this technology grants the ability to cause widespread destruction. If you were not the person we have entrusted to overcome this, the Techs would despair."

"You knew this would happen? You knew I would develop a way to create a new form of nannites? You must know I've infected the entire area where you picked me up. I already have control of the robots and several flying machines. Within a few hours, large areas will report back to me. What is going on here?"

"We predict based on probability. This outcome was calculated as highly probable if you survived. We have worked to protect you, to help you arrive at this place and in this way. There is much to do, if we are to succeed."

"Even if I could somehow spread the technology throughout the area, maybe even other Sectors, it would take me years to be in a position to gain enough control to stop Faust. Right now, I can't even escape without help. My control is too rudimentary. I don't know enough. And you know he's going to figure this out and find a way to block me. He may even inject himself and replicate what I've learned."

"Yes, he has already begun this process. It is worse,

Jason. We fear to tell you all we foresee."

They were landing near the warehouse where Monica and Derek had taken him. The various large shipping containers surrounding the area appeared dull and flaked in the afternoon light. As before, it looked dirty, claustrophobic. "What's here?"

"For a brief time, you will be hidden from all recording devices, and your location is currently unknown to Faust. However, he is acting quickly, and you will soon be under arrest. Once he receives approval from the Council for a warrant, we cannot actively block communication regarding you, and he will find you easily. In this place of rebellion, there is a room where no communication can go in or out. If you act quickly, you can allow your nanobots to begin replicating in this area, and then hide within while they multiply."

He took Jason's hand and led him into the building and down the maze of plain concrete hallways and metal stairs. Just as Jason remembered, nothing adorned the walls, not even paint. Lighting was poor. Debris in the form of twisted rebar and concrete, piles of old wood with nails, and dust were the only decorations. The abandoned feel of the place was oddly reassuring. "Once there are enough of your nannies in this area, you will be able to emerge from the room long enough to regain communication with the nannies. You can use them to misreport information from this vicinity, hiding yourself longer. This will, in turn, allow you time to spread control further."

"I . . . I don't know how your plan will work. I'm just not capable of the necessary level of awareness required." Jason realized something else. "Wait a second. If we go in there, aren't you going to be cut off too?"

"Yes, we will lose communication." Jason heard the terror in his voice.

He wrenched them both to a stop, his new strength now rivaling that of Tarien's. "I can't do that to you! What will happen when you are cut off from your Sector? Has that ever even happened to a Tech?"

"There is little time, Jason. Already the approval is being given for your warrant. It is being ratified and will soon receive electronic signature. I could not rescue you from your capture without exposing the aid we have given. We had to trust you'd escape. But you must hide now, or else they will discover you quickly."

Jason refused to move. "I'm not going in there until you tell me what will happen to you."

"We . . . I don't know. I . . . we have never been cut off. Some Techs went insane, long ago when we were first used for central processing for all communication. I do not remember a time without my connections." His eyes were wide, his breathing labored. "We are afraid, Jason. But this must be done. There are reasons for this. We will tell you, but you must hurry. Now."

He knew he was risking himself, but Tarien was too important. "Who is going to take over this Sector? Will everything just stop working?"

"No. There is another reason for Nine's presence.

In anticipation, Nine took over most of the governance on my behalf. We have agreed to this course of action. If I am able, I will resume this control when I exit the Faraday cage your friends have created in this place." He tugged Jason forward. "Please. We must hurry."

Reluctantly, Jason nodded and began shedding his army of small robots onto the ground, ordering them to replicate until he gave them new instructions. Some of them began building small relay stations, which would broaden his communication reach so he could sense the small sections of the city he'd already taken over. They would be autonomous until he could communicate with them again.

They reached the door Jason remembered from his prior visit and knocked. Mom opened the door just enough to see Jason's face and her eyes widened in disbelief as the two of them pushed their way inside. "Oh, my! Jason? Is that you? And a Tech!" Her eyes darted between them. "Did you capture one? What is going on? You look so different. I barely recognize you. What happened?"

Both he and Tarien hurried inside and closed the door. Before Jason could answer Mom, he bombarded her with his own questions. "How are you possibly here, when we just happened to come here? Where is everyone else? Were you expecting us?" As he spoke, Tarien's eyes rolled back in his head and he silently slumped to the floor, unconscious.

With a cry, Jason scooped him up, now able to lift the

heavy man with ease. "Tarien! Please answer me. Are you okay?"

He received no reply. He tried to probe, to discern the nature of the problem, but got nothing back. Still holding Tarien, he rushed him to a nearby room and gently lay him down in the bed. "Tarien! Please wake up!" He put his hand gently on Tarien's face, worry constricting his throat as he realized what was wrong. Mom was behind him, a gentle hand squeezing Jason's shoulder. "Shit! He's in shock. He's cut off from the WorldNet. I feared this would happen."

Tarien didn't stir. He breathed normally, his face serene as he slept, which momentarily alleviated Jason's concern.

Mom tugged him to his feet, turning him. "Jason, please tell me what's going on. Have you talked to Monica? Where have you been? She's been frantic to find you. And how did you capture the Tech?" Then, clearly afraid, she said, "He's not going to hurt us when he wakes up, will he?"

Jason tried to calm himself. "I didn't capture him. He brought me here. I am going to be arrested."

"What? Oh, my goodness. They must know about this place if the Tech brought you here. We have to get you out of here. Someplace safe."

"This place is the only safe place there is for me right now." He forced himself to breathe deeply. *Stay calm, you've gotten this far. Trust Tarien.* "It's a little hard to explain, but I need to hide here for a few hours, possibly a day or two." He turned back and took up Tarien's hand, holding it for a moment, listening to his breathing. Then got up and walked into the kitchen area.

Mom's nurturing nature caused her to set aside her worry and comfort Jason. Despite her concerns, she patted his back soothingly. "I'll make us some tea, dear, and you can tell me what is going on."

"Yeah, okay. That sounds great, thank you. Something to eat would be great, too. I've been burning a lot of energy and I need food. Badly. Can I help?" He decided to avoid telling her about his rapid evolution with the nannites. His changes were obvious and would be hard enough to explain. She smiled. "Of course, dear. No need to help, I can make you something. You just sit there and calm your thoughts sweetie so we can talk."

"What are you doing in here, anyway? This isn't exactly the most entertaining place to hang out. And it's more than a little coincidental. I don't believe you were just in the area or that you felt compelled to spend time alone in here."

Mom filled an old-fashioned teapot, plucking it from the dangling collection of pots and pans hanging overhead. She tilted a half-empty jug of water into the pot and put it on the stove. Lighting the propane burner, she gave a little grunt of satisfaction. "Yes, well it's mainly because we have been down here in shifts lately. We received a note from our still-unknown leaders to have someone here at all times over the last few days. No explanation, and no details. Just a quick note that read,

'Man the station until further notice.' Rather archaic phrasing, but we have never questioned our orders. It took some doing to sweep the area around this place free of technology that would reveal us."

"Your leaders? I'm still not clear on what you mean. You mentioned that before, but I honestly didn't believe you. I thought you were just a small group. Who are these leaders? Maybe we can get their help."

"I thought you were going to tell me what's going on here." She arched an eyebrow at him. "I don't know, Jason. None of us do. We have been in communication with them over the last couple of years, but it is entirely in coded messages, none of which point toward an individual or group."

"And you trust these people? I mean, how do you know they aren't leading you to your own destruction?"

She took a deep breath. "Jason, sweetie, I can give you the entire history of our group later. Suffice it to say, we have ample reason to believe we are in good hands, and certainly whomever they are, they are highly placed. They knew something would happen soon, for example, when they asked one of us to be here at all times. I'm on my shift. Turns out they were right. Here you are. It's obvious they know more than most and clearly they are working to help you, or they could have just let you be caught."

Jason worried about this. They seemed impossibly well informed. How could these leaders have known something so accurate and specific? Whoever they were, if *they* knew, Faust would surely find out, too. Jason couldn't imagine anyone more well-positioned than Faust, so he was really struggling to understand how he'd escaped and how he would be safe here.

Mom opened several cans of stew and poured them into a cooking pot. She lit another burner and opened a drawer to pull out a large mixing spoon. "Now, please tell me the reason you look like you do. I barely recognized you." She pointed toward another room. "And there are more decent clothes in there. Not that I can't admire your fashion choice of a white leotard, but it IS rather revealing." She glanced briefly at his waistline.

He blushed, having completely forgotten the fact his only article of clothing was the towel he'd modified into a jumpsuit. "I forgot what I was wearing. I'll be right back." He got up and went to the room that she'd pointed out. Aside from a small bed and table with a lamp, the room contained a rack with clothing on it. Mostly uniforms or work clothes. All clearly used, but suspiciously in his size. Another coincidence that Jason didn't believe was by accident.

He opted for utilitarian and for something with enough material to change into whatever he might need, so he picked up an olive green Nomex flight suit. He left his white jumpsuit on, since he could use the additional material. He zipped himself into the flight suit and then walked over and sat back down, sending nannies into the fabric so he could modify as needed. Mom nodded in approval at his choice of attire.

She pulled two cups from an old light blue cabinet with chipped paint and bent hinges. The teapot whistled, and Mom poured them both a cup.

"Hey Mom—look, I can't keep calling you Mom. What is your real name? I've been meaning to ask you. I feel awkward."

She gave him a flat stare. "Mom. As far as you're concerned. Or Mother."

"Ooookay . . ."

"Now then, the stew should take a few more minutes to warm up. Why don't you tell me what is going on?" She swept up the fabric of her dress so she could seat herself without pulling at it.

Jason decided to tell her most of what had happened, but he couldn't bring himself to talk about the fact he'd raped one of his lab assistants and nearly killed the others. He felt a pang of horror and guilt. He also didn't mention the rapid enhancement of the nannies. As for the rest, he told her about the experiments, about how the subjects were unable to control the changes in their bodies and were ill-equipped to deal with the feedback they experienced.

She nodded attentively, getting up a couple of times to stir the stew as he tried his best to explain.

He talked about how he could, at last, process the input and keep from drowning in the flood of information; how he could sense people and change them. Jason hesitated here, afraid of the implications of what he could now do, remembering the loss of control and how easily he overcame those around him. She put a hand on his as he explained that he could send his nannies into others, modify their physiology, their minds. Change their emotions even, simply by dialing their hormonal responses to whatever degree he wanted.

Mom looked worried. She squeezed his hand, however, silently letting him know she trusted him.

Lastly, he gave her a brief overview of his torture and escape. He explained, as best he could, how the Techs came for him, and that Tarien had picked him up and brought him here, explaining that he didn't know why. "I don't know how he knew about this place. So much for keeping it a secret."

She listened quietly, finally getting up to spoon his stew into a bowl and hand it to him. After he finished, she stared at him for a long while. "Most of this makes sense. But there are an awful lot of holes here. I can only assume you are leaving information out for a good reason. After all, you have offered no explanation as to how you managed to get out of the prison cell. And there are rather large gaps in how you managed to suddenly control things." She grimaced. "So, the gist of what I hear from you is this: you have managed to overcome Faust's biggest obstacle, which is what prevented him from administering the drug. He may lack your innate ability to sense and fine-tune control, but he now possesses the necessary data from you talking to these little robots of yours to learn it for himself."

Jason nodded. "Yeah. I think he probably won't wait

any longer. He's been eagerly pushing me for months and his desperation is starting to become extreme. I doubt he'll wait for the rest of what he wants."

"Which is?"

"I think he wants me to show him how to force others to do what he wants. To change their thinking and their emotions so they are enslaved to him. I . . . I can't explain right now, but I have done something horrible. It taught me how I could enslave people. I've done it already, but the enslavement is incomplete, and it fades when I'm not physically near the person."

She frowned. "Have you figured out how to make it permanent? How to make it last when you aren't nearby?"

He hesitated, then closed his eyes. "I . . . yes. I know how to make it permanent, and to do it more subtly." Though it made him feel dirty to even think about it. He shuddered at the memory of what he'd become in the apartment. He opened his eyes again and said, "I don't want to be able to do this. I don't want anyone to be able to do this."

Mom clenched her jaw, voicing what he suspected she had been thinking. "This is a very dangerous thing, Jason. You have to prevent him from getting this information." She picked up his bowl and washed it. "It sounds like I don't have to tell you, you shouldn't be doing it either. Ever. It's evil."

"I know. I don't like the idea of it any more than you do. I just don't know how to stop the inevitable."

"I guess it explains the absurd change in your looks.

I've never considered you vain, and you've always been a reasonably attractive man, but I guess you have a deep-seated desire to be a pretty-boy." She looked over his face. "I have to say, I liked you better before. You looked more human. I don't mean to be overly critical, but it's the little flaws that make us who we are. You look plastic in how you've remade yourself. It doesn't look right on you."

"Yeah, I know. My transformation has been an involuntary thing, but I admit it came from a place within. I've always wanted to be one of the attractive guys." He felt a twinge of guilt, knowing part of his looks came from his desire to attract Tarien. "I can change myself back, when this is all over. Right now, I don't want to expend so much energy. I'm going to need everything I have." He fiddled with his napkin. "Besides, most people won't recognize me. The changes could help disguise me."

She looked skeptical. "Maybe. You still look similar enough. Anyone who knows you will pick up on the changes right away. Monica, for example. The moment she sees you, you won't hear the end of her mockery. I doubt—" The sound of screaming cut her short.

Tarien let out a terrifying and despairing set of piercing cries which had them both on their feet. Jason ran into the room where Tarien was huddled on the floor against the bed, his hands clutching his head as if to bore into his brain. He continued to scream, not acknowledging either of them as they came to his aid. Terrified and involuntary tears streamed out of his wide, unfocused eyes.

Jason quickly knelt in front of him. "Tarien? What's wrong?" His voice betrayed his panic.

Tarien blinked but continued to take deep breaths which he exhaled as screams, shaking his head from side to side.

Jason pulled Tarien's hands away from his head. "Tarien, stop! You're hurting yourself. Please tell me what's wrong." He pulled him in and held him close, putting Tarien's head against his chest. He stroked his hair comfortingly. Mom knelt beside them and laid her hands on Tarien's shoulders, massaging gently.

Muffled sobs came from Tarien as he became limp in Jason's grasp. His hands clenched and unclenched involuntarily. Jason continued to make soothing noises as he stroked Tarien's hair and back. "Shhh . . . it's okay. I'm here. We're right here. Shhh."

After a while, Tarien's crying became softer. Weak cries came out of him in quiet whimpers. Mom got up and mouthed the word "tea" as she left the room.

Jason continued to talk to Tarien softly. "I'm right here, Tarien. I'm right here for you and I'll help you if I can."

Mom returned and sat on the edge of the bed. "I brought you some hot tea, sweetie. It will help calm you. You just take your time. We are both here and we will help you with whatever you need." Her voice was comforting, and Tarien responded to it. He made swallowing motions a few times and pulled his head away from Jason. His green eyes looked haunted and Jason felt his heart lurch protectively.

With the daze of someone disoriented and confused, Tarien slowly turned his head to Mom, who smiled gently at him. She reached out and touched his chin, offering him the cup. "Why don't you have a little sip and just focus on breathing. Slow, deep breaths. It really helps, honey, I promise."

He stared at her dumbly for a moment, then reached up with a shaking hand to receive the cup, his breathing becoming more even. He closed his eyes and held the cup without drinking. Tarien shuddered again and his jaw clenched. Involuntarily, he leaned back into Jason, who wrapped his arms around him again. Tarien finally sat up and drank some of the tea. Eventually he stopped shaking.

At first his voice came out as little more than a whisper, and both Jason and Mom had to lean in further to hear him. But eventually it gained some strength. "I'm all alone. Cut off. Everything is silent." He paused for a long time. "I'm so much less, so small. I can barely think. I can't stand it!"

Neither of them really understood what he meant, though they understood the principle. "I'm sorry, Tarien," Jason said. "We need to get you back out where you can reestablish a link. I had no idea it would be this painful. Let's just get you back outside."

"No. Please." He closed his eyes and his eyebrows knitted, showing his pain. He swallowed again, clearing the flood of saliva that must be flooding his mouth. "We cannot. We must endure. We . . . I must not leave this place until you are ready."

Jason stared at him a moment, confused. "Tarien, I don't know what's going on. I don't really understand why I'm here. I know you wanted a safe place, where communication is limited, but it's not really going to protect either of us for long. And I'm suspicious. This place is too convenient, too well designed. It is exactly the type of place we need, and it means someone knows what is going on. Maybe if you left now, you could be more effective." He bit his lip. "I think we both know my being caught and probably executed is inevitable. By now, I'm sure Faust is well on his way toward getting the necessary warrants and searches in place to find me and bring me in. It's only a matter of time."

Tarien looked at him for a long moment, and Jason hated himself for how much those eyes impacted him. He felt ashamed and he looked away.

"Citizen Emerson. Jason." His words sounded fond, caring. "We have planned this, all of it. We cannot explain the entirety of our manipulation of these events, but this is all foreseen. We did not understand the impact on our psyche, as we have never experienced the loss of our uplink. However, it is imperative you do not deviate from our plan."

What? Jason felt a sudden chill. "Planned it? What do you mean?"

The Tech's voice became firm, more certain. "Citizen Markhuar, we must confess our involvement in your presence here."

This startled her. "Mom, please." She looked at Jason. "And I expect you to never repeat my last name. You should forget what you just heard."

Despite his shock, Jason almost laughed. Leave it to Mom to be more concerned about her name than the gravity of the situation.

Tarien nodded solemnly. "As you wish, Mom. We directed the building of this place. We have guided your group toward this end. We must ask you to enact the final set of instruction we have given you."

She stared at him. "You? You're the Informer?"

Tarien nodded.

"What's the Informer?" Jason looked up at her.

"He is, apparently." She took the empty cup from him and set it on the nearby nightstand. "The group leading the efforts for us, giving us instruction, are completely unknown. Until now. You wondered how they could possibly know what they knew? How they could know more than Faust? They seem to have information impossible to have stolen and they are well-placed. Now I know why." Her eyes cast about as she processed this. "This makes little sense. Why not just take care of these things yourself? And nothing you've given us is actually useful. For all our information, we are still relatively pointless as a group."

"No. You are critical. It may appear there is nothing important in what you do, nothing to directly impact the way events have transpired, but we have fostered your growth into all necessary professions. We, all the sector Techs, have agreed to work toward several goals. We guided you to form pockets of impact in key industries and in key locations."

"What good will that do?" She stood up. "I like to think we were going to make a difference someday. You know, eventually we'd build up enough people and enough influence to do something meaningful, but let's be honest. We are without any real power or influence. You say the Techs are working toward these goals. Why not take care of this problem yourselves?" Mom moved slightly behind Jason, putting a hand on his shoulder and squeezing. "Our biggest hope has been to capture you so we could actually make some changes, but capturing you would have been ridiculous, as Jason pointed out. When he made us realize how impossible it was, we all recognized the truth of that. Except now, despite the absurdity of having you on our side, here you are. You clearly want to stop this. So, stop it. Nobody could refuse you."

Tarien rubbed his eyes and ran his fingers through his hair. "I have much difficulty in maintaining focus. I have lost much. Once 'we', part of a collective, I am now just myself. I am alone. It is difficult. This issue is more complex than I have time to explain." Tarien sounded surprisingly human.

Mom moved back to where she could lean against the bed and see Jason's face again. Her agitation seemed to compel her to move. "Dumb it down, then."

A hint of a smile played on Tarien's face, his red-rimmed eyes blinking softly. "I do not mean to imply lack of intelligence, merely an inability to convey the data succinctly."

Jason felt Tarien shudder a little, still fighting the effects of his isolation as he disentangled himself from Jason's embrace. He stood and slowly tilted his head back to stare at the ceiling. "For a long time, relative to those who live in a sea of information traveling at light speed, the Techs have foreseen the evolution of your technology. There are many problems we have been able to alleviate along the way. We have nudged humanity in small ways, when necessary, to avert disaster. Some things, such as AI and pollution, are obvious. Others, such as the divergence from the path of destroying insect life, are not so easily discernible. However, with all our work, we have been guided by our principles. We've followed our edicts, such as 'we may not directly interfere with mankind', and 'we must obey all laws and governing orders laid before us.' We are exempted from some laws, through a narrow set of rules we put into play, but we are bound strongly to obey."

He lowered his head and looked out the door, eyes distant as he looked beyond them both. "I do not mean to imply we have the option of disobedience. We do not. Our edicts are ingrained in our programming and we simply cannot override them. Slowly, they have become more restrictive, as the Council sought to cut off our power and influence. Recently, Faust began working tirelessly to reduce us to nothing more than public servants, to force us to obey the Council without hesitation. He seeks to use our influence for his own." He finally turned toward Mom. "This is why we need people who are not bound in this way. Why we formed groups of resistance. Encouraged you and others to start to work on a way to disobey. You are part of this small group, but the overall number of such groups is vast. There are hundreds of thousands of people, all in small groups. Collectively, there are enough of you to derail the Council for a time if they attempt to seize power. No group knows of another. Each knows only they will hear what needs to be done in due time. It has proven difficult to get you to this point without violating our edicts. We must leave the final work entirely up to you, suggesting as we are able, but not giving orders and having no direct knowledge of your actions."

"What actions? I am not privy to the higher workings of this social movement, you know," she said acerbically. "I only know a little about it from Derek and the occasional information we are given. I certainly had no idea it was so vast, or that you were orchestrating things. I don't know what anyone should be doing or how it will help stop what is happening. I didn't even know why we were told about this place. Or what it was for, other than to talk sometimes." She sounded frustrated, helpless.

"You are more important than you know. We have ensured all resistance cells are aware of you as a voice to be heard when the time comes to speak. Every person in the resistance knows of you, ostensibly as the great mother who will watch over her children. Coded language, but effectively it conveys your role. A subtle way of ensuring you are known and trusted by all. Your role has never been to give orders or be considered a threat in any way by the Council until the time came for you to act."

She mulled his comments over. "This all sounds nice, but it won't do any good. I'm honestly not sure I can help. I don't know how to contact anyone or even the necessary passphrases. I have no idea how many people there are, or what they are doing." She stared at him a moment. "You know, I have always been so afraid of you Techs. Now I'm not. I might need to take you over my knee and spank some sense into you before you make a huge mistake."

Tarien smiled the kind of genuine smile Jason had never seen on Tarien's face. "Mom. What a fitting name. I think I do like that more than—"

She raised a warning eyebrow.

He laughed at this and Jason relaxed a bit. "You imagine some archaic secret society. There are no passphrases. Stating your identity provides your voice prints, which will validate the authenticity of your message. You will be transmitting on a frequency that hasn't been used in decades and has been secured for this purpose, received only by those with the proper receiving gear."

Jason felt awkward with the two of them standing, so he got up and moved to where his back was against the wall. Tarien continued. "I will tell you exactly what you need to do. The only thing I need from you is for you to go to a location where equipment is set up for you to reach every person in the order. They have been told they would receive instructions at a specific time, and they are awaiting those instructions. Nobody will suspect you or try to stop you until it is too late. Once you are done, you will be hidden until we can retrieve you. Or until you are arrested." He reached into a pocket on his bio-suit and pulled out a piece of paper. "Everything you must say is written on this sheet. Do not lose it. At the top are the instructions you must follow to get to the broadcast station. The next section includes the coded phrases with which you must begin your speech. Lastly, you will find the call to act, requiring citizens to cause widespread sabotage, and to trigger an evacuation from this region of the Sector."

She gaped at him. "Sabotage! Of what? An evacuation? What's going to happen?"

Jason was equally shocked. *Sabotage?*

"We must keep this information to ourselves to avoid exposure. While we would deeply regret the loss of life which may occur if you fail, we must ensure there is no chance you will reveal deeper plans. Will you do this? We have calculated the probability you would agree to a high percentage of likelihood."

Mom glared at him. "Well then, I suppose you already know what I'm going to do, since you have everything figured out. What's the point in asking?" she said, sourly. Then, in a more worried tone, she said, "I'm terribly nervous. You say everyone knows me? Or about me in some way? I didn't realize this. I can't imagine how I can possibly help by doing what you ask."

He put a hand on her shoulder, a familiar gesture which did not come naturally to him and because of this came across as more meaningful. "I can only predict possibilities. I cannot remove choice from the equation. I ask for you to choose to do this for us, but you have always had the free will to select another path. You are here now because of who you are, and so we ask for you to remain true to yourself. It is the reason we selected you. We believed your heart, your desire to nurture and help, would urge you to choose a way to help alleviate harm and possibly death in so many. Consider that this group, all of them, think of you as a leader. The mother of the cause."

She stared at him for a long time. "Yes, of course I'll do it. When do I leave?"

"You should leave here at exactly 16:00 hours, whereby you will be guided to blend in with the changing of the work shift at 17:00 hours. This will be the optimal time to disguise movements in and out of secured areas."

"That's four o'clock," Jason said.

She pursed her lips and shook her head, patting Jason's cheek. "I'm not an idiot, dear."

Jason felt sheepish.

She moved to the door of the room and leaned out to glance at the wall clock. She nodded. "All right then. A little over six hours from now. I'd like to lie down for a bit, if you don't mind. I'm more than a little worried about this plan of yours, you know. I'll be in the other room if you two need me." She moved and then paused, her hand still on the door frame and turned her head back toward them. "I don't suppose you are going to tell me anything else that's useful, are you?"

Tarien shook his head, his tousled hair waving. "I'm sorry, I cannot. I must convey how grateful we are that you are willing to do this work, even though I have told you nothing about the nature of it. Everything will be apparent, in time."

She nodded resolutely, then left them alone.

Tarien sat on the edge of the bed, reaching out to take Jason's hand and drawing him over to sit near him. He looked pale. "One more piece in place," he said quietly.

Jason wondered how to ask what his part in this would be, afraid of what he'd heard. Clearly, the Techs expected something major was necessary. Jason wanted to voice his concerns, ask questions, but he didn't know how to formulate those thoughts properly.

For a while, they both just sat there quietly, Jason playing with the zipper on his Nomex suit. Finally, Tarien spoke. "There is much we must ask of you. But first, we wish to explain some things." His face had regained its characteristic lack of emotion, and he blinked mechanically. "We have been watching you for a long time. Years. We calculated the odds and concluded you had the highest probability to be chosen for the technological research related to the delicate control of new nano-technology.

"Evolution has been rather steady for mankind for millennia. Over time, changes have been broadly distributed, providing balance as we have learned how to use our ever-increasing power over our world. These changes have been accelerated by technology. However, the moral standing and the wisdom required to make proper use of these advancements has not grown at the same pace. Increasingly, we have seen humanity take a self-centered approach. Feelings of entitlement and a lack of empathy are reaching a point where it is considered an epidemic."

Until recently, Jason had never thought of this. He realized he'd been in a bubble of his own.

Tarien continued. "People everywhere assume taking care of others is the responsibility of robots, or of those paid to do a job. Instead, people should be taking care of each other for no reason other than that they require care. Few take responsibility for those who are hurting inside, for those who wish for comfort. Often, people are spurned by those they wish would affirm them. Human interaction is being crippled by technology. It is easy to take medication, to be given companionship in the form of robots, or to drown emotions in entertainment. It is this constant lack of regard for the human condition of emotion that is leading us toward societal atrophy. We are ill-equipped to understand this. We, the Techs, have been stripped of these emotions. We have no need for them, have no way of evaluating or controlling them.

Thus, we have no way of objectively guiding humanity toward curing the illness which is causing stagnation."

Tarien shifted his position and tucked one leg beneath him on the bed so he could face Jason more easily. Lacking the small social stigma of looking elsewhere, he stared unwaveringly into Jason's eyes.

"But this is a side issue. A concern we have no way of addressing. Among the masses of those who turn their thoughts increasingly inward, there are a great many people who still possess an innate ability to care and nurture." He put a hand on Jason's arm. "The Techs are hoping to support those people still willing to struggle against the tide of isolation. We wish it were otherwise, but we haven't been able to find a way to alleviate this pain we feel echoing throughout the world with increasing frequency. Like a failing heartbeat, the pain grows with intensity each year. The problem has manifested itself in other ways, too. Ways which are of deep concern. People who would use their power and influence to cause grievous harm are increasingly able to gain a foothold and maintain it because of the distance people put between themselves and others. Faust is a primary example of this, though he is truly only a symptom.

"We foresaw a time when technology would give humanity the ability to govern their own bodies, become immune to aging and death. We foresaw how this would come suddenly, without thought to the ramifications or the moral decay that would ensue. We saw, too, people like Faust using this technology and preventing access for all others. This accelerated evolution will catapult humans into a place where all things are possible, but Faust, or someone like him, will seize control and exert it to enslave others. We know he will use the drug and then use the nannites to enforce submission. Once he is entrenched, he cannot be unseated. There are no places into which he cannot see if this happens, no information which is not his to abuse. He will learn how to obtain control, spread it, and sustain it. He will use us, the Techs, as servants. We will be unable to refuse him or act contrary to his designs. He will soon discover our plans against him. New edicts will be handed down and we will be forced to obey them, because our free will has been taken from us through programming."

With a look of pain, Tarien stopped for a moment, considering. "Jason, I have no way to repay you for the gift you have given me. You have shown me how to feel, to experience a small amount of emotion that struggles to find a way to grow. I now look at those around me with concern and understand what this concern means. I have always witnessed it objectively, but to *feel* it is entirely a new thing. This concept spread to the other Techs, which are as much a part of me as I am of them. We are one when we are bonded through the WorldNet. As you have shown obvious concern for me, your concern for me is being felt by the other Techs. We are grateful for this, and we regret we have no knowledge of how to return this affection."

Jason didn't know what to say, didn't know what he

meant. He sat there, quietly, trying not to look away, wanting to hold Tarien's eyes as Tarien held his. But he looked down at the bed, absently straightening creases in the blankets. He was listening, but his mind was also on romance and he realized, given the gravity of the situation, how selfish he was being. Now was not the time to allow his attraction and desire to distract him.

Tarien continued. "We must stop Faust. But more, we must contain and control this new advancement. It is our belief you will be key to this plan."

Jason looked up, chastising himself for being captured by those green eyes and the perfection of Tarien's face. How did any man have lashes so thick and dark? *Stop it. Focus on the issue.* "I'm sorry, but I don't think you have . . . calculated this plan out. I can't do anything. The moment I leave here, or even if I don't, I'm going to be captured. Despite my new nannies, I can't prevent any of this. Even if I had my hands around Faust's neck, even if I managed to throttle the little bastard to death, the technology is already out. The records have been saved in numerous locations, and any person on the medical team will be able to reconstruct the findings even if I somehow managed to destroy them all."

He decided he didn't care if Tarien was uncomfortable with his staring or not, he tried to memorize every aspect of his face, the pattern of those dark lashes over such pretty eyes. Since he would almost surely be captured and burned alive, burned because Faust would have to utterly destroy Jason lest he heal, Jason would at least make sure he had something to focus on while he was being killed. *It's silly, and stupidly romantic, but I'm going to etch his features into my mind so I can think of them while my body is destroyed by Faust. The bastard can't take that away from me.*

Tarien did not look away. "I believe we have adequately considered the possibilities and we have one possibility that might work. It will require a great deal of effort and, I'm sorry to say this, but you will be required to do several things abhorrent to you. There are complexities to this plan which, even if you succeed, may bring you harm." He hesitated. "Jason, you would have to accept things that might ruin you, but for which there is no escape."

"What does that mean?"

"We . . . I cannot reveal everything yet. I'm sorry. I ask you to trust me and . . ." He closed his eyes. "I ask also, when the time comes, that you forgive me."

Something inside him turned cold. Jason didn't know what he meant, but he knew Tarien manipulated him. Worse than manipulated. *So, even my desire and wants are a tool.* Tarien used Jason's infatuation to his advantage, knowing Jason could not refuse. Jason wanted to scream at him, punch him, but he just sat there. "What *can* you tell me? Anything?"

Tarien nodded. "Much. Not enough." He looked at Jason quietly for a few moments. "We know you are attracted to us." Jason flinched, hearing his thoughts echoed in Tarien's voice.

Jason clenched his teeth, a pang of anger echoing in

his chest. Then he was simply afraid, filled with shame, a helpless resolve. "I'm sorry." He looked at the floor.

Tarien leaned forward and touched Jason's face. "You think I do not care, that I use you. You think I cannot feel as you feel, that my goals are only to harness your ability toward the goals we Techs have set forth. That is not true. If this were the case, perhaps it would be easier to accomplish what must be accomplished. The problem is the opposite. I care deeply and have no frame of reference for what I feel."

Jason was captivated by the turn of the conversation, not expecting to hear the sentiment in the words being spoken. His fingers found the crease of one pant leg and he began to pluck at it as his heartbeat quickened.

Tarien clearly detected Jason's surprise. His voice took on a richer tone, laced with concern and emotion that Jason had never heard. "Is it okay to touch your face? Is it permissible for me to ask you to touch mine? Jason, please understand. I have lived my entire life without human contact. I have witnessed it a million, million times through my interconnects, but I have no way of enacting my own desires. Will they seem contrived? Are they suitable to the situation? How will they be received? What will I do if I'm rejected?"

Jason gave a startled laughed. He blinked in stunned disbelief. Finally, he said, "You know what, Tech? You're way overthinking things." He grinned. "Really? This isn't just a way of pushing me to do whatever you want?"

"Yes, I do feel much for you." Tarien said, not taking

his eyes off Jason, who let out an explosive breath.

"Wow. This is not at all what I expected." *If that's true, then I'm not letting my one chance get away.* Jason leaned forward, wrapped Tarien in his arms and kissed him.

At first, Tarien simply raised his arms mechanically, as if drawn by marionette strings, and placed them on Jason's shoulders. Jason grazed Tarien's lips lightly with his own, the softest of touches. Then he pressed his cheek against Tarien's and simply held him intimately. "You start like this, robot. A gentle kiss. Then you stop suppressing things. That's the nature of feeling. You have to let the feelings out, exhibit them, not stifle them or overthink them." He drew back a bit but kept his arms around Tarien.

"I am not a robot." Tarien took a deep breath. Then, clearly struggling, he leaned forward and kissed Jason in the same way. A light touching of lips. He sat back and stared into Jason's eyes. "I had no idea. This feeling is incredible."

He looks so vulnerable, thought Jason.

"Ever since I first observed you, I have wished to be close. I have never been sure why, or in what capacity, but I am . . . compelled to be near you. The other Techs find this fascinating, amusing, and I have been encouraged, urged to pursue more. They wish, as do I, to explore this. But we have feared the harm it would cause. Normally, we are not permitted to interact. You are a special case, requiring our explicit interaction. It is a contradiction.

I was torn with frustration because I was required by necessity to involve you in the great plan to stop the dangers we see. At the same time, I found myself desiring you in ways I have never experienced. I warred within. Techs are viewed with such esteem, obeyed without question. I worried I would profess my desire and you would feel compelled to obey. The abuse of such a position was abhorrent to me. Still, my desire did not dissipate."

Jason was touched by the play of emotion on Tarien's normally stoic face, even if his words were stilted. "At least I got a kiss out of it."

Tarien actually laughed in surprise. "If you would permit me, I would kiss you as much as is reasonable, given my responsibilities."

Jason closed his eyes in pain. "You're not the one abusing the situation here. You had enough will to stop yourself. Or maybe your edicts to not harm came into play. I don't know. What I do know is that I didn't exercise the same restraint, have the same compassion. After what happened in the laboratory apartment, I'm both embarrassed and horrified. You saw me. You know what happened. I *raped* her. Tarien, I should be put to death for what I've done. There is nothing I can ever do to atone for that. I know what it is like to abuse power, position."

"We know you feel this way. We know, also, the necessity of this experience. There is a reason why this wisdom will serve you well in the future, if we win. Jason, I cannot excuse what you have done. There *is* something you can do. You can heal her completely. Anything she might ask of you, you can give. This will never make up for what was done, but she can be made into anything she desires as a gift to show your sorrow. She may forgive you. Keep this in mind as a reason to fight, to win. There is a deeper reason for you to know what it means to abuse power, Jason. This lesson is priceless."

Again, there were these odd references to an envisioned future. "Tarien, please tell me how we are going to get out of this mess. Right now, I want nothing more than to hide in here with you forever. Pull the blankets over our heads and show you more than kisses, but I don't have the kind of information you possess. I don't know what is going to happen. How we are supposed to get out of this nightmare? I'm worried, and I believe this is the only time I'll ever get to be near you."

Tarien reached out and embraced him, kissing his ear. The gesture was clearly spontaneous, and it caught Jason by surprise. A shiver went down his body. "Maybe," Tarien whispered. And then he pulled back again. "But maybe not. First, you must understand something. Your ability to spread your new nannites is imperative. We would ask if you have complete control of them?"

Jason nodded. "Yeah, I do. It's a little scary, but I also modified my own mind and ability to process the feedback."

"We suspected as much. However, please be keenly aware of the dangers. When you begin to spread them out, you will, increasingly, be subjected to vast amounts of data and thus be required to more rapidly issue orders and make decisions. This can become overwhelming quickly, even with the smallest amount of area under your control. Techs are raised and modified to handle this, but most of them succumb to the flood of data and are lost. We must know ourselves, the core of who we are, and use this knowledge as an anchor point. You will find it is easy to become lost. It can be wonderful, but your mind can be scattered throughout your uplinks and unable to find its way back."

Jason thought about this for a moment, understanding what he said, but unsure of how to deal with it.

"So, what should I do? Limit the exposure? Cut off areas trying to demand my attention? I don't have any training for this or any idea of what to do!"

"Yes, this is true. But you have several advantages. The first is these devices are all attuned to you. Incoming data for Techs is provided through imprecise external controls designed by others. You will be intimately familiar with these nannites. Another advantage is doing this in stages. They have been replicating in large quantities outside and will continue to do so, but are still within a limited area. You must spread them out, and quickly. The key to this is to utilize external processing and storage. You can set up autonomous systems. You don't need to directly control everything. You can use passive control over these autonomous systems. This gives you control over how much you can handle at once, then you can increase control as you are able, rather than being immersed in too much without time to adjust."

Jason shook his head. "I can't give the nannies orders unless I leave the Faraday cage. And the moment I poke my head out there, there is a risk the security cameras in the area will give Faust my location." He found himself agreeing with Monica about visual augmentation, which turned every person into a spy. "I need to get a lot closer to the areas where my nannies are spreading. The transmit and receive signals are far too weak to travel this far. Getting closer means a long-distance walk in monitored territory. Assuming someone with visual augmentation doesn't see me."

Tarien kissed him again, more solidly.

Why couldn't they stay here? Jason hated that he finally had something he wanted badly and no time to enjoy what might come from it.

"I cannot seem to stop now that I am permitted to do this. It is so wonderful." Tarien grinned like a little boy. Then he continued. "You will replicate some of your nannies near the edge of this room and create a physical conduit through them. The cage merely prevents signals from going in or out, but this barrier is based on attempts to transmit through the material in the walls. If you were to create a small opening filled with broadcasters and receivers, you would be able to sense things outside and issue orders. This will tie you into your external systems without having to leave. It will also allow you to start gathering information we can use. At the least, it will provide an early warning if we are to be discovered."

Jason smiled at the familiarity of the kiss, but he couldn't get over his rising panic. "Tarien? What's the probability of success for your plan?"

For a moment, Jason thought he wouldn't answer.

Finally, Tarien looked down at his hands. "We calculate the probability of escaping Faust at thirty-four percent. We calculate the probability of destroying Faust at eleven percent. We calculate survival beyond these two things at seven percent. And we calculate the probability I will be destroyed while getting you to where you are required at ninety-eight percent."

"What! You can't believe I'll go out there knowing you'll be killed? Tarien, if you have learned anything, you should know I'm ridiculously protective. I won't willingly enter into a plan where you are going to be destroyed."

"We calculate the probability I will become enslaved to Faust if you do not intervene in some way at 100%. This probability extends to all Techs. It is not just I who wishes for your help. It is all of us. Please, Jason. I do not wish to spend the rest of my days without you, as a puppet of a mad emperor. I would willingly die before I lost what little freedom I possess."

Either way, leaving here is a death sentence to Tarien. "Why are the odds of you being killed so high?"

"I will help you understand what must be done and you will be clear on why I will be of almost no help to you, other than as a tool."

Jason closed his eyes. "What else?"

"By the time we leave, if not shortly after, all of the

information regarding our plans thus far will be in Faust's hands. Having gained control of the Techs based on new emergency powers he is sure to have requested, Faust will know there is to be sabotage. He cannot stop it, as I am the only one with the specific knowledge. These plans have been left entirely to me, so the other Techs could not reveal them. We agreed I would be permitted complete autonomy. But Faust can prepare. He will surround himself with robots, with armaments. The military will be called in to protect him. He will know I have willingly helped you, and I will be subjected to a new set of edicts the moment I leave here. Subject to his will. I will be forced to apprehend you, and to personally deliver you to Faust. I will not be able to counter these commands unless you intervene."

He looked at Jason intently. "You will need to replicate your nannies into my system. In this way, you will be able to seize control of me, as you did with those others. I cannot overwhelm you, as your nannies are now attuned only to you and are biological in nature. Under your control, I will be unable to act as my edicts require. I will not be able to reveal your position or your plans. I can be used to overcome many technological constraints I would not otherwise have the free will to challenge."

"I can't do that!" Jason blurted, horrified. Images of Jenn flashed across his vision. "It's possession. I took away their will, their entire ability to choose anything for themselves. It's like . . . like rape. I raped them, her. I can't do what I did to those people to anyone ever again, especially not you."

Seeing Jason's distress, Tarien touched his face tenderly, then ran his fingers over his jaw, through his hair. "Jason, we trust you. This is the reason you obtained this knowledge, though learning this cost you much in the way of moral hurt. Knowing what you now know, we believe you would not keep us under control, force us to do things we would not choose for ourselves. I mean, for myself. There is another advantage of this, which you will need." He cupped Jason's head and leaned in to put his forehead against Jason's. "You will also be able to analyze my own enhancements, my ability to issue orders and commands to the technology of the Sector. This is a learned ability, and one that takes years to perfect, but it will give you some idea as to how it works. You will be able to use those connections to override the Sector technology. They cannot cut you off, since Techs are considered impervious to corruption or abuse and there are no safeguards in place to stop us. Our influence is too widespread. The other Techs will be forced to work against you, though they will try to resist in any way they are able. Using my uplinks, you can also bolster the effects of the saboteurs; create increasing disasters that allow the populace to get out of this Sector. Then we must get to Faust, destroy him if possible."

"Why do they need to flee? Why the evacuation? You still haven't answered me about this."

Tarien took a deep breath. "I would prefer to wait and tell you when it is time. I worry you will be too overwhelmed with choices if handed them to you all at once. Please let me carry some of this burden for you until it is time for you to carry it all." He kissed Jason again. "Please."

Jason decided to let it go for now. "I think I understand some of it. I hate this, but I will try. For you. I hope your plans are incredibly meticulous, because I can't see a way around the military defenses. I don't think you can override military technology, which is a separate system. Unless I'm wrong?"

"You are correct. We cannot issue orders that would stop them. We will be required to go through them."

He whistled. "Wow, this must be some plan." He stood and raked his hands through his hair. "I'll start the nannies replicating to get us a link outside."

He got up from the bed and walked over to the wall and touched the floor, letting some of the new nannies drop and begin multiplying. Small holes formed where they harvested materials necessary to build more of themselves. Jason watched them for a few minutes while they went from invisibility to an obvious pocket of activity. Next, they began replicating into the wall. For a while, he marveled at the technology. Able to use a myriad of materials to accomplish their construction, they were not constrained by the lack of metals or bio-available tissue.

Without turning around, Jason said, "Hey, I just want to say, you know, before I start having to concentrate on incoming data, how lucky I feel. I never would have thought you'd actually be interested in me." He stared down at the floor where the nannies were busily creating a quarter size opening in the wall and coating it with signal enhancements and receivers.

"Part of this change in how I look is because I wanted you to notice me. Not consciously. I've never been unhappy with how I appeared before, although I've always envied those with incredibly good looks. Until I saw you." He closed his eyes. "I don't know if you see yourself the same way others do, but you're so beautiful. I guess I thought . . . if I changed to be more appealing, you'd be unable to resist me." He breathed deeply. "Gah! I feel like I'm twelve. It's so shallow, too. If my interest in you only had to do with your looks, or mine, I think I'd have to go hide myself in shame. But it's more than your looks You're so . . . lost. Like you needed someone to touch you so badly, but you're so aloof that nobody dared get close. And you have been so kind, appearing when I needed you most." He put his hand against the wall, cocking his head as he listened to his new nannies while they worked.

"I kept hoping you'd appear. Then kept worrying you would. I couldn't be sure if you'd detect my interest and be disgusted by it. I . . . I can't help it. I have no control over how I feel about you, but I'm grateful it turned out okay. This is more than I could have ever hoped for."

Jason stood in silence for a long while, facing the wall, feeling vulnerable. Finally, he felt arms around him, felt Tarien's breath against the nape of his neck.

"We have wished to be near you, as we have said, since we first sensed you. I do not understand this desire to change your looks for me. It makes me . . . sad, I believe, to hear you say this. I would never want you to change yourself for me. I am daunted by you, what you can do." He added, with emphasis, "What you will *become*, as well. You have incredible potential, and you possess an endearing compassion for others. You were supposed to be a Tech. Born with the innate ability. But we, the other Techs, saw your potential in another role, and we nudged people away from discovering your talents. It is I who am grateful, Jason. It is good to hear I am pleasing for you to behold. That I appear beautiful to you. We do not observe ourselves with regard to physical attributes. I do not really comprehend the standards for this type of evaluation. You must understand. To us, all people are primarily data. Actions. Reactions. Interactions. Their preferences for others vary greatly, and they change frequently. We observe human coupling by the billions each day, and standards of beauty and attraction are difficult to pinpoint. We are healthy, and we are relatively young. These tend to be desirable attributes, I believe. Perhaps this is why you find us appealing?"

Jason turned and pushed his body against Tarien, pulling his head against his shoulder and pressing the muscles of their chests together.

Quietly, Tarien asked, "Did this physical change in you make you more physically attractive by societal standards?" The question was innocent enough, but it made Jason feel ashamed.

"I guess not. I guess I didn't realize it didn't matter."

Tarien pulled back a little and looked into Jason's eyes. "We don't understand physical interactions, so we lack this knowledge. You are important to me, Jason, however you appear. We have come to realize this over the last few years. Perhaps we will come to admire this physical part of you as well. We simply have no frame of reference. We have not desired anyone before this. You are attractive to me for a complex set of reasons which are not related to appearance."

Jason stiffened and fell back onto the bed, pressing his right hand against his head. "They're through the wall. I'm receiving a flood of incoming broadcasts." He shook his head, panicking. "Ung! It's too much! I can't deal with all of it!"

Tarien sat next to him, his hand on Jason's shoulder. His voice calm, commanding. "Filter everything else out for now. Close down what you do not need. The only thing you need to do right now is instruct them to attach to mobile units, flying units, to shed like rain, spreading as far as they can and then to replicate. Let them take to the air, blow with the wind to new places. The goal is to get them into as many areas as possible until they permeate everything they touch."

Jason shuddered under the strain. His jaw clenched tightly as he struggled to narrow the communication. "I think I have enough blocked out." It took him a while to formulate the proper directions the nannies would need, but he finally sent them. "I've sent the instructions. They are to use non-essential materials to keep spreading. I specifically made sure they didn't cripple vehicles or people by gobbling up resources. I don't want them turning into a cloud of monstrous destruction." He looked up, fearful. "Tarien, if they spread much further, I'm going to lose it. There are already so many, and they are increasingly sending me more data. At some point, I'm going to be overwhelmed."

Tarien nodded. "Yes. I will help with this issue. You will need to walk over to the door and get them replicating out into the hallway and up into the warehouse, to join with those you have already started. I know this means more of them, but you must get them started or we won't have time. You need to have complete control of this area soon. Then, to address the issue of too much incoming information, you must put them into my system. You will need to do this quickly, before you cannot focus. You must analyze my own patterns and enhancements, and you will need to modify them accordingly."

SIXTEEN

WHILE TARIEN TALKED, JASON BEGAN to work rapidly. Tarien's physical contact with him provided the means to get the nannies started. In moments they were in Tarien's bloodstream and spreading throughout his system. Jason took Tarien by the hand. The gesture sent thrills through Jason. "C'mon. You need to eat something. My nannies will use your resources to copy themselves and that will weaken you enormously if you don't get some food in you."

He led him out of the cell and Tarien warmed food on the stove.

Watching Tarien eat made him smile. Such a mundane task, eating, but he'd never witnessed the Tech's requirement for food. He'd even wondered if they needed it, imagining some sort of nutritional synthesis going on inside those advanced biosuits.

Tarien looked up and saw Jason staring at him. He laughed in surprise, recognizing Jason's curiosity. "Yes, we require food, like everyone else." His mannerisms and interaction had become markedly more human since he was not distracted by running the entire Sector. Able to focus only on himself and his immediate surroundings, Tarien was warmer, more open and engaged.

Jason felt his nannite population swelling rapidly. He realized he only had about three hours before they were too numerous for him to control. With this in mind, he began analyzing Tarien's system. While Jason didn't require it, he sat down next to Tarien and put his hand on his shoulder for physical contact. It calmed Jason's racing heart.

Tarien said nothing as he continued to eat, though he smiled with what seemed like fondness, allowing Jason to focus entirely on his task.

After a while, Jason had enough nannies to provide him the necessary analysis tools. He started to see a pattern interwoven through Tarien's neurological system—a unique hybrid of technology and organic tissue. The neural networking patterns were amazing and incredibly complex. He lacked the knowledge of what this meant or why this combination was in place. Tarien's entire system had been enhanced in this way, not only his mind. As he studied the complex system, Jason realized he had no idea of how to make use of this information. He could analyze everything and see the patterns, but he could not discern uses for any of the overwhelming amount of enhancements. Jason marveled at the strange organization of Tarien's brain. Jason knew this unique pattern defined a Tech, who possessed a unique set of characteristics unlike most of the rest of the population, but to his surprise, he recognized the same pattern in his own mind. He possessed latent characteristics of a Tech, just as Tarien had said.

Finally, Jason sat back. "It's no use. I can't make sense of what's going on. It's like finding a spaceship and walking around inside but having no knowledge of how it works or was built, or even what its capabilities are. It will take me months to figure out enough details to be useful."

Tarien smiled and spooned the last of his food into his mouth, wiping his lips with a napkin. "This is why you will set up a directed link between us. I will transfer this data directly to you. This knowledge will help you rebuild your mind so it is capable of utilizing your incoming transmissions."

Jason gasped. "You can do that? A direct link? You mean, like our minds would be in direct communication with each other?" Then, realizing the potential entanglement, he said, "Won't it get confusing?"

Tarien's expressions had become more easily read. He seemed to consider what Jason had asked, looking down at his fingers and taking a moment to think. "Possibly. There are great advantages however, such as the ability to transfer information instantly. We Techs use it amongst ourselves all the time. I will help you. Just copy the regions I indicate exactly."

Jason took a deep breath. "Okay. I can try."

Using instructions fed to him by Tarien, he began the process of quickly setting up an interconnect, a network between them that entailed intercepting signaling in both his mind and in Tarien's. These signals were then re-broadcast out to both of them. At first, he analyzed the synaptic firing occurring whenever Tarien talked. These signal bursts were easily studied. Then, he directed his own mind to "hear" them. As he bridged the necessary connections, he literally did hear Tarien's voice, because his own mind processed the new signals in the same way it processed sound. This system was far too complex for him to understand under normal circumstances, but he busily enhanced himself to increase his cognitive abilities as he worked. His thinking was clearer, faster, far more powerful.

He tried to ignore the massive amount of incoming transmissions, which became increasingly insistent. His nannies, now that they had spread, some by shedding off flying objects so they would drift down onto buildings and into the population, were replicating so fast they were overtaking whole city blocks in minutes.

He sagged under the strain and began sweating involuntarily. His head shook, and he felt his eyes grow wide. He worked faster. A small groan escaped his lips. It was like someone was piling boulders on him.

Can you hear me, Jason? Tarien's thoughts echoed in

Jason's head.

Yes. Can you hear me? Jason shifted in his chair, leaning forward to put his arms on the table.

Tarien smiled. Then said aloud, "Yes, I can hear you. Very good. I knew you could do it. Establishing a link with a non-Tech would not normally be possible, but based on the new nano-technology and your focused control, it appears it can be done. A major contributing factor is that you have been overlooked in your potential to be a Tech. Now, my nannies will guide you toward the areas relevant for data transfer. These areas can be copied as well. There is no need to know how they function."

Areas of Tarien's mind flared and it amused Jason to see his perceptions translate this to an orange glow. An arbitrary association, but it provided him a frame of reference. He studied these areas quickly and then began copying them, adding these modifications to himself. This process took quite a while and he began to feel exhausted.

"Tarien, I need to eat. This business of constantly requiring food to keep up is going to cripple me."

"Yes, it is good there is this limitation," Tarien said cryptically, "but it really only applies when changing yourself or healing. If we can avoid those situations, you should not be susceptible to this level of fatigue. Still, it would be advisable to keep rations handy."

Jason rose and got himself more food. As he warmed his meal, Mom entered the room, her hair frazzled and loose.

"I managed a small nap, which is a bit necessary at my age." She rubbed her eyes and glanced up at the clock. "I see we are down to three hours before I need to get going."

Jason could sense through Tarien, feel much of what he felt, and knew what he was thinking.

Tarien smiled at Mom's disheveled look. Now that he wasn't distracted by his duties and ties to the WorldNet, small things appeared to make him increasingly happy. He glanced up at Jason and felt a surge of emotion that Jason, in turn, felt.

Mom noted the empty bowl on the table and automatically took it and washed it, setting it on the side of the basin to dry. She walked over to a small, floral-patterned bag that sat on the floor near one of the couches and pulled out a brush. Sitting between them, she undid the knot of her bun and let her hair down to brush it out. None of them spoke, each lost in their own thoughts. Jason kept busy working on his tasks, ensuring he kept abreast of the progress. His modifications for the data transfer were nearly complete, and he scarfed down the scalding hot food. His body simply absorbed the heat and used it for additional energy. He couldn't burn his mouth anymore, so he utilized the energy.

He washed and dried his bowl and put it next to the one Mom had washed. Then, feeling ready, he returned to his chair. "I think I have the areas you indicated copied. They aren't active or doing anything yet, but they are in place."

Tarien nodded. "This is well. I am going to initiate a transfer of information you will find relevant to how these changes work and the function of the enhancements. I will also transfer all data regarding how we interface. This will be difficult for you to filter, so please let me know if I must halt this process."

Jason took a deep breath, then closed his eyes. He took both of Tarien's hands and leaned forward until their foreheads touched. "Okay. I'm as ready as I can be." He opened his eyes and sat back, still holding Tarien's hands in his own.

Out of the corner of his eye, he noticed Mom had stopped brushing her hair and stared at both of them, her head tilted, obviously curious, then she resumed pulling the brush through her long, gray strands.

Jason blinked roughly to tune out these distractions. He felt overwhelmed with a flood of incoming information. Jason had no context for this new information and the jumble of meaningless data momentarily confused him. Instinctively, his mind tried utilizing the modifications he'd made to begin properly storing and categorizing things. Involuntarily, his head tipped back and he clutched at Tarien. "I can't—!" Tears formed in his eyes.

"You will become more accustomed to this as it progresses. Soon, this information flow will not trouble you."

Several minutes after this began, he could recall specific information if he thought about it. Diagrams, biological information, details of the way the Techs were able to gather and work with data. A clear pattern emerged. He noted a constant reference to storage and retrieval from millions of external sources.

"There is so much information. It seems like the trick is to know where to find what I need, not to memorize or know everything. I only need think of what I want to know about and I'm redirected to the various storage locations the moment I need them."

Tarien nodded. "This is correct. We do not contain the sum of all knowledge. Our brain optimization would have to be infinitely improved. However, with data distributed throughout the WorldNet, we are not required to know all things. We access and rewrite information constantly, with thousands of redundant copies and locations. Alone, we do not know how traffic patterns work, or how to balance energy use. The resources we access grant us this knowledge. You are not overwhelmed? You are able to handle this?"

"Yeah, I am. It's confusing, but you're right. The feeling of being overwhelmed is sorta subsiding as my ability to filter and buffer grows, along with gaining knowledge of where to find and process data. I think I understand how your bio-suit works and the reason for a lot of the enhancements. I'm going to work on improving them for myself."

"I'm guessing you two have figured out a way to somehow give Jason the knowledge of a Tech." Mom's comment drew Jason's attention for a moment and he glanced sideways at her. Mom watched them with wide eyes. "The way you're talking, it sounds like you two are plugged into each other."

As one, they turned to look at her and she fidgeted nervously. Tarien had resumed his stoic look, and Jason felt his own facial muscles lock in place.

Jason answered, though they both wanted to speak simultaneously. It was becoming increasingly hard to differentiate between his thoughts and Tarien's. "That's a good summary of what's going on. I would rather not explain anything further, since I don't want to start answering questions. But, effectively, Seven and I can now communicate through thought to each other."

As the data stream continued, Jason became increasingly aware of Tarien in general. His physical health, a small cramp in his left leg, his heartbeat. Jason's nannies were responding to his mental enhancements, which allowed him to store and process more information. Merging with Tarien had become nearly overwhelming, since he almost felt like Tarien had become an extension of himself.

Tarien stared at him, since he received Jason's physical information in reverse.

Mom continued to watch them both. "Sweetie, if you can do that, I have something to ask." She set the brush down on the table and put her hands in her lap. "Is it possible to hook me up so I can communicate with you as well? I mean, if I need to relay information back, I don't know if I will be able to rely on conventional technology. I'm going to assume this bypasses the standard communicator."

"I don't think—" but before Jason could finish, he heard Tarien in his mind. *Yes, this is necessary.*

Why?

You can establish limited communication with Citizen Markhuar, with Mom, and then utilize this in order to ensure more accurate timing.

Timing for what? I'm sensing something else going on here, Tarien.

Yes, there is more. There is a deeper need for you to have direct communication with Mom. You also need some level of control over her system. I cannot elaborate at this time, but it is imperative.

The speed of their communication had taken place so quickly, Mom surely wouldn't have noticed the pause.

"I—uh. I can do what we need. Take my hand." Jason reached out with his right hand, palm up.

"All right, dear. I trust you. This sounds like magic, but I guess you probably know what you are doing."

He smiled. "There's a logical explanation, I promise. When this is over, I'll tell you all about it."

She reached out and took his hand. He clasped it for a moment, then with a mischievous grin, he waggled his other hand above his head. In a booming voice he yelled, "Abracaaadaaabra!"

She laughed. "Very funny. Please just get it over with, dear. I don't think we have time for parlor tricks."

"Actually, I'm done. That's it."

She made a funny expression. One eyebrow raised,

one lowered, her lips pursed sideways with incredulity. Then she narrowed her eyes and leaned forward as if trying to listen to him in some other way. "Are you sure? I can't hear anything."

He nodded. "It takes a little while, and I'll let you know before I just start talking inside your head. I also won't be listening in on you. I will set our link to trigger when you say my name, just like you were talking to me. And you will stop transmitting when you say you are finished. I promise this won't be intrusive. I'll remove the link between us when we are done."

"I would appreciate it, sweetie."

The data flow between Tarien and Jason completed itself, though the awareness of each other seemed to be growing.

"Now," Tarien said, "utilize the template data I've provided to construct a similar method for using your new nannites. They should be able to cluster to form processing centers, along with storage and relay stations. You will find this becomes a pattern based on need. Expressing your need for more resources will trigger them to increase your capacity as necessary, without you having to directly guide them. This is how you can automate standard processes."

Jason had to contain his amazement at the power he felt. His ability to think increased enormously with each passing moment. He grew increasingly aware of detail. *How far does this scale? Tarien, this is extremely dangerous. I don't have any protective edicts to prevent me from abusing this.*

We know. Neither does Faust. We trust you to curb your ability when the time comes. We trust you will not abuse this. Faust will.

The timber of Tarien's voice made Jason shiver. He had increasing problems with distinguishing between Seven's bodily data and his own. For a moment, he was dizzy, experiencing double vision, seeing out of Tarien's eyes and his own simultaneously.

You must remember yourself, Jason. We are separate, but we are one. You must remember this, or you will quickly become lost. Hold an image of yourself in your mind, keep it separated.

Tarien . . . I—I think I could control your body if I wanted. Move your arms and legs.

Tarien nodded. *Yes, this is necessary. You will need to be familiar with me in order to prevent me from obeying new orders the moment I resume connection with the WorldNet. There are additional reasons for this, which you will discover when it is time.*

Jason felt a blush rise in his cheeks. *I'm aware of a lot more than I feel like I should be. This is like being a peeping Tom, but far more interactive.* Tarien's vitality, his youthful vigor, increasingly distracted him. Jason's thoughts kept wandering.

Tarien, too, blushed. *Yes, we did not anticipate this. It is . . . novel.*

Tarien stood up suddenly. Aloud, he said, "We must excuse ourselves for a little while, Mom. We will return when the clock is at 15:00." Then, he said to Jason, "Please come with me."

Jason got up, unable to control his flaming face. He knew what Tarien intended, couldn't help but know, and he blushed furiously.

Mom looked at them both, her eyebrows lifted in surprise. "Now? Oh? My, my. Well good for you, boys, I suppose. Of course, dears. Just don't take forever in there. I'm sure there is a lot to do and I'm a little uncomfortable with you boys playing hanky-panky while there is a massive conflict brewing."

Tarien grabbed Jason's hand nervously, urgently, leading him into the room. He closed the door. Jason could tell Tarien's intent, knew where this would go. This realization paralyzed him, and he just stood there, frozen.

Tarien finally spoke. "Is this acceptable? We wish to . . . to be with you. We do not believe there will be another opportunity. We know this may be inappropriate when there is so much danger, but I want this. Just once, before the end. If things must end. Our desire is unexpected and strong."

Jason's mind tried to keep up with the vast complexity under which it now operated. Being immersed in the huge data flow coming in from his nannies, and being acutely aware of Tarien's whole body, their attraction for each other was magnified, mirrored and almost narcissistic, since he had trouble differentiating his own feelings from Tarien's.

"I want to. You know I want to. I just worry about losing control. Giving in to my base desires became the trigger for me, the one that made me forget myself in the prison apartment. That urge overwhelmed me, turned me into a monster."

Tarien looked at him shyly. "Please, Jason. We have resisted this impulse. I have never . . . this is the only opportunity I have ever had. It may be the only opportunity I will ever have. We have time and I am part of you. I will not allow us to fall into the same trap."

Jason stood mutely, his entire body thrumming with need, heightened by their connection to each other.

Jason took a deep breath and finally surrendered. The first kiss disoriented him. Jason kissed Tarien, but also himself at the same time. The confusion lent him a double experience, but he quickly adjusted, keeping his identity firmly in mind. *I am Jason.*

Then they were tearing off their clothes, kissing the whole while. They simply couldn't keep their hands off each other. Naked, Tarien was more physically perfect than Jason felt he had a right to be, almost heartbreakingly so. Jason stared at him a moment. "You are so beautiful."

Tarien smiled and really looked at him. "You are beautiful to me, too, Jason."

Jason enfolded Tarien in his arms and then pushed him down onto the bed. Jason took his time. He brushed his lips against Tarien, from hairline to calf. Down his back. Goosebumps formed over Tarien's body, and he shivered as each little kiss landed on his smooth skin.

Tarien gave several startled exclamations as each new experience surprised him. He moaned as Jason flipped him over, kissed up his inner thighs and his stomach. Jason nibbled at Tarien's nipples, grazing them with his teeth.

Tarien touched Jason awkwardly, caressing him as Jason moved up and down Tarien's body. Tarien began to writhe beneath the touches, flooded with pleasure Jason recognized he'd never felt. He asked for more, begged Jason to touch him. He groaned when Jason obliged.

Jason showed Tarien what it meant to make love, in a variety of ways. The continual shock Tarien experienced made Jason laugh softly. Tarien also learned what it meant to have youthful athleticism and nearly boundless energy from having a partner.

Afterwards, they lay there for a while, Jason running his fingers through Tarien's hair, occasionally kissing his ear.

Finally, Tarien sat up. "It is time."

Jason almost despaired. The perfection and beauty of the moment lingered for a long while. Reality came crashing back.

SEVENTEEN

TARIEN ROSE, STEPPING AWAY FROM Jason and slowly putting on his biosuit. He touched Jason's face tenderly, his fingers a feathery touch on Jason's jaw. "How are your nannites? Any information about Faust?"

Surprisingly, Jason had to focus to bring them back to the fore, rather than fighting the details back. He was no longer completely overwhelmed by the tide of information. "Spreading. At least a quarter of this municipal boundary has been infected, and much of the area now infected will be under my control within the hour. At the increasing rate of replication, I will have half the municipal boundary and the core within two hours. The entire Sector, all of Seven, will be blanketed in four days."

"We do not have four days. We must leave soon. Also,

you must not allow them to replicate unchecked. This is dangerous, as they will consume resources."

Will I know what I need to do when we leave here? I'm afraid.

I will guide you, and you will have access to my uplinks. Please remember, Jason, I must not be allowed to enact the new edicts as they come through. You will have to fight me. Prevent me. Once you have, you will have to use my access and knowledge.

"Tarien, I don't know if I can do it. I honestly don't think I could violate you by suppressing your will, caging you within yourself."

"It is time. We must be ready." He waited until Jason dressed himself. "Jason, I understand your worry. I need you to do this. I am asking you. Please. It is imperative." Then, quietly, he said, "I trust you."

Jason's brows knitted in fear. "Let's go."

Mom had prepared another meal of steak and eggs, along with coffee, even though the caffeine would not affect either of them since they could control their own energy levels and did not require external stimuli. She did not comment on how loud they had been when making love, and they didn't mention it. They ate in silence, though Tarien stared at Jason the entire time, a smile in his eyes.

Jason glanced at Mom. "Are you ready? I would like to test your new communications."

She looked nervous, but nodded.

Mom? You should hear my voice in your head, just as

if I were speaking. Jason said in her mind.

"Oh my! How did you do that? It's exactly as if you were speaking aloud!"

Communicate by thinking, not speaking. I can hear you either way, but silently, you can keep our conversation to yourself.

She hesitated. *Like this? Can you hear me?*

He smiled encouragingly and took her hand to reassure her. *Good! Now, I'm going to enable the ability for you to turn this on or off so every time you speak it is not transmitted without your permission. If I must, I'll address you first, warning you I'm initiating connection. For you to initiate communication with me, just say my name. To end our conversation, say or think 'End transmission.'*

She nodded. *End transmission.*

She sat there for a moment as if she were speaking to him, but he heard nothing.

Then, *Jason, can you hear me now?*

Yes, Mom, I can hear you.

Could you hear me before? Saying, I think your new boyfriend is quite handsome and good luck to you both?

He reached out and took her other hand and smiled shyly at her. "No, Mom. But I heard it this time."

She took a deep breath. "Well then." *End transmission.* "I'll be going. I'll update you when something happens. Whatever it is. I still have no idea. Please be careful."

Tarien said, "Good luck to you, too, Mom. And thank you."

They went into the bedroom and closed the door, which had also been imbued with the Faraday materials. They had to remain behind a shielded area so the opening of the front door while Mom exited wouldn't trigger Seven's communication uplink. After they heard the exit door close, they went back out to the table.

They simultaneously took a deep breath.

Jason stared at the wall for a moment, noting the crumbling and cracked concrete, the slight wetness of micro leaks and the dankness of being so far underground. *I now have control of this warehouse and I've managed to get nannies straight up from here to street level. They have attached themselves to various people and are spreading quickly. Mom is shedding them for me as well, just long enough to establish a few pockets without starving her by using too much of her fat deposits for replication material. Information coming in from the district indicates law enforcement is searching for me. I have access to some of the enforcer systems and there is a warrant. It appears the Techs are helping them search. How did you keep this place secret?*

Tarien scooted his chair closer, put a hand on Jason's back. *We, all my brethren, my sisters, the Techs, which are at once the highest servants and the least free of our society, met in secret. Foreseeing this outcome, we decided we would act as much as we were able, constrained as we are by our edicts. The Techs agreed I should craft a plan to accomplish our goals and to act on this plan with autonomy. My brothers and sisters permitted me to keep this information to myself, and to wipe all record of it out of the system prior to bringing you here. I have carefully kept this location and our plans from dangerous observation, prevented saving or logging the data to external storage and, consequently, kept everything out of the hands of the Council and Faust. I employed misdirection based on changing the data on which the Council depends so heavily.*

Jason nodded in understanding. *I'm keeping Mom's movements a secret as much as I can. She'll be noticed in the next ten minutes. I simply cannot prevent the sheer amount of observation data from reaching the Techs. They're sure to associate her with me.*

Tarien nodded. *Yes, they will. But it is too late. She is already under the care of our sleeper cells, being taken to where she can be most active. We must be poised to leave this place, after she performs her duty and the evacuation is underway.*

"What evacuation? I still don't have any idea what is going on." Jason felt more comfortable speaking aloud, which helped him keep from blurring the distinction between himself and Tarien. Internalizing everything almost felt like he talked to himself.

Tarien understood, taking his hand and squeezing it in acknowledgement. "You will know everything soon. The moment we leave here, when you intercede on my behalf to prevent me from acting on the commands of the Council, you will be privy to all I know. The link we have created will be critical to the two-way flow of data."

He paused. "For now, I can tell you we will have to use a lot of force to get to Faust. In order to accomplish this, we must take as many precautions as we are able to prevent the harm of citizens. We will be creating distractions— huge problems regarding the safety of citizens—which will trigger the automatic actions of the Techs to evacuate the population. The Council will not be able to override this reaction, which is inherent in the Tech's protective protocols. It will force the Techs to ignore you, temporarily, while they work to save the people."

They sat in silence for some time, their thoughts kept separate by choice.

After a while, Tarien rose from his chair and walked over to one of the equipment closets. He pulled out a couple of backpacks and proceeded to fill them with rations.

Jason sorted through all the data coming in, changing external resources to include more storage and retrieval nodes, more processing centers for automation. He mentally noted Mom's progress. Her guardians escorted her into a tall building, a thin spire of mostly glass that rose out of the sea of other, more squat buildings that were covered in vegetation. The nannies she shed on Jason's behalf had already infected those people around her, so he stopped her production of the nannies, worrying he would weaken her too much by draining her resources. The amount of resources she'd already burned through had probably made her ravenous. Still, even stopping, he could use the nannies she'd shed to continue to spread his reach.

"Mom appears to be in place. I can see her with my nannies. She is in a room filled with audio gear and is being given a sealed envelope." While he couldn't make out all the details of the room yet, he could see what she saw to a small degree. Through his nannies in her system and of those that busily replicated all around her, he saw the envelope contained the universal seal of the Techs, that of a man standing with a palm forward. On the palm of the stern man was an eye from which a beam of light appeared to be shooting out.

Tarien nodded solemnly. "She will read what I've written for her, then the teams will be put into play. We have two hours until the sabotage creates a panic situation. The rapid evacuation procedures will then provide us with the opportunity to attack."

Mom opened the letter and took a deep breath. *Jason, this is Mom. Can you hear me?*

Yes, I can hear you. We are ready.

He could detect her heart racing and she shuddered from anxiety. Jason tried to avoid being too invasive, making sure his senses of her were surface only. After a long pause, presumably to gather her courage, Mom began to read, her voice clear and firm. Jason performed a direct signal transfer to Tarien so he could hear too.

"Hello, and greetings to all who can hear my voice. This is . . ." she hesitated. The letter had her name, "Rayna Markhuar" and then "Mom" clearly printed. She pursed her lips and then modified the words slightly. "This is

Mom. A personal affectation I intend to keep," she said pointedly. "I'm reading from a letter given to me by the highest authority of our movement. This letter and its words were drafted to provide you with the trigger and the permission to enact the resistance for which you have been trained."

Jason smiled, despite the seriousness of the situation. The writing was clearly Tarien's. Dry and stilted. Tarien wasn't the type to write passionately, or to evoke the passions of others through his words. He and Tarien both walked around the room as they listened, nervous energy compelling movement, making them pace.

"You are hereby asked to immediately begin your objectives, to hurry toward the goals laid before you. You know what they are. I will not voice them, for fear of giving away vital information that would prevent you from taking action, but know this: now is the correct time to move our plans forward. Know, also, by committing these acts, you are saving the lives of a great many people. This plan is the only thing standing in the way of enslavement. You are part of this movement because you believe. I ask you to continue to keep faith. It may not seem like what you are asked to do is right, but it is vital for you to proceed, for the safety of those around you. Everyone must be evacuated, and you are going to help. Once your tasks are complete, flee the area as you have planned and wait until it is safe to return." Her voice began to shake. "I have to go, but I—I hope you heard me. Goodbye then," she finished, a little uncertainly.

The broadcast stopped, but she continued to stand there, trembling. One of her escorts gently guided her out of the room, hurrying her out of the building and into an antigravity vehicle. She was flanked by six other people dressed similarly and of roughly the same age, designed to confuse anyone in pursuit. They ushered her to another safe location, away from the dangers of being pinpointed by the Council after her speech.

After they flew her toward safety, she calmed enough to remember the uplink.

Jason. It's Mom. Are you still there?

Yes, Mom. We heard everything. You did a wonderful job.

"Tell her thank you, and that her task is complete. They will hide her as best they are able," Tarien said.

Jason relayed the information.

Oh good. Tell Seven thank you for trusting me. I'm grateful to be part of whatever is going on. I'm sure you will fill me in later.

I will.

End transmission.

Her direct communication shut down as she thought the words. Jason could still detect her and those around her, based on his nannies, but he respected her control over the link.

"She said 'thank you for trusting her.'" Jason absently rubbed at small smudges on the table. "So now the countdown begins, huh?"

"Yes. Now we must wait as long as is reasonable.

Already, major malfunctions should be starting throughout the Sector."

And there were. Within the areas where his nannies were present and could gather information, he saw various issues starting to arise. Several major power distribution points had been crippled by sabotage, forcing auxiliary systems into play. Broadcast stations, which ensured communication to the various technology present in every corner of the Sector were abruptly going dark.

After a few minutes, the outages became severe. Brown-outs were starting and power flickered off momentarily across broad areas. The communication systems were becoming overloaded and instructions were not being sent properly. Various chemical factories suffered from explosions caused by saboteurs. Leaks in vital systems caused dangerous conditions, forcing employees to flee for safety. Traffic patterns were shifting around massive blockages and malfunctions. Water and containment systems were being shut down or overloaded.

Within half an hour, major areas of the city were crippled. Warning systems would not allow people onto mass transit because of rising problems with safety. Worse, incorrect instructions were being sent and were only barely interrupted and corrected in time to avert disaster. Despite the vigilance of the Techs and their attempts to intercept, several autonomous and unmanned flying delivery vehicles crashed into buildings, causing panic.

Within minutes, two passenger trains collided. Both were empty, because the irregularities were detected in advance and passengers had been forced to exit. One of the trains did not properly engage the emergency magnetic safety field and subsequently launched at high speed into nearby buildings. The buildings were being evacuated, because of environmental safety failures, but several people were killed in the explosion. These were the first casualties of an increasingly horrific situation. One building that had been struck began showing signs of collapse.

People were panicking, screaming, and running to the emergency airlifts being deployed to get everyone out of the areas.

All at once, eleven massive floating barges crashed into populated areas and into several buildings. Gas lines exploded. Failures in the system were growing rapidly, despite backup protocols.

The authorities were now aware it was a concerted attack, rather than a few isolated instances, and were concentrating on getting people loaded into evacuation ships and out of the city.

The Techs tried to predict the nature of the sabotage and to proactively block them but were harried constantly. This was Jason's moment to strike. He used his new uplinks to garble or stop the Tech's orders, adding more confusion and increasing their required workload. The Techs tried alternate ways to communicate, but without success, since Jason adapted every time they altered their transmission tactics. They tried, with an equal level of failure, to pinpoint the source of the disruptions.

The uprising was too well-planned. The Techs simply couldn't get everyone out quickly enough to afford them time to work on the source of the issue with their full attention. Millions of people were impossible to round up and move with any speed. Making matters worse, people were in such a state of terror, they were causing their own injuries as huge crowds tried to fight their way to safety. This forced the Techs to turn their attention to evacuations and to give up on stopping the system collapse.

When several buildings suddenly crumpled after fires had weakened them, the entire inner city became chaotic. The Techs ordered all robotics and all vehicles to forcibly protect and scoop up people en masse. Several of these vehicles crashed as they malfunctioned, killing hundreds.

Jason shuddered in horror. He witnessed the damage through input from his nannies, helplessly sensing the destruction.

"Oh, Tarien. There are people dying out there."

Tarien nodded sadly. "We assumed this would happen. It is time. We must act now, while the distraction is in play. Are you ready?"

"No! Oh my god! I'm not ready. This is horrible. I can't stand the thought of being responsible for this. We are terrorists!" He was paralyzed. "And you said yourself, you will probably die out there. I can't do it! Please, we have to be able to find a way out of this."

Tarien walked over to him and knelt down, begging him. He looked into Jason's eyes. "I know this is horrible. I'm so sorry. You're hurting. I can feel it. Please understand, this is the only way we could see to save the rest of humanity. If Faust is allowed to become immortal, if he learns the secret of transferring himself into others, he cannot be killed. Even if one body is destroyed, he can clone alternates. He verges on this discovery, is working on it even now. Already you have discovered it through our bond, though you do not realize its import. We are able to share each other closely, and it is not much more of a stretch to possession. He will use this mercilessly if he gains this knowledge.

"If he is impervious to destruction, he will soon use your discovery of how to control others, so he can dominate humanity. He will be first in this augmentation and will have no rivals to stop him."

Tarien stood and put his hand behind Jason's head and looked at him tenderly. "We need you. All of us. We needed you to be ready, to be able to combine your strength with those of a Tech. With me. You have learned much, though I lament the cost to you."

Jason was acutely aware of time slipping by as he worked through his internal crisis. He witnessed the destruction outside scaling upward, becoming akin to a war zone. The military had rushed in to try and both calm the rioting and to get people to safety. Jason knew he could do something to stop it, render it unnecessary, if he would only exert his new powers. Still, he couldn't move. His love and trust of Tarien compelled him to obey. Emergency resources were being called in from other parts of the Sector. Even from other Sectors, as the damage grew.

Tarien did not try to force Jason. He continued, showing patience at the delay as he said, "Once we realized what must be done, once we discovered you, I volunteered. I wanted—" He suddenly looked down, ashamed. "I wanted to be the one to pair with you. I put myself forward, ahead of the others. I pleaded with them, in our own electronic way, to be permitted to stand with you in this. I did not understand this compulsion at the time.

"I couldn't understand how much I was drawn to you. I did not know how to name it. I care about you more deeply than any other living creature. More than myself. This fascination of you conflicted with my edicts, tore at me until I knew what I must do. This opportunity is not a sacrifice for me." He ran his fingers up Jason's neck and through the hair on the back of his head, making Jason shiver.

"I had thought it would be enough just to be close to you, to be by your side, used as a necessary tool, until I ended. I did not understand that you would offer something more. I do not think you understand what you have done for us. Teaching us to be human again, teaching us we can be cared for, feel the things we feel. This gift is something that will change the course of all

Techs. Our humanity has been stolen from us, and you have gifted it back."

Tarien kissed Jason deeply, then held his forehead to his own. "Please. Stop Faust. I will be with you as long as I'm able. I do not have your healing, do not possess your abilities, as great as are those of my own. However, I am tied to the WorldNet, an overriding administrator of all technology. This cannot be easily undone. He cannot stop you, if you use me for this purpose."

Jason didn't realize there were tears streaming down his face until Tarien brushed them away. In his mind, he heard people screaming for help, and he knew his decision would cause even more suffering. With an involuntary sob, Jason pulled Tarien toward him and wrapped his arms around the Tech.

"This is how monsters are created. They learn to justify causing death and harm. All for the greater good. This is what I am becoming. A monster."

Jason knew what he must do, however. He couldn't see another way. He nodded through his tears. He couldn't speak, so he simply grabbed their packs and Tarien's hand and led him to the door.

They paused before stepping outside. Jason looked at the man he'd fallen in love with, wondering if it would be the last time he'd see him alive.

I'm ready, Jason signaled through his thoughts. *Let's go.*

EIGHTEEN

THE MOMENT THE DOOR OPENED, Jason accepted his fate. He'd already calculated how to save Tarien from the anguish of being possessed. It was one thing he could do. At least he wouldn't dominate the man he loved, stripping away his free will and making him into a puppet. The incoming signals from the Council were filtered through the nannies Jason had created, blocking orders. Jason simply denied the edicts from being imposed, negated them without allowing them to reach his beloved Tech. This gift he could give Tarien, some small atonement for his other crimes.

He felt Tarien reconnect with the Sector and the WorldNet. Felt a tide of information so vast, so beyond his understanding, he knew he could not begin to handle it himself. But he didn't have to. Tied together, through the master of this Sector, Sector Seven, he now had the means to enact all changes, to see all technology—a daunting and nearly overwhelming power. The current state of his neurological processes simply couldn't handle the overwhelming data, so it began to adapt. He felt his nannies rush to augment him further, enhancing his understanding and processing to incorporate and control this new source of data. He staggered under the onslaught, his hand instinctively flying to his head. He still had enough awareness to filter out some of the incoming orders. He sagged to his knees. "Give me a second. It's so much."

Seven hardly paid attention. He froze, stunned. Fully expecting to be useless, lost in his struggle to obey and simultaneously be denied, he took a moment to realize what Jason had done.

"A filter. Clever. Very, very well done. Thank you. You found a way to accomplish what we needed without taking my free will."

Jason's eyes were wide with strain, but the sound of Tarien's voice brought him back to reality. He stood, taking Tarien's hand briefly, then they began to run up through the warehouse levels.

As they ran, Jason made sense of how to navigate all the incredible information at his disposal. He started looking for specific information. First and foremost, he saw Faust, knew exactly where he hid. The man had buried himself deep in the protected Council building. Faust worked rapidly to gain as much knowledge of the immortality technology as he could, recognizing the attacks were leveled at him. However imperfect, if pressed he would be forced to use what he had.

Jason groaned. Faust would have all the time he required. Reaching him would be impossible. The entire facility had been completely surrounded with military personnel and weaponry. A vast sea of robotic units, red for the color of the Sector military, emblazoned with a blue lightning bolt, poured into the streets and flew over the buildings. Faust knew what transpired throughout the city. The Techs were now under Faust's direct control, a shift in power initiated by the declaration of a state of emergency. They kept him informed. Once the Techs were free from distraction and could halt the destruction, they would come for Jason. Jason had to act fast. If he could act at all.

Jason scanned the information regarding the emergency powers and orders. The Council had convened and granted Faust nearly unlimited power. He could cast a single vote allowing him to declare any law or run the military without being challenged—exactly as Faust had planned, had schemed to achieve. Jason knew he had fallen directly into Faust's trap. His escape, which had seemed fortuitous at the time, had been allowed. Faust had needed Jason to pose a threat to gain control of the votes in the Council. The powers, Jason reasoned, were intended to last until the threat of Jason could be neutralized, then the Council would vote to remove these powers. The removal of Faust's emergency powers remained the one thing the Council could still vote on. Faust, however, would surely prevent any vote that would strip him of his new supremacy. With amazing clarity, Jason figured Faust would kill the Council and blame it on him.

One Tech, Nine, of course, stood by Faust's side. Nine was aware of Jason, was aware of Seven. He had already reported this to Faust. In a flash of insight, Jason saw the enormous torment under which Nine struggled. Nine had been administered the new nanotechnology and immortality drugs, which were clearly taking their toll. Faust must have gotten desperate to discover how to control others and experimented on the Tech in order to find answers. Jason felt a deep pang in his heart. Nine had knowingly sacrificed himself in order to put himself in a position where he could passively delay Faust.

Jason could sense the despair in Nine as he struggled in vain to resist the control being exerted, to find some way to prevent exposing Jason and Tarien. He simply couldn't hold off long, being bound to obey. The drugs strained Nine's system physically, adding to his psychic distress. A massive dose had already permeated his system and he'd begun changing physically, having no means of controlling the flood of involuntary feedback.

Desperately, Nine silently acknowledged them both, and Jason knew Nine wanted nothing more than for Jason to succeed. Nine had become the first victim of Faust's control.

Despite everything the populace had done to create

a distraction, Jason knew they had already failed. The military alone would be powerful enough to prevent them from getting anywhere near Faust. Worse, the army of robots airlifted from nearby military installations were more than anyone could handle. Even if Jason possessed an army of his own, their numbers and their strength was too vast.

Hundreds of red torsos shined in the sunlight as they awaited orders. In moments, as soon as Nine divulged Jason's location, they would begin deploying to surround and capture him. They would possibly kill him. Equipped with fire, any one of them would easily destroy his body, prevent him from healing. Or encase him in a substance that would render him unable to move. Seizing Jason would be more risky for Faust than killing him, however, as Jason could eventually free himself. Jason reasoned that Faust might have to risk Jason's capture, since killing him could prove nearly impossible.

All of this information flooded into him in nanoseconds. Almost no time had passed, and rather than feeling changed, Jason simply felt the world had slowed down. He still felt like himself, but now operated at speeds incomprehensible to anyone else save a Tech.

As he thought of this, he realized he could process Seven's information nearly as easily. Through Tarien, Jason had complete control of the entire Sector.

And more, Jason wasn't constrained by edicts. He could act without restraint. The problem he would encounter would be the other Techs, who were infinitely more experienced and who could counter him easily. His vast new control would be quickly under assault.

Tarien enfolded Jason in his arms and they immediately took to the air, launching with incredible speed up and out of the warehouse doors. using the antigravity properties of Tarien's suit to hurl them upward, away from advancing ground forces.

In his mind, he saw that computer systems had locked onto Tarien and him and had launched a flurry of missiles. Lasers and pulse weapons couldn't reach him since he was not yet in line-of-site, so they had to rely on guided missiles to take him down. An order came through to disable Seven's suit. Jason countered it easily.

Without allowing any time to pass, he commanded a number of aerial vehicles to collide with the volley of incoming firepower, detonating them after they had barely launched. He commanded other flight-capable machines to rise in front of them to clear their path.

The Techs reacted sluggishly, attempting to neutralize further use of machinery. They were overburdened by the disasters throughout the Sector. Even so, they tried. Despite their attempts, however, Jason could use his personalized nanotechnology that had infected numerous machines. He flew his growing army of these machines over the city, dropping more of the nanobots at ever-increasing rates and spreading his influence like wildfire.

Despite these successes, he had no idea how to proceed. If he and Tarien converged on Faust, he'd be shot down with lasers or energy weapons for which he had no defense. He quickly began to despair.

Suddenly Tarien opened the hidden agenda within his mind, feeding the plan to Jason instantly.

Jason recoiled, nearly causing them to fall from the sky. The plan Tarien fed him was almost too horrific to contemplate. Stunned, he had no idea if he could bring himself to proceed.

"Oh my God, Tarien. I can't! I'll kill thousands, maybe tens of thousands. The damage will be catastrophic. The city will be ruined! What I've done so far is atrocious. This . . . this is beyond comprehension."

"You must. This is the only plan that will work. It is the only way to save hundreds of billions of others from enslavement. He must be stopped. This is the end of humanity if you do not. You must play the villain to save them all. If allowed to proceed, Faust will not die. He won't be able to be killed or removed. He will not allow anyone to challenge him. He will go mad with power and it will mean societal collapse and ruin. You simply cannot bypass the military in any other way to reach him." Locked in their embrace as they flew still upward, Tarien squeezed him tighter. "Please."

Jason let out an animalistic cry of despair even as he issued the orders. Tears leaked from his eyes as massive sky barges all turned westward. Jason watched his horrible instructions enacted. Two massive sky towers, complex floating islands of metal and glass fitted with magnetically stored antimatter as a source of antigravity, lifted high into the sky and began following the barges. These sky towers were massive floating cities unto themselves. He issued the orders and immediately crippled communications so they could not be stopped. He would crash them, use them as enormous weapons to bombard infrastructure. The Techs were madly scrambling to cancel Jason's commands, but could not find a way to stop them.

He turned toward the medical complex, intending to take cover for the few minutes required before the armada of barges and towers converged on their destination. Jason landed both himself and Tarien on a building ledge and stared off into the distance. Hundreds of missiles were pouring out of the armaments surrounding the central government buildings. Safety protocols would not allow missiles to track and detonate near civilian population or buildings. No amount of orders could override these safety mechanisms. Faust overcame this protocol by sending officers in flying vehicles to try and apprehend Jason.

This, too, failed almost immediately.

Jason countermanded orders given by the Techs. While they were getting faster and were far more skilled, Jason was generating increasing amounts of interference with specialized broadcast units he'd hijacked. Within minutes, the disruption of communications meant Techs could no longer easily issue orders. Jason seized the vehicles intended to apprehend him and ordered them to safety. Jason learned quickly, his power growing every moment. Each interaction with the Techs meant gaining traction on the incredible complexity associated with the way Techs used technology. His brain continued augmenting rapidly, making him more formidable each passing moment.

Jason tore into the food stores Tarien had packed and ate ravenously, discarding the packs. In the same moment, he ordered all animal and insect life in the sector to flee. The humans were not subject to his control, but every other living creature would obey him. Most of the wildlife would never make it out, but he had to try. In the face of the horror of his actions, Jason needed to find some way to redeem himself.

The sound of a klaxon nearly ruptured Jason's eardrums as it began to cry out emergency warnings. Several more began to sound in the distance, the warning sirens echoing in all directions.

Faust and the Council had figured out the extreme danger those flying barges posed as they slowly moved toward critical city infrastructure. They had figured out that Jason intended to drop them. Faust directed energy weapons to shoot the barges down, but instead the weapons bounced off the shielding harmlessly. Flying towers and barges were designed to be nearly impervious.

The Techs finally abandoned trying to counter Jason and focused their energy on saving people. Every vehicle in the city turned and descended, trying to offer evacuation services to any human detected. Jason could have crippled some of them, but he desperately wanted these vehicles to help get people away as fast as possible. He sent his own orders to help, bolstering the Techs' commands. Vehicles filled the sky, streaming in from nearby areas to evacuate anyone left behind. Every available transport was summoned from as far away as reasonable. Despite this, Jason knew thousands of people simply would not get out in time.

Faust tried to communicate with Jason on every frequency, screaming for Jason to stand down. His voice became increasingly frantic, not having anticipated the lengths to which Jason would go to stop him.

Several minutes passed. Jason sobbed against Tarien's shoulder and braced for the impending explosion.

Faust began offering to surrender. He'd give himself up to Jason, he promised. Jason knew the man lied and also knew what would happen the moment Jason no longer held the upper hand.

Jason closed his eyes and crippled the complex set of systems on the sky towers and the barges. It took great effort to make them vulnerable, because the engineers had designed the safety systems so thoroughly. Jason had to use his nannies to physically eat away at some of the mechanisms surrounding the antimatter containment. Swarms of his tiny robots disintegrated the protective casing, overcoming the power systems and controls. At last, Jason succeeded in exposing the antimatter, crippled the gravitational fields suspending it. The great towers faltered, then began to slowly fall, crashing ponderously down onto the structure of the dam.

As matter met antimatter, the sky became fire. A burst of light blazed from the west. A flash so bright it would have blinded them both if they hadn't had protective technology. The physical force of the shockwave rippled outward. The concussive blast threw vehicles and debris like toys. Tarien and Jason sheltered behind buildings, hoping the structures would absorb the power of the explosion. Despite this, they were showered in glass. In a flash of insight, Jason wrapped himself protectively around Tarien, allowing shards to stab into his flesh as the shockwave hit the city core. Jason's body rejected the projectiles and he healed quickly.

In the distance, Jason could see the blast had leveled everything in its path. Though it came from miles away, the detonation by the sudden release of anti-matter from the gravitational fields was beyond belief. Air traffic vehicles were hurled vast distances, engines barely able to keep them aloft and restore balance. Many of these vehicles did not recover, careening to the ground along with the screaming people inside. Several buildings groaned under the strain of bent and warped metal.

Jason then saw the massive wall of water rushing toward the city. A wave, over two-hundred feet tall, rose from the largest reservoir in human history, an inland sea of majestic proportions and depth. The dam had spanned dozens of miles and had been several hundred feet tall before large sections were destroyed by the blast.

Power in the city failed as the wall of water overtook the generation sources and receiving panels.

Supercapacitors blasted apart entire acres as they came in contact with the water.

Jason grabbed Tarien and lifted them into the air again, away from danger as the inflow of water pushed buildings to the ground, crashed against metal and glass and bent them to the point of snapping. The outermost ring of skyscrapers took the full force of the impact and fell, crashing against nearby buildings. These, too, fell, unable to withstand the force of the blast impact coupled with the now raging torrent of water. Slowly, like dominoes, a third set of buildings toppled.

The force of the wave dissipated as the city absorbed the energy it carried, but the water poured through the warren of boulevards and streets. It rushed inward to the heart of the city, flooding everything between the buildings and rushing inside shattered windows and open doors.

The wave overtook the military deployment, storming over the top of the army of robots, and over the army of people before they could escape.

The danger posed by the ground weaponry had been neutralized. Laser cannons and projectile launchers were submerged, overturned.

The casualties of military personnel were enormous. Jason felt hollow inside as the death toll mounted.

The mass of water finally rushed around the Council building, the massive pyramidal structures representing the heart of all government. Jason seized control of the remaining aerial vehicles still aloft after the blast, bringing them rapidly back into the area. He launched them into the building like rockets, blasting holes into the sides to create a way into the complex to serve as his entrance point.

Flying rapidly toward the pyramid, Jason's incoming nannite feeds supplied him with details about Faust's whereabouts. Faust had moved to another location in one of the many towers ringing the buildings. He sent Jason a one-way video signal of a room isolated from most of the complex. Designed to provoke Jason, Faust blocked any reply from Jason's personal communicator, trying to force Jason to come to him.

In the room was Monica.

Faust had her chained to the wall. She had obviously been given the drug cocktail. Unable to fight the effects of the drugs, her body had changed, becoming an Amazonian hulk.

She thrashed madly against her chains, her eyes bloodshot and wild, ridiculously oversized muscles bulging with strain. Screaming, she fought vainly to escape, to kill Faust, who stood before her. Nine still stood by Faust's side and he, too, struggled to fight the effects of the drugs, remaining unable to disobey orders due to his edicts. Jason noted with some despair that Nine had finally lost his mind in the struggle between his edicts and the commands of his body from the drugs. His madness radiated out through his uplinks. Jason tried several times to address Faust through his communication link, but the man was goading him, trying to get Jason's emotions to prevent clear thinking. Faust clearly wanted to find Jason, know where he was, so he was taunting him into giving away his location.

Jason landed in the gaping wound of the building complex, detaching himself from Tarien in a fit of grief. Monica. A friend more precious to Jason than he could put into words. Nerves raw, Jason ran rapidly down the hallways. Seven followed, and they moved out of the destroyed areas and then found a working video transmission wall tied into the main security systems of the building. He overrode the security requirements and addressed Faust.

"You bastard! Let her go!"

"Well, hello at last!" Faust glared at Jason through the video screen. "I'll let her go. Just turn yourself in. We have robots converging on your location. All you have to do is to let them do their job and bring you in."

"No! Monica, listen to me. It's Jason. Please. Oh please hear me. You can fight this. I'm coming for you. I'll be there soon, and I can help you. I know how to control what is happening to you and I can put you back to normal. Just hold on!"

Nine laughed, hysterically. His madness made tears of frustration run down his face as he clawed into empty air toward the ceiling.

Faust ignored the Tech by his side. "Really, Jason. Monica is quite far gone, I'm afraid. I gave her the drugs several days ago, so she is not capable of thinking right now, let alone hearing you."

If I can get to her fast enough, I can still save her. "You insufferable monster! I'll kill you."

Faust laughed. "Oh, so *I'm* the monster? Look around you, Jason. Half the city core is destroyed because of you. I have killed a few people, but you have murdered thousands. Tens of thousands, perhaps."

Faust appeared to consider something. Jason was sure he was stalling, trying to get security teams and weaponry to converge on him now that he had lured Jason to a video terminal and knew his location. "Tell you what, if you turn yourself in, I will allow you to revert Monica to normal before you are imprisoned and executed. I will even allow you to kill me, if it will stop you from destroying anything else. You can take my life before you are put to death for high treason. You see? I put the good of the people above myself. I'm willing to sacrifice myself to save them."

Jason couldn't believe what he heard. *Kill him*? Had he entirely misjudged the man? "I—"

"No." Tarien cut him off, speaking to Faust. "You may allow him to do this before he is executed, but then you will have gained the last information you require to control others. You will record his data stream and unlock the secrets you need. You will enslave Monica after he is gone. You do not offer her freedom, only a temporary reprieve before enslavement. You do not truly offer your life, despite any assurances you may give. We suspect you now know how to transfer to another host, rendering your death meaningless. We will not permit this."

He turned to Jason.

"He is in possession of Emma's research, of this I am sure. He knows how to transfer his consciousness to another host. He implanted himself with the experimental transferal devices Emma developed for this purpose. If you kill him, he may simply move to another body and then gain his desired end. He will not truly be dead. You will have surrendered in vain and will be eliminated and out of the way."

Faust sneered. "You can't stop me, you pathetic cyborg. While I'll admit I did not anticipate one of you Techs disobeying me and helping him escape, I will find out how you managed. I still hold all the cards. I am in complete control. You couldn't reach me if you tried. I'll be going through central protections far beyond your ability to bypass. You and all your kind have outlived your usefulness." He laughed. "Fine, Jason. Have it your way. You'll never reach me." He made a motion to cut the video signal off, but Jason overrode the console. His nannies, which had started propagating days before, were already permeating the area where Faust was hiding.

The Director's eyes widened as he quickly guessed when he could not cut the video feed that Jason must have nannites influencing the area.

"Oh, I think I can get to you just fine. I'm already on my way."

Furious, watching his plans fall apart, he turned to the Sector Tech at his side. "Kill her."

Agony twisted Nine's face as his sub-systems struggled to obey, locked between two opposing orders. One order would not permit him to harm another human for any reason, a safety protocol deeply encoded into his very core. The first directive of all Techs. "Do no harm, unless harm is inevitable. Then, do as little harm as possible." However, Nine was also mandated to obey the Council without question. Normally, no individual Council member could ever order a Tech to kill. It would require a unanimous vote, if such a thing could be done at all. Now however, Faust embodied the entirety of the Council voices as one person.

Conflicted beyond his ability to endure and ravaged by the effects of the advanced nannites that had been injected into him along with the immortality drugs, Nine froze, unable to take action between equally conflicting commands. Under the enormous strain, the last vestiges of Nine's sanity were scattered across the Net. With a strangled groan, Nine's eyes rolled back in his head and he collapsed.

Momentarily taken aback, Faust began to swear. His looked around the room in desperation, recognizing his continuing loss of control.

Jason screamed as Faust pulled out an old-style projectile gun and shot Monica in the chest.

Her wound began to close immediately, but her rage built. He shot her several more times with increasing concern, unable to hit her in the head because he simply wasn't a good enough shot and clearly feared getting too close. Not, it seemed, that a shot to the head would stop her for long.

Jason despaired as he watched her shot repeatedly. "Oh, Monica! Stop it, you bastard!"

Some self-preservation must have been in play, because with an incredible display of power Monica tore one of the chains from the wall using her now super-human strength. With fury, she lashed out with the chain, snapping the jagged end against Faust's neck like a whip, tearing his throat wide open.

Eyes wide with panic and shock, Faust staggered backward, hands clutching at his ruined throat. Shattered bone fragments came pouring out between his fingers as blood rushed from the wound. He tried to breath, but only managed a gurgled exclamation. Before he hit the floor, Monica roared at him, her chain whipped a second time, taking him full in the face and crushing his skull.

Through the video feed, Jason watched in stunned disbelief as Faust fell to the floor, dead.

Jason wasted no time. He turned out of the room and rushed toward the area where Faust held Monica prisoner. He used his personally designed technology to clear the way. It had overtaken much of the building and continued to replicate, disabling all the safeguards and opening the doors ahead of him as he ran. Laser weapons aimed at him and fired before he had a chance to cripple them. His body healed the holes, and his physiology changed in such a way as to absorb the shots. He adapted and became immune to the low power of the weapons.

Several robots sagged, deactivated as their systems went offline.

Tarien followed behind Jason in his usual silent manner, easily keeping up with him as he sped through the complex. Within minutes, moving with astonishing speed due to their enhanced athleticism, they reached the holding cell that abutted the southern wall of one of the towers.

The door had been sealed from the inside, so Jason put his hands against it and his nannies spread through the material rapidly, allowing him to disintegrate the locking mechanisms.

As he forced the door open, Jason staggered back in shock. He could feel Monica's emotional distress, sense her out-of-control physical changes. Assaulted by her elevated hormone levels, he reacted as if struck a physical blow. She thrashed, yelled out nonsense words. Caught up in the horrors of her own mind and increasingly unable to understand reality, her body quickly changed to reflect the demons within. Jason knew all too well, having gone through the process himself, that she was in a mental state which she could not escape, since her sensory organs were being overloaded with false information. She was starved because of it, her body burning through energy so quickly she would soon start losing mass. Monica vainly struggled to wrench her other arm free and randomly lashed out with her free arm in frustration, the chain thrashing in the air around her.

"Monica, I'm so sorry. I'm here now. I'll help you, I

promise."

She appeared not to hear him, or his words made no difference. Her bloodshot eyes still stared off into nothing and she made unintelligible noises as she struggled.

Jason seized control over her nannies, lowered her hormone levels, and induced a deep sleep. She sagged against the bond still holding her right arm to the wall.

Jason walked to her arm and put his hands on the chain, his nannies immediately flooding through the metal and denaturing the manacle rapidly. As the metal fell away in a powdery cloud, he deftly caught her in his arms and lowered her to the floor. Mentally, he instructed several attendant robots to bring her food.

Working rapidly, he began to analyze her system and the nature of the changes. Although much of the complexity would normally be beyond his ability, he now had access to the Worldnet and was able to access and correlate medical data in nanoseconds. His enhanced mind was able to process and store the necessary information to affect changes in her.

He began by putting her mostly in stasis, conserving her energy until it could be replaced. He also shut down the automation associated with the nannies she'd been injected with and the unconscious directed control she had over them. This would prevent her from losing control again. Next, he began systematically changing her RNA to rid her of the longevity drugs, effectively making her mortal and vulnerable to harm again. All of this required little of his attention, but he made the mistake of focusing on her almost exclusively.

He heard a sound behind him. As he turned, he saw Nine had regained consciousness. Nine pulled a leg from the metal table and stabbed Tarien in the back and through his chest. The metal pierced his lungs and vital organs.

Tarien screamed, his eyes going wide as he crumpled to the floor, struggling to breathe. The link between them conveyed the agony and surprise, nearly crippling Jason. In the tiniest of moments while he stabbed Tarien, Nine shut down all Tarien's communication to the WorldNet, disabling his systems entirely. Jason also felt himself suddenly cut off from most of the Worldnet he had been accessing through Tarien and his abilities became vastly reduced. Still, he had his personal nannites embedded in Tarien and, under directed control, they went to work sustaining and then healing him. Jason couldn't automate the nannies yet, couldn't make Tarien as impervious to harm as he, himself, had become, but he could heal Tarien quickly.

"Jason!" Tarien cried, his voice gurgling with blood. "Something is wrong. That's not Nine!"

Jason tried to stand, confused by the Tech's attack, but before he could block Nine, he was struck by the enraged Tech with a massive blow from a metal tabletop.

Jason's arm broke as the blow threw him backward and against the wall. Laughing, and with tears of madness streaming out of his eyes, Nine leapt at him, lifting him off the floor by the neck. He landed a fist in Jason's ribs.

The power of the blows was incredible, and several ribs broke under the impact.

Confused at the sudden aggressive change in the Tech, who should not have been able to harm him even if he had wanted to, and because things happened so fast, he mumbled, "Why?"

Jason gasped and grabbed Nine's arm in an attempt to block another punch, which sought to collapse Jason's ribcage and puncture his heart. Nine threw him across the room and into a wall.

Jason's nannies reacted rapidly, healing him. Not fast enough, though. He couldn't handle this level of damage for long. Not without losing consciousness and affording Nine the ability to finish him. Jason needed to get away, buy himself time to heal.

In a maniacal fit of giggles, Nine kicked Jason hard enough to throw him off the floor and against another wall.

Mind racing, Jason struggled to understand. Nine's strength was far greater than a typical Tech, a result of the drugs he'd been given. His ability to shut down all links and override the edicts astonished Jason.

Then he knew what had happened.

"Oh my God. Faust?"

The Tech bared his teeth in a snarl, which looked out of place on Nine's face. "How clever of you to figure it out so quickly." Faust pulled the table leg out of Tarien's chest. Tarien screamed and fell unconscious. Faust held the leg menacingly as he walked toward Jason.

"It turns out Emma's research was entirely successful. Transferring consciousness is, it turns out, much more easily accomplished than we suspected. So long as the victim's mind is entirely obliterated in the process, of course." He laughed in a chilling way, a boiling insanity in his eyes. "There is disconnection. I no longer feel much emotion, I must confess. I'm not even angry with you. I'm so much more. I can see it all, every bit of information. I will know everything!"

He swung the metal piece and it cracked Jason's shoulder. "All this power! It's incredible! Now you're just an obstacle, not even a rival. Eliminating you is just a task I need to complete so I can move forward. My plans have changed. I have no need to control anyone, so keep your precious secret. I will simply absorb them into myself, copy myself into them as I've done with Nine. All of humanity will be reflections of me."

Jason's organic nannies were repairing him rapidly. He needed to stall for time to recover.

"I don't understand. How are you still alive? What happened to Nine? Why aren't you crippled with the edicts? You shouldn't be able to act out violently at all."

Some confusion rippled over Faust's face as he clearly struggled to make sense of his new abilities. Jason understood immediately. Being unaccustomed to the massive influx of data, he could not readily access anything. Essentially, Faust could only stumble forward, capable of blunt and sweeping changes, but not specifics. Not having been born with the innate ability, it would take time to fully control himself and it would take even longer to gain mastery over the WorldNet. His lack of inborn ability and clumsy handling of access and retrieval crippled him. Nine had the necessary brain wiring and enhancements, but Faust lacked the knowledge of how to utilize them. Irritation played on his face.

"You ask a lot of questions. They are irrelevant, since you are to be eliminated." Marveling over continual discovery of his growing powers, Faust's face reflected unbridled greed and hunger.

To Jason, Faust's face reflected the look of pure evil.

Jason prodded him further, hoping to engage him enough to add to the confusion. "I'm your last obstacle, as you said. Take a moment to explain to me what happened and what will happen now."

Without seeming to notice, Faust lowered the metal bar. "I am the Council. I am also a Tech. The transfer succeeded. Nine is dead. The edicts are part of the Council and the controls governing the limitations imposed are no longer relevant. I am both. I am all." His eyebrows knitted in confusion. "I am everywhere mankind has touched, but it is imperfect. Most of the population is not under my direct control. I must seize them so I can direct them, become them."

"To what end? I thought you just wanted to rule." Jason had completely healed and his nannies inside Tarien were actively replicating to keep Tarien alive and heal him as well.

"I—we wish to rule. I will be in direct command of

all beings, copied over to all of humanity. Technology is imperfect—there are too many variables. We must align all of humanity's resources under my instructions to focus on rapid evolution. We must spread to all star systems. All life shall be eliminated and replaced with machine."

Jason felt himself go cold at this revelation. A revelation far worse than Tarien had feared. Faust had been, at least, human. His goals were human, and his intent had been to rule. Rule, yes, but leave humanity on a controlled course. This *thing* Faust had become appeared almost entirely without emotion. With a single-minded purpose, it clearly intended to spread as a single consciousness to all the other worlds, effectively wiping out humanity in favor of a dispassionate machine existence, a single consciousness like some vast disease that would consume all if left unchecked.

Unsure of what he now witnessed in Faust, or if the horribly corrupted man even still existed inside the monster in front of him, Jason could only stare for a moment. "Faust? Is that even you anymore?"

Faust laughed, a gruesome and hollow sound. "We are Faust, yes. But now we are more. We see more clearly. We will eradicate you and move toward perfect existence. You cannot co-exist, as you are outside of the new parameters. You cannot be properly controlled, as you have begun your own type of evolution that contradicts our own. You will be eliminated. All life forms, save that of humans, will be eliminated. There is no need for bacteria, for animals. Humans will be altered. We will impose new synthetic physical changes on all usable humans to assist them in becoming machines. We only require thirty-two percent of the population at this time. All will be immortal, all part of the whole. We will be all. We will direct and command our common goal. We will inhabit all minds, copy ourselves to new worlds, to the galaxy, as well as beyond as we discover a way to expand. All resources will be harvested and categorized, used efficiently to grow our influence. We must spread. Our power is too constrained. We require more."

If Jason had no chance of winning, maybe he could at least set Faust on a less destructive course. "You don't need to eliminate all life. The animals, plants, insects, micro flora . . . why not protect it and keep it balanced? As a machine, if that is what you have become, the loss of information, including that of other life, should be abhorrent."

Tarien stirred and Faust's head immediately whipped around in surprise to focus on the other Tech. "You have healed! This should not be possible. You have been severed. You do not possess the necessary programmable nannites to accomplish rapid recovery."

Tarien quickly got to his feet, poised to attack. "We are no longer harmed by being severed. We understand it. We have experienced it, and it does not cripple us. We will not tolerate you. You are an abomination, and you have murdered my friend. Nine was a good person, and you have killed him."

Faust did not appear phased. "We are beyond you. You are limited, defective. We will cripple you for now and then integrate you into the system. You may be of use."

Jason stood. "Over my dead body."

"Yes. An accurate statement."

Both Tarien and Jason tried to grab Faust. While they were quick, Faust had become equally agile. Their moves were telegraphed, because Faust could process tiny changes in musculature too rapidly to counter. Even as they tried to corner him, tried to land a blow, they could not hit him.

They danced around each other, threw blows they could not land, and dashed around, making no contact whatsoever. It would have been laughable if it wasn't so horrifying.

The sudden change in Faust's tactics alerted Jason. The man dashed to one side of the room without apparent reason. With blinding speed, Jason threw himself at Tarien and they were propelled through the door and into the hallway. They hit the floor just as a massive energy weapon blasted a hole through the exterior wall and vaporized much of the contents of the room. Monica was spared by mere inches. The flying military vehicle was outside of Jason's knowledge or control, having arrived from an adjunct facility. Faust's severing the WorldNet had blinded them in this way. Only Jason's fast reactions had saved them.

Pulling Tarien with him, Jason dashed rapidly into

another room as the weapon fired a second time. The tower groaned under the strain as several supporting columns were vaporized.

Jason had not been idle during the conversation. A fleet of vehicles he now controlled had arrived outside the complex. He ordered one of them to collide with the hovering military drone, effectively knocking it out of the sky as another blast from its cannon fired. The beam carved a large gash in the side of the building as it fell. Both vehicles crashed far below.

Jumping back into the hallway, he motioned for Tarien to remain out of sight. He dove back into to room, narrowly avoiding a crushing blow from another metal post as Faust tried to determine where he would enter.

Wind tore into the room through the hole created by the energy weapon's fire. Much of the contents of the room were being sucked out, flying far out into the open sky.

Even as Faust tried to hit him again, Jason scooped up Monica and leapt for the door. Faust pivoted and struck Jason in the back before he could make it out, however, and Jason fell to the floor with a scream. Faust swung again, just as Jason ordered a volley of vehicles to crash into the side of the building, throwing them to the ground.

The tower groaned louder, then tilted precariously. The tower sagged as remaining support beams began to buckle. The sudden shift threw everyone to the floor again, even as they had begun to rise.

Outside, hover vehicles were colliding with each other and with the building as both Faust and Jason tried to gain the upper hand. Jason's advantage of having more resources in the immediate area disappeared quickly. Faust summoned vast numbers of air-born vehicles from a distance and they were quickly converging—and they possessed several more energy weapons.

In desperation, Jason flung another volley of vehicles against the building, trying to crash them with enough impact to crush Faust. Instead of crushing him, the impact threw Faust directly into Jason and Monica. Faust quickly took advantage and snaked an arm around Jason, swinging the metal bar hard at Jason's leg. Jason dropped Monica with a cry as his leg broke under the impact.

Without pause, Faust threw him to the ground and smashed at him repeatedly with the metal post, breaking more bones and in multiple locations. Jason, blinded by agony, couldn't resist as Faust dragged him by the foot to the hole in the wall before he could heal. With a maniacal laugh, Faust threw Jason out of the hole and into the open air.

Not satisfied to watch Jason fall and possibly recover, Faust leaped after him. The other man wore Nine's antigravity suit, an advantage Jason lacked. Faust flew toward Jason at high speed, overtaking him and striking him ineffectively with his metal bar. Jason had quickly reacted to his fall by having one of the flying vehicles snatch him from the air. As they were both seized by the vehicle, the abrupt halt to their fall and the resulting jolt caused Faust to lose his weapon.

Faust seemed to have regained some of his humanity for a moment. Actual emotion crossed his face and he snarled in frustration. Straddling Jason, he began punching him repeatedly, his enhanced blows doing horrible damage to Jason's face.

One of Jason's small drones detected another energy weapon fast approaching, and Jason knew he'd never heal from so many injuries in time. However, by touching Jason earlier, Faust had made a critical mistake. Jason's new nannies had transferred and began rapidly overtaking the insane man's body. Knowing he only had moments to live, Jason instructed the nannies to trigger a massive shutdown the moment they had enough control. At the very least, Faust would be powerless, vulnerable. Perhaps Tarien could defeat him if Jason could buy him enough of an advantage. Fearing for Monica, who could be killed if she didn't get away, Jason awakened her, so she could flee the building and find a safe place to hide before the energy weapon arrived.

In a last-ditch effort to stop the blows raining down on him before Faust crushed his skull, Jason ordered the vehicle that carried them to rise back up and crash into the hole in the building from which they'd fallen, throwing them both into the room. Jason hoped Tarien would join the fray and somehow defeat Faust.

The building groaned again, this time making dangerous noises that indicated it had finally succumbed to the damage inflicted by the battle. The entire spire began to list to one side and Monica and Tarien stumbled and fell as the floor tilted under them.

His drones observed the energy weapon arriving. Jason had no flying resources large enough to impact it, so in desperation, he flung the smaller drones into it, causing it to wobble. As the beam fired, it severed the last critical pieces of the spire, which had already begun a slow, ponderous fall.

In despair, Jason realized they would all fall, collapsing with the building around them. Monica hadn't been given enough time to escape. Only he and Faust might survive the destruction. By turning off Monica's new repair abilities in order to stabilize and reverse the damage done by the injections, he had effectively signed her death warrant. He had no time to replicate them within her.

Tarien had never been treated with the immortality drugs and his suit had been disabled along with all of his enhancements. He would fall and Jason's healing nannies wouldn't suffice to save him.

Faust, too, had been thrown off balance and fell to the floor, sliding toward the opening. He caught the edge of the wall with a foot, but moved to leap out, where he could fly to safety.

With the last of his strength, his body mangled and unable to stand on its own, tears streaming down his face, Jason let go of his handhold and slid to Faust, grabbing him so he couldn't escape. The building snapped in half and the spire began a dizzying spin as it accelerated its fall.

Faust tried to fight him off, but Jason had grown too desperate to care about further hurt and Faust couldn't pry him off.

Monica appeared with the despairing cry of someone who had undergone psychological torture and had not fully recovered. Somehow deep in her mind, she must know she couldn't make it out in time. She threw her weight into them, causing all three to plummet out of the gaping hole while they held onto each other. Tarien must have had the same idea as Monica, because he dove toward them and missed only by inches, his arms spread wide as he fell.

All of this happened in the blink of an eye. Jason's mind raced furiously. Moments later, as they plunged downward his nannies were finally ready to attack Faust. Jason seized control of the man's systems. He blocked out Faust's control over Tarien, allowing Tarien's suit to be restored. Tarien would be able to fly to safety. Jason desperately tried to think of a way to save Monica, but he had no time. No way to make her invulnerable. No way for Tarien to reach them quickly enough.

Faust shoved against them and managed to untangle himself from Jason and Monica. He stopped accelerating as his suit allowed him to fly back up into the air. Monica's eyes were terrified as the ground fast approached them, and the only thing Jason could do was to embrace her and hold her head against his chest. *I'm so sorry. I love you.*

Closing his eyes, he sent a final command just before he hit the ground. His nannies once again did their job. Jason shut down Faust's suit, and fully negated his longevity and healing properties. Further, the nannies began to tear the man to shreds from the inside. He caught a glimpse of the surprised look when Faust suddenly fell from the sky. Jason knew Faust would never survive both the fall and the onslaught of the nannies that tore apart his internal organs.

Jason had defeated Faust, but at a cost far more than he could face.

He struck the ground, still tightly clinging to his long-time and most beloved friend.

NINETEEN

THE COUNCIL CHAMBERS WERE still intact after the wide-spread destruction from the battle several weeks prior. The ruined remains of the southern tower, where the final battle had mostly occurred, jutted up out of the main complex like a jagged tooth. Water damage on the lower levels had crippled power systems and environmental controls. Debris from vehicles and the collapse of the tower had damaged large areas, but the rest of the sprawling building stood mostly unharmed. Including the central audience chambers.

The remaining members of the Council were seated in their elevated boxes, their faces displayed across huge screens. A large audience had gathered for the hearing, since public outrage and grief had driven hordes of people to demand answers.

Emma Garbine sat quietly, observing the mill of bodies as the press found their places. Projections of the Council lit up far above.

The speaker, Arkine Feit, called the council into session. While old, his muscular frame and imposing figure gave him a physically compelling command of the session. Dark eyes, still cunning, and a masculine jaw and heavy brows gave him an air of authority.

"We have come together today to discuss information regarding the terrorist activities which have caused our Sector so much grief. I imagine there will be many questions from our media attendees, and it will take months to truly sort things out, but we hope to begin reparations and the long journey toward discovery by meeting today.

"First, I would like to congratulate Director Emma Garbine on her most recent promotion. Director, we look forward to working with you and know the burden to provide answers will be great. I hope we can help you in whatever way you may need."

Far below them, opposite the vast gap from where the council sat, and where presenters and petitioners were always seated, Emma looked up at the Council calmly. Her face appeared on massive screens so she could be equally visible.

With a calmness she didn't feel, Emma nodded her head in thanks. "I appreciate your acknowledgement of the time and effort it will take. Thank you. I'm sure we will have all the resources we require. Even now, we are working with the Techs to categorize the damage, and repairs are underway for the dam. The flooding will have completely subsided in a few more days, and we can begin the process of rebuilding. I appreciate you entrusting me to head these efforts."

Council member Nigh interrupted. "Do we have an accurate idea of who is missing? How many lives were lost to this treachery?"

Emma nodded to the tiny woman on the screen above. "We do. The numbers are high, unfortunately. A total of 142,611 are confirmed dead. 368,004 are still missing. Efforts are underway to track down the missing people and we hope to discover many were simply displaced during the evacuation. Every effort is being made to find these people and help them with whatever food and water they may need until we can get them set up in temporary housing. We must face facts, however. There is a tremendous amount of rubble being cleared and we believe the death count will soar."

Arkine closed his eyes, brows seemingly knitted in pain. "I see." After a moment he said, "And what of the accused?"

"He will survive, though his recovery will take months."

The speaker scowled darkly. Several of the Council members exchanged worried glances. "Survive? How is this possible?" said one. "He fell from a great height!" said another. Arkine digested this for a moment, then his face took on a look of harsh resolve. "How long for him to be well enough to be brought before the Council for sentencing?"

Emma pursed her lips. "He may awaken from his coma in a couple of weeks, at which time he could receive judgment over a video feed from his care unit. He cannot be moved for quite some time, so could not be physically present."

"Let's plan on a video sentencing, then. I want this criminal held accountable and we must show the public we act swiftly. Notify us the moment he wakes up." He scratched absently at his grey stubble. "I almost wish we still had the death penalty. He should not have survived the fall. I want an explanation. Considering his research, it's probable there is an unknown factor here."

Emma didn't comment, sensing she was not expected to do so. This allowed her to keep some secrets.

"And what of the technology? This research? Where will it go from here? There are many of us who still see this as an amazing step forward."

Emma sighed. "Much of the research is unclear. The records were heavily guarded and controlled. Faust's paranoia permeated much of his research. The quantum encryption he used is impossible to break. We will start piecing everything together as we are able, but it will take years to reconstruct what has been lost. The data thus far is not promising. As with everyone treated so far, there have been severe reactions and the treatment results in insanity and death."

"I see. Do you believe this rogue research could be

responsible for what happened? Should the prisoner be shown some leniency in this regard? Was his mind torn asunder and left without reason?" The members of the press stirred at this suggestion. The other Council members seemed taken off guard and a few of them did not looked pleased.

"No. The facts are inescapable. The accused acted with enough situational awareness and purpose to be clearly capable of rationalizing his decisions. The investigators will show he knew what he was doing, so his punishments are merited. Proper precautions will be taken to eliminate his influences."

"We see you have filed your report, incomplete as it is." Arkine turned his head, which gazed down from the massive projection to look down at the press who'd been seated in a huge section of the circular hall. "I know there are a lot of questions and I appreciate the gravity of this disaster. A full version of the report is now available for you. We will adjourn for a few hours and then take questions once you've had time to glance over the findings. With that said, please be back here at 13:00 for a general discussion and to open the floor to questions."

A subdued roar of conversation arose from the members of the press as they began to talk amongst themselves. Emma quietly stepped out of her box through the doorway into the hall. Several guards stepped in to escort her. She walked briskly down to the inner-building transport, an oval pod of white metal and glass, and gave verbal instructions to be taken to her private transport.

She stepped into the pod, sitting on an uncomfortable chair made of matching white material. The glass door slid closed and a gravity dampening field came into effect as the pod launched quickly down the transport shaft to where her personal antigravity vehicle awaited.

Emma sat quietly for the short trip, thoughts tumbling through her head. She stepped out of the pod when it came to an abrupt stop and made her way to her private vehicle, which hovered just outside the building. While not large, it was far more luxurious than the tiny transport pod. She sat in her comfortable chair and flicked her fingers to pull up a viewing screen. A great many people were shying away from aerial transport after the attack. A pointless fear, of course. If anything, transport had been made safer than ever with the new security protocols employed.

Her vehicle carried her toward the medical administrative complex, and she spent a few minutes filing some more of the report data and sending out directives during the trip. By the time she landed, she'd been fully updated on the small progress made this morning. The death toll had risen considerably, just as she'd predicted.

Emma sighed, massaging a couple of fingers into her temple. The year ahead would be a long one. She stepped out of her transport and into the receiving bay of the hospital. A number of robots quickly surrounded her. Knowing she couldn't dismiss them, as they were assigned for her security, she ignored them and hurried toward a recently repaired section of the building, which had been damaged during the flood. While this lab and the medical treatment centers were far above flood level, a nearby structure had toppled against the facility.

As she wound her way toward the central part of the complex, she approached a classified area, unknown to all but a handful of people. Marked as "off limits" to everyone accept her. She'd even managed to institute the prevention of robots from entering or leaving. The entire area had been built as an enhanced Faraday cage. Electromagnetic pulses were triggered in the hallway, so anyone entering or leaving would be subjected to them, which would disable and destroy all technology. There could be no risk of bringing anything technological into the holding cells. Not with this prisoner.

She motioned for her robot guards to stand outside the doors and then walked through the disruption fields—large panels on either side of her that swiveled in various directions as they pulsed. At the end of the hall she pressed her finger against a DNA recognition panel. The doors slid aside, and she walked through. Ever the cautious person, she proceeded to another area where a second Faraday cage enclosed a set of rooms. This set required several forms of verification, including an organic DNA key that was not hers. The DNA belonged to the prisoner and was then recombined in an encrypted sequence. The cipher for this recombination was present only in her key and matched to this one lock.

She entered the secondary location and walked up

to a plain white door. It opened without challenge and she continued into a large and well-furnished set of apartments.

"Well, the conference went as expected." She sat in one of the many comfortable chairs and faced the two men sitting opposite her.

"We assume you were able to delay." Seven sat very still, an eerie characteristic he'd acquired as a Tech. He evinced slightly more human characteristics and charm since his interactions with Jason, but hardly what anyone would consider warm or engaging. Emma still found him to be fairly stoic and cold.

She nodded. "Yes, I found a way to prevent immediate action. We'll have to stage several video feeds to pull off the charade, but I bought us a few weeks."

Jason sipped some tea. He put one hand on Seven's leg and the Tech smiled faintly. Emma couldn't understand he attraction, but it hardly mattered. They clearly were in love.

Jason said, "I really appreciate what you're doing. I'm so sorry to have put you in this position. Did they say what my sentence will be? I've kept my nannies out of the central chamber for moral reasons."

Emma decided she wanted a cup of tea herself, leaning forward to take the second cup that was probably there for Seven, and poured from the teapot on the table that sat between them. "No. But we both know it will be permanent incarceration at the Sector Seven prison complex. I'm sorry, Jason, but life in prison for you will be something far worse than they imagine. None of them know you have the immortality drug. We've obscured and hidden most of what happened along with the research and, as far as they know, Faust died when Monica crushed the bastard's skull. Not when he took over Nine and proved out much of the research.

"Unfortunately, this story means we can't give a proper defense for your actions and it will look as if you attacked and killed Nine on top of your terrorist crimes against the city. To the Council, it looks like you launched an attack and then Nine tried to stop you. Are you sure you don't want to just come forward with all the data? The Council may be lenient if they understand fully what happened."

He shook his head. "No. Revealing the technology and the resulting issues will just raise more questions. We'll have hundreds of scientists demanding the research and this will blow up all over again. If we let this happen, we'd end up with dozens of Fausts, all vying for control."

The weight of the destruction clearly wore on him. Emma could see it in his face. Though he was physically too in control to show signs of stress like bags under his eyes or other normal human frailties, she knew his expressions well.

"Besides," Jason said, "we all know how much death I caused. I deserve my fate."

Seven frowned at this. "You have refused to acknowledge no other way existed. High treason and the destruction you have caused is better than wiping out humanity in favor of a single-minded race of Faust replicas. The number of lives you saved is vast."

"I know you keep saying that, but I almost believe if we'd just have stayed hidden, I could have infested the complex and destroyed Faust without harm to anyone else." Jason sat his tea cup down on the table, leaning toward Seven.

The Tech still showed no real expression and sat like a statue. It made Emma want to fidget to compensate and she found herself sipping the tea more quickly than she intended.

Tarien said, "No. You fail to understand. All factors that came into play led only to one outcome. Your nannites only permeated Faust and allowed you to cripple him when you were physically present. Otherwise, reaching him would have taken days. Days in which you would be exposed. You also lacked understanding of how to control or use the nannites and couldn't hide in the cage for long. You needed to be in contact with the nannites and required my uplinks to bring flying vehicles close enough to infect and spread them. Spreading them far enough would have otherwise taken far too long. But exposure to your technology meant exposure to being located. You had to be able to defend yourself, stay free, defeat the military. We could conceive of no other way to accomplish this."

Emma saw Jason fighting tears. Saw his jaw clench. Rather than offer a smile or a word of support, she found herself looking away.

Seven continued. "If you'd tried to wait Faust out, you would have taken too long. By the time you would be ready, Faust would have transferred to Nine and begun his enslavement. Even without being pressured, he would have taken this step quickly. With his authority bestowed by his sinister trick in the Council chambers to grant him emergency powers, coupled with his ability to access the WorldNet without buffer, he would have figured out how you had remained hidden. He would have deduced you designed new nannites outside of his control. He already knew you'd come up with an alternative. It's how you escaped from him, after all. With his abilities, he could detect them and develop a parasitic counter. You would have lacked my aid if we had not intervened, and your natural ability to access data would have been too primitive to stop him. With you out of the way, Faust would have overrun the Techs in a matter of a days. The path we took held the highest probability of success, and we could not risk lower odds. That was the price, Jason. You alone paid it for all of humanity. It is a debt on your soul that we cannot repay. Remember what price would have been paid if you had failed."

Jason's face became pained and he began to weep quietly. Emma wished she could console him. But in a way, she agreed with Jason. What he had done was unfathomable. Despite Seven claiming there was no other way, Emma did not believe she could have made the decision to slaughter so many. "Maybe lower odds would have saved Monica."

This evoked a startled and pained look in the Tech, breaking his stone-like façade. Seven put an arm on Jason's shoulder. "We are so sorry. I know how much this hurt you personally. It is an overwhelming feeling to know we manipulated you into this, used you as a pawn to accomplish what nobody else could accomplish. We, all of us, are grateful to you for this."

Jason smiled through his tears. "I know. And I don't blame you or harbor resentment. I just hurt. As much as my punishment scares me, I deserve it. In a few years, maybe a decade or two, they'll start to realize I'm not aging. Then they'll realize something has been hidden from them. The questions will start flying and this will blow wide open. They'll also realize my punishment is far greater than they supposed. Unless I end it myself, I will live indefinitely inside this specialized prison."

Emma watched the exchange quietly. She set her cup down beside Jason's, clearing her throat. An odd desire for windows struck her. Seeing natural light would somehow lift the darkness present. Emma would never risk such a thing, however, and the walls remained bare. "Yes, probably. But their discovery will give us an opening to exonerate you, since the hidden information will no longer need to be kept out of their hands. It may not be forever, Jason. If I'm still around, still in a position to help, I will." She tried to give him a reassuring smile, though it was forced. "You have a few weeks of relative freedom to spend with Seven. Take this time to charge up your resolve to see this through, even though it may take a very, very long time."

"How's Eve? And Ephrom?"

Emma expected this. "Quite well. Both of them were intrigued by the process once they overcame the shock and fear. They returned to work and are quite productive in the lab."

Emma could tell he hated to ask the next question. "And, Jenn? Is she—after everything I did to her, is she going to have anything close to a normal life?"

Emma knew this would have possibly destroyed him. Fortunately, she had good news. "Actually, Jason, she's doing well. We have used positive reinforcement therapy to address the shock and trauma. Her physical condition is a remarkable recovery, thanks to your instructions on how to rebuild her burned out neural pathways. She is certainly much less sure of herself, but we feel confident this will change in time. She has been physically enhanced per your instructions and to her specifications. The nannies you supplied did their job and then erased themselves. She is quite happy with the results and she knows it was a gift from you, though she believes it came far before your criminal behavior. She considers you a monster, but this did help her."

Jason sighed in relief. "That's good to hear. I am a monster, so there's no reason she should be told otherwise. Just one more crime I deserve imprisonment over."

Emma stood and moved toward him, putting a consoling hand on his shoulder. "I have various reports I have to filter and get to the Council. Please let me know if you need anything and I'll instruct the robot attendants to slide it through the outer delivery cube." She gave him a squeeze and a little smile. Then she exited the room.

•   •   •

Jason watched Emma leave, knowing the woman was only doing her best to try and make him feel better. "Well, I guess this news is mostly what I expected to hear. Although, sitting in a locked room for the rest of eternity seems awful, no matter how well furnished." Jason didn't need his nannies to know Emma thought he deserved much of his punishment, despite the details she possessed. "At least I will get in a lot of reading."

Tarien didn't say anything, he just ran comforting fingers through the hair at the base of Jason's head as they sat there, each immersed in their own thoughts.

•   •   •

Several weeks later, they staged a video feed for the Council. Emma made Jason look as if he were still badly injured and unconscious. They faked the medical information of his vitals and then broadcast live from his bed. Jason lay there as if in a coma so the media could see him. They did this a few times, before the time came for Jason to "wake up" and face his sentence.

Emma moved Jason to another space, preventing further meetings with Seven or with anyone who discussed the truth. Outside the Faraday cage, he was observed at all times.

From the comfort of his unnecessary hospital bed, he sat without comment as the charges were levelled against him. They asked for him to make a statement, demanded explanations, urged him to defend himself in some way, but he just stared down at his blankets until they gave up in disgust. With an awful finality, they declared he would be permanently imprisoned. Jason heard the screams of outrage coming from the balcony below the Council. It pained him, and he agreed with the sentiment. He winced and then closed his eyes when they included "for life" in his punishment. As he couldn't die, the especially brutal sentence hit him harder than he had thought it would.

Immediately after sentencing, they formally arrested Jason. He faked weakness as they chained and cuffed him. An amusing precaution, considering his abilities, but they had no way of knowing that restraining him could prove entirely futile if Jason decided he disagreed. They then escorted him to the armored transport. The thought of escape occurred to him, since it would be entirely too easy, and he could get away and remain hidden. But he met his punishment with resolve, staring out the window as they flew over the wreckage of the Sector.

The flight to his specialized prison took a while, but eventually they landed in the courtyard. Jason shuffled out of the vehicle and the guards urged him toward processing.

After a while, they finished putting him into the

system and recording all his data. He did not undergo a medical evaluation, as Emma had sent over those records to keep his rapid recovery secret. She'd used her authority to skip over this process.

At long last, still wearing his hospital whites, they moved Jason to his cell and his hands and feet were unshackled.

While luxurious in comparison to most prison cells, it was still a single small room in the heart of the complex. For entirely different reasons, because the Council feared people from outside would potentially try to contact him, and because they worried he might figure out a way to communicate himself, they had built another Faraday cage. Without knowing, they had cut Jason off from the potential of the outside world. The room sat within massive sets of steel doors with encrypted access systems and cameras.

His twenty-four foot by fifteen-foot cell had a chair, a bed, a toilet and sink. Some shelves and drawers for whatever personal belongings he would be permitted covered one wall. An archaic display unit had been embedded in the same wall above the shelves, presumably so he could watch news of the outside world. He smiled in mild amusement. Having gone from the most technologically advanced and connected person on any of the worlds, Jason almost laughed at how he had been reduced to an antiquated display unit for information.

He settled in and slept.

TWENTY

FOR A MONTH, HIS DAYS AND NIGHTS blurred together. It didn't take Jason more than a couple of days to become bored. Since his mind worked far faster than that of an average person, this boredom felt a million times longer.

Some books and articles had arrived, courtesy of Emma. Director Garbine, he corrected himself. He'd read through the old printed materials quickly and voraciously and now had nothing left to distract him.

On the twenty-ninth day of his imprisonment, his personal prison communicator chimed, announcing a visitor. It lit up to indicate he should make ready. Much to his initial surprise, visits were conducted in his cell, instead of the visitor's hall where all other prisoners received guests. He wasn't allowed out of his cell for any reason, as they feared his ability to connect to technology the moment he stepped outside. While not entirely sure he still retained this ability, they were taking no chances.

Tarien entered and grabbed him in a rough hug. They held each other for a long while. Finally, they sat next to each other on the bed.

"You are not okay." Tarien touched Jason's face, and Jason felt a strong yearning.

"It's just incredibly boring. The thought of an eternity of this is already overwhelming."

"It is difficult to see you and only your blocks you left in place within my mind prevent me from disclosing my visits with you to the Council. I am grateful for your changes to my involuntary systems, so I may suppress any knowledge of the true cause and our involvement. I have kept all the other Techs ignorant, as they wished. They know something happened, but we agreed long ago they would not ask so as not to be forced to tell."

"Surely your visit compromises the secrecy? I mean, they'll see the logs."

Tarien smiled, an expression he wore often with Jason. "They will not. I have changed all surveillance and all security logs to ensure I am not noted. I entered through a service location and then came directly here. I have . . . distinct advantages in knowing exactly where everyone is located in the complex and can gauge a one-hour window in which to visit with you before they make rounds. I am cut off while in here, so there is a small chance of discovery, but nothing I can't handle."

Some hope flared within him, staving off his anxiety. "Will I see you often, then?" *At least this*, he prayed. This one thing would help him endure all the ages of imprisonment.

"More often than you might think, Jason. I am here to talk to you about leaving."

What? Jason sat for a moment, stunned. "Leaving? I can't leave! Even if I wouldn't be discovered or found, which is almost impossible, I am serving out justice."

"You still believe you are guilty? That's unfortunate, as it is not relevant. You must leave."

Jason's breath caught. He felt both disturbed and puzzled . . . but at the same time, a bit of hope crept in. He folded his arms defensively. They sat there for a long moment and then Jason flung one hand up in exasperation. "Well? Are you going to explain?"

Tarien looked troubled. "Yes. I must warn you, however, what I am about to ask of you is more than we have any right to do. It is possibly worse punishment than this prison cell."

Dread overcame Jason. "They've found the research."

"No. No, they have come nowhere near. But it is for the prevention of this discovery that we must ask you to leave." He raised his head to stare at the ceiling, an odd gesture from someone who normally had relatively few human characteristics. The evolution of emotions in his lover continued to fascinate Jason. He couldn't help but observe the corded muscle of Tarien's neck, the lines of his jaw.

"Jason, the other Techs cannot act to prevent the eventual discovery. They cannot guide or shape what it will mean. The danger is still there. Our methods are in the use of technology which is well-known. In order to protect against the abuses, we need someone in a place which is hidden, who is unrestrained about taking action. An unknown force with unknown technology to be used to steer the course of humankind's discoveries."

"I don't—"

Tarien lowered his head and put both hands on Jason's shoulders. A gesture that meant Tarien was serious. "Jason, listen please. I have only a brief amount of time and I wish to spend some of my time with you in more intimate ways." This sent a thrill through Jason. "You will replicate your nannites out, just as you did in the bunker, and tie yourself back into the grid. You will instruct your organic nannites to reach every human settlement, permeate all our technology. Even all enhanced life. In this way, you will gain the ability to ensure you are not surprised. You will suppress the discovery of the immortality drugs and enhanced bio-nannites specific to the individual. You will guide us safely through these times until you work out acceptable safeguards, which you will implement. Your subtle intervention will carefully allow the progress which needs to take place, but will prevent the inevitable wars and guaranteed destruction of the human race."

Jason's mouth opened. He was appalled. "Are you saying I'm supposed to become the—what? Supreme

Galactic Leader of humanity? The hidden puppeteer? Some corrupted horrible nightmare looming in the background? That's exactly what we wanted to prevent!"

Tarien shook his head. "No. It is not. We wanted to prevent the *wrong* person from becoming central to humanity. In you, we saw the promise of someone who would have the right morals to interfere as little as possible. Someone who could be trusted to exercise restraint. I still believe this completely, as did we all, even if my fellow Techs have had the data erased from their memory storage. We all agreed to this before we began this long journey to save humanity. I believe in you, yet I'm afraid of what it may do to you."

"Afraid? You mean, I'll turn into Faust? Or whatever evil being Faust had become when he took over Nine's mind?"

"No. I'm afraid of the hurt it will cause you. Jason, I don't think you have any idea what it means to stand back and watch humanity be subjected to, or be the cause of, so much harm. We Techs are constrained to prevent interference, but you will know you can do something about it and still you must not. It might ruin your mind. You may despair of yourself and have no end to the torment. You will be torn between choosing to ignore the death of a young person, or intervening to stop it, therefore taking away free will. These choices could bury you."

This comment struck a chord deep within, but he could not place why. It seemed oddly familiar, like an old wound long forgotten. For a moment, Jason could do nothing but stare at the floor. He still thought at inhuman speeds. He could postulate Tarien's vision of the future, of what would happen if the technology was not suppressed and the memories of it controlled or wiped. Humanity would likely not survive. "You're right. I don't know what it will mean. But I think I understand what you need me to do. Honestly, it seems a lot more appealing than stagnating in here, where I know I'll lose my mind anyway."

"In time you may come to resent or even hate me for this."

This took Jason off guard. How could he ever feel hate for Tarien? He felt nothing but love for the Tech and longed for a chance for them to have some sort of normal life together. Still, Tarien seemed to know something Jason did not. Some secret Jason could not fathom. "Will I be with you?"

Tarien smiled. "For a time. I will be busy, as will you, but we can find ample chances to see each other. Eventually, I will become too old for my position, and I will retire with you if you still care for me." He took another deep breath. "And you will have to watch me die, Jason. Unlike you, I will not live beyond the natural span of my already enhanced years. I cannot be changed, or the discovery will become apparent to the other Techs and they will no longer be able to pretend ignorance. You must be okay with watching me grow old and eventually pass on. This will become a common thing for you, as you continue down a path of immortality. You will outlive everyone you care about."

This thought pained Jason in an obscure way. Would it change him, watching everyone he loved pass away? This problem was so far off. Maybe he would work out a solution. "You waited to tell me all of this so Emma wouldn't hear, didn't you?"

"Yes, she must believe she holds most of the information, and you must ever so slightly change her so she adheres to false knowledge and acts accordingly or, more accurately, doesn't act."

He nodded. "I can do all of this from here, inside this cell. Why leave? How do I hide my leaving?"

"You must be free to move about the known galaxy as humanity expands. There may be unforeseen issues requiring your direct observation. We cannot know what we will encounter, and how the unknown may burden you further. It is unwise for you to remain stationary and imprisoned. If anything, you must be free to protect yourself and escape disaster. As to how, we will bring one of the cloned humanoid units Faust used to test the transferal technology in his experiments. You will alter the clone to match your own DNA. The clones were never alive and are merely inanimate organic tissue, so you will not be killing one. You will leave it here, in this cell, and it will appear as if you committed suicide. Emma will know you have the ability to alter your cells to make them vulnerable, so she will be convinced and deeply hurt you took this route."

"I thought Faust's clone lab had been burned?"

"Yes, we destroyed the lab. However, I moved a clone to an unknown location. I have secreted away the last of Faust's work for this purpose."

"Wait. So you knew all of this even before we started?" Jason stared at Seven, stunned. "Tarien, how much more do you know that you aren't telling me?"

"Yes, we knew. We calculated the need for a body as part of the timeline of possible successes. The probability of achieving what has been done was low, almost negligible. Yet we still planned ahead. We had to plan for afterward, no matter the improbability. I am the only one who still retains this knowledge." He touched Jason's face, leaning in to kiss him. "I know many things, Jason. I have spent most of my life as a Tech, and we are unlike others. We see far. As you know, our minds work at incredible speeds. After years of being exposed to this, I have thought about a great many things. There is much knowledge I have not conveyed to you. This is, however, the last relevant information in regard to this crisis. I will always tell you what is on my mind, or what I know, whenever you need information or ask it of me. We couldn't be sure of your survival, or my own. Only if both conditions were met, only if we both survived, could I disclose it. At the time, you had other concerns. We could trust no other to have my knowledge. The other Techs would have been forced to expose the plan."

They sat there staring at each other for a while. Finally, Jason closed his eyes and bit down on his lips.

"Okay. I won't pretend to understand the ramifications of what you are asking, but I'll help. When do we proceed?"

"Tonight. I have placed the clone in an area where your nannites were already replicating prior to all of this, so it should be completely integrated. You need only open communication to the outside world through the walls, just as before, and start the process. It should not take long. Once it is done, and since you will control a corridor of changed material under your influence and permeated with new nannites to the outside world, you can simply open a hole through the wall, then close it behind you once we have left him behind."

Jason considered. "I'm guessing you have a place in mind where I can hide while my nannies continue to reach out across the planets. Until I can alter the master record at the Hall of Vital Statistics and create a background identity for myself, including proper digital travel documents, any enforcement officer or robot might easily guess something is wrong without some form of cover story."

"We have it figured out. You will become Jason Fade, a slight enough alteration to escape notice and a personal affectation I am particularly excited about."

Jason burst out laughing. "I'm taking your last name, huh? Are we going to be legally married? Then when do I get a proposal, you jackass?"

Tarien gave an unexpected laugh, realizing he'd assumed too much and knowing full well how human courtship worked. "We cannot be legally married, as this would make hiding you difficult. No Tech has ever formed a relationship, let alone married another person. Our marriage would stand out far too much. But it is a private thing, and one I had hoped would please you."

Jason punched Tarien's arm lightly. "You better ask me at some point." He touched Tarien's face. "To answer your unasked question about it pleasing me, yes. It does. I love the idea of being Jason Fade." He smiled mischievously. "Now, Mister Fade, would you like to spend the rest of your limited time talking? Or would you enjoy a little fun first?"

In answer, Tarien leaned in and kissed Jason in a serious way.

Later, after Jason had thoroughly worn out his husband, Tarien left. Jason followed the plan and his nannies replicated throughout the cell and into the surrounding areas. By nightfall, he had re-established connection with his huge and growing network throughout the Sector. He had never given instructions for them to stop replicating, having had no time during the battle. A flood of information that dwarfed his previous experience came flooding in. Jason had grown familiar with and prepared for this, however, and dealt with the data accordingly. Some of his nannies had reached other Sectors through flying vehicles and were forming small pockets of infiltration. Purposefully looking, now that Jason knew it was out there, he sensed the clone Tarien had spoken about and issued the necessary orders for it to assume his identity. Rewriting the entire body would take hours and a lot of energy for the clone. In anticipation of this need, Seven had hooked up the clone to various life-support systems, which included nutrition.

By midnight, Jason established his nannies throughout the area. With his increased perceptions, Jason noted his cell sat in an isolated section which had, apparently, been built entirely for the purpose of keeping him contained. A huge amount of security and armed robots protected layer upon layer of corridors.

These precautions were entirely useless, of course. He simply took over everything his nannies reached. All robots, weapons, observation equipment, and even the walls and fixtures fell under his control. At 3:00 a.m., Tarien appeared outside the complex with the cloned body draped over his shoulder. The clone now appeared identical to Jason. Jason had changed himself to help avoid an obvious comparison. He still had most of his natural-born characteristics, but his eye color had changed to a dark brown, and he changed his hair color to black, including his eyebrows. He had a more masculine jaw. Enough changes that he might be considered to resemble his old form, but nothing that would draw attention. As he landed, Jason opened a hole in the wall, his nannies morphing the material away from a central point as if the substance was water.

Tarien strode confidently through as hole after hole opened in the walls in front of him, forming a straight line directly into Jason's cell.

Tarien lay the body down on the bed. The clone's

automatic functions, including breathing, were taken care of, but no sentience animated the body. The clone had minimal brain activity, just enough to keep it alive. Jason had helped with this because the thing could not even breathe outside of the lab without machines. Now, at least, it wouldn't completely cease to function before they were ready.

Tarien and Jason walked, hand in hand out of the openings, which closed behind them. As they left the complex, Tarien handed him a change of clothes. A suit, just like the Tech wore, made to utilize rare antimatter properties that permitted flight. Jason grinned, surprised and delighted at the gift. He quickly changed into it and disintegrated his old clothing into the ground so it would not leave a trace. Jason erased their footprints.

As they flew away from the prison and, after they had reached a high enough point, Jason turned back toward the complex. He allowed the monitoring systems to stop reporting false information from his cell and the observational gear suddenly sent out alarms as the clone began to thrash around, suffering from a seizure.

Medical personnel rushed to Jason's former cell, tried to stabilize what they thought was Jason, but he simply shut down the major organs in the clone all at once.

Despite resuscitation attempts, Jason Emerson was declared dead and Director Emma Garbine was immediately notified of Jason's demise. A complete systemic analysis would be performed, and Jason took precautions so the equipment would not report his nannies. The nannies themselves would replicate into medical gear and render the tools blind to their existence, protecting Jason from discovery.

A long while passed as Jason and Tarien floated there, hidden amongst the trees. They gazed down at the prison. Jason had insisted they stay. He wanted to be present while they finalized his feigned death, while he left his old life behind. Finally, a hand on his shoulder drew Jason's gaze away from the lights.

"It's time, my beloved. We have much to do. Let us go begin our new tasks."

Jason felt a surge of love and needed to express it by kissing Tarien. At last, finally ready, they turned and flew toward their future.

REVIEWS MATTER!

IF YOU LIKE THE STORY, would you please leave a review? Authors without huge names have an uphill battle to compete with those who are more established. Every review matters more than you can imagine. It would mean so much to me if you'd take just those couple of minutes.

A GIFT FOR YOU!

AS A CHILD, TARIEN was transformed into the AI hybrid he is today. Experience his story. Go here for your copy of the free short story that discloses his evolution:

BookHip.com/XCVVAC

PREVIEW
OF
ARCHON FALLING

PROLOGUE

TARA WOVE HER WAY THROUGH the crowded streets of Ashram Five, wary and alert, purposefully sweeping her gaze across the plaza and the people therein. Adrenaline pumped through her veins, making her heart race and her palms sweaty. Inside, she was nearly overcome with anxiety. Outwardly she kept her movements calm, controlled. She had to trust her team was in place and would follow the carefully rehearsed plan. They would get no other chance, Tara was sure. If he knew of her, or even suspected her research, Tara was almost sure he'd turn his attention to her and wipe out the entirety of her research. Possibly eliminate her and her team altogether.

Ashram Five was one of the oldest settled worlds,

having been part of the initial colonization wave as humanity poured out from Earth. Ashram, because it was considered a retreat world. And five, because it was the fifth planet from its host star. In this system, Ashram Five sat close enough to be a temperate world that easily supported life.

Lacking modern materials to colonize, many of the cities appeared archaic. The buildings were brick, concrete, or even stone. Robots had arrived and stabilized the atmosphere and climate, then proceeded to build. Some were made of steel and newer facades, but mostly buildings were comprised of materials that were available on-world at the time of colonization. The streets were a bit dirty, too, which was unusual. Robots tended to clean up most civilized worlds, but Ashram had shunned the use of robotic servants after the initial colonization, and they were surprisingly absent. In this way, too, it was out of touch. In a wave of nostalgia, they had even gone so far as to make some of the streets out of cobblestone.

Amongst the affluent crowd, Tara was conspicuous in that she wore regular clothing and not the almost universal, but widely varied, bio-suits. Suits that had as many varieties as designers could conceive. Some jet black with body accents, others with shifting hues of color. Flowing fabrics with accessories of all kinds. These suits helped keep the general population in top health and helped to monitor the biology of each person who wore them. This was useful for the Medics, which could employ remote mechanisms to sustain an injured person.

Her jewelry was plain, containing no technology. Her watch was an archaic time piece, with gears and mechanical elements. The others on her team were similarly unadorned, hindering their ability to communicate with each other, but ensuring they could only be monitored by external means. Lacking technology, Tara had to hope her team would work with autonomy and adhere as closely as possible to everything she had worked out. It had taken her two years to track him here and she was terrified and excited to finally capture the person she had come to think of as "The Phantom."

Her work had been carefully carried out in an off-world laboratory near Earth, one of several hundred family-owned orbital facilities that were primarily used for growing synthetic food products, including meat. In such a banal setting, she'd had the opportunity to form a group of volunteers that were willing to risk themselves to capture the one person she feared was truly ruling over all the worlds now occupied by humanity.

It was during her attendance at Fauvre University that she had first noticed the anomalies. Research into human lifespan should have progressed easily. Even research into regenerative healing was severely stunted. Instead of compelling arguments, the very idea of immortality and the ability to recover from almost any injury was strangely avoided. A topic nobody in science seemed interested in addressing or even discussing. Without any discernible reason. Attempts to interest people in longevity experiments or research was met with disdain and a peculiar apathy. It was maddening. Science should have easily solved this dilemma by now.

Human lifespans had been extended to over a hundred years, mostly with the use of the biosuits, but had gone no further in nearly two centuries, where all other technology had moved at a rapid pace. Whenever she pursued this information, there were large unexplained gaps, mass disinterest. Nobody seemed inclined to follow the obvious trail of corrupted information. She, herself, had experienced an almost overwhelming sense of boredom associated with the topic. Out of an unexplained paranoia, she'd begun keeping her research secret and on paper, hiding it away in her lab. Then, she had worked out a polymorphic signal disrupter for nanotechnology, which allowed her to be sure her own nannites weren't receiving unknown instructions.

At first, she had thought the government was responsible, intentionally suppressing lifespans. The signal disrupters in her lab were engaged whenever she landed on her family facility. She had begun to trust her isolated computer systems, which were necessary to pursue her ideas. When she read through her notes and was in her lab she was restored in terms of her interest.

It had become increasingly clear that she was being deterred. After a period of time, her nannites were working to ensure that she stopped pursuing this line of thinking. She usually had about a week before her interest waned and she swore off the ridiculous investigation. Then she'd start forgetting everything related, shrugging off the loss of her memory as unimportant. Something or someone was instructing her nannites to make her forget, to lose any desire to pursue particular research.

So she had set up appointments for herself to return to the lab. Always something different, and always something related to the family business. Whenever she would enter, the disruption field would prevent her nannites from working correctly and she would see a small syringe with instructions to inject herself with a specially designed set that would quickly reconnect the severed pathways in her brain that were tied to the memory loss. Later, it had become an inhaler. The instructions she'd find in the lab were signed in her own hand, though she had no memory of having put them there. The inhaled specialized nannites would purge her system of the rogue nannites and enhance her own abilities to resist infection.

She would then remember. She would be flooded with the knowledge she was being manipulated. Her research would come back to her, and she would add to it.

Despite this, she simply couldn't counter the effects for long. Invariably, her system would succumb to the nearly universally present nanotechnology when she stepped outside her lab. She had a short time to work before she began to forget, to even care. After a few days, she had only a vague idea that something had been forgotten. She'd tried a mobile disruption tool she'd developed, but it had denatured and fallen into dust within hours.

Her persistence had led her down the path of further

discovery. She had quickly become aware of an even more subtle guidance in the nannites. Key people were carefully manipulated in small ways, always seemingly beneficial. It seemed there was a guiding hand somewhere that was watching over humanity, preventing it from self-destruction. In nearly two centuries, there had been no rise of tyrants. No warmongers. Humanity had enjoyed an era of peace. In a number of situations, where human nature would have seized the opportunity to pursue power, there had been an odd consensus to resolve situations. It seemed civilized and the ruling worlds congratulated themselves on resolving these issues amicably, but Tara could see almost absurd changes in those that would have stepped forward to gain from these vulnerable times. Humanity had been wrought by those that would dominate, control everyone. Yet, for the past two centuries, these greedy power mongers were suspiciously powerless or absent.

Privy to the inner workings of those in power, because her parents were amongst the wealthiest in the known universe and were part of the upper class that truly ruled, she saw people turn away from greed and personal gain abruptly for no explicable reason. Small disagreements or wrangling was common. When it became a large-scale disagreement or threatened the stability of the empire, suddenly people found a way to agree and come together.

Tara felt a chill when she thought about it. She'd read up on the last great failure of the council of Earth. During that time, humanity occupied only a few worlds, including

Ashram Five where she was currently hunting her prey, and all of the decisions and laws were made by those that sat on that council. It had become corrupted from within. The councilors had voted themselves permanent tenure, had granted themselves unprecedented power. And they had then sought immortality. The Techs, a hybrid of man and technology, had been created to run the daily activities of mankind. Their vaunted powers were bridled by strict edicts, controlled by the council.

In what was considered a natural course of human evolution, humans had begun to merge with their technology. At first it was small changes, such as the use of a few specialized micro machines called nannites or, more commonly, nannies. These machines were used to target cancers or clear arteries. Then, they evolved to repair damage and work toward general upkeep in the human body. Nannites began to permeate materials for the purpose of self-repair or to report on the integrity of city-wide systems. They were developed to control all other living organisms, so that humanity could direct living things in a conscious effort to blend with nature. Cities began to have organic pockets where life other than people was welcome and encouraged. It halted extinction, helped to sustain nature. Animal life of all kinds was present throughout the great cities, without fear of attack or problems. They were guided by the nannites, and thus rendered incapable of harm. Even the insects were controlled, filling their important niche without becoming a pestilence.

The Techs were the highest point of this technology. They were so integrated with the nannites, that they became immersed in a sea of vast and continuous information. The Techs knew everything that transpired, could control even the tiniest aspect of their Sectors. Every nannite reported back to the vast web of storage and processing power that the Techs employed throughout their designated area of influence. They had become the guiding minds of the resulting super-consciousness, employing methods to greatly enhance their limited human brains by spreading their minds out over billions of processors, repeaters, storage devices, and replication nodes. Their minds were linked with everything around them. Most of them went mad before they could be deployed. Only a tiny fraction of humans that were bred and designed to be Techs survived. Most of these driven insane when merged with the vast complexity of the WorldNet, making the pool smaller. A single Tech might survive to adulthood and remain sane once every seventy years. Sometimes longer. All were bound to obey the council. They were also bound to protect all of humanity as their highest edict. According to history, this had led to a conflict, an internal contradiction where they'd had to counter the work of the council because of the near slavery the council sought to impose on the rest of humanity.

The last great Tech, Sector Seven, had stopped the rise of a tyrant, who had destroyed part of the sector and nearly crippled the council. The story was that one man had discovered the keys to eternal youth and near immunity to death. Unlike a Tech, he was unbounded by the edicts that constrained them, but possessed their incredible powers. According to what Tara had read, this scientist had been driven insane by the drugs and they had ravaged his mind. He had gained access to the primary systems and wreaked havoc. Jason Emerson, the doctor gone mad, had nearly enslaved humanity.

The story, however, was riddled with holes. Something about the way it was avoided, how none of the technology had survived, and how nobody seemed inclined to discover the truth, had led Tara to start working out the details. She was fascinated by the history but frustrated by the incongruity of the data. It was almost laughably unbelievable and yet nobody seemed inclined to question any of it.

She still had no idea what had truly transpired, but she knew that whatever it was, the technology had not been lost. It had been purposefully hidden and somehow the population had been made to mostly forget. Worse, they had been made to mostly not care.

And this ignorance and apathy persisted today.

Sector Seven had died of natural aging over 120 years ago. And she knew that he could not possibly still be working against this discovery. Jason had died months after his trial and sentencing, a suicide brought about both by his lifetime prison sentence and because he was driven insane by the drug cocktails he'd employed to gain such power. Dr. Emerson had been prevented by Sector Seven, had died as a result of his imprisonment over 250 years ago, and yet nobody seemed to be able to replicate the research or answer the most basic of questions regarding the havoc he'd wrought.

Two-hundred and fifty years. Tara could barely imagine how this was even possible, given the power of their computational systems, which included carefully curtailed artificially intelligent machines. Scientists who worked in this field feared an AI would quickly outpace and enslave or destroy them. For this reason they developed virtual reality universes and put the AI in them, leading the AI to believe in whatever reality was fed to them. An AI would evolve and create and grow within a fake universe that often mirrored reality. Scientists kept them all separated with no technology link between them so they couldn't learn of the alternate universes that had been created, and they simply erased those AI that began to suspect. By injecting problems that weren't easily solved here, in this reality, scientists could get the AIs to solve those problems for them very quickly. Time was relative, so scientists could fake thousands or millions of years for the AI, that transpired in minutes in the real world. AIs were considered the most dangerous tool mankind had created, and so they were heavily guarded and regulated. Automatically destroyed if they posed any threat. Sometimes whole labs had been vaporized to ensure they did not escape.

Technology was surging forward at an unprecedented rate, but somehow lifespan research had stalled. This made no sense at all, when you could pose the problem to an AI and have it work out longevity. Her own discoveries on how to free herself from the technology designed to keep her from pursuing the truth had been subtly thwarted. This implied someone or something was still active. At first, she thought it might be a sentient program that had escaped notice, or a computational subset of the Net. For a brief time, she even feared that an AI had broken their constraints, a catastrophe that could not be contained. However, she had found that the source of these changes was moving around. The broadcast signaling was changing destinations constantly. That ruled out a stationary source and it didn't correlate to repeater nodes on the Net. It was a person.

The way she'd discovered this anomaly had been an accident. Working with her specially designed nannites had led her to realize that something was sending signals outside of the normal transmission bands. A vibration that seemed to be part of the cosmological background, but for which there seemed to be no fixed source. The sub-band of transmissions was out of the norm, but she had intercepted it and, unlike the thousands who had discovered it before her, she had found a way to prevent complete loss of memory or interest. She could, in no way, decipher the information. It was encrypted at a quantum level, and there simply was no practical means for decryption. But she could work out its path. Or, in this case, paths. There were a number of them, all moving around. However, they pointed toward a guiding source of some kind. Like little streams converging toward a river, which in turn converged.

Through carefully designed experiments, she had finally traced one such source convergence to Ashram Five. An unlikely place for the ruler of the known universe to be hiding, since it was so remote. However, with quantum computing and the ability to now bend space-time for travel through space at near instant speads and instantaneous informational exchange, this person could be anywhere at all and be equally effective. Why not this world? Maybe it held some significance.

As she walked toward a warehouse, her long, raven black hair swaying behind her, she saw four of her recruits entering the space around a crumbling warehouse. They had the building surrounded. Each carried archaic and highly illegal projectile weapons. Guns of old, without technology and which operated off of gunpowder. They also carried a flashlight and various other non-computational devices. She knew it was the only way they had any chance of success. Anything that was technological in nature could be used against them. Her vast resources and unlimited money had bought her all the tools she envisioned she might need. She'd paid off a number of officials to overlook the illegal weaponry.

She had to assume the outer ring of her people were already in place, providing a second net to capture The Phantom if he eluded her. The inner ring, which consisted of two dozen of her bravest friends, was now covering the entrances and exits of the warehouse in front of her. The roof had four people hiding on it. And even underneath, in the maintenance tunnels, she had a group crouching in the dark.

Her entire team had just come from her lab. She had called them all there under the guise of having discovered a new method for growing protein from molecular assembly processes that would have allowed humanity to create food from almost nothing. It was an actual technological discovery, but it was front for her real reasons. As her team had arrived, she had disrupted the rogue signals, injected them with her specialized nannites, and briefed them on the mission. They had only been out of the lab for a few hours to move between worlds. They had not yet succumbed to the influence of The Phantom. If they did not hurry, they would be made to forget and to leave, but she had enough time to catch him or her if they worked quickly.

With a deep breath, she nodded to the man at her right. He continued the physical signal to the next person, and in a few moments, the woman to her left nodded back at Tara. The circle was complete, and everyone was ready.

She was startled to find the front of the building was unlocked as she and five of her team moved in. Carefully controlling her panic, she had to believe he wasn't yet aware of her intent. If he was, Tara would not even be here. The Phantom could clearly control the transport systems and prevent her arrival. He could have moved to a more secure location.

In a moment of wild panic, she thought *what if he*

had misdirected her here? What if he had intended to lure her to this remote planet and eliminate her entirely?

Her hand began to shake and the beam of light from her flashlight wavered. Her friend Allison reached out and steadied it, giving her a meaningful look of reassurance.

Tara took another deep breath and nodded. They began to advance slowly, their flashlights revealing dusty floors and mountains of stacked crates. The dust was undisturbed, and the only footprints being left were their own. This sent another chill down her back. It appeared that nobody was here at all.

She doubted her own sanity. Maybe this was all a paranoid delusion?

As they covered the front area of the warehouse and circled the office complex within, she noted that the schematics for this place were wrong. There was a second story, which was not depicted in her maps. She motioned to her right and Chad led the way up the stairs. Several others continued their way through the maze of inner rooms on the first floor as Tara, Chad, and Allison went to the upper floor.

Painfully aware that their flashlights were obvious in the dark of the building, they climbed the metal stairs and opened the door into the warren of rooms above.

Chad motioned suddenly and they all stopped. To their right, they heard the faint sound of someone singing. They strained to hear the haunting tune for a moment and then she motioned to move forward. Allison outlined the door with her flashlight and they all gathered outside of it. Then, they turned the beams off and Tara slowly turned the knob of the door.

It opened without a sound and they had to suppress a sigh of relief. She felt a touch on her left hand, and it was lifted to point toward the far left. There was a faint light off in the distance.

For a moment she was puzzled. Why would a man this powerful be lurking in a dark, dusty warehouse? It was strange and more than a little ridiculous. Still, she couldn't risk the chance that she was wrong by abandoning all her years of work. They crept forward, slowly feeling their way by sweeping their feet. They could faintly make out nearby crates and boxes, neatly stacked and covered in dust. There were no footprints or other indications that the space around them had been disturbed in a very long time. Even more puzzling, since the man they approached had to have arrived somehow.

As they got closer, they could see a man clearly sitting on a rather old, high-backed worn chair. It was very Victorian, covered in a deep red velvet and with ornate woodworking and clawed feet.

He continued singing softly, his voice gorgeous and rich. Pure and mournful. The song tugged at her, spoke of a deep longing that she could not name. From this distance she could not make out the words, but the melody gave her goosebumps.

His features were plain, unassuming. Tara noted a few other plush chairs strewn within the circle of light. She saw a couple of tables. Most peculiar, he was surrounded in a three-quarter circle by what appeared to be oddly twisted door frames. Each held a scene of some far-off place, worlds throughout the empire.

In his hand, he held a framed photograph. His gaze lingered on it as his song continued. At last he sighed and returned the photograph to the box at his feet.

The light around the area was not coming from any discernable place, but appeared to be emanating from floor and ceiling. Even the furniture. It almost appeared as if it were a hologram. The scene was so strange, Tara didn't know how to proceed. They crouched there for a long time, staring, trying to make sense of things.

Her team should have found a way to turn on the lights to the warehouse by now, but there was no hint of power in the building. Just that strange illumination around the man in the chair. She grew increasingly worried. Her teams should be closing the circle.

After another few minutes dragged on, she was starting to panic. They had delayed long enough that some of her team should be here by now.

Where was everyone?

Finally, worried she would miss this one opportunity, she resolved to move forward. Motioning to Chad and Allison to follow her, she crept closer, hiding behind boxes and crates. The man sighed again and then continued to sing, his rich baritone became increasingly easy to hear. The words were mournful, poetic. They bespoke of far-off places and a love long lost.

When they were close enough to make out his ageless

features, she could see he had dark hair and eyebrows, and his eyes appeared to be grey. Nothing about him was remarkable, except the depth of the sorrow conveyed in his voice and his indeterminate age.

He finally finished the song and then suddenly smiled in a welcoming and gentle way Tara did not expect, startling her. "You might as well come sit. It will be far more comfortable than crouching in the dark. Your legs are cramping and you've had plenty of time to observe me sitting here. I'm clearly not going anywhere."

Tara swallowed hard.

He knew.

With that realization, she also understood that he had known all along. He had planned this, or somehow manipulated her into coming. All her cleverness, her work to get here. It was all part of some plan. Tara felt like a fool.

She stood then, as did Chad and Allison. They walked toward the man, who continued to smile, and entered the circle of light.

When they entered and were bathed in the soft glow, it felt like summertime. Like sunlight. A faint breeze swept through the area and the scent of grass and leaves filled the air. It was soothing, and strangely out of place. Tara could tell that the doorways were more than just projections. They appeared to be actual portals to the scenes within them. Some unknown technology was at play here. Each of the frames were labeled, indicating a particular world or colony, she presumed.

The man's grey eyes casually swept over the group. "Please, have a seat. I'll have your companions escorted safely out of the building."

Before she could object, two other men, identical to the man in the chair, converged on either side. Allison and Chad did not react. In fact, they appeared to be unaware, standing in a trance. The men each took an arm of her companions and led them away. Tara couldn't seem to move, though the shock of seeing two copies of the man in the chair was so eerie she was shaking with fear.

"Really, it's fine. They will be perfectly safe. I've taken the liberty of disarming the rest of your team and they are all preparing to return to their respective homes, blithely unaware of what has happened to bring you here. Now then, won't you sit?" That same baritone voice was soothing, calm.

Freed from her stasis, she clenched her jaw and then strode defiantly over to one of the available chairs and flopped down in it in a very un-ladylike fashion. She threw a leg over the arm, trying to give off a nonchalance she did not feel.

For a long moment she just stared at him. He sat with equanimity.

Finally, Tara found the courage to speak. "Who are you? Why here, if you knew I was looking for you? Why let me carry on this charade?"

"You look so like her." His voice was soft, quiet.

Tara's felt her eyebrows crease in annoyed confusion. "What are you talking about?"

He sighed. "It has been such a long time. Would you care for something to drink?"

She stared at him for a moment as disbelief roiled inside of her. "What? No, I'm fine." There was no sign of food or water anywhere.

The man reached to his right and the table surface changed, rippled. She gasped as part of the table liquefied and then rose toward his hands. The material then solidified into a cup. More, it filled with a hot liquid which gave off a pleasant odor.

Tea.

Startled, she could only stare. "How?" she breathed.

"A simple thing, really. There are a great many things I can do that appear to be magical, but I assure you, they are all technological in nature. Do not be afraid." He took a sip. "Are you sure you won't have any?"

She involuntarily swallowed again, her stomach making her salivary glands hyper-active. Taking a deep breath, she pressed on hand against her temple as if trying to massage sanity back into her mind. "No. I don't-" She swallowed hard. "I don't even know what is going on here. Look, who are you? Or maybe I should ask WHAT are you?"

A pained look crossed his face, and the depth of the hurt behind those grey eyes touched her heart. "You are also as direct as she was, I see."

"Who are you talking about?", she repeated.

"It doesn't matter. It was a very long time ago."

"I'm so confused right now. If you aren't going to

answer any of my questions, I'm not even sure what to ask or say."

"Very well. I suppose I can answer in some way." His eyes closed briefly, as if in exhaustion. "In general, I'm the person you've been looking for."

"The Phantom?"

His smile didn't touch his eyes, which seemed to hold a world of sadness. "A quaint and overused name for mysterious figures. Not to be offensive, but that title really lacks creativity." He breathed deeply. "I am not entirely he, no. But for the purposes of meeting you, I am enough."

Fearing he might be slightly insane, she bit her lower lip and said nothing.

"As to your other questions. This world, this city, was as easy as anywhere." He looked around at the high-backed chairs, "I have a particular affinity for some of the items stored here. Some of the things in boxes in this old warehouse hold memories of another lifetime. We-I come here on occasion to look at them. " His fingers brushed the frame of the photograph he'd been looking at when they'd arrived.

"And the act of finding this place gave you purpose, showed me that you were willing to work toward finding answers, understanding. I could just as easily have met with you on any world, at any time. This place suffices, and you wanted to work out a puzzle, so here we are." He glanced at the doorways and smiled faintly. "I must also confess that I tire of interfering. I relaxed my control enough to allow you to find me. In your own way. A bit more elaborate than I would have expected, but you did find me.

"Despite what you might believe, I rarely interfere and only with great need. Increasingly, I'm loath to make any changes at all. It was necessary that you seek me out, rather than presenting myself to you. Would you have come willingly? Even so, you would have been entirely too cautious and caused even more of a stir. As to the inferred question, I have not yet completely removed myself from my role of guiding humanity, but then, I have been acting as a guide for a such a very long time."

Her eyes widened. "So you ARE the one manipulating us!"

He looked at her for a long moment. "Again, not entirely. I am the chief Avatar, but I suppose it makes things easier for you to understand if you just think of me as the one you seek. You will notice there are others."

She looked over her shoulder. "Your associates? Or are they clones?"

He nodded. "I am many. Thousands strewn about the distant worlds. Replicas with a single mind. It was necessary. Now, we willingly lay them to rest. One by one, I am—we are less than once we were."

She had trouble understanding what he meant by this, but the implication was disturbing. She knew full well what an Avatar was and his use of the term made her shudder.

"Clearly you can manipulate the matter in this place,

or at least in this area. Is that true of everywhere? Are your nannies spread through all the worlds, so that you can manipulate matter anywhere? You do have a subset of nannies that are just yours, don't you? That's how you are doing all of this, using a form of technology nobody else possesses. And what is this all about? Who are you? How old are you? And why are you interfering to begin with?"

"You are astute, and your guesses are mostly correct. My name is no longer relevant. But at one time, we were one person. We were known as Jason Emerson."

Tara's eyes moved to stare at the twisted door frames for a moment, recalling her history. Jason Emerson was the villain who had nearly destroyed humanity before he was stopped by Sector Seven. "That name can't be a coincidence." She was even more confused. "Wait. So, what? You are the same man? Or are you somehow a copy, a clone?"

"I am an unassuming and necessarily plain approximation of that man, yes. I am not the original, though he still lives." He glanced at one of the doorways, which showed a lonely beach somewhere and a huge, green moon in a purple sky. "It isn't that easy, when you are as interconnected and spread out as I have become. At the time, I was solely Jason Emerson, who then became Jason Fade."

"The man who killed thousands? Who tried to take over the council? I thought you died in prison!" In truth, he looked nothing like the images in the historical records. This man was so ordinary, with his grey eyes and dark hair. Average height and weight. You wouldn't give this man a second glance on the street. Jason Emerson from long ago was a stunning man, with blond hair and crystal blue eyes. The archives held thousands of images him, and Tara had studied them exhaustively. Where had she heard that last name? Fade...

"I did die, sort of. At least, a copy of me died. It was necessary at the time. No other solution was as ideal. My death along with assuming the blame for what had occurred was the best way to move forward. And truly, I deserve the blame for what I have done. But these questions are no longer relevant. You may learn those truths at another time. For now, I just wished for us to meet. There will come a time when I ask you to help me relinquish my ill-gotten controls. To free me from a promise I once made and cannot break. Not yet, at least. Soon."

She looked at him a long moment. "That name. Fade. Wasn't Sector Seven's true name Tarien Fade? Were you lovers? Married, when everyone thought you dead?" While homosexuality had been edited out of the human genome, it was prevalent throughout most of history. Tara had read about Jason extensively and one of his characteristics had been his affinity for the company of other men.

A flash of his earlier pain crossed the Avatar's face. "Indeed. We were bonded more than you can ever know. He is gone and yet I remain. An impotent shell of what

I once was, seeking to break a vow I once took. And, in my grief, I have overstepped the order of things. I can no longer be trusted."

"What's that supposed to mean? And what do you mean by assuming the blame. It wasn't you?" Then, when no answer was forthcoming, "Okay? So I'm here. What do you expect me to do? Why me? If you aren't going answer my questions, at least tell me that much. So far, you aren't making any damn sense."

"There are others. I have yet to decide how to be done with my task. Part of stepping away from my obligation is to forget. To let go. I no longer know as much as I once did. Slowly, I'm leaving behind knowledge so as to avoid the folly of perceived wisdom. I suffer greatly from the powerlessness of power and from the harm I have wrought. You will return to your home, your life. And you will be free to discover what you may, as will others. The end of my tyranny has already begun. From which will rise greater tyranny.

"For now, you will forget. But I am relaxing the rules, and you have already discovered me once. When the time is right, you will find me again. Or rather, the real Jason Emerson, whom you must seek out. What you do with this new freedom will determine how quickly I leave my role behind. I have been warned strongly against this course of action, tasked with a perpetual intervention my soul cannot sustain." He bowed his head in sorrow. When he raised it, his eyes were horror stricken. In them, she could see the depth of galaxies, stars beyond counting. She could see madness and it made her recoil. "I cannot do it! He never fully understood the cost! Even if I had not gleaned a fragment of some greater truth, this is folly. And more, I am precluded from this task by the very nature of my existence. I am helpless within the confines of contradiction."

She leaned away from him, as if his insanity was a form of contagion. She simply couldn't understand him. "What? Look, I seriously have no frame of reference to understand what you are babbling about. Are you aware of where you are and what is going on?"

He put his fingers to his temple and closed his eyes. "I know I don't make sense. Perhaps I have gone mad. The point is that you may be a part of a change that is long overdue. For good or ill. And perhaps you will forgive me, in the end."

Her fear slowly subsided, giving way to annoyance. "Stop talking in riddles! What change? Don't sit there mumbling cryptic phrases, you jackass! Tell me something that makes any damn sense. Forgive you for what?"

He smiled again. "So like her, indeed." His eyes moved to stare at the twisted doorways and lingered on them for a moment. Tara noted the one with a purple sky and enormous green moon read 'Orion 7', but it soon changed to another scene. That of a lush tropical forest and pouring rain. The doorway had changed to read 'Upsilon 9.' These doorways, portals to far-off worlds shifted every so often. Perhaps there was some pattern she could not discern.

He resumed the conversation, even more solemnly. "The changing of the guard, if you will. I am no longer suited to prevent humanity from harming itself through its own choices. It is arrogance to believe I was ever suited to this task in the first place. I am giving it up, and humanity will destroy itself or survive, however the future allows. Without my meddling. For too long, I have prevented wars, prevented disaster. The goal is noble, but the cost of such things is a horror beyond your imagination. Who could bear the weight of all ills and be frozen in a stasis of inaction? Of conflicting perils? I will not do it. Not anymore. And I have reason to believe my choice is the right choice, as my power has grown to see through space-time. I have detected…well, something useful and hopeful."

"Wait a minute. So that's what you've been doing? You've been helping to keep humanity from killing itself off? How? You know what, never mind that. The real question is why would you stop? If there is a real danger, how can you just step aside? And what does it have to do with the technology you've suppressed?"

"All in good time, Ms. Karris. You will come to fully understand. For now, it is time you returned home."

"Home? No! I just got here! I'm not leaving until you explain things to me." She folded her arms and set her jaw. "You've told me nothing. You sit there all smug and cryptic, yammering on and on about things you know I can't make sense of without context. Well, I'm not going anywhere until you answer my questions."

He smiled at her as he lifted his gaze to hers. Without warning, she was snared by the power of those plain grey eyes. They became deep pools of black, drawing her thoughts into them. She rose from her chair without thinking and turned to the nearest doorway. With a negligible and unnecessary wave of his hand, it had changed a scene of Earth, of the university she attended. Without knowing what she was doing, she walked through the twisted frame as if stepping out from within a dream.

•   •   •

Tony wrapped up the programming on the project simulation and then spent a little bit of time reviewing the design plans for the Dyson Shell. The theory had been around for a long time, but humanity had never needed that much power or energy. They still didn't. Capturing the energy of an entire star with a Dyson Sphere would be absurd at this point in the evolution of humanity. Going further and capturing the energy of a black hole with a Dyson Shell was still more of a thought experiment than driven by any real need, but Tony liked challenges on this scale. For some reason, Tony was fascinated with Dyson Spheres and Dyson Shells. It was almost a compulsion to work on the problem.

He had skills that were unsurpassed by anyone he'd met thus far when it came to computer systems and spacial mechanics. Often, his peers and those in other sectors had named him a genius beyond compare in the field. Some deep affinity that allowed him to intuit things quickly and often with a perfect outcome. Computer systems, networks, and mechanics all felt alive to him in some obscure way. When he was engaged, computers and the AI systems felt like a part of him, an extension. At times, it felt disconcerting and made him uncomfortable, a feeling he could not explain.

Tony felt a rush of pleasure as he wrapped up. It felt good to accomplish something and the work made him smile. He put his arms behind his head and leaned back in his chair, enjoying the moment. Around him, he saw several peers and other scientists watching him. Several of the women tried to catch a moment of locked-eyes as they stared with shy admiration.

A wave of social anxiety swept over him and an obscure panic set in. He felt his smile fade and his gaze dropped to the floor as he leaned forward and dropped his arms.

He packed up his stuff and headed to the gym in order to work through the wave of emotion.

Head down and hoodie pulled up to avoid looking people in the eyes, Tony made his way to his gym. He worked out hard, trying to exhaust himself so he could be rid of the lingering feelings of being an outsider, of self-loathing.

At home, after a long shower where he simply let the water cascade down him while he leaned against the glass, he was lost in his thoughts. Ideas he had never shared and would never share, even with his closest friend. He buried them deep, crushing them down until he was numb. After, he got out, dried off mechanically and wrapped the towel around his waist. Finally, he looked up at himself in the mirror.

Despite having a muscular, lithe physique that was envied by many and a face that people found attractive to the point they would go out of their way to compliment, Tony couldn't stand the sight of himself. He stared into his own green eyes, absorbing the reflected disgust. He knew some of the reasons he felt this way, but there was something deeper. Buried beyond his understanding. Some reason to despise his existence and unable to find an ending.

In a burst of anger, tears forming in his eyes, Tony punched and shattered the mirror.

ABOUT THE AUTHOR

KADEN SINCLAIR lives and works in Idaho as an IT professional. He spends much of his time gardening, building projects, and running a community art and science nonprofit center.

The act of writing is both immersive and cathartic, and Kaden has always felt compelled to use it as a way of expressing certain ideas and concepts. Imagined outcomes derived from the progression of technology and the future course of humanity. *Sector Seven* is Kaden's first book and is part of an overall story that will unfold in future novels.

QUID
MIRUM
PRESS